THE STARS ARE NOT OKAY

THE STARS ARE NOT OKAY

Kari Ingerslev

PURE&FIRE

*

* For John *

With thanks to Sally and The Star Maker

The Stars Are Not Okay
First published in the UK by Pure & Fire in 2025
Pure & Fire, England
www.pureandfire.com

ISBN: 978-1-915699-06-0
eBook also available

'Seek not so much to be oneself as to love oneself. One can only live truly once one has dared to plunge with compassion into the gulf between all that we are and all that we claim to be.' – Krispin Staniscofskin, *'A Star is Born'*

****

ACT ONE

In which Cat leaves home, breaks a promise and meets the love of her life (although she doesn't know it yet).

****

* 1 * Fun Cat makes a new start

Dotty Jay informs me that there are only seven types of people in the world.

"I'm a type one," she boasts, perching on the pile of pillows which haven't yet made their way to my bed. "That means I'm impulsive, a little bit psychic and an exhibitionist. Last year I did a naked sky dive for dementia."

I nod and try to remember where I put my room key. My stuff is everywhere. I hope I didn't leave anything in the car.

Dotty Jay keeps staring at me. "I bet you're a type three."

"What does that mean?"

"You're an introvert but you wish you were more sociable. You're creative and sensitive and you overanalyse everything to death. Am I right?"

I fix a nonchalant expression on my face. How can she possibly know that? She's only existed for fifteen minutes of my life and, for most of that time, we were carrying boxes from my dad's car to my room. I'm not even myself right now. I'm Play it Cool Cat, oozing calm. Or so I thought. Perhaps she's a witch. My mum always told me not to trust anybody. It's really hard to make new friends when I'm not allowed to talk to strangers.

"Shall I help you unpack?" Dotty Jay continues.

"It's okay, thanks!" I say this loudly. She's wrong. I'm not an introvert who wants to be more sociable. I'm an extrovert who couldn't care less.

I wish she'd get off my pillows. I don't want to have to wash them. I've never used a washing machine. Right on cue, she spots the giant box of laundry detergent with my name written in permanent marker. *Property of Catrina Berger,*" she reads aloud. "Worried people will nick your stuff?"

"No! My mum wrote it, not me. I don't mind who uses it. I bought it for everyone." That's a lie. I didn't buy it. I didn't have a clue. My mum bought everything, labelled it and warned me not to share with anybody.

"That's my room. Number 8." Dotty Jay points across the hall. "Just knock if you want anything." She finally slides off my stuff and trots into the hallway. I'm about to close the door when she turns. "Where are you from?"

"Exeter."

"I meant originally. You don't look English."

I keep smiling, jaw aching. "I've always lived in England but I have some Hispanic heritage." I wait for the inevitable blank stare before explaining, "My mum's parents were from Colombia."

"Ah! That's nice. Very multicultural!"

I shrug. "My mum's lived in England since she was tiny. She barely remembers Colombia." I don't add that she would hate to be thought of as anything other than British. She's always been ashamed of her background and she passed the discomfort on to me.

Dotty Jay keeps staring. "Long drive, then?"

"Colombia? I've never been—"

"Exeter!"

"Oh. Yes. Nearly six hours." Would've been less but my dad won't go above 50 miles an hour. Says it's not as fuel efficient. He also stopped four times to pee and stretch his legs. We listened to ABBA the whole way. His choice.

"I'm from Birmingham. You could probably tell?"

I nod, pretending all the way. The smile falls off my face as I close the door and Play it Cool Cat can finally relax.

I stare at my mountain of belongings dumped on the floor and heave a sigh before treating myself to a tour. White walls. Patchy green carpet. The basin is clean but the mirror above it is cracked. The cold tap squeaks when I turn it on. The view is of the hills beyond campus. The wardrobe is signed with the names of former residents. The desk and chest of drawers don't match and the chair has a wobbly leg. The mattress on the bed is stained. Everything smells slightly musty. I click the lamp on and off a few times. At least the bulb works. I wouldn't know how to fix it if it didn't.

My dad will be back on the motorway by now. He got all twitchy about staying too long because he wants to get home before dark. I've been abandoned. Left to fend for myself.

Baby Cat wants to curl up on the bed and cuddle Monkey Bear. She has a good cry until Fun Cat takes charge.

I'd better lead from now. You were so awkward with that Dotty girl.

Fun Cat led most of the way through high school. Until the Dark Days hit out of nowhere and Sad Cat took over. Sad Cat is pretty stubborn. I couldn't get rid of her.

I'm determined to let Fun Cat rule through university. There's no point in anybody else having a go. Nobody likes Sad Cat. Thunder Cat is a needy attention seeker. Baby Cat and Silly Cat are too young. And Scaredy Cat wants to go home despite the fact that I worked so hard to get here.

There are lots of me in my head but it's all me. Everybody does this. Everybody plays a different role around different people or in different situations. It's just that my parts are quite loud and some of them turn up when I least expect it.

I close my eyes and talk to Monica.

"How are you feeling?" she whispers.

"Nervous. It's all so overwhelming."

She gives her usual sympathetic hum. *"You'll be fine. You're going to have an amazing time."*

"I don't know if I can do it."

"Course you can! You're a star!"

I talk to Monica about everything. She always knows what to say. She's the perfect big sister.

I cling to Monkey Bear as a tear rolls down my cheek. The real Monica is two hundred and sixty four miles away in Exeter. She's probably forgotten me by now. She definitely won't be thinking about me. Won't care whether I'm a star or not. She's not really my sister. She's my English teacher from sixth form. And I never called her anything other than Miss Lucas. I only know that her real name is Monica because I looked for her on FriendWeb and found her. I didn't add her. I just browsed through all the content that she'd forgotten to make private.

Monica (Miss Lucas) was one of the few teachers who didn't laugh when I said I was going to train to be an actress. She didn't ask what my back up job was. She just told me it sounded great. We had a poetry assignment once and she called me a star and I've not stopped thinking about her since. She's been my imaginary sister for two years now. She took over from Evelyn (Miss Kingston), my favourite teacher in year seven. Evelyn got me through high school. Before her, there was Sadie who did work experience when I was in year five. And before *her,* it was Sandra, the school nurse. I used to fall over on purpose so I could have a hug from her (although it backfired when she was away and I had to have a hug from Mr Barker instead). Before Sandra, it was Davina, a Butlin's Redcoat. She stayed in my head for over a year, even though I'd only known her for three days.

I can't remember a time when I didn't have an imaginary sister talking to me in my head. I know it's not real. I've just always done this. I thought everybody did. But one day I made the mistake of asking Leah Gates whether she had lots of people in her head. She was horrified and told everybody. That's when the Dark Days began.

I am suddenly aware of noise outside my room. More new students have arrived and are gathering in the hallway. There's nervous laughter and friendly salutations and Dotty Jay's voice is the loudest of them all. "Number 6 has arrived," she announces, presumably pointing to my door. "And most of the rooms are filled upstairs and downstairs. It's just number 7 on this floor."

Somebody's mother remarks on the tiny cupboards in the hole that is the kitchen. I pray nobody's noticed the tins of beans plastered with my name. I look at my stuff, splattered across the floor. I could unpack or I could go out and meet everybody.

Come on, Fun Cat says as I slide off the bed and fix a happy smile on my face. *Let's get out there and make some friends!*

* 2 * Copy Cat nearly kills a girl

Fun Cat is charming, spontaneous and, as the name suggests, FUN! She's the part of me that enjoys the odd spot of karaoke (*'I will survive'* being my signature song) and always arrives first to a party. Fun Cat couldn't be more ready for student life. I bound into the hallway where I'm hit by the smell of perfume emanating from a glamorous woman in the kitchen alcove. She's tall and blonde with lots of make-up and knee high boots. Beside her stands a perfect little clone, many years younger but smelling just as pungent. They are unloading dried fruit into one of the cupboards.

"It could do with a good clean," the lady says, inspecting the fridge. She has a strong accent. Liverpudlian perhaps.

I halt as Sad Cat comes to peek. *Imagine if she was my mum.*

"Hello!" I shout, forcing Fun Cat back to the surface.

The girl looks across, unblinking.

"I'm from number 6." I point to the room from which I have emerged. "I'm Cat. What's your name?"

"Elle."

Elle's mother looks up from the fridge and echoes Elle's blank smile. "Elle's an actress," she informs me.

A bit audacious. Not sure we can use that title until after we've trained. But hey ho. "Me too," I say.

"Really? What have you been in?"

"Well, nothing yet. I meant I'm on the Acting course too."

"Oh. Elle's a real actress. She was Little Betty in the *Gossip Town* Christmas special."

Oh my gosh. I thought she looked familiar.

"Wow," I squeak. "That's amazing."

Fun Cat retreats and Play it Cool Cat re-emerges, aided most unhelpfully by Copy Cat. This is the awkward and stuttering part of me who is permanently tongue-tied and adapts herself to fit in with whoever she's talking to.

A pink-faced man comes puffing up the stairs. "That's everything, Elle," he says, dumping three boxes into the doorway of number 9. His accent is even stronger than the rest of his family.

Elle keeps staring at me and I wonder what to say next. I can't think of anything witty so I opt for more information. "How old are you?"

"Eighteen."

"Me too," I say, although Silly Cat wants to say, *"I'm six."*

Suddenly Elle's mother gasps. "Whose is this?" She pulls a jar of peanut butter out of the fridge and reads my mother's label. *"Property of Catrina Berger."*

"Whoops! That doesn't need to be in the fridge." I hold my hand out but Mother Elle doesn't give it to me.

"Elle has a nut allergy," she says sternly. As if I should've known. As if I'd almost killed her.

"Oh sorry! I didn't realise."

"No. That's the trouble. Nobody thinks these days."

"Sorry," I repeat.

"No nuts in the entire building," Elle's mum looks at me and Dotty Jay and an Indian girl who has popped her head out from room 10. "Alright girls?"

"Absolutely!" I try to salvage things. "No nuts except for us!" I accidentally put on a slight Liverpudlian accent.

Dotty Jay roars with laughter and the girl at number 10 grins but Elle and her mother don't look impressed.

"I hope it's alright if I dispose of this?" Without waiting for a reply, Elle's mother tucks my peanut butter into her bag.

Stupid cow! Angry Cat screams inside my head. *I didn't do it on purpose. Bet she'll eat it on her way home. What's the point in labelling my things if people just steal them anyway?*

"Type four, I bet," Dotty Jay murmurs in my ear, cocking her head towards Elle. "Uptight, insecure, a little self-absorbed, but probably nice deep down."

Elle's cheeks go red and I feel awful. I don't know whether to return Dotty Jay's grin or apologise to Elle. Squashed Cat is pressing in as number 10 comes over to introduce herself.

"Hello! What's your name?"

Play it Cool Cat takes the reins. "I'm Catrina."

"Nice to meet you. I'm Jo but everyone calls me Mad Jo."

She doesn't look mad. Sure, she's wearing three watches and shorts over trousers and she's got purple streaks in her hair so her sense of style is rather questionable. But that's not enough to make you mad. And, anyway, usually if people are mad they don't want anybody to know.

If she's mad, what would everyone think of me? Scaredy Cat whispers like a fly in my ear.

"Does anybody call you Caz?" Mad Jo peers at me.

"No. Cat, usually."

"I'll call you Caz, then!"

I cringe. My mum would hate that. Come to think of it, my mum would probably hate *her*. My mum has a lot of strong opinions about fashion. And Asians.

"What's your number?" Mad Jo pulls her phone out. "Might as well add you now. What if I forget my key or something? Better have a point of contact. Not to mention the fact that we'll probably be friends."

"Probably!" Copy Cat almost dribbles.

I find it astonishing that I am totally undone when I first meet people and yet Fun Cat rules once we're acquainted. Why can't I just be cool from the beginning?

"I'll, er, get your number too..." I fumble for my phone.

"I'll give you mine and you can drop call me." She rattles her number off. I can't bring myself to save her in my phone as *'Mad Jo'* so I add her as *'Jo Willow'* instead, Willow being the name of our block. Then I drop call her as requested.

"*Caz...*" she mutters to herself as she adds my name (or rather, *not* my name) to her phone. "What's your surname?"

"Berger."

"Burger? Like a hamburger?"

"Yeah but spelt differently." I spell it for her.

"Nice. Where are you from?"

"Exeter."

"I meant—"

"My mum's from Colombia but she grew up here."

"And your dad?"

"He's completely English," I assure her.

"I bet you think I'm Indian?" Mad Jo smirks.

"Er, I don't know."

"People always think I'm Indian but my dad's parents were from Sri Lanka. Mum's half Irish and half Norwegian and I did some research on my family tree and found some ancestors from Trinidad so I'm a proper mix..." Unlike me, she seems completely in love with her mixed heritage. To be fair, she pulls hers off better than I do. She has striking black hair (under the purple streaks) and dazzling brown eyes and perfect teeth.

I, on the other hand, am *funny looking.'* That's a direct quote from Paddy Todd who gave me a poke at Little Apples nursery and demanded to know where I was from. I didn't realise I was different until he pointed it out.

"So can you speak Colombian?"

"Er, they speak Spanish."

"Oh right. Can you speak Spanish?"

I shake my head. I don't know any Spanish except for a few swear words and a random prayer that my mother utters when she's stressed. I don't even know if my mum or her siblings have ever been back to South America. She's very secretive about it all. Once, during a sleepover, my cousin Chantelle whispered that our grandfather had been a witch doctor who was forced to flee Colombia after angering a wizard from a neighbouring village. She claimed the prayers our mothers utter are actually spells and that we have healing power in our veins. I've no idea how she came up with such an idea. Obviously that sort of thing only happens in stories. I met our grandfather once and he didn't look like a shaman. He was just a little old man. Plus, I've never healed anybody.

I have totally zoned out when I realise Mad Jo has asked me another question. "Did you bring an iron?"

"No." I don't add that I have no idea how to use one.

"I thought most people would forget! You can use mine."

"Thanks."

There's some noise on the stairwell and the door bursts open. Number 7 has arrived in the form of a short dimpled girl with fluffy blonde hair. Dotty Jay offers her assistance as the girl squeezes down the corridor with an armful of teddies, followed by yet another glamorous blonde mummy.

Sad Cat rears her head. *Imagine if she was my mum.*

GO AWAY SAD CAT!

I used to draw myself with long blonde hair, even though my hair is dark. The happiest girls in primary school seemed to be the blonde ones. The nicest mothers were blonde too.

"What course are you on?" Mad Jo continues.

I pull myself together. "Acting." I feel like an idiot. She's going to wonder why someone like me thinks they can act.

My mother's voice rings in my ears. *"Why do you want to do an Acting course? You're shy."*

I'm not shy. Not really. Copy Cat is the only part of me who is actually shy. And Lost Cat who doesn't have a voice. That's the part of me who leads most often when my mum's around. I'd like her to meet the rest of me but, for some reason, they all disappear when she walks into the room.

"What about you?" I ask.

"Art. You won't believe how hard it was to get all my stuff in the back of the car. You just don't know what you're gonna need, do you? I mean, what if we do a project on nature and I didn't think to bring my collection of leaves? Or what if we do self-portraits and I've not got my baby teeth?"

Oh my goodness she IS mad.

"I don't suppose you needed to bring much for the Acting course?" Without waiting for a reply, Mad Jo prattles on, barely coming up for breath, "Unless you've got your own costumes and stuff. But still, they've got all that here, haven't they? I saw the props cupboard when I came for my interview and it was almost as big as my house..."

I nod along and Copy Cat scratches my chin when she scratches hers.

Dotty Jay buzzes around, offering advice. She's four years older than the rest of us, having switched course twice. She's now in her final year of a Music degree and plans to be a music therapist, whatever that is.

"I had your room first," she tells me. "But I hated the squeaky tap. Sounded like ghosts going through the pipes."

I'm Play it Cool Cat again. "Ghosts wouldn't need to use the pipes. They could just walk through the walls."

Dotty Jay has already changed the subject. "There's a tree swing in the field opposite. You can see it from your window. Rory put it up last year."

I nod and wonder who Rory is. Then number 7 comes over to say hello and ask what course we're on.

"Mad Jo. Art."

"Annie Button. Dance."

"Ooh you're a dancer! I used to do ballet." Mad Jo demonstrates a pirouette and crashes into me. "Sorry, Caz!"

"It's okay." I clutch my arm.

Annie turns to me. "Hi Caz. Nice to meet you. What course are you on?"

"Acting."

"I wanted to be an actress," Annie's mother pipes up. "But I never made it. I'm a stay at home mum." She looks at Annie and reconsiders. "At least I was until today." Her voice cracks as she envelops her daughter in a giant hug. Her perfume mixes with Elle's mum's aroma and brings tears to my eyes.

"Mum, that's the kitchen," Annie says, wriggling out of her mother's arms. "No oven, see? Just a microwave."

"Phew. No chance of anyone burning the place down."

"Just make sure you don't lose your meal card," Dotty Jay advises. "Otherwise you're stuck with the vending machines and all you can get are crushed crisps and peanuts."

Elle's mother jerks her head. "No nuts in the building! Elle's allergic." She shoots me a glance.

"I'm allergic to ostriches," Annie announces. "I had a reaction to them once at a petting zoo."

"I doubt anybody's brought an ostrich!" Mad Jo guffaws.

"It's that one over there you need to watch!" Elle's dad says with a grin, cocking his head at me. "Bet you've got an ostrich with your name on in your suitcase, haven't you!"

"No, I haven't," I mutter.

"It's always the quiet ones," Mad Jo's dad chips in, even though he hasn't even met me.

My brain is jelly. Fun Cat didn't get a look in.

* 3 * RoboCat makes a room a home

Back in room 6, with the door firmly locked, I set about unpacking. I open each bag in a methodical manner. Clothes. Books. Photos. I give the wardrobe and chest of drawers a good clean, like my mum told me to, before lining it all with her special scented paper. I hang and fold everything neatly. Then I dust the three shelves and decide what should go on each one. I stick my poetry in a giant collage on the back wall. Right in the middle is the poem on which Monica wrote *'You are a star.'* I surround my poetry with my collection of buttons, blue-tacked to the wall in rainbow colour order.

I am focused throughout, with RoboCat on autopilot. I don't even stop to go to the toilet even though I've needed to go since I arrived. The toilet is all the way down the hall next to Elle's room and, even though I'm pretty sure her parents have left, I don't want to risk it.

I finish off by taping my inspirational quotes around the mirror and organising my shoes in a neat line under the window. I hide my giant butterfly hoodie under my bed because it suddenly seems like a stupid thing to have brought.

When I glance at my phone it is already past seven. I hadn't noticed the time fly. I poke around in my bag and pull out the sandwich that we got at a service station on the way. I have a couple of bites but I'm not hungry. I pace around my room for a bit. Then I read all the inscriptions in the wardrobe. They go all the way back to the seventies.

'Alan was here! Acting, 1972.'

'Dance like it's your last night on earth– Shelly, Musical Theatre, 1984.'

'Juggling Jeff, heartthrob of Willow, 2002.'

There's a knock at the door, followed by someone trying the handle. I take a deep breath and go to unlock it.

It's Dotty Jay. "Hiya! Do you want to come to the—" She gasps and steps into my room. "Ooh get you! You've unpacked already! Wow. Those buttons are amazing!"

For a brief moment, Fun Cat smiles.

Dotty Jay peels her eyes away from my poetry. "Anyway, we're all going to the MB. Wanna come?"

"What's the MB?"

"The Merry Bar. It's the most excitement you can have living on campus. Unless you want to walk two miles to the Grumpy Pig. But I wouldn't go there on a Thursday as that's curry night and all the locals come out to get hammered."

Copy Cat comes back to the surface. "Right. I'll avoid Thursdays, then."

She seems to mistake my discomfort for disappointment. "Don't worry, there's a coach to Wakefield every Monday. It drops us off outside Wango's and picks us up four hours later. Plenty of time to party. Although, be warned, if you miss the coach home you're stuck. Taxis cost an absolute bomb. Especially if you use Shakey Wakey Cars. Make sure you only go with Beavers."

"Okay," I squeak.

Mad Jo and Elle have come out of their rooms.

"Ready?" Dotty Jay calls to them.

They nod.

"Right then, let's go." Dotty Jay pounds on the door next to mine. "Coming, Annie? We're all off to the bar."

Annie pokes her head out. "Do I need to bring anything?"

"Only if you want a drink."

I don't want a drink but I grab my purse before starting to take my slippers off.

"No need to get dressed up. It's only the bar. You can keep your pyjama top on."

I force a laugh. "It's not a pyjama top."

"Really?" Dotty Jay peers at me. "Sorry."

"Can I go to the toilet before we go?" I don't know why I'm asking permission. I feel like a fool.

"It's down there." She points.

I pretend this is brand new information.

"They have en suites at Wintergates but we're totally backwards on this campus. There's a petition you can sign although it's unlikely to change anything."

"Okay," I stutter. I leave my room, locking the door behind me, before squeezing past Mad Jo and Elle to enter the toilet.

"You don't need to lock the door," Dotty Jay shouts.

I pause with my hand on the handle. "When I'm peeing?"

"No, your bedroom door, silly! Of course you should lock the door when you're peeing!"

Mad Jo grins. "Up to you, Caz. We won't judge."

I hurry into the toilet and wince. *Why am I such a loser? Come on, Fun Cat. Where are you?*

I can hear everybody talking. Mad Jo asks whether the bar is far away. Dotty Jay says it's down the hill. I might as well be peeing in the same room.

Scaredy Cat is shaking. *Whatever you do, don't fart.*

"Are you done, Caz?" Mad Jo pounds on the door and I almost fall down the toilet.

I've not even gone yet but I pull everything back on and yank the flush.

"Come on then," Dotty Jay exclaims as I slink back into the hallway. "Let's all go and get Merry!" She leads the way down the stairwell and out of the building.

We're halfway down the hill before I realise I'm still wearing my slippers.

* 4 * Lost Cat at the bar

I feel like I've entered a time warp. The neon walls are decorated with film posters, the bar stools are covered in patchy pink plastic and cheesy pop from the last millennium is playing gently in the background.

Dotty Jay's eyes dart around. "There they are!" She points to a nearby table where half a dozen students have gathered. "That's the rest of our lot with Rory."

Rory made the swing, RoboCat remembers.

I stick close to Dotty Jay and Mad Jo as they trot to the bar to get drinks. The two of them order beers so Copy Cat gets one too. I kick myself when I reach our table and spot Annie's orange juice. *Come on. Be cool.*

I pull up a stool beside a tall redhead. She's emitting an invisible radar which causes me to be completely intimidated. "Shay Hannigan," she drawls in an enchanting Irish accent.

"Cat Berger," I reply, trying to return her confident smile.

"Like a hamburger?"

"Spelt differently." I spell it for her but she looks around, probably wishing she was sitting next to someone else.

"I won't remember!" She laughs. "My memory's awful!"

"Mine too. I won't remember your name either." That's not true. My memory is excellent. I remember what was in my lunchbox on my first ever day of school. I remember my brother, Aidan, taking his first steps. I even remember a neighbour called Duncan Anderson babysitting for me before Aidan was born. He drew pictures while I sat beside him on the sofa. So I only need telling once and I'll remember who all my new housemates are, where they're from and what course they're doing. The only two I am in danger of mixing up are Lottie and Lizzie. They're both dancers from London who already know each other.

The top floor are all girls, like my floor. Along with Shay (who is doing Costume Design) and Lottie and Lizzie, there's Ashley and Tanisha. Ashley has glasses and a lisp. She's doing Creative Writing. Tanisha is bubbly and brash, a typical candidate for the Acting course. She and Elle hit it off right away and I feel a pang of rejection. We're the only girls from Willow on the Acting course. I'm bound to be left out.

Then there's the boys. Five of them making up the cohort of Willow's ground floor. Bertie is dressed like a character from a period drama. He greets me with the words, "Jolly pleased to meet you! Creative Writing student here." Copy Cat articulates more than usual when returning his greeting.

Rory the famous swing-maker is in his final year doing Art. He seems to be going for some kind of Jesus look with his wavy long hair and a beard. He's the male version of Dotty Jay: weird and loud and a self-appointed leader of the pack. I assume the two of them are a couple but then I overhear Dotty Jay remarking on her on and off boyfriend, Daryl.

Wes is a second year Acting student and Mike is doing Dramaturgy, whatever that is. And finally there's Zachary. He's the overexcited skinny bean on the end of the table doing Music Theatre. This is a different course from Music and also differs from *Musical* Theatre. I have no idea how, but Zachary seems keen for everyone to know this.

We're all first years apart from Dotty Jay, Rory and Wes, although Shay took a gap year and is decidedly more mature than the rest of us for doing so. She announces that she's here to work hard, thank you very much, and has got drunken stupors out of her system. She sips her glass of wine and regards Mike with disgust. He's knocking back the pints as though he's an animal that's been let loose from a cage.

Everyone is talking loudly. I look for opportunities to join in but all I can manage is the odd nod or forced chuckle or, "I've never done laundry before either!"

"What's your name?" Mike slurs his words as he points at me from a few seats away.

I summon up every ounce of courage to drag Fun Cat to the table but she's nowhere to be found. "Cat," I say quietly.

"Cat..." He takes a swig of beer. "Like *meow?*"

"Yes."

"Surname?"

"Berger."

He thinks for a moment and I see the cogs turning. "Cat Burger!" he yells triumphantly. "Ha! Like a Hot Dog!"

"Spelt differently," I say weakly.

I've always hated my name. If I'd thought about it, I could have reinvented myself. Perhaps gone by my middle name, Carla. I glance at Mad Jo. *Maybe I should take on Caz, as common as it sounds?* I'm clinging on by my fingertips, petrified that Squashed Cat will appear and plunge me into a panic. I have the same awkward conversation about whether I'm a hamburger or a Cat Burger with Rory. I'm even more embarrassed when he asks what course I'm on.

"Acting?" he repeats. "I'd have guessed Creative Writing."

Ashley looks across and pushes her glasses up her nose. "Thath what I'm doing," she simpers.

I cringe. Yes, that would have suited me better.

Dotty Jay comes to my aid. "She must be good though. Hundreds of people audition for the Acting course. It's the toughest one to get into."

"True," Mike concedes. "I didn't get in. That's why I'm doing Dramaturgy."

I feel a swell of pride although this is quickly drowned out by Shay pointing at Elle and exclaiming, "Oh my gosh, you're Little Betty, aren't you?"

"You been in anything, Cat?" Rory asks.

"Besides a burger!" Mike snorts.

"Some school shows," I mutter. I don't add that I've never had a speaking role. My Drama teacher, Miss Bates, was more surprised than anybody when I told her I'd got into Forest Hall. She probably thought I was lying. I was never able to be anybody other than Copy Cat or Lost Cat in her classes.

I'm still amazed that I got on the course. Somehow, Fun Cat pulled it out of the bag and impressed with a rare moment of star quality. The tutor who auditioned me said I was 'bewitching.' I'd thought that was an insult until the glorious acceptance letter came through. I spent the summer riding on a wave of pure joy, with Fun Cat daydreaming about my wonderful new life up North. I'm not sure how I'll make it through the course now that Fun Cat has gone into hiding.

The talk shifts to relationships and I feel myself drifting further, like a rubber duck floating out to sea. Elle has a boyfriend called Reece, Wes has a girlfriend called Hannah and Rory's gay but currently single. Mad Jo is bisexual and Shay's taking a break from relationships and Annie's never had a boyfriend and is waiting till she gets married before she kisses anybody.

Shay turns to me. "Have you got a boyfriend, Cat?"

"No."

"You want one?"

I shake my head and say coolly, "I don't believe in love."

Shay raises an eyebrow. "Okay." She turns her chair and now has her back to me as she chats with Lottie and Lizzie.

I feel a sinking dread. Forget about Squashed Cat, I have morphed into Lost Cat. Squashed Cat and Lost Cat are twins of two extremes. One feels everything. The other feels nothing. They render me frantic with fear or numb to the core. I don't know who I hate more.

Dotty Jay is defining everybody's type and there's much discussion as she does so. Bertie is rather chuffed to be labelled a type two (wise, sincere, eccentric and melancholy) while Annie looks rather baffled about being a type five (easily distracted, curious, optimistic and gullible).

Then the chatter splits into many conversations and my head aches as I try to follow every thread at once. Lottie and Lizzie are asking Dotty Jay about the local nightlife and I listen to her spiel about the bus to Wakefield. Mad Jo is performing an uncanny Liverpudlian accent and Elle has broken into a proper smile for the first time today. Annie and Ashley are deep in conversation and are by far the least threatening of my new housemates but I'm too far away to join in. Wes looks like he's getting flirty with Shay and she seems to be reciprocating *even though* Wes just told us about his girlfriend, Hannah, and I thought Shay was here to work?

Peals of laughter hit me as Mad Jo performs a perfect Irish accent followed by a Brummie one for Dotty Jay. Then *'I will survive'* starts playing and half the table joins in. Skinny bean Zachary is loudest of them all, belting out a harmony and doing a head spin on the table as though giving a demonstration of what Music Theatre is all about.

As the song reaches its climax and, after realising that nobody has spoken to me for the best part of thirty minutes, I slide my stool out and slip away. Lost Cat leaves the bar and heads into the dark night, tail between my legs and tears trickling down my cheeks as I stumble up the hill alone.

* 5 * Scaredy Cat phones home

Oh please help. I don't know where I am.

I wasn't paying attention when we came down the hill and now it's dark and I have no idea which block is Willow. I approach the first building on the hill. *Maple.*

I turn to the next. *Beech.*

Stay calm, I counsel myself. *It's got to be one of these.*

But Squashed Cat has come screaming to the surface and I'm utterly terrified. I start to run, panic rising as I frantically check the names of the blocks I am passing.

Ash, Cedar, Hazel. WHERE IS WILLOW?

A sudden hoot of laughter causes me to freeze. Three guys are walking nearby. I duck behind a tree, clenching my fists in case they try to get me. They don't see me. I keep running. My block has disappeared and I'm in the middle of nowhere with no hope in the world. Tears choke me. The world is spinning. The dark is consuming me.

I reach the next block. *Willow.*

Oh God. Oh my God. Thank you.

I shove my key in the lock and run up the stairs. Squashed Cat retreats and Normal Cat returns, feeling stupid and embarrassed and grateful that my housemates are still at the bar so none of them saw me in such a ridiculous state. I reach room 6, unlock the door and slam it shut behind me. I don't care what Dotty Jay says. I'm keeping it locked forever.

Scaredy Cat comes creeping to the surface. *I can't do this. I'm not brave enough. Everybody's making friends and I don't fit in. I'm too weird. I just freaked out over getting lost.*

I want my mummy. I pick up my phone and call her.

She answers after the third ring. "Hello, Baby!"

I burst into tears.

"What's wrong? What happened?"

"Nothing," I blub. "I'm just scared."

"Oh!" She titters down the line. "You wanted to do the course so why are you upsetting yourself now you're there?" I fall silent as she showers me with advice. "You've just got to be confident. Smile more. No point making yourself cry. You'll look ugly and nobody will want to be your friend."

I rub Monkey Bear against my cheek.

"Did you unpack yet?"

I take a moment to admire my room. "Yeah."

"Did you put your food in the kitchen?"

"Yeah." I don't mention the peanut butter.

"Go to bed now. It's late. No wonder you're upset."

"Okay." My brain feels foggy. Scaredy Cat and Lost Cat have morphed into one.

"Love you, Baby!"

"Love you." I hang up and cry a little more. Then I close my eyes and talk to Monica. I imagine her giving me a big pat on the back as I curl up in her lap.

"*Catrina, Catrina!*" This is something Monica (I mean, Miss Lucas) used to say to me. "*Catrina, Catrina! You write so wonderfully!*" I sob as Monica in My Head says it now. "*Catrina, Catrina! You're doing better than you think.*"

"Really?" I whimper. "I barely spoke at the bar. Then I got lost coming back. I feel like such an idiot."

"*You're only just getting started. I believe in you, Cat. And I'm so proud of you. Never forget: you're a star.*"

I cling to Monkey Bear, choking over tears and snot. I alternate between fleeting moments of comfort from Monica in My Head and deep longing for Monica in Real Life.

Suddenly there's a knock on my door followed by a loud, "Yoo-hoo! Are you awake, Cat?" It's Dotty Jay. I can't let anyone see me like this. I will pretend to be asleep.

"Cat!" She pounds on the door. "Are you in there?"

Angry Cat rears her head. *Leave me alone!*

I drag myself off the bed and open the door. "Hi."

She gives a goofy grin. "Sorry. Did I wake you?"

"It's alright. I wasn't asleep yet."

"We're all off on a midnight walk. Want to come?"

"A midnight walk?" I echo. "I, er, dunno. I'm quite tired."

She peers at me. "It's okay to feel homesick, you know. Ashley's been crying too."

"I'm fine, honestly. I just..." A tear leaks out of my eye.

"Come on." Dotty Jay grabs my arm. "Put a coat on and some wellies, if you've got some. You're about to get muddy!"

* 6 * Thunder Cat arrives

Forest Hall is set in the middle of a sprawling estate in the Yorkshire countryside. Dotty Jay is keen to show us the giant weeping willow in the field behind our block.

"Behold, the mighty willow!" she roars, embracing the tree. "Legend has it that those who befriend you will never weep again!"

My housemates laugh, except for Ashley who keeps sniffing. Within seconds, Drunk Mike has given the tree a snog and Zachary the Music Theatre loon is halfway up it.

"And here's the swing." Dotty Jay points to a plank on a rope attached to a nearby tree.

Rory grins as everybody takes a turn. Silly Cat watches in envy and makes a mental note to come back alone. Tanisha and Elle are discussing the Acting course. I linger like a shadow as they talk about the books on our reading list.

"I read two," Elle says. "But I didn't manage the rest."

"Me neither!" Tanisha assures her. "I doubt anybody will have done. Seriously! Who wants to read books all summer?"

I back away. I don't want them to know that RoboCat read the whole lot. Some of them twice. And made copious notes. And highlighted them to death. And has already arranged them in alphabetical order on my shelf.

Mad Jo has an arm around Ashley. Shay has hit it off with Lottie and Lizzie and is telling them about her gap year travels across Asia. Wes is staring at her with a dopey grin. Nobody asks me why I left the bar early. I swallow back the tears, Scaredy Cat still present. *I should've refused to come on this walk. Nobody likes me.*

"Do you want to go on the swing, Caz?" I look up to see Annie staring at me.

"Er, no, it's okay." I force a smile.

I watch as Annie trots over to have a turn. She giggles with enviable freedom as she soars through the air before resuming her place beside me. "That was so cool!"

I force another smile. Dotty Jay and Rory hurry us on. Apparently, there's a lot to see. There's a waterfall by the lake and a bat cave in the woods and sculptures made by local artists hidden through the trees. Annie walks beside me. Her pace is slower than mine and I feel clumsy as I try to keep in step.

Suddenly, she announces, "God says you're going to be my friend, Caz."

I stare at her beaming face. I don't know whether to be flattered or freaked out. "Thanks," I mutter.

I should probably tell her my name isn't Caz.

"Where are you from?"

I take a deep breath. "My mum was from Colombia. My dad is English so I'm half English and half Hispanic."

She looks at me blankly. "I meant where do you live?"

"Oh. Exeter."

She rummages in a pocket before offering me a sweet. I'm about to say no but then I realise they are *Jumping Jupiters*.

"Oh my gosh. I've not had one of those for years!"

"Take as many as you want."

Silly Cat wants to take a handful but Play it Cool Cat just takes one. I stare at the purple ball of sherbet encircled by pink liquorice. A million memories of childhood parties explode through my senses as I bite into it. I feel excited and forlorn and lonely and nostalgic all at once.

"Here it is!" Dotty Jay stops the parade with a wave of her hands. It's clear from the look in her eyes that we're about to see something special.

We stop in our tracks. Nobody speaks apart from Shay and Lottie and Lizzie who are dawdling several paces behind and don't seem remotely interested in Dotty Jay's marvellous tour.

"This is my absolute favourite spot on campus," Dotty Jay says, rubbing her hands together.

I crane my neck to see what she's getting so excited about. All I can see is a wooden clearing surrounded by vines. Annie offers me another *Jumping Jupiter* and I pop it into my mouth just as Dotty Jay announces, "Welcome to Fairy Land!" She darts into the wooden clearing and stomps hard on the ground. Music begins to play, as though the ground is a grand piano. I watch open-mouthed as Dotty Jay prances about, sending the most enchanting melody into the dark night.

A few of us venture in and leap from one plank to another. And suddenly, as the sherbet explodes in my mouth and my jumping feet make music beneath me, Thunder Cat arrives.

"What the *flip*, this is amazing!" I start running up and down, sending waves of music into the air. I laugh and squeal and dance with fairies, pretending I'm the leading lady in an epic movie as all my inhibitions fade away. *I LOVE this place!*

I don't want the fun to ever end but Dotty Jay reminds me I can come back any time. "We've got lots more to see," she says as we leave Fairy Land and head down to the lake.

Annie offers me another sweet and I take a handful. It's only now that I realise I am ravenously hungry. I trot along, feeling merry and bright, party tunes singing in my ears.

Ashley has stopped crying and has gathered a few feathers. I pick up a long white one and add it to her collection. I feel like a hero as she smiles. Bertie isn't wearing the right shoes and decides to venture back. I remind him that Willow is between Hazel and Laurel.

"I got lost on the way back from the bar," I say with a careless laugh. "I almost died!"

Shay and the dancer girls are still bringing up the rear, missing all the fun because they're too cool to join in. I call out to Shay that I like her boots and she grins and returns the compliment. I beam and stomp along in my bright yellow wellies, a wise purchase by Fun Cat in the run up to uni. Comfortable and stylish, the only irritation being the fact that my mother wrote my name on the heels in permanent marker. I drag my feet through a patch of mud to cover her hasty scrawl.

We reach the lake and look out over the moonlit waters. Not too far away, there's a stream and a little waterfall. The sound of running water tinkles magically through the quiet night. I scramble onto the wall to get a better look.

"Watch me!" I yell as I walk along the wall.

Elle shoots me a funny glance but I don't care. I don't need her.

"Steady on!" Rory laughs. "How many beers did you have?"

Dotty Jay helps me down. "You don't want to kill yourself before Fresher's Week. You'll miss out on all the freebies."

"Look up!" Zachary yells suddenly.

I tip my head and am just in time to see a shooting star soaring through the sky. My heart leaps. It's a sign! Proof that this is a whole new beginning. A whole new me. The past is behind me forever. Something new and unfamiliar stirs in me. A feeling I've never known before. Is it joy? Or excitement? No. It's something else... *Hope.* I can almost feel Monica with me, walking with the pack, cheering me on, her eyes always on me.

Sad Cat sighs in my ears but I drown her out by declaring with great gusto, "The whole sky is about to fall down!"

"I've never seen so many stars," Ashley agrees.

"Welcome to Yorkshire!" Rory booms.

We move on. I brave it into the bat cave and declare that I can see four. Rory says they are rocks and I smirk as everyone laughs. Then we pass some metal sculptures on the way back through the trees and I poke my head between the legs of a giant copper man and wave to Annie. "Yoo-hoo!"

I take selfies with my new housemates. "For the memories. We'll want to remember the night we met."

Dotty Jay poses with me. "You've come out of your shell!"

I shrug and pretend this was me all along.

Anything is possible. My old life doesn't exist any more. Nothing matters except this moment.

My brain is buzzing, full of a thousand ideas. I'm going to get up early and go to Fairy Land. Then I'll go on the swing. Then I'll have a proper hunt for bats and impress everyone by finding one and bringing it back to our block.

As soon as I get back to my room, I throw my wardrobe open and grab a pen. Then I scrawl in big letters, *'This is my first night! Bring on the adventure!'* I date it and sign it with Thunder Cat's special super cool autograph, the one with a giant curly C and a star for an A and the perfect little cross for a T.

* 7 * Copy Cat joins the Christian Union

My blissful sleep is hijacked by The Dream.

It's as it always is. A mysterious woman stalking me in the dark. Grabbing me. Pinning me down. She's a stranger and yet so familiar. I can't move or speak or fight and, when I finally break free, I awake in a puddle of sweat and shame. There's crying in my head and I can't stop shaking.

My chest pounds as I scramble to sit up. *Where am I?*

It slowly dawns on me. I'm at university in my new room. I'm doing the Acting course at Forest Hall. My room is 6 Willow. The events of yesterday come back to me. The long drive from home. Meeting my housemates. The bar. The walk. Fairy Land. I sink back under my covers. Just a stupid dream.

The distant dinging of the tower clock marks the passage of time. Three o'clock. Half three. Four. I stay awake, listening to the squeaky pipes and thinking about the ghosts of 6 Willow. Alan, Shelly, Juggling Jeff. What are they doing now?

When I wake again, it's past eleven. I dress quickly before opening my curtains. The late September sun glistens through the trees and a swarm of swallows dart across the blue sky. And my parents said Yorkshire would be grey and miserable!

The corridor is silent. In the kitchen, there's a box of cornflakes with my name on (literally) but I don't feel hungry. There's noise coming from outside so I venture down and peer out. My housemates are gathered on the step.

"Hey, Caz!" Annie waves at me. "We're about to go to the Freshers' Fair. Want to come?"

"Definitely," I say. "Do I need to bring anything?"

"Just arms," says Dotty Jay. "To carry all the freebies."

I laugh and flex my muscles. Can't wait.

Ten minutes later, we arrive en masse at the mansion in the middle of campus. The doors are open to two large rooms full of busy tables. A wave of fear washes over me and I'm almost swept off my feet by the reappearance of Copy Cat. I plaster a fake smile onto my face and pretend that I couldn't be happier as I make my entrance with my lovely new friends.

Dotty Jay acts as our tour guide, dragging us from stall to stall, introducing us to students in the years above and making sure we each pick up a carrier bag to stash our freebies. She supervises the mass signing of the en suites petition before urging us to join The Forest Hall Pudding Club which meets at the Grumpy Pig on Sundays.

It's not long before we all split up. Shay and the dancers get talking to some beefy guys manning the table for the Breakdancing Society. Zachary is bouncing from stall to stall, behaving as ridiculously as Thunder Cat in a sweet store. Tanisha and Elle are signing up for bank accounts. Mad Jo is on the hunt for the Running Club. Dotty Jay herself has got side-tracked with entering a raffle to win a waffle maker.

I'm left with Annie and Ashley. I flit between Copy Cat and Play it Cool Cat, depending on the person at each stall and how persuasive they are at getting me to join their cause. Without meaning to, I sign up for the Pillow Fighting Society, Greek Club, the Vegan Association and Capoeira Club. I don't even know what that is. At some point, we arrive at a rather basic table decorated with Bibles and religious paraphernalia. I wrinkle up my nose and prepare to move on.

To my surprise, Annie greets the girl at the table with a cheery, "Hooray! I've found you!"

The girl grins. "Are you a Christian?"

"Yeah! I'm Annie."

"I'm Nina. So good to meet you!"

They embrace one another like long lost sisters and I pretend to be interested in a leaflet entitled, *'Lost? Try Jesus!'*

When I look up, Annie is busy writing her contact details on a piece of paper. Nina smiles at me as Annie drops the pen. In the awkward silence that follows, Copy Cat picks the pen up and writes my own details down.

"Are you a Christian, Caz?"

I regard Annie's dopey grin with confusion. "I suppose. I went to a Catholic primary school so I know all the stories. And I was christened."

Annie's face drops.

"And my parents are both religious," I add.

What I mean is that my mum used to go to mass every Sunday until she got offended with Father Derek because he was eating dinner when she wanted to see him and she felt that a priest who wouldn't stop his dinner for someone in distress clearly wasn't fit for the job. And many times I've waited outside the church while she's gone in for confession. She comes out looking teary and fragile and I used to think she'd had a heart to heart with Jesus himself until I grew old enough to know better. And my dad usually sits round the house crying and yelling at God. So I expect he believes in him. And I'm no stranger to Holy Cat. She appears whenever there's a crisis at home. I pray. I weep. I beg for forgiveness. And I try really, really hard to be good.

Nina gives an overzealous smile. "You're welcome to join us any time!" She hands me one of the *'Try Jesus'* flyers.

Well that was awkward. And the freebie wasn't worth it.

We move on and I warn Copy Cat not to sign up for anything else. At some point we lose Ashley to the Knitting Club and it's just me and Annie traipsing around for a long time before finally admitting the whole thing is distinctly less thrilling than Dotty Jay promised. I peer in my carrier bag. I've got five pens, a keyring for a bank that I don't bank with, a ball of fluff with googly eyes, a packet of popcorn, two lollypops, six boiled sweets, four bookmarks, a white balloon, Nina's wacky Jesus leaflet and a plastic lemon.

"Are you hungry?" asks Annie. "Dotty Jay said the refectory do the best bacon butties." She pauses. "Sorry, Caz. I forgot. You're a vegan, aren't you?"

"No, I'm not. I just really wanted the plastic lemon. I don't speak Greek either."

"Caz! You're hilarious."

I snort. "My name is Cat, not Caz. I didn't know how to say no to Mad Jo!"

Annie giggles before confessing, "I can't decide whether I am totally excited or totally terrified to be starting university. It all feels so grown up."

"Far too grown up," I agree, waving my plastic lemon.

We look at one another and laugh. Then, somewhere between leaving the mansion and entering the refectory, Fun Cat finally arrives.

* 8 * Fun Cat likes butterflies

How wonderful it is to be Fun Cat! My head is no longer swimming, I can have a conversation without feeling like a blushing fool and I'm humming *'Dancing Queen'* as we skip into the campus canteen.

We spot Dotty Jay and Rory in the queue, swinging their Freshers' Fair carrier bags and glugging bottles of pop. Rory finishes his before he reaches the till and hands the empty bottle to the dinner lady. I'm famished and start salivating at everything on offer. There's a pasta table, salad bar, more sandwich fillers than I have pairs of socks, four meal options with chips, rice or mashed potato, a fridge full of colourful desserts, a crisp rack, several rows of chocolate bars and three types of bread roll. I load up my tray with lasagne, chips, green beans, sweetcorn, a banana milkshake, a packet of prawn cocktail crisps and a chocolate muffin before presenting my meal card to the dinner lady at the till.

"Hiya, Petal," she says in a thick Yorkshire drawl. "Is this everything?"

I look around. *What else is there?*

"Oh, and these," I say, picking up a cookie and a sensible apple for later.

The dinner lady swipes my card and hands me my receipt. "There you go, Petal."

I stuff my meal card back into my pocket. It feels like free money. I've got a card with hundreds of pounds on it, pre-paid by my parents, to use in the refectory as often as I choose. I can have a banana milkshake every day if I want!

Annie follows me with a bacon butty. We join Dotty Jay and Rory at their table and I feel rather indulgent as I unload my tray. The two of them are sharing a sausage roll.

"You need to be careful!" Dotty Jay wags a finger at me.

I'm about to explain that I've always had a fast metabolism and can eat anything I like without putting on weight. Lucky Fun Cat. But she continues, "It's not as much money as you think it is. You'll feel like a queen for a week and eat till you're stuffed. But, if you're not careful, you'll use it all by Christmas."

Rory gives a sombre nod. "Last year, I had to survive on leftovers for a whole term." He points to the metal trolleys by the kitchen that are stuffed with dirty plates and surplus food.

I take this on board but I'm not worried. My parents have already said they'll top up my card if I need them to.

I look around the busy hall. My welcome letter and accompanying brochure had led me to believe that a 'refectory' was something refined. But it is, in fact, just one huge school canteen. It even smells like one. I feel like a small child as Silly Cat comes bobbing to the surface. It's my first day of school and I've got my cheese sandwich, chocolate in a blue wrapper and red flask filled with water. The freedom to choose what order to eat everything in makes me dizzy. I give myself a shake. A few swigs of my milkshake and Fun Cat is back. I guzzle my chips, giggling as Dotty Jay treats Annie and me to a series of strange superstitions.

"Never go to Fairy Land in a thunderstorm because Willow will be struck by lightning if you do... If you buy an orange, take it from the back of the bowl because the front ones have been contaminated by everyone's eyes... Don't step on the fourth step outside Hazel because a rat died on it once and it's cursed so you might break a bone... And never, ever look at the tower clock when it's striking midnight..."

Dotty Jay is the weirdest person I've ever met. She has some kind of ethereal quality to her, as though she was dug up from the ground instead of being born like a normal person. And she has an opinion on absolutely everything which she gives whether you want it or not. Still, she's being very nice to me and I could think of worse housemates (cough cough, Snooty Elle.)

In the evening, Posh Bertie sticks up a map of the UK on the boys' corridor and invites everyone to put a pin on their home town. Bertie's idea of an ice breaker.

Despite only coming from Leeds, which is a mere thirty minutes away, Annie turns out to be hideous at geography and needs a lot of help working out where to put her pin.

Dotty Jay is on hand to help, singing, "Typical type five!"

I join the game, choosing the brightest pink pin in the pot.

Mad Jo comes up behind me. "Exeter's miles away!" she remarks as she stabs a pin north of London. "Is it nice?"

"Quite nice." I try to think of something nice about it. "We've got a few beaches nearby."

She shoots me a look of envy. "Lucky you!"

I feel an irritating pang of sorrow and hurriedly stuff Sad Cat down. "Did you find the Running Club?"

"Yeah! They meet for a sunrise run every morning."

Copy Cat would have pretended this sounded fun and probably would have been roped into joining. Not Fun Cat.

"Rather you than me," I say with a grin.

There's some scuttling in the stairwell and Shay, Lottie and Lizzie appear in the doorway, dressed up to the nines.

"We're off to Wakefield," Shay announces.

Dotty Jay looks up from the map. "The bus leaves at—"

"Half past," Lottie chips in. "We know."

"And you get off at—"

"The Fishy Fishy Chippy," says Lizzie. "Some of the guys from Laurel told us earlier. We're going to start at The Old Hag then head to Wango's when the clubs open."

Dotty Jay looks rather put out that they have organised their night without her input. Still, she pulls herself together and says, "Great. Willow trip to Wakey!" She sprints out of the boys' corridor and dashes up the stairs, yelling, "Wakey night out in ten minutes!" as though it was her idea.

Mad Jo is hot on her heels. "I'll get changed!"

Shay looks at me and Annie. "You girls coming?"

I hesitate. I don't want to go. The idea of being in a strange city after dark terrifies me. Plus, we went to the bar *yesterday*. How many nights out do these people need? But I don't want to be a loner weirdo either.

"I don't fancy it," Annie says beside me. "I'm quite tired."

"Sure you are," Shay laughs. "Coming all the way from Leeds. You must still be recovering from the journey." She gives a melodic giggle. Her yellow pin sings proudly from the mysterious green fields of Ireland, the furthest travelled of us all. She's crossed land and sea to take her place. And I can't even stomach a bus ride to Wakefield.

"I'm pretty tired too," I say. Then Fun Cat takes a stab at being honest and adds, "I'm not a fan of clubbing."

Shay and the dancers look at me like I'm an oddity but Fun Cat doesn't falter. Wow, I'm strong today.

With a burst of courage, I go to my room and grab my giant butterfly hoodie. I pull it on and dance back down, standing shoulder to shoulder with Annie as we wave everybody off.

"Have a great time!" I yell, flapping my wings.

There's the sound of someone popping up behind us and Ashley says in a whisper, "I've got some crafts if you're interested? We could make posters to brighten up the halls?"

So while everyone else gets boozy in Wakey, the three of us have a creative session in the middle of the top floor corridor. Ashley has a box full of card and stickers and glitter which she shares with reckless abandon.

"Do you want some money for this?" I ask, after using half a bottle of glitter glue on my picture of a giant butterfly.

"Of course not!" she exclaims. "I brought it for everyone."

This kind of frivolous generosity feels wild to me. I was always taught to hold things tightly. I feel like I need to give her *something* so I run to my room and grab my extra cookie from lunch. I split it sloppily into three.

We hear marching on the stairs and Zachary the skinny bean pops up with a cheery smile. "What are you doing?"

I hold up my poster. "It's for my door," I say proudly. Then I explain, "It's a butterfly," in case my clumsy efforts aren't clear.

"I gathered that." He laughs before reading the inscription beneath it. *"High in the sky the butterfly sings, 'Only the bravest caterpillars get their wings.'* Did you make that up? It's nice."

I'm even more chuffed when Ashley tells me it's good. She's on the Creative Writing course so that's high praise indeed.

Zachary points to my hoodie. "I take it you like butterflies?"

"Yeah. They're the craziest creatures. A hairy caterpillar tucks itself into a cocoon only to transform into something entirely new, nothing like it's former self. Everything about it is changed. In fact, there's a point where the caterpillar literally turns into mush before becoming a whole new creation!"

Annie looks up from her painting of a hedgehog.

Zachary gives me a funny smile. "A miracle, indeed."

Ashley pats the floor. "Wanna join us, Zachary?"

He reaches for some yellow card. "You girls didn't fancy going to Wakefield then?"

I shake my head. "Not our thing."

"Me neither."

It turns out Zachary is quite an artist. His piece of card is soon covered in the most mesmerising maze of spirals and stars. I watch as he colours it in with neon pens before slicing it up into triangles.

"What are you making?" I ask.

He grins. "Bunting."

I give an incredulous laugh. *Bunting?* I know from the pin on Bertie's map that Zachary C Fenn is from a tiny village in Norfolk. Perhaps the boys are different there.

"What's the 'C' in your name for?" I ask as I watch him doodling over a sheet of electric pink.

"Conway. My mother's maiden name. It means 'holy river.'"

I nod. "Mine is Carla. I don't know what it means."

Annie's is May after an old aunt and Ashley's is Sue after her grandmother. I'm not named after anybody and I'm glad about that. If I could, I'd cut off my silly burger surname and just be Catrina Carla. That will be my stage name anyway.

By the time we go to bed, every common wall in Willow is decorated with brightly coloured butterflies and birds and hedgehogs and Zachary's psychedelic paper bunting. I have so much fun that I don't notice that my phone battery is dead and I've missed the phone call I had scheduled with my parents. A good thing really. I don't fancy being Lost Cat or RoboCat right now.

* 9 * Sad Cat is not sheltered

I'm proud to say that Fun Cat has held the reins for three whole days. It looks like she's here to stay!

I'm being friendly with everyone in my block and most of the time I don't feel intimated by Cool Shay or Lottie or Lizzie. I let Annie share my cereal when she ran out of hers. At first, Angry Cat was a little miffed at how quickly my stash was shrinking. But then Annie surprised me with a chocolate bar from the vending machines and Fun Cat decided that being generous is definitely the way to make friends. I know my mum wouldn't approve of me sharing my food so I don't mention it when she rings.

Each morning after breakfast, I take a stroll around campus, following the path that leads straight to Fairy Land. Thunder Cat has a bounce before coming back via the library. I've checked out eight books which RoboCat plans to read before our lessons start on Monday. I've sampled all the yoghurts at the refectory and lemon mousse is my favourite. I survived my first shopping trip to Wakefield (with Dotty Jay as my omniscient guide). I can get to the Merry Bar and back without getting lost. I was bold enough to order a blackcurrant soda when Mad Jo tried to buy me a beer. I held my cool when Mike teased me for admitting I've never been drunk. And, thanks to Rory, I'm a dab hand at bumping the vending machines to occasionally score myself an extra packet of crisps.

I've also done laundry for the first time ever! My dirty clothes were piling up so I summoned up the courage to ask Dotty Jay where the laundry room was. She kindly took me and showed me what to do.

"Set a timer for an hour and come back to put it in the dryer," she'd said after popping my money in the slot.

"But what if it's done before I get back?" I asked.

"It'll just sit there unless someone needs the machine and takes your stuff out." Dotty Jay pointed to a pile of damp clothes on a bench. "But it will probably be fine. My stuff hardly ever gets moved."

I didn't fancy my chances and waited in the laundry room for the full hour. Then I rang Dotty Jay and she came back and showed me how to operate the dryer and I waited another hour until it was done. All in all, I'm amazed at how simple the whole process was. I'm pretty sure I'll be able to remember it.

Everyone else seems to be settling in too and this afternoon we're enjoying a block picnic under the weeping willow. Dotty Jay has impressed everyone with a batch of homemade cookies and some potato wedges. It's astonishing what you can cook in a microwave! I still don't know whether Dotty Jay is her full name or whether her first name is Jay and 'Dotty' is a description. What I do learn at today's picnic is that Dotty Jay had a rather tragic childhood. She's been in and out of foster care and has an alcoholic father. You'd never know it to look at her. She always seems so jolly. I see her quirks in a whole new light and feel a surge of shame for not being more grateful for my own life.

I hear my mum's voice in my head. *"I've given you everything!"*

She really has. Clothes, shoes, swimming lessons, fancy phones, trips away, healthy meals, haircuts. She's said she'll pay for driving lessons and buy me a car as soon as I pass. You can't get more generous than that. My dad is sending me fifty pounds a week and most parents don't do that. Dotty Jay and Rory have part time jobs at the Merry Bar and Mad Jo has said she needs to find a job swiftly. So I'm lucky really, even if Sad Cat wants to know whether good mothers leave their children as often as mine does.

She does her best. Holy Cat appears, the voice of shame and endless good intentions. *And if God is real, then he loves her and you're meant to forgive her.*

Speaking of God, Annie has asked if I want to go to church with her at the weekend. I might have to go to be polite unless it clashes with something else. Perhaps Dotty Jay's pudding club. I wonder what kind of desserts they have at The Grumpy Pig. My favourite is rhubarb fool. It's one of my mother's specialities. I also like rice crispy cakes. I actually know how to make those. Next time I go to Wakefield, I'll have to remember to get some cooking chocolate. Perhaps I can make one for all of my housemates as a way of being friendly—

"Watch out!" I am startled by a shout, quickly followed by a blow to the side of my head.

"Sorry!" Wes comes running over to retrieve his frisbee.

I clutch my head and blink back the tears. I'd zoned out without realising.

Everyone is still discussing families. It turns out the man I took for Mad Jo's father is actually her stepfather. And her real name is Jocelyn. Why she chooses to be known as Mad Jo when she has such a lovely name as Jocelyn is beyond me. I feel Sad Cat burning behind my eyes. I always feel like crying when people talk about their families. Happy families or unhappy ones, it makes no difference. Both make me feel left out. If I'm not careful, Sad Cat will open the door to Squashed Cat or Lost Cat and Fun Cat will be gone again.

I reach for one of Dotty Jay's cookies in an attempt to shut Sad Cat out. "These are so yummy," I say loudly.

Waves of approval ripple round our housemates and Dotty Jay beams. "I'm the queen of microwave cooking," she tells us. "I've had three years on campus to practise."

I have a brainwave. "Can you cook eggs in the microwave?"

"Of course. Just crack one into a mug and put it in for four minutes."

"What about a boiled egg? Then you wouldn't need a mug."

Dotty Jay gives me a funny look before creasing up.

"A boiled egg?" Rory repeats. "You mean just bung an egg in without cracking it?"

"Yeah... Why are you all laughing?"

"You can't put an egg in the microwave!" Lottie exclaims.

"It would explode," adds Lizzie.

"Oh my gosh!" Shay shoots me a pitying smirk. "You're so sheltered."

I feel a surge of self-pity as Sad Cat rears her head.

"I'm not sheltered," I snap.

"You are *totally* sheltered!" Shay laughs. "You've never done laundry. You've never been drunk. You were afraid to get the bus to Wakefield. And now you reckon you can cook an egg by putting it in the microwave!"

My housemates are grinning at me.

"Don't worry. We'll teach you the ways of the world," Mike offers.

"Don't feel bad, Caz," Mad Jo adds. "It's sweet."

I force a careless shrug. Inside, Angry Cat is reeling.

I am not sheltered. I know several swear words in English and Spanish. I've seen some very scary films, thanks to my cousin Chantelle. I've run barefoot through the streets of Exeter hunting for my runaway mother. I've been my father's therapist since the age of seven and, so far, I've kept him alive. I know many things about my mother's childhood and the horrible things that happened to her.

Unspeakable things.

The kind of things that break a person.

I've seen my mum beat my dad with a plank of wood. I watched her threaten Duncan Anderson from down the road with a knife. I've crossed my fingers as she's been rushed to hospital multiple times for collapsing for unknown reasons. And I've made a contingency plan for if both my parents disappear and Aidan and I are left in the custody of Aunt Sonya. In fact, the first thing I'll do when I finish university is find a flat of my own and apply for housing benefit. I've got it all worked out and I've done a lot of research.

So I'm not sheltered. Not really. I just don't know how to boil an egg.

* 10 * Creative Cat saves the day

The rest of Fresher's Week is a blur of crazy activity.

Willow comes second at the Merry Bar pub quiz, with RoboCat's knowledge of homeopathic remedies (courtesy of my father) coming in handy for the first time in my life. During an open mic night, Fun Cat takes the stage with Zachary, Mad Jo and Dotty Jay for a rousing rendition of *'I will survive.'* Ashley and I have another craft night and I make a dragonfly poster for Dotty Jay because they're her favourite. Shay and the dancers try to tempt me with a selection of cocktails during a birthday barbecue for Tanisha. Mike teases me but I feel vindicated when he gets drunk, falls down a drain and ends up in A&E with a fractured ankle. Bertie blows his student loan on a grand piano. It takes up so much space that there's no room for his bed and he now sleeps on a duvet under the piano. His room is below mine so I'm treated to live music day and night. I have a trumpet lesson from Zachary and I make crispy cakes with Annie and I even do another load of laundry all by myself.

My parents phone every day although Lost Cat has very little to say except that I'm fine, thank you, and yes, I'm taking my vitamins, and, no, it's not too cold up North, and, yes, I'm keeping my door locked and, no, nobody's stolen any of my food and of course I'm not letting anybody use my meal card. I feel unsettled after their phone calls but it doesn't take much to recover my joy. A milkshake. A bounce in Fairy Land. A gaze through my window at the beautiful green fields.

But university isn't all about making friends and not getting drunk. There are lessons to be had! And my actor training starts today.

Monica counsels me in my head all through campus. *"You can do this, Cat. You were born for this. I'm so proud of you. Just get out there and shine like the star you are!"*

But the moment I enter the large airy room in the heart of the mansion, Fun Cat shrinks away. Copy Cat is back and a creeping dread spreads over me. *What am I doing here?*

The room is filled with about thirty five others. I recognise a few of them from the Merry Bar freshers' events. The rest must be from Wintergates, the campus in the heart of Wakefield. They have to get the bus in and out every day. I can't imagine anything so stressful. I rarely got the bus back in Exeter, and certainly never for school. My dad always drove me. My parents are reliable like that. Won't ever let me go anywhere alone.

I follow Tanisha and Elle to the back of the room where a gaggle of Wintergates girls are recounting some escapades from the night before. Apparently, someone got so drunk that they climbed out of the window and the warden had to be called. It sounds like their campus is a lot wilder than ours. The students are cooler too. Half a dozen of them are still outside having a smoke. I chew my nails, begging, *pleading* with Fun Cat to come back. But it's no use. My chest is pounding and my eyes are welling up as Copy Cat and Scaredy Cat, the hapless duo, take my hands.

Then Terry Marvel walks in. He's the one who auditioned me. He has fluffy white hair which hovers on his head like a cloud, a scruffy chin and eyes like emeralds. He catches my eye and I feel a flutter in my belly as he gives me a look of recognition. Following behind him are a lanky middle-aged man in an oversized shirt and a serious-looking lady with steamroller straight blonde hair and immaculate clothing.

"Good morning first year Acting students!" Terry booms. His voice fills the room like a flood and everyone falls silent.

My head swims as Terry welcomes us to Forest Hall. "You have all accomplished something incredible simply by being here today. For every one of you, there were fifteen hopefuls who didn't make it. Do you hear that? Fifteen?"

Far from feeling proud, Scaredy Cat is shaking. *There must have been some mistake. I can't act. I'm too shy. I've never had a decent part in a show. When Terry noticed me earlier, it must've been because he never meant to admit me. He's going to come over afterwards and ask why I'm here.*

Sweat floods my armpits as Terry goes on, "You worked hard to get here. Now you've arrived, we expect nothing less than complete dedication. We will not accept laziness or unaccounted absences. While you're here, you'll learn the skills and discipline required to be a working actor and none of you, *none of you,* have made it yet. I don't care if you were the lead in your last school show or whether you're Little Betty from Gossip Town." He shoots Elle a wink.

There's a gasp as people turn and notice her.

Elle sniffs.

"Whoever you are," Terry continues. "We expect you to work hard and do yourself proud."

Terry waffles on about the course and our classes. I try to pay attention but I get tired and RoboCat ends up counting the number of students with black hair, brown hair, blonde hair, ginger hair, green hair and multicoloured stripes.

Finally, Terry gestures to the two people beside him. "This is Pat and this is Jodie."

Pat gives a goofy wave but Jodie just stares stony-faced. Terry invites them to introduce themselves and Pat does this with great gusto, using phrases such as 'blisteringly glad to be here' and 'jolly old fellow from Brighton.'

When he's done, Jodie smiles tersely and says, "I'm a former Forest Hall Acting student myself so I speak from experience when I say you're about the have the time of your life. Don't waste it. Your university years are sacred and you'll never get them back. It's already ten years since I was sitting where you are and, believe me, the time has flown. You can get as much out of Forest Hall as you want. It can be the making of you or the breaking of you. We're all here to help but, ultimately, it's down to you."

My chest aches. I'm desperate to be made and not broken.

"As you can see, there are rather a lot of you," Terry says. "So we'll be dividing you into two groups. Group A will be led by Pat and group B will be led by Jodie."

Thunder Cat wants to be in group A because A sounds better than B. Scaredy Cat agrees because Jodie is very stern and Pat might be kinder. But Silly Cat can't help wondering whether Jodie might like to be my mother. That's stupid. She's nowhere near old enough.

"The moment of truth!" Terry whips out a piece of paper and puts his glasses on. "If I call your name then you're in group A with Pat and he'll lead you through to Heather next door."

For a moment, I wonder who Heather is. Then I remember that the rooms in the mansion are all named after flowers. We're in Primrose right now. I concentrate on staying alert as Terry goes down his list. This would be a really bad time for RoboCat to zone out. Several students arise as their names are called and Pat welcomes each one with a high five. Meanwhile, Jodie stands looking frosty and I am more and more desperate not to be left in group B. Tanisha's name is called and she shoots Elle and me a grin before grabbing her bag and joining Pat's party.

Finally, Terry rolls up his piece of paper and says, "And that's everyone. So the rest of you are left with the Ice Queen."

Jodie gives him a punch on the shoulder. "Off you go," she says to Pat and his gang. "Clear off, all of you."

Pat blows a kiss before leading group A out of the room. Terry follows behind and shuts the door, leaving twenty of us staring at Jodie as she paces the room, muttering to herself, "...taking forever over introductions... only ten minutes left."

Elle is frowning. The rest of our group look equally dismayed to have missed out on being with Pat.

"Right then!" Jodie claps her hands. "Get into a circle."

My heart sinks as she introduces a getting-to-know-you game. One by one we're to leap into the centre of the circle and announce our name while performing an action corresponding with our first initial. Then everyone else has to repeat our action and say hello to us. I hate this sort of thing.

What did you expect? Angry Cat scolds. *You can't sign up for an Acting course then go all shy when they ask you to perform.*

Jodie begins with an energetic bounce, "I am Jumping Jodie!" She finally looks pleased to be here.

"Hello, Jumping Jodie!" we reply as we mimic her.

The others take to the game with great enthusiasm but I can't think straight. *What should I choose? Cooking Catrina? That's daft. I can't cook. Clapping Catrina? Pathetic. Crawling Catrina? Too weird. Cartwheeling Catrina? I've never done a cartwheel in my life. Choking Catrina? Crying Catrina? Cut me up into little pieces Catrina? What's wrong with me? It's a game. Just pick something!*

I'm pretty sure I'm going to go with Cooking Catrina as it's the most normal thing I can think of. But then Cooking Clemmie introduces herself and I am flooded with terror as I only have a matter of seconds to think of something else.

"I'm Electric Elle," my housemate says as she steps into the centre of the circle and does a little wiggle.

I feel a surge of irritation as everyone laughs and wiggles. "Hello, Electric Elle!"

Egotistical Elle, more like, Angry Cat snaps.

Think of something! cries Scaredy Cat. *It's my turn next!*

And, in the nick of time, I remember mine and Ashley's craft sessions and save myself with a wave of the hands and an awkward bellow of "I am Creative Cat!"

"Hello Creative Cat!" Everybody copies my careless wave and I breathe a sigh of relief as I leave the circle.

When everybody's had a turn, Jodie says, "I don't expect you to remember anybody's name just yet. I certainly won't. Except for you, Vibrating Viktor."

Viktor repeats his action and everyone laughs. Everyone, that is, except RoboCat who has absorbed all the information perfectly. Along with Elle and Viktor and Cooking Clemmie, there's Roaring Rose and Snorkelling Simeon and Kite-flying Kimberley and Weightlifting Will and Dancing Donna and Sneezing Sky and Smoking Sienna and Murdering Marsha and Poker-playing Poppy and Horse-riding Heidi and Foxtrotting Faye and Praying Pranjal and Boxing Blake and Partying Pip and Abseiling Arthur and Owl-watching Otis.

Jodie checks her watch and scowls. "We've run out of time. I'll have to set you the other task as homework."

I feel another surge of anxiety but the assignment isn't too awful. We just have to read the first chapter of 'The Actor Wears a Mask' (which I've already done) and create a short mime of making our bed which we will be asked to perform in different emotional states.

Our first lesson is over. We'll be having Jodie for our main workshop every morning, then skills classes in the afternoons. After lunch today we've got a movement lesson in another of the mansion rooms followed by a voice class led by Terry.

Elle leaves pretty swiftly. She doesn't even ask if I want to walk with her. Which I don't, anyway. A few of my new classmates hang back to chat with Jodie. They want her tips on student life and where to shop in Wakefield.

Jodie catches my eye. "Remind me your name?"

"Cat," I mutter.

"Oh yes. Creative Cat."

My throat goes dry. Eventually, Copy Cat asks stupidly, "When did you study here?"

She gives me a funny look as if to ask why I wasn't paying attention earlier. "Ten years ago."

I nod and ask the question I had actually meant to ask. "Did you live on campus?"

"Yeah. I was in Willow."

Silly Cat feels a surge of excitement. "I'm in Willow! So are Tanisha and Elle. Tanisha's in group A. Elle was Little Betty in *Gossip Town*. Which room was yours?"

Please say 6! Please say 6!

"7."

"That's Annie's room," I stammer. "She's doing Dance. I'm room 6."

"Lovely. You're going to have a great time." Jodie smiles before turning to another student.

Sad Cat wants to keep talking but I don't have anything else to say. Perhaps I could ask a question about the assignment. But then she'll think I wasn't listening. I should ask her something about Willow, like whether the stairwell was as cold in her time.

Don't be stupid, Sad Cat. Just go away.

"See you tomorrow," I squeak.

But she doesn't hear me. She's too busy discussing Shakey Wakey Cars with Smoking Sienna and Cooking Clemmie.

* 11 * Sad Cat makes her bed

Thunder Cat makes her entrance known as soon as I'm back in the safety of Willow.

"I am Creative Cat!" I leap into the corridor and give a crazed swipe, far more dramatic than the one I managed for my classmates.

Dotty Jay greets me in a tatty jumper. "Did you have a good lesson?"

"Yeah. It was great. How was yours?"

I realise I don't care and Thunder Cat prances down the corridor in search of food while Dotty Jay tells me about musical theory. Or something.

I enjoy a microwaved egg in a mug before scurrying back to the mansion for the afternoon. Thunder Cat is left behind and I'm Copy Cat again, bumbling my way through the movement lesson and staying silent through the voice class, despite the fact that Terry doesn't demand to know why I'm here and, in actual fact, smiles and says, "Catrina Berger, right? I remember your audition." I want to cry. According to Wes, Terry Marvel has a drinking problem. That'll be why I'm here. He was drunk when he auditioned me.

Terry leads the class through some breathing exercises and then we slowly chant vowels in unison. I mouth along but, all the while, Squashed Cat is a tangled knot in my throat.

And then my first day is over and I am Normal Cat again, trotting to the refectory to have dinner with my housemates, my head a jumbled mix of shame and self-doubt and frustration and just the teeniest bit of hope because what if Terry Marvel *wasn't* drunk when he auditioned me? And what if I really can do this? And what if Forest Hall could truly be the amazing place of freedom that it promises to be?

Annie is feeling glum because her ballet is not quite up to scratch. Ashley's mind went blank during a writing exercise and she only wrote two lines. And Zachary accidentally passed wind during a dance class. So it's not just me who flunked the first day. It could have been worse. At least I didn't fart out loud. Not that Zachary seems bothered. He jabbers away with careless confidence and eats two whole plates of food as well as mine and Annie's leftovers.

The next morning, Fun Cat is determined to try again. Along with the rest of the class, I mime making my bed as Jodie stands at the side and calls out emotions.

"Excited."

I let Thunder Cat take over for this one and remember how I felt on the day I found out I'd got into Forest Hall. I don't even put the duvet over the bed. I just toss it carelessly into the air and bounce around on it.

"Heartbroken."

Sad Cat takes over as I remember one of the many times when my mother has left. Instead of making my bed, I slowly mime peeling back the sheets and crawling under the covers. I curl into a tiny ball and bury my head in my arms. It's so good, I almost shed a little tear.

"Hungry."

Thunder Cat is back. I spring into action, shaking my imaginary sheets and pummelling my pillows before rooting around under my bed for my emergency chocolate.

Scaredy Cat takes on 'nervous' and RoboCat does 'spaced out' and Angry Cat makes a rare appearance to mime smashing my bed to pieces for 'furious.'

I feel a little dizzy once it's over and slide back into Copy Cat for the rest of the lesson.

We have a dance class in the afternoon and I feel ugly as Scaredy Cat gets her left and right muddled up. Later, hidden in my bedroom, Fun Cat will dance this routine perfectly.

Then we have a singing lesson and, as I stutter along with the group song, I think back to my Fresher's Week rendition of *I will survive* and wonder why it is so hard to be myself.

The week goes on and I alternate between being Fun Cat out of lessons and stupid Copy Cat or Scaredy Cat in class. Jodie must think I'm a loser. I often notice her staring at me when we're rehearsing. Everyone else in my class is loud and proud and keen to have a go. I never volunteer for anything.

The following Monday, we're in pairs and have been given twenty minutes to rehearse a duologue. I'm working with Kite-flying Kimberley, a large bubbly girl from Manchester.

"I know this one," she says, glancing at the script. "I did it for one of my exams at college. I'll be Yvonne."

"Yeah, okay," I mutter. I haven't even read it yet.

"You start." Kimberley flaps the script at me.

My eyes scan the text. Yvonne is thinking of leaving her husband and my character, Diana, is begging her to reconsider. I feel a stab in my heart. I remember being seven years old and watching my mother gather up her possessions into four large suitcases. I remember standing by the front door with my arms outstretched. As though that could stop her from leaving. I remember her saying coldly, "Get out of my way, Catrina. I don't love you any more."

I take a deep breath before letting Sad Cat out.

"Please don't do it," I read, my voice wobbling and sounding strange to my ears.

"I have to. I've got my own life to think about," Kimberley reads carelessly. *"Andrew's just holding me back."*

"He loves you more than you'll ever know."

"Oh, he doesn't love me," Kimberley sings gaily.

I remember my dad sobbing on the stairs after she left. I remember him smashing his head repeatedly against the wall. I remember him calling Father Derek round, as if he might have the power to pray her back.

My voice cracks. *"I don't know what he'll do without you. I don't know what any of us will do."*

I feel rather shaky as we reach the end of the script.

"Hey, that was quite good," Kite-flying Kimberley says flippantly. "You just missed this line..." She points. *"At least wait until after Christmas."*

"Oh yeah, sorry."

We read the script a few more times and then it's time to show the rest of our class. We perform the scene just as we rehearsed it, with Kimberley dancing through her lines in loud confident tones and Sad Cat muttering through mine. Everyone claps politely when we're done and I keep my head down and scurry back to my seat.

As I watch everyone perform the same script over and over, the ache in my chest grows ever more painful. I put my hand up and ask if I can go to the toilet. Jodie nods and I sprint out of the room, tears falling all the way down the corridor. I don't know why I'm so sad. It was just a stupid memory from a long time ago. And she came back. She always comes back. And of course she loves me really. She wouldn't buy me nice things or write my name over my belongings or promise me a car if she didn't.

I stuff Sad Cat down and wander back to Primrose where RoboCat takes over to get me through the rest of the lesson. When Jodie dismisses us, I prepare to run away but she calls me back. "Can I have a quick word, Cat?"

My stomach churns. *She's going to tell me off for disappearing for so long.*

"Can we chat outside? I'm desperate for a cigarette."

"Yeah... Sure..." I follow her through the back door and into the drizzling rain. The tears have welled up before she's even lit her cigarette.

But, when she speaks, her tone is gentle. "Are you alright?"

I'm about to say I'm fine, but Scaredy Cat bursts into tears instead. Jodie watches me and I feel all kinds of stupid.

"I spoke to Terry about you," she says, taking a long drag on her cigarette. "He said you were bewitching in your audition."

Smoke wafts over me and I try not to cough.

"You've read all the books on the reading list, haven't you?"

I blink at her. *How does she know that?*

"It's obvious. I can see it on your face every time I ask a question and yet you never answer. Why not?"

I shrug, cheeks burning.

"I tell you what... Tomorrow I'm going to ask you something from '*The Truthful Actor*.'" She has one last puff on her cigarette before tossing it to the ground and stamping it out. "I'll ask you a question and I want you to reply, okay?"

"Okay," I squeak.

"And, whatever you do, promise me you won't quit."

I shake my head. Of course I won't quit. I never want to go home again.

* 12 * Scaredy Cat makes Little Betty cower

The next day, as planned, Jodie poses a question and picks on me. "According to Krispin Staniscofskin in *'The Truthful Actor,'* what is the key to truthful acting... Cat?"

I gulp before replying, "Truthful living."

"Which means what?"

"Knowing what you know and feeling what you feel."

"Excellent!" Jodie punches the air. "That is the right answer." She shoots me a little wink.

I feel a shiver of excitement and Fun Cat peeps to see what's going on. *I'm going on! That's what! I just answered a question in front of my whole class!*

I feel smug as my classmates write my quote down. Then Jodie tells us to get into pairs as she hands out some scripts and Fun Cat slinks away, expecting to be left behind.

"Want to work with me, Cat?"

I look up to see Owl-watching Otis grinning eagerly.

I stare at him in surprise. Owl-watching Otis is part of the Wintergates gang. He's friends with Roaring Rose and Murdering Marsha and several other cool kids. I manage a nod before turning to today's script. It's about a couple making up after a fight. I think about the frightened relief I always feel when my mum comes home and use that as inspiration.

"I'm not sure what you're saying, Mitch."

"I'm saying that I love you, Sarah. I know I've been an idiot but I can change."

"Don't mess me about, Mitch. Please don't do this."

Otis looks up from the script and grins. "You're really good at this, Cat."

I shrug off his compliments. "You too."

We go over the script several times. I've memorised my lines by the time Jodie calls us all to sit down. Thank you, RoboCat. Yet, somewhere between sitting down and waiting for our names to be called, anxiety sets in.

I need to tell Jodie we're not ready, Scaredy Cat whispers. *We need more time to rehearse. I'm not good enough.*

"Cat and Otis." Jodie calls our names and I'm shaking as I follow Otis to the front.

I don't want to look like I'm showing off by doing it without the script. At the same time, it feels clumsy in my hand. I can concentrate better without it. I drop the paper and look Otis in the eye before beginning our scene.

"I'm not sure what you're saying, Mitch..."

He gives a nervous cough before glancing at the script in his hand and reciting, *"I'm saying that I love you, Sarah. I know I've been an idiot but I can change."*

"Don't mess me about, Mitch. Please don't do this..."

With my hands free, I am untethered from the script. The words feel fresh and new, as though they are flowing from some deep, true part of me.

"Please, Sarah. I won't let you down."

"I can't," I whisper. *"You were my first love and I'll always love you. But I can't do this any more."*

We reach the end and I feel a giant wave of relief.

I look up. My classmates are staring at me. At first, I am horrified, afraid they are about to mock me. But then Smoking Sienna swears and says, "That was amazing."

"Mesmerising," whispers Poker-playing Poppy.

"It made me cry," adds Horse-riding Heidi.

"Me too," says Vibrating Viktor.

"It was beautiful," Jodie says firmly.

Several of my classmates give murmurs of agreement and Elle is staring at me, looking dare-I-say-it frightened.

Jodie catches me at the end of class. "See? Did you hear what your classmates said?"

"Yeah." My ears go hot. "I didn't think it was any good."

"Why not?"

"I don't know... I wasn't very good at acting at school."

"Weren't you?"

"Well, my old Drama teacher didn't think so. I never played the lead or anything."

Jodie snorts. "Then your old Drama teacher obviously doesn't know how to spot potential. You're exactly where you need to be, Cat. You belong here."

Scaredy Cat does a somersault in my belly. "But I... I don't... I mean, I'm not like everybody else."

Jodie gives a funny laugh. "Honestly, Cat. The only difference between you and the rest of the class is that you're slightly more talented."

I think my heart actually stops beating.

"The rest of them..." Jodie gestures wildly. "They all think they're brilliant. They're used to being the best in their school so most of them just aren't bothering to try." She screws up her nose. "But you... You have no idea how gifted you are. It's all in there. Just waiting to be released."

This, right here, is going to be one of the moments I relive for the rest of my life. Forever I will remember Jodie with her grey suit dress and clunky bangles, thick fringe flapping in her long serious face, staring at me keenly with piercing blue eyes and reeking of cigarette smoke.

I don't know what to say. Sad Cat wants to cry happy tears. Silly Cat wants to give her a hug. Thunder Cat wants to get it all down in writing so I can send it to Miss Bates, my old Drama teacher. Scaredy Cat wants to check that this isn't some cruel prank.

"Right, I've got to go." Jodie picks up her bag and shoots me a rare smile. "You can do this, Cat. You're a star." She trots out of the room without a backwards glance.

I slide to the floor and put my hands to my cheeks.

What just happened?

After sitting in a daze for goodness knows how long, I scrape myself off the ground and wobble out of the room. Something has come to life inside me. A little spark has been lit. A tiny seed of hope fizzing in the dark.

Jodie's words echo in my ears all the way to the refectory. *"You're a star! You're a star! You're a star!"*

I pass Elle and she gives me an awkward smile. "Well done on your scene." There it is again, that little look of fear.

I stare at her for a moment before muttering, "Thanks."

Then I turn on my heels and trot on, Thunder Cat roaring like a lion. Well that's a turn of events. Who'd have imagined that a real actor like Elle could be intimidated by a fake one like me? Although, you have to admit, I'm pretty good at it. Bewitching, some might say.

* 13 * Fun Cat doesn't run

The weeks fly by and Catrina Carla is finally alive!

Fun Cat isn't always very loud. Most of the time I am just me. Normal Cat. No big fanfare. Just a quiet contentedness. I feel a peace I have never known. A sense of being safe. Free. Home. There's a song in my heart and a skip in my step.

I love everything about Forest Hall. I love my lessons. Acting skills, dance, singing, voice, movement, accents and even some stage combat. I'm soaking it all up and I'm *good* at it. Miraculously so. I can't believe it. People like me. They want to work with me. They praise me.

I'm not the loner, the misfit, the caterpillar.

Sad Cat is no more! This butterfly is taking flight!

I'm able to bring Fun Cat to class more often than not, although Thunder Cat sometimes turns up in knee high socks. Creative Cat has taken on a life of her own and every now and then she appears with an idea that is nothing short of genius. We've started a module on storytelling. I'm working with Sneezing Sky, Foxtrotting Faye, Abseiling Arthur and Murdering Marsha (who is not as scary as she sounds). My group love my ideas and I've not been shy at all. Outside of lessons, I'm doing a student film, a play with the Shakespeare Society and a cameo in a third year directing piece. It's non-stop activity and I love it. I love my teachers. Especially Jodie. The icy coolness was all an act. She's the greatest teacher ever! She's always telling me how well I'm doing. I'm SO glad I didn't get put with Pat in group A.

I love my housemates. Okay, I'm still working on Elle. And I could take or leave most of the boys. But the rest of the girls on my floor have become true friends, especially Annie who often gives me a friendly knock through the wall.

I love our campus and all the staff. Especially the funny team of dinner ladies at the refectory. There's one who calls everybody 'Petal.' One who whistles the same tune as she clears our trays away. One who can never manage to get the till to work. And another who is always snarling and speaks in a low gravelly Yorkshire accent. She looks utterly terrifying yet often slips out a smile when Rory affectionately calls her Windy Wendy.

I'm also rather fond of Bob the housing officer. He's the one to go to for maintenance issues, like sticky locks and broken plugs. Regrettably, he couldn't do anything about my squeaky pipes but he did give me a new light bulb when the one in my lamp stopped working. He even came and put the new one in for me, chuckling kindly when I said I'd never changed a bulb before. Bob handles the post so I go to his office once a week to pick up the latest parcel from my mum.

"Somebody loves you!" he says when he hands it to me.

The parcels are full of toiletries and food. The toothpaste is mounting up. I need to tell my mum to stop sending peanut butter. Most of her letters sit unopened for a few days on my desk. I don't have the time to reply. I mean to, of course, but I never know what to say. How do I put into words this whole experience of coming alive? She wouldn't understand. And how do I share my joy of discovering I am talented? She'd only ask why I didn't know it sooner.

It feels like I've lived here forever. Everything is so familiar, so comforting and wonderful. I can't believe I got lost on the first night! These days, I could find my way around the whole campus with my eyes closed.

One of my favourite things to do is to get up really early and go for a walk while everybody else is sleeping. I can walk through the entire campus— to Fairy Land, the tower clock and the library— without seeing another soul, except for Mad Jo's Running Club who pass me on their way to the lake.

Mad Jo always waves when she sees me, her face looking pained and focussed. She never asks what I'm doing up so early. We have an unspoken agreement not to judge each other for being odd enough to set our alarms for the crack of dawn. It's these early morning meetings that bond us and, as late Autumn sets in and the mornings grow colder, the two of us can often be found in the refectory huddling over two hot chocolates before the breakfast rush begins.

We begin with mutual silence: Mad Jo puffing and panting as she peels off her running gear and me thumbing through my newest library book or practising lines.

About halfway through our drinks, Mad Jo will say something like, "Good book?"

And I'll reply with a quote which she pretends to be interested in before asking, "How was your run?"

And she says, "It was so good, Caz. You should join us."

Then we laugh because Fun Cat never runs.

All is well in the world until one Thursday evening when a phone call from my father catches me out of the blue.

"She's gone, Cat. She's gone. She means it this time!" My dad's screeching panic stabs me straight through the heart.

Scaredy Cat starts freaking out. *She's gone. She's gone for good. I'll never see her again.*

But RoboCat takes over on the outside and gives my father the same, calm advice that I always give him. "It will be alright. She will come back. She always does."

"I can't cope! I've had enough!" My dad is shrieking now.

I hold the phone away from my ear and take a deep breath. Scaredy Cat is wailing too but I stuff her down.

"It will be alright." RoboCat continues. Firm and monotonous. "It will be alright."

"Find her, Cat," my dad begs.

"I will," I promise. "I'll call her now."

"You know her heart isn't good. What if she collapses? What if she's in a ditch? If you don't find her I'll—"

"I will," I repeat, a little louder. "But I need you to get off the phone so I can call her."

He hangs up. The daggers in my heart twist but there's no time to cry. I hurriedly call my mum. No answer. I try again before sending a text. *'Are you OK? Where are you?'*

I stare at my phone, chest thumping, mind spinning. I fall to my knees and I'm Holy Cat, bargaining with God.

I'm sorry for being proud when Jodie said I was talented. I'm sorry for letting my guard down and not phoning my parents for a while. I'll try harder. Please make her come home. Don't let her collapse from the stress of it all. Please stop my dad from killing himself. Please look after Aidan. Please. If you're real. Please, please please...

My dad rings. "Did you find her?"

"Not yet. I will." RoboCat is super calm. "It will be alright." I hang up and pace my room. I can't do anything all the way up here. It's not like when I was younger and my dad could drop me off at her work with the instruction to talk her round. I try phoning again. No answer. I want to scream. But I don't. I can't. I need to bring her back.

I send another text. *'Trying to call you. Are you OK?'*

I only have to wait for an hour. Nothing like the time she was gone for a week. But it's still agony.

'Hi Baby! I'm in Tiverton. I got you a dress.' My mum's text is accompanied by a photo of a skimpy red dress. Not my style. Too Shay or Lizzie or Lottie.

The poison in my chest oozes away. Most of it.

RoboCat replies. *'Thanks. Just checking you're OK?'*

'Of course.'

Then, another hour later, a text from my dad. *'She's back.'*

No *'Thanks for your time,'* or *'Sorry for upsetting you.'*

I grab my pillow and scream in silent fury. Angry Cat wants to smash things. I thought I'd left this behind.

I need to get out. I run out of my room. I don't stop to grab shoes. Nor do I bother to lock my door. I just run. Outside. Into the cold, damp dark. I run and run across the fields, tears streaming down my face, mud splashing up my bare legs. The cold air is both numbing and refreshing. I run with no plan except to get as far away from myself as I can. Which I can't. I can never run fast enough.

Eventually, I tire of running and sit exhausted under a tree, hugging my frozen legs with shaking arms. Then I cry until there are no tears left and I'm empty and numb. When I return to Willow, everything is just as I left it. My room did not suffer for being left unlocked. Nobody has noticed I've been gone. Why should they?

Wes passes me on the stairwell and does a brief double take at my dishevelled state. Mad Jo and Dotty Jay are making tea in the kitchen. There's music coming from Annie's room. Giggling from the girls upstairs.

A haunting melody drifts up from Bertie's room as I lay face down on my bed. And suddenly, I can't remember ever being Fun Cat. How stupid I was to think I could be happy. How dumb to believe I belonged. I am Squashed Cat. I am Lost Cat. Nobody loves me. Nobody knows me. I am abandoned. Rejected. Alone.

* 14 * Thunder Cat has her cake and eats it

The skimpy red dress from my mother arrives in the post a few days later, along with another tub of peanut butter.

"Somebody loves you!" Bob coos as he hands me the parcel. "It's so great when parents make an effort. Some students never get any post."

Play it Cool Cat smiles until I leave his office where Angry Cat takes over with a scowl.

Holy Cat is ready with a guilt trip. *It is kind of her, you know. Postage isn't cheap. You should call to say thank you.*

Then I remember that I haven't even thanked God for bringing her home so quickly. It was very smooth, considering I wasn't there to help like I normally am. If I don't say thank you, then it might not be so easy next time.

So I purse my lips and utter a quiet, *"Thank you, God."*

The thing is, I don't know whether I am grateful to him for bringing her back or angry with him for letting her run off in the first place. I'm not a religious person. I don't understand why anybody enjoys going to mass and sitting in silence while some man in fancy dress preaches to them about being good. But obviously I pray when things are hard. That's just good sense; to pray in case. And, for the most part, God has answered my prayers. My mum has always come back. My dad has never followed through with his threats to kill himself. My brother Aidan doesn't seem too fazed by it all.

But God didn't take Sad Cat away when I begged him to. He hasn't answered my prayer about having a long lost big sister come to save me. He didn't give me lasting friendships through high school or have Monica move in next door. And he could, if he wanted to. He could make everything happy.

Perhaps, if I was more like Annie, God would like me and good things would happen to me. Annie is one of the kindest people I have ever met. She's never grumpy, not even first thing in the morning or if somebody drinks her orange juice. She doesn't yell or play loud sweary music. Even behind peoples' backs she refuses to be unkind. She just says, "Let's look for the good."

I dump my mum's package in my room before going next door to see Annie. She's sitting at her desk, a great look of concentration on her face. "I've got to write *five hundred* words on the history of contemporary dance. How am I going to do that?"

I try not to laugh. Our latest essay was three thousand words on method acting. RoboCat struggled to keep it under five thousand. But Annie doesn't like writing. Instead of books, her shelves are filled with dozens of furry hedgehogs.

One of her wardrobe doors is hanging open and Silly Cat has a sudden urge to check whether Jodie left an inscription back when this was her room. I edge towards it, getting as close as I can without looking suspicious, and sneak a peek.

Annie looks over and I almost slam the door shut on my face. I divert attention to a photo taped above her bed. "Are they your friends?"

Annie grins. "My best friends. Livi and Ruby."

"Do you miss them?"

"Yeah. They call all the time. Do you miss your friends?"

"Not much." No need to tell her that by the end of sixth form I didn't have any. The Dark Days had wiped them all out. I turn to another photo. I recognise her mother from our first day. I bet she's never run away. "Are they your parents?"

"Yup."

"Do you have any brothers or sisters?"

Annie shakes her head. "My parents wanted more but it's just me. How about you? You've got a little brother, right?"

"Yeah. Aidan. He's fifteen."

"Do you get on with him?"

"We did when we were little but he's boring now. Constantly on his phone. He hardly speaks to me."

A memory floods back of me and Aidan hiding in the park. Our mum was in one of her rages and our dad was crying and trying to reason with her. I put a coat on my brother and led him out of the house. We were going to run away but I didn't plan it very well and Aidan soon started crying. He was hungry and wanted to go home. So we did. Our parents didn't even notice we'd been gone.

"Perhaps you'll be close again when you're older," Annie suggests. "It's probably just a phase."

Sad Cat is stirring. *Why did I ask about her family? I brought this on myself.*

Annie stares at me and I start to feel nervous. "Cat... I was wondering... We're starting a new series called *'If God'* at the Christian Union. Do you want to come?"

I'm so relieved that she's not asking anything serious that I can't help laughing. "The Christian Union?"

"Yeah. We're starting this evening after dinner." Her eyes are wide and hopeful. "Oh please, Cat. I think you'd like it."

So far, I've been able to resist Annie's churchy invites with excuses about homework and headaches and rehearsals and I need to wash my hair. Today, I foolishly pause for too long.

Annie lunges on my indecision. "There'll be cake!"

My mouth waters.

"Special chocolate cake made by some of the girls at Wintergates. They have ovens, you know!"

I lick my lips. "What would I have to do? They wouldn't make me pray out loud or anything, would they?"

"Of course not! You don't have to do anything!"

I scratch my chin. She looks so desperate for me to come. What's the catch? "Will people talk to me?"

"Probably. People will say hello... I could ask them to ignore you, if you'd prefer? Someone will give a talk then there'll be a discussion but you don't have to say anything..."

I've stopped listening. Thunder Cat is dreaming about cake.

"Think about it over dinner and let me know."

"Alright."

So I think about it over dinner. And when I say I think about it, I mean there's a whole council meeting going on in my head thinking and thinking and overthinking it.

Angry Cat starts the proceedings. *I don't want to go. It's a load of fairy stories, all that God rubbish.*

Holy Cat winces. *Shhh! You mustn't think like that!*

There's going to be cake! Thunder Cat yells. *Please, please, please can we go?*

Annie's really nice, Scaredy Cat chips in. *I don't want her to feel rejected.*

Who cares how she feels? Angry Cat roars. *She hardly knows you. She wouldn't like you if she really knew you.*

Cake cake cake cake cake cake cake!

If you go, they'll think they've got permission to preach at you and send you junk about how amazing their lives are.

That's true, Sad Cat agrees. Ever since inadvertently signing up for the Christian Union at the Freshers' Fair, I've been plagued by cheesy FriendWeb alerts.

What about you, Fun Cat? Holy Cat asks, desperate for an ally. *What do you think?*

But Fun Cat is staying silent. She's been subdued since my father's phone call last week.

Let's say we'll go another time, Scaredy Cat is diplomatic.

And Thunder Cat keeps singing in the background. *Cake cake cake cake! I really like cake. Did you know I like cake?*

I eat my meal without tasting it, RoboCat on autopilot. A bunch of my housemates are at the table but I don't hear their conversation. I down the last of my apple juice and look up to see Annie grinning. "Have you thought about it?"

Play it Cool Cat shrugs and mutters, "A bit."

"So, do you want to come?"

And, because Fun Cat has lost her voice and Play it Cool Cat is careful never to let Angry Cat out, Copy Cat takes over and tries to be nice. "Yeah, I'll come."

Annie grabs my arm and squeals. "Hooray!"

Idiot, Angry Cat mutters.

"Where are you off to?" Dotty Jay asks as Annie and I get up with our empty trays.

My cheeks burn as Annie says, "The Christian Union. Anyone else want to come?" She looks at our housemates but they're all smart enough to have excuses ready.

Honestly, I'm not sure this is worth it just for a slice of cake. I could've bought some cake at the refectory, for goodness sake. Even Thunder Cat is feeling sheepish as we join the random bunch gathered in one of the mansion rooms.

"You can be as invisible as you want," Annie assures me as she ushers me into a chair. "I'll get you plenty of cake."

"It's fine," Copy Cat says quickly. "I don't mind about the cake. I mean, that's not why I came."

"I'll just get you a small piece, then."

I pretend to check my phone as Annie dashes off to a table at the back. I recognise Nina from the Freshers' Fair and force a smile. Then the door opens and my stomach does a flip as Zachary comes racing into the room and sprints straight to the cake table. He says something to Annie and she says something back and he quickly glances my way and grins.

"Hey, Cat!" he yells over the crowd.

A few heads turn to see who he's waving at. So much for being invisible. As he comes lumbering over, a piece of cake in both hands, I feel hugely embarrassed that he should catch me at a religious event. But then I realise he ought to feel just as daft if he also got lulled in by the offer of cake.

"Hi Zachary." Play it Cool Cat nods.

Zachary keeps grinning. "Annie said she was going to invite you but I said I didn't think you'd be interested. Silly me. I should have asked you myself."

I blink in surprise. "You're part of the Christian Union?"

"Yeah."

Then Annie reappears with a slice of the most decadent-looking chocolate cake I have ever seen and it takes all my energy to restrain Thunder Cat from guzzling it in one gulp.

"Thanks," I say coolly. I pick nonchalantly at the icing.

At the front, Nina announces we're going to begin and, honestly, I don't remember much after that. I know she's introduced the topic, *If God made the world,* and I assume she's planning on giving an exposition on caring for the planet and recycling and climate change. I try to listen, truly I do. It's only fair, seeing as I'm eating her cake. But without me even realising it, RoboCat takes over.

Next week is the Storytelling showcase. As the focus is on the power of the imagination, we have to tell the entire story of *Jack and the Beanstalk* without using any props or costumes. Our piece is looking great. We've got a scene where we all play parts of the giant's face (Faye and I are the eyes, standing side by side with our arms looped over our heads), a scene with a magic bean burrowing into the ground (Sky being carried around the room by the rest of us), and a scene with Arthur running through falling rocks (Marsha and Faye doing roly polys while he jogs on the spot.) But we're yet to settle on an ending. So while Nina speaks and the rest of the room debate, RoboCat enlists the help of Creative Cat and I get lost trying out ideas in my head.

At some point, I hear Nina say, "It's amazing just how big the universe is," and instantly I have a brainwave! Instead of finishing the story with the giant dead on the ground, we could end at the beginning, with the stars in the sky being depicted by a host of magic beans. I start jiggling in my seat as I map it out. Meanwhile, Thunder Cat is gazing at the cake table and wondering whether we'll be offered seconds. And Holy Cat is on her best behaviour and even nods along with a prayer. Nina calls the meeting to an end and I give myself a big shake and return to the room.

I walk back to Willow with Annie and Zachary, cringing when they ask me what I thought.

"It was alright," I say. "Some interesting points."

Zachary peers at me. "Which bits were interesting?"

"Can't remember now."

"That's alright," says Annie. "You'll get into it. Next time will be a good one."

I halt. "Next time?"

See! Angry Cat simmers. *I told you they'd try to trap you.*

"Yeah," Annie continues merrily. "In two weeks' it's *If God made you.* It's a really important one because it makes all the difference if somebody created you, don't you think?"

"I suppose..."

Zachary gives a cheeky grin. "There'll be cake again. That's clearly the only reason why you came, Cat."

"Don't be stupid!" I retort.

"You weren't listening to anything," he teases. "I bet you were just thinking about cake the whole time."

I frown. That's not fair. Only part of me was doing that.

Annie gives Zachary a nudge before linking arms with me. "You can come for cake any time, Cat. And it's fine if you weren't listening. You're still welcome. I won't judge you."

My chest feels tight as she gives me a big squeeze. She won't judge me because she's always looking for the good in people. She has no idea there's not a lot that's good in me.

* 15 * Silly Cat thinks boys are yucky

Faye, Sky, Arthur and Marsha are thrilled with my idea for the end of our Storytelling piece. We perform it on the first week of November and it's one huge buzz for Fun Cat. We have the audience rapt as we form the giant's face one last time. Marsha and Sky, reclining feet to feet as the giant's mouth, open and close their legs as we speak one by one.

"And so we go back to the beginning!" Arthur roars.

"We are all seeds," says Faye.

"We are all stars," I add.

"Waiting to be born," says Marsha.

"Waiting to be seen," says Sky.

"Waiting for our story to be told," we chime in unison.

Then we burst out of our formation and leap onto spaces on the floor. We run, jump, shake, fizz, all tiny beans in space trying to tell our story, trying to find meaning and belonging. Of course it's wacky but that's the beauty of theatre. Anything is possible. The wilder, the better.

Finally we give a unified cry, "HA!" and drop to the ground. Thunderous applause erupts. I scrape myself off the floor, Play it Cool Cat acting coy, and trot back to my seat.

"That was amazing," I hear people whisper.

"So magical," someone adds.

"I couldn't stop crying," weeps Horse-riding Heidi.

A tidal wave of joy crashes over me.

"That was incredible, Cat!" Monica in My Head can't stop raving about it. *"You were so good. The whole thing was so good. You should have seen Jodie's face. She was beaming."*

Tanisha turns in her seat and gives me a thumbs up. Her group is up next with a retelling of *'Little Red Riding Hood.'* I make every effort to pay attention, laugh appropriately and cheer loudly at the end although, if Thunder Cat was being blunt (and Thunder Cat is always blunt), there is nothing special about their performance. It is predictable and ordinary. In fact, none of the other pieces are as good as ours. This is confirmed when we get our grades the next day and my group comes out on top.

So, after a patchy couple of weeks, Fun Cat is back. And this time it's for good. Nothing's gonna topple me now. I redouble my efforts, reading extra books and signing up for more activities. I am even persuaded to partake in a daring night out in Wakefield. I have, so far, avoided the perilous coach to the city and all the shady shenanigans that take place in Wango's. But tonight I am making an exception. It's Shay's birthday and the whole of Willow is going out to celebrate.

I'm wearing the skimpy red dress from my mother even though Holy Cat feels like a tart and Silly Cat wants to cry. I had planned to wear jeans and a t-shirt but Shay didn't approve and Thunder Cat wanted to please her.

I am Scaredy Cat all the way to Wakefield. But then *'I will survive'* is playing as we enter Wango's and Thunder Cat re-emerges. The next few songs are eighties classics and Thunder Cat lets loose on the revolving dance floor.

What was I so afraid of? This is fun!

I spot Smoking Sienna and Partying Pip from my class and dance with extra vigour, keeping an eye out for Jodie. Then there's an ABBA song. One of my dad's favourites. Sad Cat stirs but Thunder Cat bats her away. I dance like there's no tomorrow until I'm exhausted and need a break. I join Annie and Ashley at a table.

"Oi, Cat. Let me get you a drink!" I recoil as sweaty Mike leans over the back of my chair.

"No, thanks. I'm not thirsty."

"Go on, Cat. Just one drink."

"Fine. Get me a blackcurrant soda."

"A what?"

Dotty Jay comes to join us, hair matted and feather boa hanging limply from her shoulders. I turn my back on Mike and make space for her before yelling over the music, "Is Dotty Jay your full name or are you just a crazy Jay or what?"

"It's Dorothy Jayne," she yells back. "But nobody ever calls me Dorothy."

"I'll call you Dorothy, then," Thunder Cat proclaims.

"No, you won't. You'll forget. Plus, you're a type three so you're too flaky."

"I am not too flaky!"

Mike returns with my blackcurrant soda and I take it from him with a quick nod of thanks.

Dotty Jay— I mean, *Dorothy*— smirks as he walks away. "He likes you, Cat."

"Don't be stupid."

"Can't you tell? Oh Cat, you really are sheltered."

Then Shay shimmies over and says, "Cat, do you want to come dance?" She indicates Mike who is gyrating and waving at me from the dance floor.

Silly Cat come to the fore. "Yuck! Boys are so disgusting!"

Mike keeps waving but I ignore him and turn back to the table. Ashley is crying and Annie is offering her advice but the music is too loud for me to eavesdrop. Ashley is nice enough but she often brings the mood down. She's been homesick all term and starts crying at the drop of a hat. Angry Cat finds her annoying but Holy Cat tries to be sympathetic. She's a type two, after all. She can't help being oversensitive.

By now, I am rather adept at identifying people according to Dotty Jay—I mean Dorothy Jayne's— types. The Acting course is packed with type ones. Confident, attention seeking, brash and neurotic. Ashley, Bertie and Rory are standard type twos: whimsical and weird and avoiders of conflict. If Dotty Jay (I mean Dorothy) is right, then I'm a type three: imaginative and insightful with a hunger for meaning and a head full of cares. Most of me can agree with that description although Thunder Cat likes to think I'm much bolder, perhaps a passionate and practical type four like Shay. I reckon Zachary is a type five like Annie because he's immature and easily bored. And despite calling herself mad, I suspect Mad Jo is a secret type six: logical and strong-willed with a strong sense of justice and insatiable thirst for knowledge. She's not as raucous as she pretends to be. I know that from our hot chocolates every morning. I blow bubbles in my soda as I watch the others dance. Lottie's boyfriend, Grant, is visiting for the weekend. He's a trainee lawyer from Oxford and is bopping somewhat hesitantly while Lottie struts her stuff beside him. I nudge Dotty— I mean, Dorothy. *Oh screw it. I give up.* "Grant... Type six?"

She grins. "Yup. You can tell he's prepared for anything. Probably brought extra socks and a spare phone charger."

I giggle. "And Lottie... Type one?"

"Totally. Bet she's a thrower in arguments and he clams up and goes cold shoulder."

I turn my attention to Elle whose boyfriend, Reece, is also visiting. I know she's a type four, self-centred and edgy. What about him? "Type one?" I guess as I watch him swinging a beer around. "He seems like a bit of a party animal."

Dotty Jay gives a wry smile. "No. He's just pretending to be that way. He's a type two really. Impulsive and a dreamer. They won't stay together. She's too obsessive and he's afraid of commitment. Mark my words. It will be over by Easter."

I raise an eyebrow. Elle and Reece have been all over each other all night. But Dotty Jay is usually right about things.

"How many types did you say there were? Six?"

"Seven."

I count them off on my fingers, scanning the room to see who I've missed. "Who's a type seven, then?"

Dotty Jay gives a wistful sigh. "I've never met one." She leans closer as though revealing a deep mystery. "Type sevens are totally good and totally pure."

"Like Annie?"

"Oh, no! Annie's too gullible. Type sevens aren't fooled easily. They are strong but not overbearing. Patient but not pushovers. Highly capable but endlessly humble. Full of love, no darkness at all."

I sip my blackcurrant soda. "Nobody's like that. Why not just say there are six types?"

She shakes her head. "I'll find one someday. I know it."

Mike suddenly reappears and elbows me. "Fancy a burger, Cat Burger?"

Without thinking, I toss the rest of my drink over him.

Dotty Jay gasps and Mike scowls. "What was that for?"

Silly Cat giggles. "Serves you right for being a poo head."

Angry Cat shudders at how childish I'm being. My head is a muddle and I wish the night was over. By now, Thunder Cat is bored and Scaredy Cat needs a wee. Baby Cat is crying, as she does from time to time. My throat hurts from shouting and there's ringing in my ears. I don't think Dotty Jay can possibly be right about there being only seven types of people in the world. There are more than that in my own head.

* 16 * Thunder Cat has a plan

"Alright, Caz! How come you're so late? I don't usually arrive before you." Mad Jo grins over her hot chocolate.

I plonk down opposite her and blink as she slides a mug across the table. "Is that for me?"

"Course it's for you, you nutter. Who else would it be for?"

"You didn't need to get me one."

"Why not? Saves you time queuing."

I feel awful. We've met nearly every morning for weeks and I've never thought to buy her a hot chocolate.

"Took longer in the library, did you?" she continues, pointing to the stack of books under my arm.

The truth is I have added a stroll around the mansion to my morning walk ever since I went past last week and bumped into Jodie having a cigarette.

She had waved and said, "You're up early, Cat!"

I went all shy and Copy Cat came out stuttering something about enjoying the fresh air. As she puffed away, I felt a wave of horror at the idea that I might be insulting her right to breathe poisonous toxins. Thankfully, she hadn't seemed offended. Instead, she asked, "How are you?"

And I said, "I'm okay." Even though Sad Cat was rearing and I had a sudden urge to cry. Then I'd given an awkward wave and walked off because I figured she wouldn't want me hanging around for too long. So, even though I haven't seen her since, the thrill of maybe seeing her is too much to pass up. I lingered a little longer today because Silly Cat kept thinking that if I walked towards the ramp outside Heather or touched the furthest post or avoided all the cracks along the pavement then Jodie would appear.

Obviously, I don't tell Mad Jo any of this.

"There was a queue at the library," I say.

Mad Jo slurps her drink. "Do you really read that fast? You're a proper geek."

"I'm just determined. I want to act more than anything."

"You'll need more than books to make it as an actor."

"I know."

Thunder Cat has it all planned out. After university, I'll move to London and get an agent. I'll work my very hardest, paying whatever I need to, to make it to the top. Then, when I'm twenty five and at the height of fame, I'll end it all. I'm completely sold out on this plan and I think it's a good one. Who wants to get old anyway? And who's going to remember Catrina Carla if she lives beyond her peak, grows up alone and quietly fades away?

"Have you got a back-up plan?" Mad Jo peers at me.

Course I've got a back-up plan. End it all at twenty five anyway. I sniff my hot chocolate before shaking my head. "No. What about you? You want to be an artist?"

"Course not!" she scoffs. "There's no money in art. I want to be a primary school teacher."

"A primary school teacher? That's so normal! I thought you were *mad?*"

"I'm not *that* mad. I'm sensible enough to know I can't make a living out of my art."

"Oh." I glance around the refectory. The dinner ladies are getting ready for the morning rush. Windy Wendy is cleaning the table behind us and Barb (the one who calls everyone 'Petal') is manning the till.

"Thanks again for the drink," I say, waving my empty mug. "It was really kind of you. I'll definitely get you one tomorrow."

Mad Jo rolls her eyes. "It's only a drink, Caz. You need to let people be nice to you more often."

Something stirs at her words. A memory flashes. My mother in one of her rages shouting, *"Nobody is nice for no reason, Catrina! You can't trust anybody in this world."*

I give myself a shake and stand up. "I'll see you later."

I'm about to take my empty mug to the trolley when Windy Wendy pops up and says with her usual grimace, "Want me to take that for you?"

"I don't mind. I'm just—"

"Give it here. Now clear off and have a good day."

"See?" says Mad Jo. "People want to be nice to you. Just let them."

"I didn't realise I wasn't letting them," I say awkwardly. "But, I'll take it on board. Thanks."

I leave Mad Jo and trot down to the mansion for this morning's class. I like to be seven minutes early. It shows keenness without being too stalkery. Sometimes Jodie is early too and we have a little catch up before anybody else arrives. Sometimes she arrives at the last minute, surrounded by Smoking Sienna and Dancing Donna and Weightlifting Will, the class smokers.

Today is an early day.

"Hello, Cat. How are you?"

"Okay." It's quite a struggle to be Fun Cat or even Normal Cat around Jodie. Sad Cat always seems to pop up, even when I'm totally fine and have nothing to be sad about.

Still, the lesson goes well. Thunder Cat emerges and puts on a bold impression of an alien when Jodie asks for volunteers. My delivery is so entertaining that even Praying Pranjal breaks into a smile, which is rare as he's usually very serious. As Jodie applauds my creativity, Thunder Cat beams because everything's going to plan. I know most people don't make it as an actor, but there's no reason why I won't.

My happy mood continues all day and I'm not even disappointed when Annie reminds me it's time for the second *'If God'* meeting at the Christian Union. If anything, I'm in the mood for some mild socialising and, of course, Thunder Cat is pretty ecstatic about the prospect of more cake.

I greet Nina with a cheery, "Hello!" as I eye up this week's sweet offering. A gooey looking lemon drizzle.

"Good to see you again!" Nina says, handing me a napkin.

"You too." I grin before heading to a seat, trying not to dribble as I unwrap my bundle of lemon goodness.

It appears that now I've dared to come a second time, Annie is less careful about looking after me. She's busy on the other side of the room and I'm soon accosted by two girls from Laurel.

"Hello! I'm Ruth!"

"I'm Charlotte!"

Copy Cat matches their enthusiasm. "I'm Cat!"

Ruth is doing Creative Writing and Charlotte's a dancer.

"Oh, you're in Arthur's class, aren't you?" Ruth says. "He's our housemate. He showed us some photos from your *Jack and the Beanstalk* piece. I bet the Acting course is so much fun."

"It is," I agree. "I love it."

We chat away and I eat my cake and Fun Cat takes over and decides that Ruth and Charlotte are genuinely decent girls. Fancy that! Two new friends without even trying!

Then the meeting starts and Ruth and Charlotte return to their seats at the front. Annie comes running over and apologises for getting lost in a conversation. I tell her it's fine. Which it is. Fun Cat doesn't need a chaperone.

At the front of the room, Nina introduces a third year called Nick who's going to be giving a short talk on today's topic of *If God made you.*

Apparently, if God made me then he knows me, loves me, and has a plan for me. It all sounds very lovely but rather disconnected from my actual life. Perhaps if God agrees with my plan to be a famous actress then I'll believe in him and maybe even go to church sometimes.

Nick finishes his speech and I mop up my crumbs as everybody else takes part in a discussion. It seems quite clear who the Christians are and who the non-Christian guests are. For a start, the Christians all speak as though they've got the right answer. And the guests talk out of turn and cause trouble. Like one girl who interrupts Nina's exhortations about God's kindness to ask loudly, "What about suffering? If God's real and good and all that? Why do people suffer?"

Yeah, smarty pants, Angry Cat sneers in my head. *How are you going to answer that one?*

"That's a great question," Nina says in unflappable tones, as though she's heard it a million times before. "And if you come back for the final session in two weeks' time, we'll cover that when we discuss *If God made a way.*"

I suppress a frown. *Come back again? Not flipping likely, however nice the cake is.*

With Angry Cat riled, the only way through is to zone out. I let RoboCat take over, mentally writing an essay and going over my lines for a piece with the Shakespeare Society.

I am stirred out of my thoughts by the sound of everyone getting up off their chairs. Annie and Zachary have gone off to mingle so I'm about to sneak out alone when Ruth from Laurel comes running over.

"It was lovely to meet you, Cat."

"Thanks. Nice to meet you too."

"I just wondered... Could I pray for you before you go?"

"Pray for me?" The offer is absurd. I'm not ill.

"Yeah. I just really felt God's love for you and I'd love to pray for you."

Her cheery face makes me uncomfortable. I'm about to politely decline but then I remember what Mad Jo said this morning about letting people be nice to me. So, although Angry Cat is sneering and Scaredy Cat is quaking, I swallow my pride and say, "Okay."

Ruth smiles. "Anything in particular?"

Thunder Cat wants her to pray that I'll definitely be a famous actress but Holy Cat is appalled at the thought. "No," I say quickly.

"Alright. I'll just pray whatever comes to my mind." Ruth bows her head so I do the same, feeling embarrassed.

"Lord, thank you for bringing Cat here tonight and to Forest Hall to be part of this wonderful campus. I pray you would shower her with your love and do a special work in her this year. Thank you that you've got great plans for her and you made her for a wonderful destiny..."

Thunder Cat perks up. *A wonderful destiny? Catrina Carla here we come!*

Ruth waffles on but I'm distracted daydreaming about fame. When she finishes, Play it Cool Cat says a polite, "Thank you." I hope I'm not expected to return the favour.

Ruth is beaming as though she's just placed an order in Heaven and is expecting the goods to arrive any minute. I want to tell her prayers don't work like that. Trust me. I've said many.

* 17 * Copy Cat becomes a vegetarian

It's only the first week of December but, thanks to RoboCat, I've done all my Christmas shopping!

I went to Wakefield with Annie and Dotty Jay and blitzed the shopping centre, picking up socks for my dad and pound shop treasures for my housemates. I thought I'd struggle to find something for Aidan because what do you buy a teenage boy who hardly speaks and just stares at his phone all day? But then I struck gold by finding a copy of the picture book *'The Bravest'* in a charity shop. It's all about a bird who's frightened to fly but who eventually rescues a whole family of mice in a storm. It was Aidan's favourite library book when he was little although I don't suppose he'll remember.

I took ages over my mum's present. RoboCat's momentum was sorely interrupted with every part of me popping up to make suggestions only to immediately veto them. Sad Cat suggested some luxury chocolates but Scaredy Cat feared it wasn't special enough. Holy Cat was drawn to a beautiful wooden box engraved with some gushing sentiment about mothers holding their children's hearts forever. But, the moment I picked it up, Angry Cat let out a growl and I quickly put it back down. In the end, I got her the chocolates and a pink scarf from the market. Of course, I won't tell her it's from the market. She wouldn't like that. If I have time, I'll write her a poem as well.

After town, it's straight to the Grumpy Pig where one big table has been reserved for me and my housemates. There's a fancy tablecloth, crackers and tinsel and a large sign proclaiming, *'Willow Christmas Party.'* Silly Cat feels super excited. I want everybody at the bar to know that we're from Forest Hall and we're one big happy family.

I drift around the table, hands on two chairs, ready to lunge in any direction. Annie slides into a seat on my right and, as I let go of one chair and edge into the one next to Annie, Shay takes the seat on my left. Dotty Jay, Mad Jo and Zachary are opposite me and Mike is relegated to the end of the table. Result!

The issue of seating resolved, I give a merry sigh and reach for the menu. A roast seems like the sensible option. This is a Christmas meal after all.

Shay nudges me. "You're a vegetarian, aren't you, Cat? Shall we go halves on the veggie platter starter?"

"Er, yeah, I can do," Copy Cat says without thinking.

I have no idea why she thinks I'm a vegetarian. She obviously hasn't paid attention to anything I've eaten for the last two and a half months.

The waitress comes to take our order and I am swayed away from my usual blackcurrant soda by Dotty Jay who insists the paradise smoothies are *'literally like drinking Heaven.'*

"A paradise smoothie," echoes the waitress in a thick Yorkshire drawl. "And the vegetarian platter. And for mains?"

"Er..." My eyes dart down the menu. With Copy Cat pretending to be a vegetarian, I can hardly order the turkey.

I opt for a mushroom pizza.

Shay approves. She's having the veg supreme.

I lean back with a sigh and think of something to say to Shay. "I love your hairband."

"Thanks." She takes it off and turns it over. "I added the sequins."

"Wow! That's amazing. How did you do that?"

"How'd you think I did it? I sewed them on."

"Oh." Play it Cool Cat tries to sound intelligent. "I suppose you learnt how to do it on the Costume Design course?"

"Learnt how to sew on my course? You're having a laugh, aren't you?" Shay roars gleefully before adding, "Let me guess, sheltered little Cat doesn't know how to sew."

I bristle but Thunder Cat gives a careless shrug and says, "Can you teach me?" I think about the simple scarf I've got my mum for Christmas and wonder whether Shay could help make it look nicer.

"Sure!" she replies. "I'll give you a sewing lesson later."

Our starters arrive and mine and Shay's platter is nice enough but I have considerable food envy looking up and down the table at Annie's meatballs and Dotty Jay's prawns and Zachary's chicken wings. Still, my pizza is delicious and, as I listen to Shay harking on about the evils of the food industry, Thunder Cat and Copy Cat are both persuaded that I should become a vegetarian. So I will. From today. I am a vegetarian.

Towards the end of the meal, Bertie arises and shocks everyone with a speech in which he thanks us all personally for the impact we've had on his life. I'm rather touched by his description of me as the *'illustrious plucky young actress in the room above who teaches one how to endure all things.'* This is a very kind way of saying I play my music too loud.

The only downside of Bertie's exhortations is that he waffles on for far too long. RoboCat zones out, but not before taking a moment to look around and breathe a happy sigh. I'm having a wonderful time; Thunder Cat enjoying being the centre of the table and the intermittent centre of attention, Fun Cat overwhelmed with a general sense of well-being, and every part of me being well-fed and watered.

But then there's the painful ordeal of paying the bill. Rory suggests we split it evenly but Ashley says she didn't have a starter and Lizzie doesn't want to pay extra for Mike who's had more drinks than anybody and I have to say I agree. I know I went wild with the smoothie but the pizza is the cheapest thing on the menu and I resisted the urge to add fries so I could keep it all under twenty quid.

"Pay for yourself," Dotty Jay yells, throwing her offering onto the plate. "It's the easiest way. Pay what you owe."

I know for a fact that mine only comes to nineteen pounds and eighty seven pence but I'm not going to quibble about the 13p. I reach across the table and lay my twenty down.

Once everybody has contributed, Tanisha takes the plate and adds it all up. "We're seven quid short," she announces sombrely, looking around to see who's to blame.

I grab a menu and do my sums again. Nineteen pounds eighty seven. Definitely. I breathe a sigh of relief. I'm clear.

A few of my housemates are doing the same but nobody confesses to owing any extra. Bertie gets a calculator out and starts asking everyone what they've had. I hope everybody saw me put my twenty down because I might be a lot of things but a thief is not one. Elle grips her purse as though afraid someone will ransack it for more. Ashley is biting her nails and Shay is speculating over who's holding out.

"Lizzie, you had a large lemonade, didn't you? Did you remember you went large?"

"Yes, I remembered!" Lizzie snaps.

"I can put a bit more in," Annie says, rifling through her purse and throwing a handful of change onto the plate.

"You shouldn't have to," says Lottie. "Either somebody's not put in the right amount or else they've overcharged us. Let me see the bill, Bertie."

Bertie sends the bill down and Lottie goes through it, asking for a show of hands for each item. Zachary causes her to miscalculate by putting both hands up.

"This is why we should just split it," Rory says crossly. "It's so much simpler if we do that."

"Alright!" says Tanisha. "Everyone take your money back. We're going to split it."

I reluctantly reach for my twenty but Ashley says with a whimper, "I literally had a bowl of chips. Can't I just put mine in and the rest of you can split it if you want to?"

"I'm not paying for Mike's beers!" Lizzie insists.

"Split the food, pay for your own drinks?" Shay suggests.

Then Zachary growls, "This is ridiculous!" and offers to stump the entire bill singlehandedly. He's halfway to the bar when Wes calls him back and tells him not to be so daft.

Still, his outlandish display of generosity appears to have had the desired effect of getting everybody to dig a little deeper and, the next time it's counted, we're over by three quid. I decide not to ask for my 13p back.

It seems Zachary still isn't happy. "Just three quid for a tip when there are fifteen of us? Seriously?"

But nobody pays him any attention. The tension eased, merry chatter resumes as we gather up our belongings and pull on hats and scarves in preparation for the long trek home. Zachary hangs back as the rest of us leave and, when I glance back, I spot him adding a tenner to the plate.

What a strange boy. He must be crazy rich.

* 18 * Angry Cat will never ever

My sewing lesson begins in earnest as soon as we get back to Willow. Shay arrives on our corridor with a cavernous bag filled with treasure, like some kind of Irish Mary Poppins.

"Show me this scarf and we'll see what we can do!"

I hand her the pink scarf and she nods her approval.

"We can add all sorts to this. Make it really pretty."

Annie and Ashley join us, like moths to a flame, excited by the prospect of another craft session. Shay tips boxes out of her bag. Sequins, buttons, swirls, beads. Velcro and zips and iron-on transfers. Spools of thread in many glorious colours. Silly Cat wants to grab a bit of everything and make a giant butterfly! I toss the scarf aside, momentarily distracted.

"So what does your mammy like?" Shay asks, watching as I poke around.

Oh yeah. Stay on task.

"She likes flowers," I say, eyeing some gems shaped like rosebuds. She buys herself a bunch every week and posts pictures on FriendWeb claiming they're from an admirer.

Shay pours some out for me. "What else?" She opens another box and reveals dozens of metal charms.

A wave of disquiet washes over me as I thumb through them. I prod the piano, the bicycle, the unicorn and the butterfly. My mother wouldn't like any of those things, however much Silly Cat desires them. I settle for a heart, a handbag and a stiletto.

After a bit of tuition in how to avoid stabbing my finger, I'm away. A rosebud here, a charm there, a sprinkling of swirls all around. I work the needle in and out of the scarf, threading a little pattern, humming contentedly as I work. It's easy! Almost as easy as cooking an egg in the microwave. Shay watches like a hawk, taking over when I get the thread in a tangle and offering her advice on where to place the charms. Meanwhile, Ashley's on a roll making Christmas decorations and I stop to admire her string of paper snowmen. Annie is busy sewing herself a pencil case out of some scrap material.

It looks like a horrible mess but she's as proud of herself as I am of my scarf so I won't burst her bubble.

"So, girls..." Shay kicks her boots off and leans against the wall. She sounds like she means business and I wonder if she's about to tell us how much we owe for her services. "Share the gossip. Who have you got your eyes on?"

My irritation for such a worthless question is hidden by the fact that Ashley immediately goes red and starts laughing.

Shay the hawk pounces. "Go on, Ashley! Who is it?"

"No!" Ashley squirms and covers her face.

Annie looks bemused. "Ooh, go on. Tell us!"

"No, no, no!" Ashley keeps giggling, her ears growing pinker. "Don't ask me!" It seems she *wants* us to pry. Why else would she be making such a silly scene about it?

I screw up my nose and keep sewing. I couldn't care less who Ashley has her eyes on. It's not like anything would come of it. Most crushes are nothing more than vain fantasies and the vast majority of relationships end bitterly. The ones that survive only do so because those involved are too proud or too frightened to break apart. That's what Sad Cat decided during the Dark Days and every relationship I observe confirms it. Like Dotty Jay and her on and off boyfriend, Daryl, who pops up for the occasional weekend only to leave in a blaze of swearing. Or flings amongst my classmates who chop and change direction faster than leaves in the wind. And, of course, there's my parents who love each other very much but never seem able to show it.

Amid more pleading from Shay and Annie, Ashley folds her arms and says, "I'm not telling you. I mean it."

Shay studies her. "It's Zachary, isn't it? You like Zachary?"

Cue more giggling and blushing and flapping of hands.

Annie grins. "I thought you liked him. I saw you go red when you tripped over his chair after the meal."

Ashley puts a hand to her cheek. "Was I really obvious?"

Annie says she wasn't and Shay assures her that boys are completely oblivious when it comes to girls.

"Especially Zachary!" Shay snorts. "He's always got his head in the clouds." She turns her attention to Annie. "How about you, Annie? You got the hots for anyone?"

Now it's Annie's turn to blush, albeit with less hysteria than Ashley. "There's a boy at the Christian Union..."

"Tell us more!" demands Shay.

Annie grins. "He's called Cooper. He barely knows me though. All the girls like him."

Nothing to shriek about there. None of us know who he is. Shay moves on. "Cat? Your turn!"

I shake my head. "Nobody."

"There must be someone! On your course, maybe?"

"Nope."

"Bertie spoke very highly of you in his speech this afternoon. Would you give him a chance?"

Angry Cat feels a surge of fury as Annie and Ashley giggle.

"And Mike is still pining after you." Shay peers at me. "Or perhaps you could fight Ashley for Zachary. He's a good friend of yours, isn't he? Always giving you trumpet lessons."

I roll my eyes. "Honestly, I don't like anybody. I'm not interested. And the trumpet lessons are a laugh but I could never fall for Zachary. He's too irritating. He's always standing on his head or showing off about something. Plus, I would never be so desperate as to fight over someone."

Ashley looks relieved but Shay gives a nauseating cackle and sings, "Sounds like you're protesting far too much!"

Angry Cat wants to throw her stupid sewing bag down the corridor and scream, *"Why can't you believe me? I don't believe in love! I never have. I never will. I would rather die than fall in love so leave me alone!"*

"What about you?" I say instead. "Who do you fancy?"

Shay sniffs. "Oh, I'm not fussed right now."

Flipping cheek. Angry Cat decides she doesn't like Shay any more. I look down at my mother's scarf and wonder whether to pick all the pieces off it. But then the hallway door swings opens and Zachary appears, scavenging for treats.

"You can't be hungry already," Shay teases, giving Ashley a sly wink. "Are you sure you're not after something else?"

Ashley goes red as a beet and busies herself with an origami tree.

My door is propped open. Nosy old Zachary peers in. "Is this your room, Cat?"

"You know it is! You know I'm number 6."

"I don't remember anyone's room number!"

Of course. Not everyone has a RoboCat to keep their world organised.

Zachary keeps staring. "It's so creative. I like all the colourful buttons on the wall. And that bear with a monkey's head!"

Thunder Cat feels smug and wants to show off my poems. But Scaredy Cat is suddenly shy and wants to shut the door. I am relieved when Zachary turns back to us. He points to Annie's sewing project. "What are you making?"

"A pencil case." She hands it to him.

"Really? There are quite a lot of holes in it. Your pens will fall straight out." He pokes his fingers through the side.

"Oh give it here, Zachary! I'd like to see you do better."

"I could do better with my eyes closed," Zachary brags.

As Zachary ribs Annie for her poor sewing skills, the realisation hits me like a brick: Zachary likes Annie! Of course he does! That's why he's always hanging out with us. And they spend so much time together at the Christian Union and their churchy events. It all makes sense. Thunder Cat immediately wants to announce this revelation but I pinch my lips shut and force myself to stay quiet.

Zachary announces he's going to make a pencil case of his own and soon gets busy with a scrap of material matching Annie's. Turns out, he can't do better with his eyes closed and within minutes he's got a bleeding thumb.

Ashley peeks at him from behind her pile of gaudy decorations, looking like a rabbit in headlights when Shay says, "You've got a plaster, haven't you, Ashley? Go fetch Zachary a plaster!"

Ashley dashes upstairs to find a plaster and returns faster than a bolt of lightning, going all dopey as a clueless Zachary takes it from her. I watch with some measure of bemusement mixed with irritation. What a quandary! Ashley likes Zachary but Zachary likes Annie and Annie likes some guy called Cooper. Daft fools. Someone is bound to get hurt. Somebody always does. This is precisely why falling in love ranks number one on my list of *Stupid Things I Will Never Do*.

* 19 * Squashed Cat is the Girl in White

The hot news around campus is the opportunity to be in a music video for a punk band called Mama Octopus. It's going to be filmed in the mansion and they need six featured actors and several extras. Everybody's talking about it in class.

"Imagine being in a Mama Octopus video!" exclaims Roaring Rose. "My friends would be so jealous."

"It would look amazing on a CV," says Boxing Blake.

"And it's a paid job," adds Cooking Clemmie. "A proper acting role!"

Not a single part of me enjoys punk rock. Angry Cat would be the closest, with her love of feisty female artists from the 80's. But with lyrics like *'Rage has a name; call me Susan,'* and *'This heart is on fire with the sound of screaming'*, Mama Octopus certainly isn't my style. I hadn't even heard of them until Jodie announced the opportunity but, after watching everybody else go loopy about them, Fun Cat is as desperate as anyone to take part. I look them up online and listen to their recent album at full volume. It doesn't take me long before I have learnt all the words to *'On a knife edge'*. For the audition, we'll need to sing along to the track. Our singing ability doesn't matter as we'll only be miming in the video but I'm determined to impress so I put in all the techniques I've been learning in my singing classes and hone it till I've got it nailed. I go to bed with angry drums and sweary screaming pounding through my brain, then I play the song on a loop all week until poor Bertie slips a note under my door pleading with me to turn it down.

The night before the audition, I have The Dream.

The evil woman is there. Grabbing me, pinning me down, ripping into my skin. I'm awake but not fully. I don't even try to get away. I just take it. It's like she owns me. Part of me is frightened of her. Another part desperately wants her to love me. I will give her anything she asks for. Anything. *Just love me.* I wake up to Baby Cat crying in my head and it's ages before I can get back to sleep. When morning dawns, I snooze my alarm repeatedly before finally dragging myself out of bed.

Why do I always feel different? Why is everything so hard? Why am I lonely, always hearing crying in my head?

I have to shake Sad Cat away. I worked so hard to be ready for today's audition. I can't crumble now. Not over a stupid dream. I have to be capable and confident and calm. I have to pretend that I belong. Even though I'm sure nobody else on campus has ever been taken out of their body by a creepy woman in the night.

The auditions take place that afternoon in Magnolia, one of the mansion rooms. I take a seat outside the room, playing it cool between Dancing Donna and Murdering Marsha. To everybody else, I am completely normal. They have no idea of the chaos raging inside me. Pumping music is coming from the closed room. The same chorus over and over.

'I'm on a knife edge, an endless life ledge,
Just one slash and I'll be gone, one slip to oblivion...'

Finally, it's my turn. As I slide off my seat and enter Magnolia, a sudden memory flashes through my mind. I'm sitting on our sofa next to Duncan Anderson from down the road. I'm tugging my white nightie and trying not to cry. A surge of terror ripples through me.

Just a flash of a memory. Over as quickly as it came.

I shake my head and walk to the spot on the floor.

I'd had every intention of coming in as Thunder Cat and rocking the place down. I'm even wearing Mad Jo's skull necklace and Dotty Jay's black leather boots. But at the sight of the serious-looking strangers sitting behind the large oak table, all my courage seeps away and I am Squashed Cat, shaking in my boots (or rather *not-my-boots)* and feeling a million miles away from capable or confident or calm.

The director gives me a nod. "Ready?"

I take a deep breath and do all I can to fight the overwhelming panic. "Ready," I say hoarsely.

The music plays. I sing. They watch. It ends.

I walk out of the mansion in a daze. Jodie's in the archway having a cigarette. "Hey, Cat! How are you doing?"

"I'm okay."

"How was the audition?"

"Okay." I want to cry but force a smile. "I think I mucked it up. It wasn't how..." I swallow. "How I practised."

She tips her head to the side. "I'm sure you did better than you think. Well done for giving it a go."

I pause but Holy Cat whispers in my ears, *Don't linger. Don't waste her time. Keep walking.*

So I nod and mutter, "Thanks," before walking on.

I wander aimlessly, taking a very convoluted route to the refectory. I feel like I'm watching the world from a distance, as though the colour and sound are muted. I forget to look as I cross the car park. When I finally reach the refectory, I have a sudden desire to be alone. I'm not hungry anyway. Squashed Cat never is. So I turn on my heels and walk through campus, striding swiftly as though I have a plan and a purpose. Walking and walking wherever my feet take me.

Fairy Land.

Not to jump. Just to tiptoe quietly across the boards.

Then to the lake.

To wonder.

About what?

Drowning?

How melodramatic.

Then to the weeping willow.

Why?

To weep?

No.

There are no tears.

I just sit under its pathetic branches, hugging my knees to my chest, Squashed Cat melting into Lost Cat as I replay my conversation with Jodie.

"Hey, Cat! How are you doing?"

"I'm okay."

"How was the audition?"

"Okay. I think I mucked it up. It wasn't how I practised."

"I'm sure you did better than you think. Well done for giving it a go."

"Thanks."

Sad Cat wishes I'd said something else. But what?

"I had a bad dream last night..."?

Don't be stupid.

Annie's door is propped open when I return to Willow.

"Hi, Cat! Are you okay? I didn't see you at dinner."

Play it Cool Cat is an expert at avoiding questions. "I was on a walk. What have you been up to?"

"I've just got back from the Christian Union. It was the last *'If God'* meeting. You remember? *If God made a way.*"

"I'm sorry! I completely forgot." This is true. I did forget. It's not that I was planning to go. But, had I remembered, I would have done the decent thing and invented an excuse.

Annie smiles. Gracious as ever. "It's okay. I saved you some cake." She skips over with a bundle in a napkin.

My mouth waters. I realise I've not eaten all day.

"Thanks," I mutter. Then Holy Cat feels guilty and adds, "I really am sorry. I should've remembered. Was it good?"

"Really good. We can talk about it some time, if you like?"

Stupid Holy Cat nods and says, "Okay."

The next day, there's a poster pinned to the board outside Primrose. I join the bustling crowd and stand on tiptoes, craning to see if I'm listed.

Tanisha turns and catches my eye. "Well done, Cat! You got a featured role! You're the Girl in White."

A few of my classmates are grinning at me. Sure enough, my name is listed right at the top. The world dims and I feel very far away. I smile. I am pleased. Of course. But I also feel oddly numb.

"Good job, Cat!" Owl-watching Otis gives me a nudge.

Play it Cool Cat, ever humble, gives a bashful shrug before slipping away. I don't want anybody to think I'm being arrogant, watching while they search for their own names.

I have a full day of lessons, followed by evening rehearsals. I'm on autopilot, RoboCat fielding praise about the music video and getting me through the day without feeling anything. It's only once the day is over, and I'm walking back through campus with the crisp winter wind in my ears, that a sense of joy settles in my heart and I remember how much I love this place.

Things are good! I've just got my first proper acting job. I'm a real actor! Like Elle!

The strange numbness melts as Fun Cat gets back into the driving seat and there's a little skip in my step as I trot back to

Willow. In a moment of spontaneous stupidity, I feel an urge to call my parents. I want to tell them about the Mama Octopus video and how I'll probably be on TV. I know my mum will be proud because it's something she could show people.

My mum is very proud of all my accomplishments, even if she sometimes embellishes them a bit. Like the time she told everyone I'd had a book published when actually I'd just come second in a local poetry contest. She's had to stretch the truth quite a lot to turn my mediocre theatre history into anything spectacular. But she won't have to pretend any more! I really can act now. Catrina Carla is on her way!

I don't usually ring my parents out of the blue. I don't usually have anything to tell them. We have a scheduled phone call once a week. Every Monday, 7pm on the dot. My dad asks about the weather and whether I'm taking my vitamins. Then my mum comes cheerily on the line and asks if I received her latest parcel and whether I'm still getting good grades. When I say yes, she trills, *"You're clever, just like me!"* and I feel a momentary swell of pride followed by sorrow. I know they wouldn't be interested in mine and Annie's midnight feasts or my trumpet lessons with Zachary or our block's Christmas meal so I just answer their questions and say nothing more. Anyway, all that fun stuff seems to disappear when my parents are on the line. RoboCat can never think of anything exciting to say. So me actually wanting to call with good news is a rarity and one I don't think to question. Stupid Fun Cat.

My dad answers after two rings with a breathy, "Hello?" It's like he's sprinted to the phone.

"Hi, it's me!" I say merrily.

The disappointment is obvious. "Oh. It's you. Oh, I thought..." He's huffing and puffing. "I'm waiting for Mum to call. She's at Angie's for a party and she'll need me to come and collect her when she's done."

Fun Cat shrivels away. "I was just calling to say hello..."

"Right, yeah, okay..." He clearly can't cope with the idea that I might be blocking the line when my mother calls.

"Never mind," Sad Cat mutters.

He attempts to compose himself. "Are you alright, then?"

"Do you want me to call back later?"

A sigh of relief. "Yeah, if you can. It's just... I don't want to miss the call. You know what she's like!" Awkward laugh.

"It's fine. Bye." I hang up, fuming.

Angry Cat makes a mental note: *Call home less.*

I picture the scene: My mum at a party, dressed like Shay. My dad at home, waiting dutifully by the phone.

My mum loves parties. She's always the centre of attention. Glamorous and vivacious, dressed to impress, with a smile that's radiant and a contagious laugh. She's nothing like my dad. Meek and awkward and antisocial. But opposites attract. So they say.

It's strange really because, for somebody so outgoing, my mum doesn't have many close friends. None, actually. Only Keith who does all her DIY and takes her on holiday because my dad is too nervous to travel. Everyone else is what she calls *'the people'* and you must never let the people get too close.

Before I left for university, she threw me a huge party. The people were all invited. There was cake and karaoke and my mum did a speech about how proud she was of her Baby. I didn't enjoy it but I felt I ought to be grateful so I sang as loudly as I could.

Someone remarked, "Your mum is so fun, isn't she? I bet it's always a barrel of laughs in your house!"

I just smiled and agreed. Because loving someone means protecting them, doesn't it?

* 20 * Holy Cat breaks a promise

I hope to be more *me* during the filming of the music video but, as soon the music starts, Squashed Cat appears again. I spend the whole time drifting aimlessly, white dress flapping, bare feet on the stone roof of the mansion, fleeting waves of panic and confusion clouding my ability to stay present. Certainly not having as much fun as Kite-flying Kimberley as the Girl in Glitter, the role I had been hoping for.

Oh well. I guess it was Squashed Cat they chose to cast. My first job as a professional actress in the bag, I pop by the library on my way home and pick up a pile of books to see myself through to the holidays. Comedy is one of our options for second year so it won't hurt to get ahead of the game. I check out *'The Tragedy of Comedy,' 'The Comedy of Tragedy,'* and *'Life in the Farce Lane.'*

I'm almost back at Willow when I remember that I left a load of washing drying in the laundry room. I'd intended to retrieve it before filming started but completely forgot! I turn on my heels and sprint down the hill at breakneck speed. How on earth did I forget? RoboCat's internal alarm system always alerts me to return to the laundry room five minutes before a cycle is due to end! I enter the laundry room where my worst fears are met. My basket is where I left it, on the end of the bench. But my clothes have been dumped in a pile on the floor. Angry Cat is furious. Furious with myself for being so complacent. And furious with whoever had the nerve to toss my stuff on the floor instead of using my basket.

I sink to my knees and begin gathering up my clothes. Then I notice a large footprint on the back of my butterfly hoodie. I swear and start crying, Angry Cat and Squashed Cat dancing a precarious dance on the edge of insanity. "How could somebody *do* this?" I screech. "I can't believe... Not even the decency to... Who the—"

The laundry room door opens and Zachary steps in. "Hi Cat!" He notices my face. "Is everything alright?"

Play it Cool Cat snaps to attention. "Hi, Zachary! I'm fine. A bit annoyed because somebody took my stuff out of the dryer and didn't bother to put it in my basket. Then they had the nerve to stand on it all, but whatever! Some people, hey!"

"Ah…" He gives a sheepish smile. "Sorry. That was me." He opens the dryer to reveal his freshly dried washing sitting where mine once was.

"Oh!" Play it Cool Cat laughs. "Right. Never mind."

"Sorry," he repeats. "Let me wash it for you again." He bends down and starts scooping my things into an empty washing machine.

"Don't be silly, Zachary. It's fine, honestly. I can just brush the footprint off—"

"I assume this is your detergent?" He grins and points to the bottle with my name on.

Angry Cat has faded away and I feel terribly ashamed for yelling so loudly. I wonder how much he heard. Zachary hums and gently pours some liquid into the tray. Then, before I can get my purse out, he drops a couple of coins into the slot and turns the machine on.

"Thanks," I mutter.

"No problem." I watch as he loads his own clean clothes into a giant backpack and swings it onto his shoulder. "I'll bring your washing back to Willow when it's done."

"It's okay. I can wait for it myself." I sit down on the bench. I'm not going to risk leaving it again.

Zachary thinks for a moment before sitting down beside me. "I'll wait with you."

"You don't have to."

"I'm happy to keep you company. Unless you'd rather be alone?" He points to the library books on my lap.

"I don't mind."

"I'll wait with you, then."

So we sit side by side, bench shaking and machine roaring, watching as my laundry goes round and round.

"Shall we sit outside?" Zachary shouts suddenly over the noise. "It's a beautiful night. Much nicer than sitting in here."

"Outside?" I don't want to stray too far from my washing.

"Literally, outside," he insists. "On the grass. We'll see if anybody goes into the laundry room and I'll follow them in and defend your washing if they do."

"I'm not worried about my washing," I lie. "I just don't want to be cold."

Zachary rummages around in his backpack. "Here. Put this on over your coat." He hands me a yellow hoodie.

"I can't wear that!"

"Of course you can. It's huge."

"I meant it's horrible!"

He gives me a playful flick and leads the way outside. Then he spreads a clean towel on the grass and we sit together and admire the quiet winter night: the mansion lit up nearby, the naked trees lining the path to the lake, the rolling hills beyond campus and the lights from the village in the distance. It's beautiful but freezing. I swallow my pride and pull Zachary's yellow hoodie on.

He grins. "The stars are incredible, aren't they?"

I nod and follow his gaze.

"The Saucepan is so bright."

"The what?"

Zachary points. "The Saucepan."

I frown and repeat, "The what?"

"Don't tell me you haven't heard of the Saucepan!"

"I know what a saucepan is. But I don't know why you're pointing up there."

"You know! Also known as The Plough... The Big Dipper..."

"Big what?"

Zachary is incredulous. "Don't you know anything about stars?"

I give a careless shrug. "No."

"Oh, Cat! The stars are amazing. Let me teach you..." He rocks back onto his elbows. "Let's start with Orion's Belt. It's easy to find. Can you see those three bright stars in a line?"

I follow his finger. "Yeah."

"Great. Do you see the slightly red star to the top left?"

"I think so."

"That's Betelgeuse. It's a thousand times bigger than our sun and some people say it will explode soon... The Saucepan is over there. See the four bright stars in a funny sort of square and the three coming off them to form a handle?"

I tilt my head to the side. "Oh yeah..."

I sit open-mouthed as Zachary scans the sky and points out the North Star and Cassiopeia and The Great Dog. "People have made patterns from the stars since the beginning of time," he explains. "They make pictures of animals or objects or mythological characters. Some stars are used to set the seasons or measure time. There are families of stars and some are absolutely massive..."

"I thought stars were just stars," I mutter, amazed at his knowledge. "I didn't realise they told stories."

"The stars tell amazing stories. Stories from the dawn of creation. There's so much I could tell you about them!"

"Wow." I stare into the sky. It looks so much more magical and mysterious than I've ever given it credit for. "I never knew."

Zachary beams. "Well now you do."

We sit in silence for so long that Silly Cat starts to feel uncomfortable. Before I can stop myself, I blurt out, "Annie doesn't fancy you, by the way. She likes someone called Cooper."

Zachary looks taken aback. "Ahh, Cooper," he says with a sigh. "Heartthrob of the Christian Union."

"Ashley likes you though," Silly Cat continues recklessly. "So you can have her." I immediately feel awful for betraying Ashley's confidence.

Zachary gives me a funny look. "Why did you tell me that?"

"I don't know. It just came out."

He looks at me for the longest time. "What about you?" he says finally. "Wes said there could be something going on with you and Mike?"

"Yuck! Don't be so disgusting!" Silly Cat blows a raspberry. "Course not," I say, quickly composing myself. "I don't like Mike. Or anybody, for that matter. I don't believe in love."

"What do you mean you *don't believe in love?*"

"Just that. I don't believe in it. It doesn't exist. It's a pointless pursuit. Can't think of anything worse."

Zachary lets out a whistle. "Why don't you believe in love?"

"I just don't."

He stares at me as though I am some strange new breed of animal. My chest feels tight and my temples hurt.

Don't say anything, Scaredy Cat warns. *Don't say anything.*

My mother's voice rings in my ears. *"We're a family and we don't tell people our secrets. You can't trust anyone."*

I've told people too much before. Back in high school when Leah Gates pretended to be concerned.

"Tell me what's wrong, Cat," she had pleaded with big caring eyes, over and over for weeks on end. And then, with suspicion and sorrow, "Please Cat. I thought I was your best friend. Why won't you trust me?"

I didn't know how to explain that it wasn't about not trusting her. I was under oath. A vow of silence. Of loyalty to my parents. I didn't know why it was important not to tell. I had often thought somebody might be able to fix things if only my parents would ask for help. But then I told Leah. And I realised why I had been bound to secrecy. Because people cannot help. And do not care. However much they claim to.

"It's my parents," I had whispered, the treason slipping out of my mouth during a sleepover. "My mum... She gets really, really angry. Sometimes she leaves. Sometimes she just threatens to go or packs her bags or stays in her room for days... And my dad... He wants to kill himself. He talks about it all the time. I can't cope with it... I can't cope with having to be perfect. Nothing I do is good enough..."

Leah got more than she bargained for. It turned out she wasn't concerned after all. She was just curious and, curiosity satisfied, she didn't have the ability to care for a troubled friend. I think she thought I might cheer up once I'd released my secrets. But, if anything, I felt even worse because Sad Cat was out of the bag and I couldn't hide her any more.

Then Leah told Jessa ("Because I can't carry all of that by myself, Cat,") and Jessa told Bex and Bex told Paige who was miffed at being the last to know. They demanded to know what had happened to Thunder Cat (although they called her *'the real Cat'*). They couldn't understand why I was constantly quiet and weepy. I was excluded from parties because they said I would bring the mood down. They whispered about me when they thought I couldn't hear them. Exchanged smirks behind my back. Claimed I was being an attention seeker for crying. They didn't understand. It was Thunder Cat who was the attention seeker, not Sad Cat! Sad Cat just wanted to die.

For two whole years the Dark Days rumbled on and I had no friends left by the end of it; their abandonment a fitting punishment for betraying my parents. Because they warned me never to tell. They warned me people couldn't be trusted.

So Sad Cat was exposed and all alone. And then, out of nowhere: Cat out of Hell. The Darkest Days of all. Endless screaming in my head. Rage suppressed in the darkness. Months of insomnia with The Dream lurking if ever I dared to drop off. And the blackest, deepest depression. A depression that didn't begin to lift until I received my acceptance letter from Forest Hall and a shard of light entered my life, a ray of hope that one day Fun Cat would live again.

So there is no way I will break my silence now.

"I just don't understand why you wouldn't want to fall in love," Zachary keeps saying. "It doesn't make any sense."

He keeps looking at me with quizzical eyes and the starry night above seems to cover me like a blanket. I suddenly feel very warm and safe inside Zachary's garish yellow hoodie.

"My mum gets so angry..." I mutter.

Holy Cat, what are you doing? Stop speaking.

I don't mean to tell. I know I shouldn't. I'm being disloyal to my mum after she's tried so hard. She does her best. She can't help it. She suffered terrible things.

Unspeakable things.

The kind of things that break a person.

I put a hand to my mouth. "Doesn't matter. It's silly stuff."

"I'm sure it's not silly, Cat."

I shake my head. I won't go on.

"My dad cries," I blurt out.

"He cries?"

And suddenly I am spilling my heart to this nosy clothes-stomping trumpet player.

"He cries and says he doesn't want to live without her. One time he threw himself down the stairs to stop her leaving. But she left anyway." RoboCat takes over, recalling the memory without any emotion. "She was gone for nearly a week that time. I looked after my dad and Aidan— that's my little brother. I followed my dad around to make sure he didn't hurt himself. And I played with Aidan and told him it would be okay. Then I packed a bag with our favourite toys because I thought our mum might come back to get us. My dad went crazy when he saw the bag. He started saying that he understood how people can get so desperate that they kill themselves and their children. Anyway, my mum came back for her jewellery and I sorted it out and explained how sorry we all were and persuaded her to stay. So she did." I grin. Like I don't care. I learnt my lesson after weeping to Leah. It's best to tell my stories calmly. *Never cry.*

From the room beyond us, I hear the hum of my dirty laundry going through the wash as I tell him far too much.

"I always have to sort it out. He threatens to kill himself if I don't. But she always comes back. We just have to be sorry enough first. Even if we're not sure what we're sorry for."

I steal a glance at Zachary. Bad idea. He looks furious.

"How can they treat you like that? That's abuse!"

"No no no!" I shake my head, Holy Cat awakening as though snapping out of a trance. "No, it isn't! They don't mean to. They try their best. My mum had a horrible childhood. And my dad's just sensitive." I scramble to my feet. "Promise you won't tell anybody."

Zachary rises. "Cat—"

"Promise!" I yell. "Promise you won't tell anyone."

"Of course I won't."

"I shouldn't have said anything. I shouldn't be telling their secrets." I march across the grass and storm into the laundry room. The wash cycle is finished so I yank my clothes out and shove them into a dryer, putting the money in before Zachary has a chance to pay for me. Sad Cat has come screaming to the surface and tears are pouring down my cheeks. I hurriedly wipe them away, keeping my back to him.

Finally, he says quietly, "What happens to you is not *their* secret, Cat. You're not betraying them by talking to me. You're allowed to tell your own story. In fact, you *need* to."

His words dance around my ears but they do not land. All I know is I've broken a promise and the last time I did this, it didn't end well. I frantically rub my eyes. Sad Cat simmers away. Play it Cool Cat re-emerges. "I'm sorry, Zachary. I didn't mean to go on like that. I'm honestly fine." I turn and smile. "And you really don't have to wait with me."

I pick up *'Life in the Farce Lane'* and throw it open. I try to read the introduction but I'm aware of Zachary watching me. I read the same passage over and over without taking anything in. Eventually, I put the book down.

"Why *do* you believe in love?" I demand. "Aren't you bothered that falling in love might mean getting your heart broken?"

"It probably will. But it's what I want more than anything in the world. I imagine meeting the right person and just knowing that she's the one. And her feeling the same way. And us falling in love and getting married and going on adventures together until we're old and grey."

"*Seriously?* Nobody actually lives like that. You're so sheltered, Zachary Fenn!"

He doesn't return my smirk.

I turn back to my book. I pretend to read until the tumble dryer finally clicks and comes to a standstill. I throw the door open, plop my basket underneath it, and tip my laundry in. Then I perch my stack of books on top and prepare to lift it all.

"Here, let me take something," Zachary offers.

"I can manage. I'm stronger than you think."

"I can see that. But you shouldn't have to carry everything alone."

I take his hoodie off and give it to him. Then I lift my load into the air. "I've got it," I insist as he puts a hand out. "You just get the door for me."

He does so and I breeze past him, fixing my eyes forwards as we make our way up the hill.

* 21 * Copy Cat is no longer a vegetarian

The last week of term is filled with performances and parties and heaps of merry banter. Mad Jo has an exhibition in the Art studio and I go along and applaud her self-directed project entitled, *'Burning Passion.'* It consists of six giant wax sculptures shaped like body parts. In the middle, one huge lit candle depicts a couple locked in a naked embrace.

"They will have melted completely by the end of the exhibition," Mad Jo whispers as I watch the hot wax running down the couple's arms.

Play it Cool Cat nods and stares at the flickering flame. I can't deny that she is very skilled, even if the subject matter is one that makes Silly Cat want to cover my eyes.

Later, I watch Annie in a dance show and the image of Mad Jo's burning candles is soothed away by Annie's graceful solo. It's so gentle that I want to cry, even though it doesn't make any sense. It's not like there's a story. It's just Annie dancing about and occasionally dropping to the floor or rolling around, a look of utter serenity on her sweet little face.

My own end of term show is a success. I play a jilted lover, a troubled teen and a bitter housewife in our showcase of Modern Drama and, as we take our bow, I peer into the audience and spot Horse-riding Heidi crying and Annie cheering and Elle looking troubled and Jodie giving me a knowing smile. And suddenly my first term is over and it has been so much more wonderful than I ever could've dreamed.

Then Zachary, who has been very nice to me since my embarrassing spectacle at the laundry room, invites me to watch his winter assignment so I go with Annie and a giggling Ashley and the three of us find ourselves sitting on a pile of damp bark watching as someone gives birth to a toaster. Zachary appears dressed in silver and plays long notes on his trumpet while several of his classmates walk in slow motion across a tin foil 'moon.'

So that's Music Theatre.

Afterwards, Zachary comes bounding over, silver face paint still visible on his cheeks, and asks, "Did you like it?"

He looks so hopeful and pitiful that I don't dare break it to him that it was the most bizarre thing I have ever seen.

Annie thinks of something nice to say. "You played your trumpet wonderfully."

And Ashley blushes all the way to the refectory.

My family are coming to collect me for the holidays so this will be my last meal with friends for a while. I grab a plate of chips and a lemon mousse before heading to Willow's table where Dotty Jay and Rory are waiting. Zachary has already eaten through his meal card so his final meal consists of a sausage and a carton of milk. Windy Wendy felt sorry for him and gave him the milk for free. My speculations about him being rich are apparently unfounded. His meal card has not been topped up by any wealthy benefactor. Looks like he's going to starve for the rest of the school year.

"How was your show, Zachary?" asks Dotty Jay. Then, before waiting for a reply, she asks the rest us, "Was it good?"

"So profound," says Ashley, shooting Zachary a shy smile.

"Zachary played his trumpet wonderfully," Annie repeats.

I nod along but then Thunder Cat blurts out, "We had to sit on damp bark and there was an awful lot of wailing. I had no idea what was happening half the time. No offence," I add.

Zachary grins. "None taken. It's okay if you didn't like it."

I breathe a sigh of relief. "It was creepy."

"But you did play your trumpet well," Annie insists.

Thunder Cat is about to make a joke but then I spot my parents and Aidan wandering into the refectory, looks of agitation on their faces. In an instant, Fun Cat disappears. Copy Cat wades to the surface, Lost Cat waiting in the wings.

My mum texted me when they left Exeter but I wasn't expecting them to arrive so early. I factored for my dad stopping his usual thousand times. I thought I had plenty of time to eat before going to my room to wait for them.

My friends are chatting away but I don't hear what they're saying. My hands have gone clammy. My head feels hot. The words *'Mum'* and *'Dad'* always sound strange when I say them. I don't know why. It's their names. It's what I've always called them. But the words sound weird in my mouth. I push my chair out and walk over to them rather than call across the refectory.

My mum sees me first. "There she is! Hi, Baby!" She embraces me. I try not to cringe at how short her skirt is. My mother prides herself on looking half her age. A bus driver once thought we were sisters and she still goes on about it.

"Hello, Catrina!" My dad looks relieved, as though he wasn't sure whether they would find me. But here we all are. Reunited. A family.

"Hi," I say, forcing a smile. "Hi, Aidan."

Aidan barely acknowledges me, eyes glued to his phone.

My dad wants to tell me all about the journey. Record time, apparently. Plain sailing apart from some idiot who undertook him on the M5. My mum titters and says it was because my dad was crawling in the middle lane. My dad defends himself. He was only there for a minute. My mum rolls her eyes and teases, "If you say so."

Copy Cat is smiling and nodding and stuffing away the familiar urge to cry.

"What happened to your hair?" my mum asks.

I run a hand through it. "I had it cut." I don't add that Dotty Jay did it for me.

She pulls a face. "Have you eaten?"

"I was just finishing." I point to my table. "Those are some of my housemates over there... Do you want to meet them?"

"Of course!" My mum is all smiles as they follow me back to my table. "Hello, everybody! We're Catrina's parents."

I note the surprise on Dotty Jay's face as she looks my mother up and down.

"I know I look like I could be Cat's sister!" My mother flashes a dazzling smile. "Nobody believes me when I say my daughter is at university."

Dotty Jay returns the smile. "Lovely to meet you."

My housemates introduce themselves. I'm grateful not to have to do it, now that Lost Cat has got my tongue. I slide back into my seat and try to smile.

"Get some lunch," my mum orders my dad. "What do you want to eat, Aidan? Go with your dad and see what they've got."

I offer to treat them with my meal card but my mum scolds me. "Don't be silly, Catrina. Your dad will pay for it."

My dad looks taken aback but doesn't argue. He and Aidan wander to the queue and re-emerge a few minutes later with a tray laden with three plates of toad in the hole.

"Ugh!" says my mum. "I don't like sausages."

"Don't you?" my dad says in surprise. "I thought you did."

"No. You know I don't!" My mum gives a careless laugh, one so loud and melodic that Dotty Jay and Rory can't help but join in. "Never mind. I'll have the vegetables." She looks at me. "Here, Catrina. Have my sausage."

"It's okay," I mutter. "I'm full." I don't add that I recently became a vegetarian. She wouldn't understand.

My mum plonks the sausage on my plate and I eat it.

Then Tanisha arrives followed by Mad Jo and Elle. Our table is a hive of activity and my mum is the centre of it all, chatting with everybody, feigning interest in which course everyone's doing and where they're all from.

Squashed Cat is getting triggered. Even though nothing bad is happening. Even though everybody is pleased to meet my parents. Even though I ought to be excited and grateful that they've come all this way to collect me. What's wrong with me?

My dad is shovelling peas into his mouth and frequently checking the time. "Have you got everything packed?" he asks me. "It would be good to head straight off."

I try to sound assertive. "I was hoping to show you around first. You know, show you the campus and things?"

He pulls a face. It's clear he's itching to get home.

But my mum says loudly, "Of course! We want to see everything!"

So my dad falls silent, shooting me only the slightest glance for ruining his plans.

* 22 * Squashed Cat on the road

Fun Cat peeks hopefully once our tour gets underway. I've been planning this all week. I can't wait to show my family the special places around campus. I take them inside the mansion and point out Primrose and Heather. Then I take the route past the costume and props department before heading back outside.

"This is the laundry room," I say, pushing the door open.

"We don't need to see that!" my mum says scornfully. "We know what washing machines look like."

My dad laughs along. "Very thrilling! A washing machine."

Angry Cat glowers as we walk on. I take them down the path towards the lake. On our way, we pass Ruth and Charlotte from the Christian Union.

"Hi Cat!"

"Have a nice Christmas, Cat!"

"Thanks! You too!"

My mum gives them both cheery waves but the moment they're gone she frowns and asks, "Who are they?"

"Just two girls from campus."

She sniffs as though it's strange that people she doesn't know should be so friendly with me. "And who were all those people in the canteen?"

"My housemates. Annie was the one closest to me. She does Dance. The ones opposite were Dotty Jay and Rory. The one who came after you was Tanisha. She's on my course."

"The black?"

I cringe and hurriedly continue, "Elle is on my course too. The boy with the trumpet was Zachary. He's given me a few lessons..."

My mother's eyes have glazed over. "Are you still getting good grades?"

"Yes. And I was the lead in a play with the Shakespeare Society. And I filmed a music video for Mama Octopus."

"Who?"

"A band—"

"Are those trousers new?"

"Yes. I got them in Wakefield." I don't add that they were from a charity shop.

"Oh." Her face tells me that she hates them. She tuts. "Don't slouch, Cat. You walk like a humpback."

I pull my neck up.

Then my dad says fretfully, "Are you taking your vitamins?"

"Yes," I lie.

I continue the tour with a selection of my favourite sculptures but neither of my parents are fans of modern art so it's all lost on them. My dad keeps glancing at his watch and sighing. My mum snaps at him to be quiet. Aidan is still glued to his phone. It's a wonder how he can walk without looking where he's going.

I reach the climax, Fairy Land, and say excitedly, "This is my favourite—"

"Oh Catrina, I have to tell you something!" My mother stops short of Fairy Land and plops down on a bench. I recognise the unrestrained glee and brace. She's about to tell me the sordid details of somebody's affair or death or other misfortune. "It's about your cousin, Chantelle."

"Oh?" I feign interest but I'm dreading whatever she's about to say. Has my cousin left home or been hit by a bus or got pregnant or been diagnosed with cancer?

"She's pregnant!"

I adjust my face accordingly. "Oh?"

"She got pregnant by a man she barely knows and now she wants to marry him. Can you believe that? I told her how stupid she is but she won't listen to me. I told her she should go to university and give her baby to Sonya to look after. She shouldn't ruin her whole life by rushing in to marry someone. She hasn't even got a job!"

RoboCat processes this information. I am supposed to agree with my mum but, as usual, it is hard to keep track.

"Maybe she really likes him," I venture.

"Don't be silly!" my mum snaps. "Of course she doesn't like him. She only just met him."

I wonder whether to remind her that she once agreed to marry a man that she had only just met. My dad popped in to use the toilet in the hotel where my mother was a cleaner, and voila it was love— or something— at first sight. Her parents said it would never last. She was barely out of her teens and he was a forty year old bachelor who packed car parts for a living. But here they are, twenty years later, still married. Proved them wrong.

"And he's a *foreigner*," my mother adds with disdain, forgetting that she herself was once a stranger to this country.

I stare at Fairy Land. "What did Aunt Sonya say about it?"

"She's not doing anything! You know what Sonya's like."

Actually, I don't know what Sonya's like. Not really. We barely see her and my cousins, Chantelle and Chris.

"Tracey agreed with me though," my mum continues. "She and Sonya aren't speaking."

We rarely see Aunt Tracey either. She last visited when I was ten. My mother's heart was playing up, as it often does, so Aunt Tracey came to help for a week. She did the cooking and washing and cleaned the house from top to bottom and nicknamed my father, 'Mr Panic' after witnessing his inability to keep calm when the oven broke. For some reason, she and my mum had a huge argument one night, all yelling and screaming, darting from topic to topic, neither of them stopping to let the other speak. I tried to eavesdrop from my bed but couldn't keep up. The next morning, Aunt Tracey was gone. They made up eventually, and they talk from time to time, but she hasn't been back since.

None of my mother's family live anywhere near us. She and her three siblings grew up in a deprived area of London until their family exploded, sending the siblings in different directions. My mum went to Devon, Aunt Sonya went up to Scotland, Aunt Tracey plummeted south to Eastbourne and Uncle Richard went the furthest of all, settling in Canada. I've never met him or my Canadian cousins, Avery and Jackson.

Obviously, I'm 'friends' with them all on FriendWeb. I 'like' their posts and my mum keeps me filled in on all the gossip. Aunt's Sonya's mental breakdowns. Uncle Richard's affair. Avery's battles with anorexia.

I only met my mum's parents once. They had moved out of London and had a small cottage in the Essex countryside. I remember my mum shouting in the car on the way. I was terrified, bracing myself for some real monsters. But my grandparents seemed normal and nice. Monsters have scary faces, don't they? Bad people are evil all the time, aren't they?

They greeted me and Aidan with giant hugs and insisted on being called *'Grandmother'* and *'Grandfather'* which sounded very strange in their South American accents.

I remember my grandfather announcing I was his favourite, an honour which infuriated my mother. She wouldn't let me go anywhere alone with him. Her mother was very emotional. She cried a lot and made long weeping speeches in Spanish. I later learnt that she was dying and our visit was arranged so my mum could say goodbye.

Their house was small and cluttered. It felt like it was short of air. Their sofa was covered in plastic wrapping that stuck to the back of my legs. They had a display cabinet that was full to the brim with British knick-knacks: thimbles covered in union jacks, mugs commemorating royal weddings, a plastic hat from the London Eye.

Lunch was an eclectic mix of roast dinner and soup and savoury bananas and beetroot. I remember my grandfather reciting some sort of prayer before the meal; a long slow chant in Spanish. We couldn't eat until he finished. He scowled at Aidan for reaching for some bread prematurely.

We only stayed one night. My grandparents expected us to stay longer and there was a scene in the kitchen with lots of shouting in Spanish just before we left. My grandmother died a month later and my mother wept for weeks. My father blamed the whole thing on her brief disappearance that summer. My grandfather lived another seven years but we never visited him again. Any mention of him would send my mum up the wall so I learnt to pretend he didn't exist.

When I'm an actress in London, I plan to find the area where my mum grew up, even though I know it was full of horrible things.

Unspeakable things.

The kind of things that break a person.

I think it would help me to feel closer to her. I have gleaned pieces of information from when she's been angry and screamed cryptically about events from long ago. I know splinters of the rows, the threats, the secrets, the strange treatments and rituals at the hands of those two sweet people who seemed so normal and nice. But there's so much I don't know. I wish I knew more. So I could understand her better. Love her better. But I'm too scared to ask. I asked her once about Chantelle's witch doctor theory and she flew into a rage and told me not to be so stupid.

We don't have anyone on my father's side. My dad's parents died before he met my mother and he doesn't have any siblings. I've often asked about his past, probing for clues on possible long-lost big sisters, but he never has anything to tell me. Sometimes my family history feels like one big jigsaw puzzle with all the pieces missing.

Fairy Land abandoned, we head to Willow and load up the car. We're about to leave when Zachary appears beside me. Without warning, he lifts me into the air and envelops me in a giant hug. "Have a wonderful Christmas, Cat."

I give a bemused splutter as he puts me down. "You too, you weirdo!" I climb into the back seat, taking one last look at Willow before my dad starts up the engine.

Zachary waves me off as we drive up the hill. I swivel in my seat and stare at him until he's a tiny dot. Then we turn the corner and he's gone. Along with Willow and Forest Hall and joy and hope and Fun Cat.

"Who was that boy?" my mum asks suspiciously.

"Zachary. I told you. My housemate. He's teaching me how to play the trumpet."

"You can't play the trumpet!" my dad scoffs.

"I'm getting quite good actually," I say. I'm not really. I'm still yet to make a proper sound with it. But I'll never play it to my parents so it doesn't matter what they know.

We've barely reached the motorway when my mother starts screaming. "You nearly hit that car!"

"No, I didn't. He nearly hit me. I'm driving perfectly."

"Don't be an idiot!"

I put my fingers in my ears. Sniping. Swearing. Snapping. Scowling. Shouting. Snivelling. Sighing. And we've got nearly six hours left to go. I am Squashed Cat. I've always been Squashed Cat. No memory or hope of ever being anybody else. This suffocating sinking suicidal sickness is all I know. All that exists in the world. My fault for asking them all to come. My mum had planned to collect me with Keith but I'd said I wanted to show them round. Silly me.

My mother hurls a final jibe and we travel in silence for the next few hours, stopping intermittently for my dad to pee.

Just past Birmingham, I attempt to chat with my brother.

"How's school?"

"Aright."

"Do you ever see Monica— I mean Miss Lucas?"

"No idea who she is."

I watch as he taps on his phone, thumb dancing wildly, his world complete without me.

Just past Bristol, my mother's cheery mood returns and she starts telling me about a holiday to France she's planning. Squashed Cat is muted and Copy Cat arises to do her job. Smile and nod and tell my mum it sounds lovely. She's going with Keith. My dad doesn't do holidays. Not since the one in America where my mum went missing in the Magic Kingdom.

It was all because Aidan spilled his drink on her camera. He didn't mean to. But he should've been more careful. He should've known it was expensive and that it was really important for her to get a good shot of us next to the castle. My dad was convinced she'd be gone forever but I assured him she would never go on the run in America dressed only in a jumpsuit and bumbag. I said she'd probably be waiting for us at the exit. Which she was. With two buckets of candy floss for Aidan and me. I ate mine in one go so she wouldn't call me ungrateful. But then she called me greedy instead.

I still remember the ache in my chest as I ran through Mickey's parade, searching desperately for any sign of my mum. But it wasn't all bad. I hugged a princess and rode on Splash Mountain five times. On our last day, our parents gave Aidan and me three dollars each for a souvenir and we decided to spend our money on a gift for each other. We were close like that when we were little. Best friends.

He got me a wind up beetle, one he'd had his eye on for himself. I got him a necklace with a bird pendant hanging off it, a reference to his favourite book, *The Bravest.* I've still got the beetle in my special keepsake box but I expect the bird is long gone.

* 23 * Silly Cat's Christmas Challenge

Christmas day is ruined.

My mum has locked herself in her bedroom. It's all because Aidan didn't want his photo taken by the pile of presents under the tree. It was brewing last night when nobody showed any interest in going to midnight mass. She said we weren't showing any respect to baby Jesus.

My dad is trying to talk to her through the crack in the door. "We're sorry! Please come out. Let's have a lovely time."

Holy Cat can't help feeling frustrated. I understand why Aidan didn't want his photo taken. He doesn't want to pose for FriendWeb and he doesn't like being told what to do. I get it. I feel the same. I just wish he would've done it to keep the peace. "Are you alright?" I ask him quietly.

He barely looks at me. "Why wouldn't I be alright?"

"Because of, you know..." I gesture upstairs.

He shrugs. "It's always okay, isn't it? She'll come down later. No point getting upset about it."

My heart splinters at the carelessness of his words. *No point getting upset about it.*

He's right. It's always okay. Eventually. After we're sorry enough. After she gets tired. After the game has been played and everybody has lost. I wish I could share his reckless abandon. I wish I had the audacity to refuse to have my photo taken. To speak my mind. To be rude and brash and moody and selfish. To shrug and not care because there's *no point getting upset about it.* But I can't help it. No matter how many times it happens, I can't help getting upset. I can't help fearing that *this time* will be the worst. This time will be the time when somebody dies or leaves for good. I can't help overreacting. I can't silence Baby Cat's screams or Sad Cat's bottomless sorrow or Squashed Cat's blind terror.

I watch my brother, wishing I knew how to connect with him the way we used to when we were children.

We used to have a game called *The Christmas Challenge.* We would take turns to hold a mirror under our chin and walk around while looking down into the mirror. The mirror would reflect the decorations hanging from the ceiling so, as we walked through the house, it was as though the ceiling was the floor. We had to leap over the tinsel covering the doorways and navigate the gaudy decorations which blocked our path like exploding bombs. It was a great game. I made it up. Aidan was so in awe of me. I like to think I was his hero once upon a time. I did my best. Playing with him. Reading to him. Packing him a suitcase, just in case. But perhaps there was never any need. Perhaps he didn't need me to be his hero. It was always okay, after all.

I glance at the ceiling. The same old decorations hang limply, the dust of many Christmasses festering in their creases. Silly Cat has an urge to go and fetch a mirror. The idea fills my eyes with tears.

My dad comes down to have a cry so I go upstairs and hide in my room. Monkey Bear has come home with me for Christmas. I cling to him, digging my nails into his furry arms, as a stone-cold numbness settles in my chest. As I stare across my room, my attention is drawn to the poem that I wrote as part of my mother's Christmas present.

It isn't the presents waiting under the tree
It isn't the turkey gawping at me
The snow could not show, the cake could be blue
It wouldn't be Christmas if it wasn't for you.

What a load of rubbish, Angry Cat snarls.

I think for a moment before plodding down the hallway and sliding it through the crack under my mother's door. Then I go back to my room, lie face-down on my bed and pretend to talk to Jodie.

"I saw you in the Shakespeare play," I imagine her saying. *"You were excellent."*

She didn't really watch me. I hoped that she would. I gave it my all in case she was in the audience. But she didn't come. I'd felt rejected, like it was a personal slight, even though there was no reason for her to come.

"Have you thought about your options for next year?" Jodie in My Head continues.

"I don't know yet," I confess, rolling over to stare at my ceiling. "I enjoyed the Shakespeare piece so I'm considering taking Classical Theatre. But I'm also interested in Comedy."

"Oh, Cat! You should do Comedy. You were hilarious in the Storytelling module. I laughed so much at your Strange Strangers skit."

"Really? I don't know if I'm funny enough."

"You are! You've got great comic timing. You should take Postmodern too. Your devising work is phenomenal."

"Thanks. I was planning to do Postmodern."

My dad has finally found a way into the bedroom. I hear his pitiful whimpers as he pleads with my mother. Her voice drifts down the hall. "I give and give and give... I was up at the crack of dawn cooking for you lot... Nobody helping..."

I feel a pang of shame. I didn't think. I didn't realise. If only I wasn't so selfish. My door opens and my dad is there, looking frantic. He doesn't knock. He never knocks. He always just waltzes in, even if I'm changing, as if whatever's on his mind is more important than checking I'm not naked. Usually, Angry Cat snaps, *"Knock!"* and he pouts like I'm being unkind. Today I just ignore him.

"Cat, can you please talk to her?" He looks at me in dismay as though I'm having a thoughtless lie down while he's working so hard.

RoboCat rises to do her job, ignoring Squashed Cat's strangled screams as I glide down the hall and into the fire. My mother is staring into space, eyes glazed and full of angry sorrow. I perch on the end of the bed and wait. I wonder whether she's read my poem yet. I scan the room and my stomach tightens as I spot it in the bin.

Finally, she turns and accuses, "You never call us, Cat. You don't care about us now you've left home."

"I do care," I say in surprise. "I'm sorry if I've been busy with uni work—"

"You never call me. Angie's daughter calls her every day and she tells her everything. You never tell me things, Cat."

I gulp. Holy Cat makes a mental note: *Call home more.*

"I'm sorry. I'll try to tell you more." I wrack my brains for something to share but I can't think of anything. "Thank you for getting up early to cook..." I peer at my mum, searching for signs that she's about to calm down, but the walls go back up again and suddenly she's livid, eyes full of rage.

"You're so ungrateful! All of you! I do everything for you and none of you care about me." She clutches her chest. "My heart is bad and none of you care."

"We do!" I cry, desperate for her to know how much. Of course I care about her heart. Of course I think about it all the time, endlessly afraid that something will happen to her; another dreadful abandonment looming in the background.

She changes tack. "All I ask is that you respect me. Is that too much to ask?"

"We do respect you! We know you've done so much for us. It's amazing how much you do..."

I feel myself floundering but RoboCat presses on. I've developed a wide array of magic powers over the years. I know all the ways to get her to crack: Look her in the eyes and hold her gaze with a beseeching stare. Appeal to the goodness inside her. Tell her Aidan needs a mother; he's only four, six, ten, fourteen. Thank her for her years of endless sacrifice and resolve to try harder from now on. Say sorry over and over. If she starts to cry, then we're almost there.

I note the slight shift in her body language, arms loosened as she wraps them around herself, not quite so fierce. Her face quivers. She looks distressed and dazed, as though stuck in the torment of events from long ago. Not fully here. Any minute now she'll open her arms and tell me to come and give her a hug. Then we're okay again. Forgiven. I fix my eyes on hers, squeezing her soul with my magic stare.

At last, the dam breaks and she starts to cry. "Come here, Catrina," she weeps, her arms wide. "Give me a hug."

And Sad Cat begins to weep too as I crawl across the bed to embrace her. "I'm sorry," I blub. "I'm sorry."

"I'm crazy, Cat. I'm not well."

"It's okay," I assure her. "It's okay. I love you."

She mutters something in Spanish; the familiar prayer that she clings to in moments like this. I have no idea what's supposed to come from it but I repeat it too, in my head. I let her hold me for as long as she needs and panic fades to nothing as Lost Cat takes over.

* 24 * Sad Cat looks ugly when she cries

I pinch the tears from my eyes. "I'm sorry I didn't help you with lunch. I can do something now if you want?"

"Don't be silly, Catrina. You can't cook." My mother pats me on the arm and sits up, her face distorted from crying. "Do you want to open your presents now?"

I have to feign the right level of excitement. I don't want her to think I'm not grateful for the mountain of gifts she's so lovingly provided. But nor do I want to appear too eager, as though opening presents is the reason I came to talk her round. "Okay."

"Come on then." We wander down together. "Aidan!" she calls. "Do you want to open your presents?"

I'm scared that he'll set her off again by refusing but, thankfully, he and my father spring into action and within minutes we're playing the role of happy family, passing presents between us. My chest is tight and my head is a mess but I fix a calm expression on my face as I open my gifts.

There are some tops that I will never wear. Too Shay or Lizzie or Lottie. Four bags of chocolate coins and a tub of peanut butter. A make-up bag. A pen. And several months' worth of sanitary towels and shampoo.

It's not that I'm not grateful. I am. Clearly nothing says, *'I love you,'* like a supply of sanitary towels. I just can't shake off this angry, overpowering urge to scream.

"Do you like your presents?" my mother asks.

Copy Cat fakes a huge smile. "Yes, thank you so much. Do you like the scarf? I sewed all the bits on myself."

"I've got lots of scarves already," she says carelessly.

I watch as Aidan opens *'The Bravest.'*

"It was your favourite book when you were little," I say. "Do you remember it?"

He grunts. He shows no sign of appreciating it but, even so, I note that he sits and reads it from cover to cover before opening anything else.

After presents, we eat the meal my mother dutifully prepared while the rest of us were sleeping. It's a tradition that each year she and my father count how many vegetables have graced the Christmas dinner. This year it is thirteen.

"Wow!" my dad gushes, gravy dribbling down his chin.

"I think this is the best I've ever done the Yorkshire puddings," my mum says proudly and we all agree. She rises to take a photo for FriendWeb.

I shoot Aidan a glance. To my relief, he doesn't protest.

My parents gossip about cousin Chantelle's upcoming wedding. It's scheduled for March so that Chantelle won't be too heavily pregnant. My mother is adamant we won't be going. "Not driving all the way to Scotland to show my face at such a farcical event."

"Can't think of anything worse," my dad agrees.

"I don't know what Sonya is thinking, agreeing to it. It's because Martin left her, of course. What do you expect your children to do if they're raised in a broken home?" According to my mother, the worst thing you can do is raise your children in a broken home.

After the meal, I sit in my room and talk to Jodie in My Head. I wonder how she's spent her Christmas. I'm suddenly overwhelmed by a ridiculous longing to be loved by her. It's not enough that she said I'm a good actor. I want to be her favourite. I play back every poignant moment from the last term. The first time Jodie walked into the room, all ice cool and stern. Our first bumbling conversation and the discovery that she once lived in Willow. The day she called me back after class to see if I was okay. The little wink she gave me when I answered the question about Krispin Staniscofskin. The moment she told me I was talented. The thrill of every surprise meeting around campus.

The realisation hits that I have started talking to Jodie in My Head more than Monica. I think this means I am over Miss Lucas. She has finally been relegated to the long list of *People I used to be attached to*. Along with Evelyn and Sadie and Sandra and Davina, none of whom matter any more but who were once my entire world. Now it's all about Jodie.

I curl up on my bed and hug my knees, giant tears rolling down my cheeks as I obsess over my teacher.

She doesn't really like me. She just has to pretend to like me because it's her job. She won't be thinking of me today.

My head is pounding. My eyes land on my open suitcase and the little purse filled with homeopathic remedies that has slipped out of the top. My dad doesn't trust doctors and never gives us normal medicine. When I left for Forest Hall, he loaded me up with his best selection of alternative cures. Gelsemium for headaches. Belladonna for coughs and colds. Pulsatilla for period pains. Ignatia for depression. Dotty Jay laughed when she saw it all. She laughed even more when I said most of them take a few days to work.

"A few days to cure a headache? Try a paracetamol, Cat!"

But I couldn't do it. I've never swallowed a pill before and the very thought of it made me gag.

I unscrew the bottle of Gelsemium and slip a couple of tablets under my tongue. Then I wander to my window and put my head against the glass. The cold window soothes my hot head as I stare into the dark sky at the stars. They are not as bright here as at Forest Hall. It's like my whole world has turned back to grey. I locate The Saucepan and Betelgeuse and The Great Dog, all hanging serenely without a care in the universe. I want to text Zachary and see if I've got them right. He must be psychic or something because my phone suddenly beeps and he texts me first.

'Happy Christmas, Cat! How was your day?'

I look at my phone, wondering how to answer.

We had thirteen different vegetables.

I've got enough sanitary towels to last me till Easter.

My mum didn't like the scarf.

I want to die.

I settle for, *'Average. Can you see the stars right now? I think I can see The Saucepan.'*

'Yeah! I can see it too. Isn't it amazing? We're looking at the same thing even though we're miles apart.'

'Yeah. Crazy.'

A few minutes later: *'We're having a party for New Year. You should come! Get a train! I'll meet you at the station.'*

A train?? I've never got a train in my life. I roll my eyes and toss my phone aside. Then I stare out of the window until tears have clouded my vision and the stars are no more.

My dad appears and asks if I want to watch a film with them. Something funny, apparently.

"No thanks. Feeling ill."

"Oh no! What's wrong?"

"Headache."

"Make sure you take some—"

"Gelsemium. Done it."

"Take two and another dose in—"

"Four hours. Yes." I keep staring out of my window.

He lingers in my doorway, a bundle of nervous energy, my pain an extra inconvenience in an already miserable day. "Oh dear. Oh dear. Another thing for me to worry about." Then, in a pathetic whisper as he leaves, "I'm sorry."

My phone beeps again. It's Zachary with a proposed itinerary of how I could travel from Exeter St David's to Berney Arms in Norfolk and arrive in time for his party. I don't know whether to laugh or cry. He's so daft. I pick up the bottle of Gelsemium and give it a furious shake. How many would I need to take to knock myself out for a bit?

I took a whole handful once, during the Dark Days. I wasn't really thinking. Sad Cat just wanted to block the world out. I had tried telling my parents I felt depressed but they didn't believe me.

"Don't be daft," he'd said. "You've got such a nice life."

"Don't make yourself miserable," she'd scolded. "You look ugly when you cry. You don't want to go crazy like Sonya."

So, after weeping a river of secret ugly tears, Sad Cat had raided the medicine cupboard and emptied the dregs of a bottle of Ignatia into my mouth. Ten pills exactly. I counted them fastidiously as they went in. Upon swallowing them, I was immediately filled with dread. I thought death might be imminent and was afraid of where it would lead. But, when I ran to tell my father, he grumbled, "Don't waste them! They're not cheap, you know." So any fear that I might have done something foolish was immediately replaced with frustration that my cry for help had gone unnoticed.

I lean over and kick my suitcase, causing the rest of the homeopathic remedies to spill onto the floor. Sometimes I am so sick of being Sad Cat. So sick of lonely Christmasses. So sick of endless headaches and being so ugly when I cry. Ten hadn't been enough. Perhaps fifty would do it?

****

ACT TWO

In which Cat plays games, uses her magic powers and goes through a door.

****

* 25 * Angry Cat is so ungrateful

Sometimes I forget that I have a wonderful life at Forest Hall. I get all moody and miserable for no reason at all. After the little blip over Christmas, Fun Cat is back! Now I'm on my way back up North, suitcase in the boot filled with four month's worth of sanitary towels and a brand new bottle of Gelsemium. My father is singing along to ABBA and I'm texting Annie to see whether she'll be back by the time I arrive.

Halfway into the journey, my dad launches into his favourite topic of conversation. The football. "I suppose you heard about McGrath's latest gaffe?" Without waiting for a reply, he treats me to a minute by minute recap of Exeter City's most recent match. If it was my mother speaking, I'd have to pretend to be interested. No need with my father. I can yawn all I like. He doesn't notice. He just keeps talking.

Somewhere past Sheffield, he moves on to more miserable matters. "I hope Chantelle sees sense and calls off her wedding. You know what your mother's like when she gets her mind set on something. I don't want it sending her up the wall."

I frown. "Why should it matter if Chantelle gets married?"

"Don't ask me!" He pulls a face, a cross between a grimace and a smirk. "I don't know why she has to involve herself in everybody else's business. She'll end up upsetting herself and she really can't afford to do that with her heart." A self-pitying, long-suffering sigh. "I don't know why she can't keep her nose out. She was on the phone to Sonya till midnight when she first found out. You can imagine how angry she was! All for something that's nothing to do with her."

I stare at the road. "Why don't you tell her?"

"Don't be stupid!" He gives a bitter laugh as though I have lost my mind. "You know I can't *say* anything."

"Then why are you telling *me*?" Angry Cat storms to the surface, preparing to be caught in a trap.

"Oh, Cat!" He winces as though I have hit him. "Don't be like that. I'm just telling you what's been going on. You have no idea. Now you've left us. No idea what she's like." He lowers his voice, confiding in me whether I like it or not. "I think she's getting worse. She doesn't make sense half the time. And I can't take much more—"

"Why don't you get some counselling?" I butt in.

"Don't be ridiculous. You know I can't do that. It wouldn't help! Besides, she'd go berserk if she found out I was talking to people about her."

This has been our game for as long as I can remember. My dad dumps on me his emotional turmoil, I produce the best advice I am capable of— honesty, counselling, mindfulness, hobbies, friends or medication— and he tells me, without giving it any thought, exactly why my ideas are foolish and will never work.

I turn in my seat and press my head against the window. There is loud swearing raging between my ears. Angry Cat is not supposed to come to the surface. I learnt years ago that the most important thing to do is to keep the peace. That means not speaking my mind. Not showing irritation. Not making my needs known. Angry Cat is usually content to sit in the passenger seat, whispering in my ear, hating everyone and everything. She very, very rarely speaks out loud.

My dad is confused over my sudden change of behaviour. "Cat? Are you alright? What are you doing, Cat? We were having a conversation and now you're acting all funny."

Tears have sprung to my eyes. Angry Cat shakes them away and silences any whiff of neediness from Sad Cat. "I don't like it when you make threats."

"What are you talking about? I haven't made any threats."

"You do it all the time. You say you're going to kill yourself if she leaves or if she's angry."

"I don't do that! Why would you say that? Don't lie. I think you're being silly all of a sudden!"

This is another of our games. If I summon up the courage to confront him, he immediately throws the blame on me.

"I'm not lying," I snap, Squashed Cat and Angry Cat taking hold of my brain and shaking it around.

"I don't know what you're talking about. You're going crazy. Perhaps you're not feeling well. Do you still have a headache?"

"Shut up! Just stop talking to me."

He gives a flabbergasted moan. "Sometimes you're just like your mum."

If it wasn't for the fact that in just under an hour I will be back at Forest Hall, ready for my second term as a first year Acting student, on my way to becoming Catrina Carla the famous actress, and back within hugging reach of Jodie, I might have done something regretful at that moment. As it is, I stuff Angry Cat deep, deep down and allow RoboCat to take over. All emotion drains away as I sit numbly for the rest of the journey. My dad puts ABBA back on and sings along as though everything is merry and fine.

Finally, the gates of Forest Hall appear on the horizon and I let out a wistful sigh as we drive down the hill, past the fields and into the parking lot. I leap out of the car within seconds of the engine turning off. I am home!

Fun Cat stirs as though waking from a slumber and I feel a giddy smile creeping over my face as I look up at the great, welcoming arms of Willow. I race to the boot and yank my suitcase out. My dad reaches in to help and somehow cuts his finger on a piece of metal on the side of the car. He gives a loud squeal and I wince at the sight of his blood oozing. I wince even more at his pathetic crying.

"My finger! I've cut myself! Oh! Oh! My finger!"

"I've got some plasters in my room," I say. I hoist my backpack onto my back, tuck a box under my arm and grab my suitcase with the other hand before leading the way into Willow. My dad follows me up the stairs, empty-handed, clutching his finger and whimpering like a baby.

I hope nobody will be around to see him carrying on like this but, to my embarrassment, Dotty Jay appears as we reach my room. "Yoo-hoo!" she calls. "You're back!"

"Hi!" I greet her with a hug before shooting her an apologetic smile. "I just need to get a plaster for my dad."

My dad sniffs miserably behind me, shaking as though he's close to death.

Dotty Jay peers at him. "Oh no! What happened?"

"He just cut it on the car," I say quickly before sprinting into my room to find a plaster.

My dad follows me in, still crying.

"Wash it first." I direct him to my sink and he makes a great show of wailing and splattering blood everywhere.

I hold the plaster out. "Here."

"Can you do it for me?" he whimpers.

"Do it yourself!"

"I can't! I can't!"

"Fine. Hold it still." I rip into the plaster and strap it round his finger, fuming as he winces. I'm so embarrassed. Dotty Jay must think he's a freak. Crying over the tiniest cut.

After a sit down and a toilet break, he is ready to leave. I retrieve the last of my belongings from the car and prepare to send him off. "Thanks for bringing me," I say, recoiling as he goes to hug me.

He's keen for me to know how traumatised he is. "I hope I'll be able to drive without crashing. You've no idea what it's like driving in a suicidal state."

"There!" Angry Cat is triumphant. "That's what I was talking about. Making threats. You're doing it now."

"I wasn't! I was just *saying—*"

"You do it all the time and I hate it. How do you think it feels to be constantly afraid you're going to hurt yourself?"

He hangs his head and starts to sob. Giant man-size tears. When I say nothing, he repeats wretchedly, "I'm sorry! *I'm sorry!* I can't do anything right. Perhaps you'd be better off without me..."

"Don't. Just don't."

I see the bewilderment in his eyes. He has no idea what he's done and is helpless to know how to fix it.

"I love you." When my father tells me he loves me, he always says it as though it is a question. What he really means is *"Do you love me?"*

I don't reply right away.

"I love you? *I love you?*" His eyes are frantic.

I pat him on the shoulder. "I love you too."

Sigh of relief. "See you at Easter, then. Don't forget to take your vitamins."

"Yup." I stare vacantly as he gets into the car. My hand waves him off. Then I trot back into Willow, stomping Sad Cat away as I bounce up the stairs.

Dotty Jay is waiting furiously on our corridor. "You were so rude to your dad! I can't believe the way your spoke to him!"

Angry Cat is momentarily riled. I want to tell her it's none of her business. But Holy Cat is there too and I am covered in shame as she chastises me. This is precisely why Angry Cat is meant to hold my anger without ever saying anything. It always comes out wrong.

"I'd give anything to have my dad care about me the way yours cares for you," Dotty Jay harks on. "He's so sweet, driving you here from Exeter. Now he's got to drive all the way home by himself and you didn't even say thank you."

"I did say thank you," I mutter. "Just now, outside."

"Good. You don't realise how lucky you are. You take your dad for granted."

I bite the inside of my lip. "I don't," I say in a small voice. "I just got cross with him. It annoyed me that he couldn't put the plaster on by himself."

She sniffs and keeps frowning, splattering me with judgement. I am such an awful person.

"I'm going to unpack," I say quietly.

I go to my room and snip the tip of my finger with my scissors.

Holy Cat is distraught. *What if my dad crashes on the way home? What if I never see him again and that was our last ever conversation? I should've been more sincere when I told him that I loved him. Of course I love him. I was just cross and lost perspective in the heat of the moment. I'm always doing that. I'm such a horrible daughter.*

I send my dad a text. *'Sorry about earlier. I hope your finger is OK. Thanks for driving me. I really appreciate it.'*

It's alright. He forgives me. He always does. Long-suffering and all that.

* 26 * Silly Cat still wants to play mermaids

Zachary arrives just before midnight on the bus from Wakefield, having got a train all the way from Norfolk. Annie and Ashley and I greet him at the top of the hill. He's dragging a giant suitcase with one hand and clutching a holdall with the other. His trumpet is on his back, there's a rug slung over his shoulders and a pair of cardboard wings have been strapped to his coat. I marvel at him carrying everything across the country and wonder what his parents are like, sending him off laden down like that. Were they unwilling to drive him, lacking the generosity of my own sweet father?

"What are the wings for?" I ask with a grin.

"They could come in handy for a show or a party."

"And the rug?" asks Annie.

"To brighten up my room." Zachary waves his holdall. "I also brought my camping stove."

"Just the essentials, then?" I joke.

I take the wings and Annie and Ashley carry the rug between them as the four of us trot merrily down the hill. Ashley doesn't speak. It seems the Christmas break has only intensified her attraction to Zachary. She keeps giggling and nibbling her fingers. At least she's not homesick any more.

Dotty Jay meets us in the stairwell and asks if we want a microwave brownie. We go up to our corridor where some of our housemates are already tucking in.

Thunder Cat grabs a brownie for each hand. "Zachary brought a camping stove!" I announce. It feels important that everybody finds it as funny as I do.

Zachary laps up the attention. "So I can cook for myself," he says proudly. "I don't need to be a slave to whatever the refectory has on offer. I can eat what I like, when I like."

Shay raises an eyebrow. "So what's on the menu, Chef?"

"Soup. Macaroni cheese. Perhaps some beans."

We roar with laughter.

"You can cook them in the microwave!" Dotty Jay exclaims.

"I've just remembered!" I nudge Zachary. "You've already used up your meal card. You're going to starve this term!" I reach for another brownie and wonder how I can tease him further. We're being very loud and Holy Cat is aware that Elle is probably trying to sleep. But nobody else shows any sign of having a conscience and Thunder Cat is just so excited to be back that I cannot restrain myself from shouting.

And then, because we are students and free and foolish, we stay up chatting until 3am. I drop into bed with a belly full of brownie and a head buzzing with glee. Before turning off my lamp, I check my phone and notice I have a message on FriendWeb from my cousin Chantelle.

'Hey Cat! How was your Christmas? I'm guessing you've heard my news?'

I have to ignore the question about Christmas. It would be a cardinal sin to tell family secrets to family. As for responding to Chantelle's news, I can't say anything that might get back to my mother so congratulations wouldn't be appropriate. I think before responding, *'I heard! How are you feeling?'* I'm about to put my phone down when Chantelle's profile picture lights up to signify that she's come online. It would be rude to disappear so I pause and await her response.

'Sick as a dog. You're coming to the wedding, aren't you?'

'Hopefully.' I don't add that it depends on if I'm allowed.

'Uncle Richard might come with Avery and Jackson. Imagine all the cousins together for the first time!'

I'm surprised at the prospect of our relatives coming from abroad. When we were little, Chantelle and I often talked about Avery, our Canadian counterpart, speculating over what she was like and whether we would ever meet her. Being a couple of years older than us, we viewed her as incredibly cool. I still do. Even though she shocked everyone by becoming anorexic. That's not the sort of thing you expect your heroes to do.

'Really?' I type as quickly as I can, which isn't very fast at 3am. *'Avery's coming over??'*

'It's not confirmed yet. Mum was discussing it with Uncle Richard yesterday.'

I frown. Aunt Sonya discussing something doesn't mean a thing. Uncle Richard didn't even come over for our grandfather's funeral so why would they come for a wedding, especially one as scandalous as Chantelle's? There have been endless discussions over the years of family reunions and holidays to Canada but nothing ever comes to anything. Someone usually gets offended or the ideas run out of steam because nobody wants to organise anything.

We've never even been to Aunt Sonya's house as they live all the way up in Scotland. Before Uncle Martin left, they travelled down to us every summer. Chantelle would sleep on an airbed on my floor and Chris would share Aidan's bunk bed. Our nights would be filled with whispered secrets and our days would be packed with trips to the beach and the park and the ten pin bowling centre. At some point there would be a huge drama, usually between Aunt Sonya and Uncle Martin but occasionally between us kids. I never knew anybody fight as awfully as Chantelle and Chris. They went for each other like cat and dog and drew blood on more than one occasion. I remember Aunt Sonya going mental and offering them both a knife so they could finish each other off.

For that one week every summer, Chantelle was my bestest friend in the world. But then Uncle Martin left and Aunt Sonya was too nervous to make the journey by herself. My father couldn't stomach the drive to Scotland so they compromised a couple of times by hiring a cottage in North Wales. There was always conflict over who ought to pay for what, and the prospect of going on holiday left my dad in a state of panic for the entire month leading up to it, then my mum and Aunt Sonya had a major bust up at Conwy Castle and we haven't holidayed with them since.

The last time we were together was my grandfather's funeral when I was fourteen. The Dark Days had just begun and Chantelle was going through her own moody teenage phase so neither of us spoke to each other. My parents didn't want to stay very long so we left after a brief slice of cake at the wake. Aunt Tracey was particularly put out, having organised the whole event, and I remember a rather snide letter arriving which my mother burnt on the stove.

Perhaps if we all lived closer things would be different. Perhaps if my mum and Aunt Sonya and Aunt Tracey were better friends. Perhaps if Uncle Richard hadn't moved to

Canada. Perhaps if their childhood hadn't been so painful. I wonder if Chantelle ever feels as lonely and odd as I do?

'Do you want to come to the hen do? We're hitting the clubs and casinos in Edinburgh.'

Scaredy Cat recoils. *'When is it?'*

'First weekend in February.'

I check my calendar and breathe a sigh of relief. I have a rehearsal. I can say no without feeling guilty.

'I'm so sorry. I'll be needed at rehearsals all weekend. We're not allowed time off unless we have a doctor's note. It's so strict because if one person is away it lets down the entire cast.' I've hammed this up because I don't want Chantelle to think I'm being flaky like our mothers.

She doesn't reply right away and I'm petrified she might offer to reschedule. Thankfully she responds with, *'I'll see you at the wedding then! I can't wait for you to meet Haroon!'*

I stare at my phone. The last time Chantelle came to Exeter we pretended to be mermaids on Exmouth beach. She said boys were disgusting and that she never wanted to get married. Silly Cat was thrilled to have found someone who understood. And now she's up the duff and going clubbing and visiting casinos. I put my phone down, feeling strangely abandoned. *We were never meant to grow up.*

I have restless dreams. Dreams of being chased, dreams of searching for something out of my reach, dreams of almost falling and dreams of losing all my money in a casino.

When I see Jodie the next morning, scurrying through the rain with a textbook over her head, the ache in my chest explodes with full fury as I beg God or whoever is listening, *Please, please let her be my long lost sister.*

"Hi, Cat!" she calls as she dashes by. "Good Christmas?"

I can't imagine that she cares for the answer. She'll be soaked if she stops to listen. I give a shy nod and hurry on, as though I've got somewhere important to be. As though I wasn't just wandering around in the rain in the hopes that we might meet.

* 27 * Thunder Cat the snow wrestling champion

"Wake up, Cat!" Some lunatic is pounding on my door at the most unreasonable hour. "Look out of the window!"

I realise it is Zachary. I am about to tell him to go away when he yells a word that triggers everything childlike in me to spring to the surface: "SNOW!"

Silly Cat leaps out of bed like a child on Christmas morning. A happy child, I mean. Not me. I yank my curtains open and give a whoop of amazement. The entire campus is covered in a thick blanket of cotton white snow. The sun hasn't even risen yet and everything looks spooky and serene. We *never* get snow in Exeter. Certainly not as abundant or as magical as this!

Five minutes later, I'm outside Willow, donned in coat and hat and scarf and I'm hurrying to scramble together a snowball before Zachary can get his gloves on.

"Can you believe how deep—"

SMACK!

Zachary stops mid-sentence, his jaw hanging open as my hasty snowball hits him right between the eyes.

Silly Cat gives a triumphant giggle and reaches down to scoop up another snowball. He beats me to it and within seconds I've got a mouth full of snow. I scream and try to run, stumbling and staggering and flinging as much snow as I can in Zachary's direction while he pelts me and laughs.

Then Wes pokes his head out of his window and yells, "Guys! It's half six!"

"Look at the snow!" we exclaim, turning with dripping faces.

I'm expecting him to jump for joy out of his window but he just swears before slamming the window shut.

"Let's go a bit further from our block," Zachary suggests.

Silly Cat wants to go on squealing until everybody is awake, but I grudgingly agree. We crunch through the snow, making footprints that nobody has ever seen as we carve a path to the field. The tip of my finger stings but is soon numbed by the biting cold. We reach the giant weeping willow and wander in and out of its branches. Without warning, Zachary shakes the branch closest to my head and showers me with snow.

I scream as a frozen clump slithers down my neck. "Zachary! Stop it! No more snow fights unless we both agree, okay?" I put my hands on my hips. "I'm being serious."

"Alright." He gives a cheeky smile before grabbing a stick and drawing a giant ring in the ground around us. "First one out of the circle loses. Unless you're too scared. If you're too scared you can just walk out of the ring. I won't judge you."

Thunder Cat is affronted. "I'm not scared!"

He claps his hands together and snow flies off his gloves. "Come on, then!"

I look at his makeshift wrestling ring. "No, thanks. I'm far too dignified to roll around in the snow." I pretend to walk away before turning back at lightning speed and lunging at him. His eyes widen as I catch him off guard and shove the side of his legs with all my weight. He stumbles and falls and I give a roar of victory as I take the opportunity to stuff a handful of snow up his nose.

"I win!" Silly Cat yells, bouncing up and down on his tummy before getting up and performing a triumphant dance.

"You haven't won!" he exclaims, yanking me by the foot and causing me to faceplant beside him. "The winner is the last one to leave the ring."

Next thing I know, he's rolling me through the snow towards the edge of the circle. I give a yelp and aim a kick at his backside. I catch the side of his head instead.

"Ow!" He lets me go and clasps a hand to his head.

"Sorry not sorry!" I shout, scrambling to my feet and pushing him as roughly as I can.

"Cat, stop! Stop!" he pleads. "Seriously. Stop!"

But I keep pummelling into him, pounding him with my fists and elbows until I've edged him over the line. "Ha!" Thunder Cat is jubilant. "I've won! I beat you! I'm stronger than you! And better than you! Look, I got you over the line!"

"Aright, alright." Zachary sits panting on the ground. He rubs his head. He has a slight purple bump and blood is trickling down his glove.

"Oops," I say. "Sorry." I plop down beside him and try to look repentant. Then Thunder Cat adds with a grin, "At least you've got some ice on it."

He rolls his eyes. "Very funny."

I can't work out whether he is angry or not. I feel momentarily troubled as Holy Cat wonders what on earth is wrong with me, wrestling a boy to the ground and kicking him in the head. But then he elbows me in the ribs and says, "I'll win next time."

Silly Cat breathes a sigh of relief and giggles merrily.

"Hey, look!" Zachary points over the hill. "The sun is coming up. Isn't it incredible? I love sunrises!"

I follow his gaze. A bright flash of orange is peeking over the horizon. "I don't think I've ever seen one," I admit.

"Never seen a sunrise?" He is aghast.

"I mean I've never sat and watched one."

"Oh, Cat! You're missing out. Every single morning God paints a brand new masterpiece in the sky. It's like a glorious kiss from Heaven."

I snort. "If you say so."

"Look over there! That flash of purple. And there... Those red ripples of fire. It's stunning. And it's just for us. Nobody else will ever see it."

We sit and watch as the colours explode across the sky and a new day dawns over Forest Hall. Zachary is right. It *is* stunning. And mystical and majestic and far too powerful. It makes me want to cry. So Thunder Cat pretends to be bored. "How was your New Year's party?" I ask.

"Great! I was an angel. That's what I made my wings for. You should have come."

I flick some snow off my leg. I could say I was busy or that the fare would've cost too much. Instead, I confess, "I've never got a train by myself. I'd get completely lost. I can't even remember which stop to get off when I get the bus to Wakefield."

He thinks for a moment and I brace.

"It's easier than a bus because the conductor announces where you are before each stop. It might feel scary as it's a long journey but you'd actually be fine."

I summon up the courage to look at him. He doesn't appear to be laughing at me for being sheltered or stupid.

Zachary gets to his feet, still gazing at the sky. "That was amazing," he says, as though he's just witnessed the universe being born.

Thunder Cat wants to tease him for being so soft over a sunrise. But I shove her away. I can't tease him. He didn't tease me for being too scared to get a train.

Zachary offers me a hand and helps me up. Then we make our way back across the field, crunch crunch crunching through the blanket of white, neither of us speaking.

"Is your head okay?" I ask as we climb over the fence. "I really am sorry for kicking you."

"It's fine." He grins. "Let's get a hot chocolate."

Windy Wendy gives a loud tut as the two of us enter the refectory. "Look at the sorry state of you!"

"Sorry, Windy Wendy!" I sing.

"I beg your pardon?"

"I mean, Wendy," Scaredy Cat quivers.

She points at the cut on Zachary's head. "Had a fight with a polar bear, have you?"

Thunder Cat is back. "Actually it was a Cat," I say smugly. "And the Cat won."

"A cat?" Windy Wendy looks at Zachary in horror. "You had a fight with a cat?"

"It was a wild cat," says Zachary, giving me a mock glare. "Completely mad."

Hmmm, Wild Cat, muses Thunder Cat. *Nice name. Perhaps I should reinvent myself.*

"Well I never! You'd better report it to Bob, you had. A dangerous cat on the loose clawing students in the head!" Windy Wendy is salivating. "Hey, Barb! Have you seen his face? A cat attacked him!"

"He deserved it," I say, peeling off my soggy gloves. "He started it." I trot to the nearest radiator before Zachary can respond. My hat and scarf are soaked through. My face is so cold that it burns and I've lost all feeling in my hands. I shake off my coat and drape it over the radiator, pausing to warm up my hands and bottom. Then I brush my hair out of my eyes and survey the room. Several of our housemates are gathered at our usual table. Mad Jo is in her running gear although I'd be very surprised if she's managed to run in this weather. Annie and Dotty Jay are eating bagels for breakfast. Shay has a coffee. And Ashley is wrapped head to toe in a giant grey scarf.

"Go and sit down," Zachary offers, catching up with me after breaking free from Barb and Windy Wendy. "I'll grab us both a hot chocolate."

"Okay!" I'm halfway to our table when I remember he hasn't got any money left on his meal card. "Oh, Zachary!"

He turns. "Yes?"

"I'll pay." I whip my card out of my pocket and hurl it at him. He tries to catch it but fails. I giggle as it hits him in the chest before falling to the floor. He grins and picks it up.

"Well!" Shay gives me a funny smile as I approach our table. "You look like you've had fun." She glances across the refectory at Zachary. "So, what's the situation, Cat? You two getting it on?"

Ashley shoots me a startled glance.

"Don't be silly. We were just enjoying the snow." I shrug before adding, "I never get snow in Exeter."

Shay points at my dishevelled hair. "Enjoying it quite a lot, by the looks of it."

Silly Cat melts away. I comb my fingers through my hair and scowl. "I don't know what you mean by that." When she keeps staring, I add irritably, "I've told you before that I don't want a boyfriend."

Shay smirks. "I forgot. You don't believe in love. You're a complete anomaly."

I feel a surge of anger but, before I can respond, Zachary appears with our hot chocolates.

"Thanks, Cat!" he says as he tosses my meal card to me. "I hope you don't mind but I got a couple of bananas too. I thought you might be hungry."

Shay catches my eye and grins.

"Yeah, that's fine," I mutter, avoiding Zachary's gaze as I stuff my meal card into my pocket.

I am suddenly really angry. I'm angry with Shay for suggesting there's something going on with me and Zachary, as if two people can't enjoy a spot of wrestling without it descending into romance. I'm angry with Zachary for taking liberties and buying bananas with my meal card. I'm angry with Ashley in her stupid fat scarf, looking all pathetic just because she hasn't got the guts to tell Zachary she likes him. I'm angry with Dotty Jay because my finger is hurting again and it's reminding me how she judged me when my dad dropped me off. I'm angry with my dad even though I haven't spoken to him for days. And I'm angry with myself for feeling angry. Angry Cat is accompanied by Squashed Cat who suddenly feels very stressed that my knees are soaking and my hair needs brushing and my coat is on the other side of the room.

When nobody's listening, Mad Jo nudges me and whispers, "Ignore Shay. People always judge what they don't understand. You can be whatever you want to be, Caz."

I force a smile as her words dance over me.

You can be whatever you want to be.

It sounds very lovely. But it's not true. I can't be brave just because I want to be. I can't be a bird or a horse or a star. I can't be happy or whole or free.

* 28 * Lost Cat in the classroom

It's the first day of our second term and the start of a new module: Theatre of Fact. Sounds boring. I much prefer fantasy to fact. That's why I'm training to be an actress, after all, and not a doctor which is what my mother hoped I would be. Several of my classmates want to work with me. There's Cooking Clemmie and Foxtrotting Faye and Horse-riding Heidi and Owl-watching Otis all clamouring for my attention.

The thing is, Fun Cat isn't here today. I don't know why but I woke up as Lost Cat and I can't shake her off, no matter how hard I try. It doesn't make any sense. I was fine when I went to bed. I just woke up this way.

"Can I work with you, Cat? We've not worked together yet." Clemmie shoots me an eager grin.

"You always create something beautiful," gushes Heidi.

Thunder Cat would love this. But not me. I'm rubbish. I can't make theatre. I can't make friends. I can barely think straight. All I want is to be left alone. I am saved by Jodie announcing that she'll be choosing our groups this time. There's a hush as she divides us up.

"Donna, Viktor, Pip and Will. Go over there..." Jodie glances round the room before pointing a finger at me. "Cat..." She gives a wry smile at the sight of Clemmie and Heidi and the others standing very close to me and says, "Alright... Cat, you go with Clemmie, Heidi and Pranjal..."

Faye and Otis slink away as Clemmie and Heidi whoop and Pranjal blushes. I follow my group to a corner and try to return their smiles, Play it Cool Cat working double time.

Jodie explains our assignment. "You have three weeks to devise a short performance on a social issue of your choice. Let's hear some examples of social issues?"

"Animal rights!" yells Donna.

"Women's rights!" adds Kimberley.

"LGBT rights!" shouts Pip.

"Indigenous rights," suggests Arthur.

"Prisoners' rights," says Blake.

"Students' rights!" Viktor laughs.

Why did I sign up for the Acting course? I should have done Creative Writing with Ashley.

"You need to decide on a topic by the end of this lesson," Jodie says loudly. "And remember: this is Theatre of Fact. So your piece needs to educate as well as entertain. Make sure you pick something you care about."

I try to force Fun Cat into the room. "Heavy stuff, hey? So... What should we do our piece on?"

Clemmie, Heidi and Pranjal just stare at me, as if they expect me to already have something up my sleeve.

"Animal rights?" Heidi suggests finally.

"What about modern slavery?" Clemmie says. "That's a huge issue that people never think about."

"Globalisation and trade?" says Pranjal. "Or government spending? Or maybe high interest lending?"

Fun Cat disappears and I'm Lost Cat again, watching mutely as my group bounce ideas back and forth. Then Elle arrives late, having had an appointment, and Jodie carelessly thrusts her into my group without realising that Elle won't appreciate the opportunity to work with me. She scowls as she joins us in our corner. I can't decide whether I am thoroughly miffed or whether it will be a good opportunity to get to know her better. If I could summon up Fun Cat, I'd say something friendly. Perhaps ask if her appointment went okay. But I still can't think. Can't speak.

Pranjal's on a roll. "Seriously, I think we should consider doing it on corporate accountability. It's a subject with heaps of scope and it touches upon so many other issues."

Elle screws up her nose. "What's going on?"

"We need to choose a social issue for our piece." Clemmie fills her in. "Pranjal wants something political."

"I'm just saying it's important." Pranjal folds his arms. "I almost did Economics so I know what I'm talking about."

Heidi's making notes. "What did you call it? Corporate...?"

"Accountability. It's all about how companies avoid harm to the environment or to people."

I finally find my voice. "Wouldn't it be better to pick an issue that we're passionate about? Rather than something we don't understand?"

"I understand it," Pranjal says petulantly.

"The rest of us don't. And it's not exactly very emotive."

"Cat's right," says Elle.

Deep inside, Thunder Cat pulls a party popper.

"What do you suggest, then?" Pranjal looks at me.

I wrack my brains. What am I passionate about? Getting up early and reading library books? Listening to eighties pop? Snowball fights with weird boys in my block? Dotty Jay's seven types of people? Talking to Jodie in My Head? *Don't think about that!* I try calling on Creative Cat but I can't find her. Sometimes I think she doesn't exist.

"What about racism?" Clemmie says. "Some of us will have experienced that."

"All the time," agrees Pranjal.

"People always think I'm Chinese," Clemmie adds. "Even though I've lived in England my whole life and just happen to have a Vietnamese father."

"That's not necessarily racism," says Elle.

"But it doesn't feel nice," Clemmie counters. "It makes me feel like I don't belong in my own country."

"I know what you mean," I say. "People always ask where I'm from." We share a laugh. A laugh that only someone who is fully British but isn't fully white could understand.

"Agreed. Let's do it on racism!" Pranjal says triumphantly.

"But I've never experienced racism," says Elle.

"Me neither," says Heidi.

"You could be the racist ones," Clemmie suggests.

They don't look very happy about that.

"There must be a topic we *all* care about," Elle insists. "What about terrorism?"

Pranjal wrinkles his nose. "As long as you don't make me play the terrorist."

Elle blushes.

"That's racism," says Clemmie, wagging a finger at Elle.

Elle sighs. "Alright. How about climate change?"

"Pip's group is doing that." Pranjal points across the room.

Heidi is looking at me. "No offence for asking, Cat," she whispers. "But where *are* you from?"

Before I can reply, Elle says loudly, "What about mental health? That affects *everyone* at some point."

There's a pause, then Clemmie says, "Yeah, alright."

Heidi nods and I hear myself saying, "Great idea!"

"Let's each have a different disorder," Pranjal suggests. "We could be five friends all hiding a secret illness."

"Okay," says Elle. "I'll have anxiety."

"Shotgun depression!" says Heidi.

"I could have OCD," Clemmie offers. "Because I think I have got that a little bit. What about you, Cat?"

"Er... " Even though Fun Cat just agreed mental health was a worthy cause, Lost Cat is threatening to return. I should argue that corporate accountability is a good idea after all.

"You could have an eating disorder?" Heidi suggests.

I guess I could draw inspiration from my cousin Avery's struggles but the prospect doesn't exactly fill me with delight.

"What about me?" asks Pranjal.

"I know!" exclaims Clemmie. "Multiple personalities!"

"Ooh!" Elle squeals. "One of Pranjal's personalities could kill us all!"

Squashed Cat comes screaming into my ears. *Don't let them know. Don't let them guess. Don't let anybody come too close.*

Don't be ridiculous, mutters Angry Cat. *I don't have multiple personalities.*

"I don't want multiple personalities!" Pranjal sneers.

"How about a phobia?" says Elle.

"I'll have a phobia," I say quickly. "You have the eating disorder, Pranjal."

"Great," says Clemmie. "That's sorted. What phobia will you have, Cat?"

A million thoughts explode through my brain. *Being alone. Bad news. Strangers. The dark. Crowded places. Being buried alive. Fires. Dentists. Big dogs. Drowning. Choking. The Dream. Going crazy. Being abandoned. Being attacked. Knives. Blood. Love. Myself.*

But I just force a shrug and mutter, "I don't know. Spiders, I suppose."

* 29 * Holy Cat loves her mama

I look stranger than I thought. I'm watching the Mama Octopus music video for the first time and I'm amazed at how big my eyes are. We're gathered in Rory's room for the premiere. He's got the biggest TV. Dotty Jay has made jelly and several of my housemates have come along (not Elle, of course). Thunder Cat is particularly keen to impress Shay. I also want Mike to know I'm an excellent actress because he's always making jokes about cats getting stage fright.

Every part of me is in attendance for the screening. Thunder Cat is very excited and is leading the show, bouncing up and down with glee. Fun Cat is also at the surface, feeling proud and soaking up the praise. Out of sight from my housemates, the rest of me is watching. Copy Cat is acutely aware of the reactions around me: Mad Jo nodding along to the beat, Shay scratching her cheek, Annie blushing at Kite-flying Kimberley's glitter bikini (I'm *so* glad I didn't get that role), Ashley gasping as the chorus kicks in, Tanisha looking a little envious, Zachary guzzling jelly at my feet. Holy Cat is worried that Annie will find the song offensive. Creative Cat marvels at the video's special effects. RoboCat is calmly reciting the lyrics. Baby Cat is crying. Squashed Cat is embarrassed. Angry Cat is strangely numb. The video comes to an end and everyone turns to congratulate me.

"Well done, Caz!"

"I can't believe you were in an actual Mama Octopus video. I'm so jealous!"

I stuff all the unwanted parts of me away and give a merry sigh. There were several close-ups of me walking along the mansion roof and the camera panned in such a way to make it look more dangerous than it really was. I am particularly proud of the real tears that gathered in my eyes for the final verse. Not exactly Little Betty but I'm on my way!

"You were wonderful, Cat," Annie says kindly. I'm relieved she doesn't mention Kimberley's bikini.

"I can't believe how close you got to the edge of the mansion!" Ashley whispers.

I don't tell her it was an illusion.

Zachary pats my foot. "Good job, Cat."

"Yeah, it was great. Well done!" I'm elated to have Shay's approval. I want to ask her which bits she liked but, before I can say anything, she slides off Rory's bed and heads for the door. "Gotta dash. I'm off to the bar."

I don't know whether I'm flattered that she squeezed me into her busy schedule or disappointed that she's not staying for jelly. Sad Cat is triggered, feeling rejected and confused.

"I didn't realise you were so talented," Rory remarks. "You're a dark horse."

"You mean a dark cat," Mike jokes.

Sad Cat disappears and Thunder Cat is back on top, aiming a spoon for the top of Mike's head.

"Odd name for a band," Zachary pipes up. "Mama Octopus. I wonder why they called themselves that."

"Yeah, it's weird," I agree. "I would've expected more of an edgy name for a punk band."

Wise sage, Dotty Jay, gives a hum. "It's a comment on how mother octopuses die as soon as they give birth. Once an octopus lays her eggs, she stops eating and stays by the eggs until they hatch, protecting them and giving them oxygen and slowly starving to death."

"What?" I gape at her.

"No way!" Tanisha exclaims.

"It's true." Dotty Jay licks jelly off her wrist. "If she leaves her eggs, they'll die. So she gives all her strength to their survival. Her final act is to blow the newly hatched octopus babies out of the nest." She demonstrates this by blowing a mouthful of jelly across Rory's bed. "Then, as they swim away, she dies of starvation and exhaustion."

There's stunned silence as we take this in.

"Wow. That's beautiful," says Ashley. Her beady eyes are twinkling. It's her thinking face. In a week or two she'll produce a Creative Writing assignment inspired by the mama octopus.

"So tragic," murmurs Annie.

The atmosphere is too solemn. "It's quite freaky," Thunder Cat says. "And not exactly nice for the octopuses to have to grow up without their mother."

"It's the perfect picture of sacrificial love," Dotty Jay insists. "Giving everything so that someone else can live."

"That's what mothers do," says Mad Jo. "My mum was a single mum for years and she's absolutely incredible. The stuff I put her through!"

"And mine!" agrees Tanisha. "I was a right pain. You don't realise till you leave home just how much they do for you."

Annie is looking forlorn. Ashley's eyes have filled with tears. Mike is staring at us like we're all a bit soft. Zachary is gobbling jelly and Rory is fiddling with his television.

"You boys don't get it," Mad Jo scolds them. "It's a woman thing."

"The bond between a mother and a daughter," Tanisha adds. "There's nothing like it."

Angry Cat is reeling. *Since when did this evening become a meeting for The Mothers' Appreciation Society? Can we please get back to my video?*

But then Annie says, "My mum is the kindest person I know," and Holy Cat somersaults into my chest.

My mum is kind too. She's so generous, always sending me things and asking if I need any money. She took me and Aidan everywhere when we were younger: to clubs and parks and to the library. She wanted to give us all the things her parents had denied her as a child. She took us swimming every week, even though she couldn't swim herself. She let me get my ears pierced for my sixth birthday (even though my dad wasn't keen) and she said I could choose any of the earrings that I wanted. She painted my bedroom walls purple because it was my favourite colour. She worked tirelessly on endless costumes for World Book Day, always rising to the challenge even when I left it till the very last minute to decide who I wanted to be. Once, she walked the entire length of Exmouth beach looking for my lost teddy even though her heart was bad and she kept getting out of breath.

When I got into Forest Hall she gave a big beam and said, "Well done, Baby! I knew you'd get in. I can't wait till you're a famous actress." On the day that I left for university, she gave me a book full of quotes from mothers to daughters and she'd highlighted all the ones that were particularly pertinent to her. Things like, *'There is no love like a mother's love,'* and,

'My daughter is my best friend.' Things I'm sure she wanted to say in person if only she could find the words.

She tries so hard and gives so much. It can't be easy being a mother. Especially *my* mother. I never do things right. I don't smile enough. I'm too sensitive. I'm ugly when I cry. I'm selfish. I keep things to myself. I am very hard to love.

I realise with a pang of shame that I haven't phoned my mum this term. I should ring her; tell her about the Mama Octopus video and how it's reminded me about how self-sacrificing she is. Once the jelly is eaten, I go to my room and call her. She is thrilled to hear from me.

"Hello, Baby! It's so nice of you to call me. I was just thinking about you."

I want to cry.

"Thanks. I just wanted to say I love you."

"I love you too, Baby! You know that. I always love you."

I hang up and cling to Monkey Bear. Thunder Cat swapped his head for a monkey in sixth form but the original teddy was a childhood present from my parents. The very same teddy that almost got swept away by the sea but was rescued in the nick of time by my selfless mama.

* 30 * Fun Cat is completely fine

Good news! My mum has decided we will go to Chantelle's wedding. My family will pick me up on the last day of term on the way up to Glasgow. I am thrilled. Especially because it transpires that the rumours about Uncle Richard coming with our Canadian cousins are true! I will finally meet my hero, Avery. Annie has offered to come with me to Wakefield to buy an outfit and Shay has promised to do my nails. It's not for another two months but I can't wait.

This weekend is Chantelle's hen do. From the pictures plastered across FriendWeb, I am very glad I couldn't go. I send Chantelle a cheery message along with a selfie from my rehearsal to give credibility to my absence.

I'm in the mansion with Elle, Clemmie, Pranjal and Heidi. We managed to secure Primrose, the most coveted rehearsal space, but we've wasted the first hour by being on our phones and generally ignoring each other.

The Theatre of Fact showcase is next week. I wish we'd never chosen mental health. Our representations are clichéd, shallow and impersonal. Elle's depiction of anxiety is of a girl who can't even stand up straight without shaking and bursting into tears. Heidi's version of depression is a character who cries non-stop, wears a black hoodie and is constantly trying to take her own life. Clemmie's idea of OCD is somebody who won't stop washing her hands. I couldn't persuade Pranjal to have an eating disorder so he's depicting a lunatic with multiple personalities who switches identity with great drama every other sentence. And my presentation of phobias is of someone who is so afraid of spiders that they collapse even if somebody utters the word.

It's all one big farce. There is nothing truthful or realistic about any of it. But I can't suggest we be a little more honest because, quite frankly, I don't want to be honest. I don't want to admit I am struggling. I don't want to tell Elle that the worse thing about anxiety is not the pain of falling apart but the agony of keeping everything together. I don't want to tell Heidi that it's possible to be drowning in despair while laughing the loudest at a party. I don't want to explain to Clemmie that sometimes OCD looks like having the same conversation over and over with imaginary People in My Head. I don't want to prove to Pranjal that it's possible to switch between parts without anybody noticing. I don't want to tell them that one of the biggest challenges of mental illness is hiding it from everybody else.

But surely they already know that? Surely they're all doing it too? Surely Clemmie isn't as jolly as she always appears to be? Surely Pranjal and Heidi have had their fair share of struggles? Elle had another appointment this morning. She was late to a rehearsal last week too. I'd assumed she'd had a dentist appointment the first time. But nobody goes to the dentist twice a week. Surely she's got issues behind her mask?

We finally start rehearsing and, as we run through the opening scene, I find myself freezing.

"It's you, Cat. It's the bit where you scream because Pranjal's character has a tattoo of a spider," Heidi prompts.

"I know... I just... Do you think we're being realistic enough? Some of our characters are a bit over the top, you know? It's not very relatable."

"That's theatre," Elle insists. "We're doing it over the top on purpose. To make a point."

Try being real, Holy Cat suggests.

But Fun Cat is repulsed at the idea of being real. After all, I'm completely fine. I know so many people struggle with their mental health but I want to pretend that I don't.

A voice whispers, *"Why?"*

Because nobody cares about me and my high school friends rejected me when I told them things and it's all my fault anyway and other people have more serious things going on and I don't want to be an attention seeker and nobody would even understand because I'm more broken than they are and I can't explain all the—

Heck. Stop thinking too deeply, Sad Cat.

If I'm not careful, I will cry.

I meant be real for the sake of others, Holy Cat chastises. *Not for your own sake. They could all be depressed and you've not even asked. Elle looked a bit glum when she came in this morning. What if her appointment was with a therapist? Or a bereavement counsellor? Or an abortionist? What if she has nobody to talk to? What if—*

Just get on with it, Angry Cat sneers. *It's only a stupid play. Nobody even cares. Just scream at the flipping spider.*

"Are you alright, Cat?" asks Clemmie.

Fun Cat gives a cheery smile. "I'm fine."

I switch into RoboCat and convince myself that this module doesn't matter.

We work on the ending. Pranjal's character has killed me and Elle. Heidi's character has killed herself. And Clemmie is frantically mopping up the blood.

"One in four of us will struggle with their mental health this year," Heidi says as she scrapes herself off the floor.

"Someone you know might need more help than you realise," RoboCat drones as I scramble to my feet. I sneak a noble glance at Elle and wonder what's going on behind her eyes.

We finish with several more miserable facts on mental health and a quote from Krispin Staniscofskin.

'Love for oneself is the rarest love of all. And the mask we are most fooled by is the one in the mirror.'

* 31 * Sad Cat and her suitcase

I lie awake for hours talking to Jodie in My Head. We talk about everything and nothing. The Theatre of Fact pieces and the fact that ours is not very truthful. The choice of yoghurts at the refectory and how lemon mousse is my favourite. My opinions on laundry room politics. The futile petition for en suites. Fairy Land. My parents.

The dinging of the clock shakes me out of a monologue at 3am. I had been telling Jodie in My Head about the debacle over Christmas. Suddenly I am slapped out of my stupid stupor with the realisation that I am only talking to myself.

Wasting time.

Alone.

Talking to myself.

Idiot.

A sob bubbles out of the depths of my soul and chokes me as it gurgles out of my throat. I shuffle under my duvet and pound the sides of my head. Then, before Sad Cat collapses completely, I shut my eyes and turn back to Jodie in My Head. "She was in bed until about two in the afternoon," I whisper, picking up where I left off.

Jodie in My Head listens with compassion. *"That sounds horrible, Cat. I'm so sorry. Has it always been like that?"*

"Yes..." And suddenly I am recounting a plethora of memories of my mother leaving or almost leaving. The look in her eyes when she tells me she doesn't love me any more. The letters she sends detailing why she left and why she'll never return. The time she threw an ornament and a shard of glass cut my leg. The time she—

And then I stop. And realise. Again. I am talking to myself. I let out another sob. The only people who have ever understood me are the pretend people that I talk to in my head. No neighbours or teachers or family friends ever noticed when I was hurting. One of the neighbours once peered over the fence and asked if everything was alright. I dutifully replied that it was and she never asked again. Keith once tried to make me laugh when he witnessed my mum throwing a mug at the wall but I didn't find it funny.

Sad Cat is wallowing in self-pity, giant sobs rocking my body, constricting my throat and squeezing the life out of my lungs. *Nobody loves me. Nobody notices me. I am invisible.*

Someone saw me once. At Disney World. I remember standing in awe of one of the princesses. She was beautiful in her dazzling blue dress and tiara. Her blonde hair was so shiny. I wished my hair was blonde and shiny. I couldn't stop staring at her. My mother snapped a photo and told me to hurry on but the princess just smiled and asked if I wanted a hug. It was like being hugged by love itself. A hug from a real princess! We saw her again in the parade and, as she floated past, she caught my eye and waved. "I remember you!" she mouthed.

I remember you.

I see you.

I know you.

I love you.

No, of course she didn't love me. But for a month my thoughts were consumed with Cinderella in My Head.

I wrap my pillow over my face and try to stop speaking. Stop thinking. Stop feeling. I need to go to sleep. *Jodie in My Head is not real. The real Jodie does not care.*

Sleep never comes easily for me. I'm often awake for hours as the parts of me who have been silent all day force themselves upon me, vying for attention. Tonight, Sad Cat weeps the tears that were suppressed when Annie's doting mother came to visit last weekend. Baby Cat screams a silent fit of rage over goodness knows what. Holy Cat recounts the day, replaying all the foolish things I did or said and rehearsing the things I should have done instead. And Silly Cat daydreams about Jodie. Over and over and over. Fantasising about ridiculous scenarios like finding out we're related. She's invited me to live with her thirteen times so far. Silly Cat gets so involved that I actually shed a little tear when Jodie in My Head tells me that she loves me.

You're so stupid, Angry Cat snarls. Angry Cat doesn't need anybody. Hates the very idea of ever needing anybody.

A memory stirs. I am ten years old. It's my first time away from home. A school trip to the Isle of Wight. We've had four days of playgrounds and farms and mazes. I'm rather fond of a floppy hat I purchased at the farm. It has a rainbow-coloured lamb on it. It's our last day and I'm struggling to pack my suitcase. Everything fit when I arrived but, for some reason, it won't fit now. The coach is leaving any minute and everybody is waiting for me. Perhaps they'll leave without me.

Mrs Granville stands in the corner of the dormitory and snaps, "What on earth is the matter, Catrina?"

"My stuff won't fit," I splutter, tears blurring my eyes. "And nobody's helping me."

"Why should anyone help you?"

"Because I can't... I don't know how to..."

"For goodness sake, pull yourself together." She grabs my towel and stuffs it into my case. "What on earth is this?" she mocks, indicating the hat.

My mum will say the same thing later. *"What a waste of money, Catrina!"*

I hoist my suitcase off the bed, shame cascading over me and pooling in my shoes. It's so heavy. But I mustn't complain. Mrs Granville's words echo in my ears, *"Why should anyone help you?"*

I was planning on wearing the hat on the coach home. But now I feel stupid. Ugly. I shove it into my backpack and drag my suitcase all the way to the coach. It's my own fault it's too heavy. My fault for having so much junk.

I never wore the hat. And even though I am all grown up— sort of— the memory of Mrs Granville still fills me with shame. Her words fill my darkened university room, screaming the accusation that has followed me through the years. *"Why should anyone help you?"*

Why should I be so vain, so pathetic, so foolish as to lie awake longing for someone to talk to? I don't need help. I can carry my own stuff. Because that's my job and why should anybody help me? I let out a moan and bury my head deeper into my pillow. *I don't need anybody. I don't need Jodie. I don't need anybody. Nobody cares anyway.*

Before I can stop myself, I'm talking to Jodie in My Head again. *"I'm so sorry, Cat. So sorry you've had to go through all that alone."*

I put on a brave smile whilst simultaneously milking the tears. "It's okay. I'm okay."

"If there's anything I can do to help..."

"I don't know. I just want someone to talk to sometimes. I need... I need help carrying my suitcase." Tears gush out of my eyes and soak my pillow. I hug it tightly. I pretend it's Jodie.

"Oh, Cat. Of course. You can talk to me any time. In fact, I want us to schedule a time to talk once a week. Is that okay? Come and see me every Monday. 7pm okay? We can go for dessert at the Grumpy Pig."

"Thanks. I know it's silly but I've always... I've always wanted a big sister."

"I've always wanted a little sister. I'm so proud of you, Cat. You've been through so much. It's amazing you're so normal—"

I feel sick.

Oh. God. Not normal at all. Go to sleep. Stop talking to yourself.

The next day, we perform our piece. Afterwards, Owl-watching Otis taps me on the shoulder. I'm petrified that he's about to ask about my mental health. But, no. He just wants to tell me I did a good job.

A good job. A good job at lying to the world with a performance that screams, *I am fine! I can carry everything all by myself! I don't need anybody!*

Jodie grins at me. I desperately wish she would hug me.

I smile politely. Sad Cat stuffs my pain into a suitcase.

* 32 * Play it Cool Cat the astronaut

An opportunity for Zachary to don his angel wings arises in the form of a Valentine's fancy dress disco at the Merry Bar.

I was going to wear my butterfly hoodie but, at the last minute, Thunder Cat had a burst of inspiration and enlisted the help of Shay to create a unique costume. I've got black cat ears, a tail and a shiny red cape over a black leotard.

My housemates are gathering in the stairwell and I'm all set to party when my phone rings. My stomach lurches at the sight of the word *'Home'* jiggling across the screen. That one little word sends me into a panic, like a dog trained to dribble when it hears a bell. It's not a Monday night. It's not 7pm. It's not a scheduled call. I swallow a few times before pressing the answer button.

"Cat, oh Cat! I don't know what to do..."

An icy coolness rushes down my spine and a veil comes up and cuts me off from the rest of the world, like an astronaut's helmet in outer space.

"She's packing her bags. She's got the cases down from the attic. Can you try phoning her mobile? Please, Cat?"

I sprint to my room, picturing the scene. I know it well. A throng of mismatching suitcases thrown open on the bed. My mother raiding the wardrobes and tossing everything in. Her best dresses crushed and creased, still on their hangers. Toiletries carelessly flung in. Diaries and dusty old trinkets tangled in her underwear. Handbags and high heels. Bank cards. Make-up. Her passport. I learnt as a child that if she left without her jewellery, then she would soon return under the guise of needing to collect it. And, once she was through the door, I could use my magic powers to get her to stay.

RoboCat asks calmly, "Has she packed her rings?"

"Yes, yes," my father weeps. "Everything."

Panic floods my chest. I stuff Squashed Cat away and force myself to stay calm. I know not to ask what happened. I know all that is required is that I fix it.

"It will be alright. Have you tried—"

"Hold on." My dad cuts me off before muttering, "She's coming down... I'll call you back."

A single tear dribbles down my face as he hangs up.

"Cat! Are you coming?" Annie pounds on my door.

I wipe my face and fix my smile. Annie's dressed as a hedgehog. She beams her usual carefree beam as I answer my door. "Let's go... Are you okay?"

I tighten my helmet. I'm flung further into space, no signal at all with the earth. "Yeah, I'm fine," Play it Cool Cat says coolly. "I'll catch you up. I'm not completely ready yet." I fiddle with my tail, as though it's not quite right.

"Want me to wait with you?"

"No, it's alright. I'll see you there."

I close the door on one of the nicest people I have ever known. I don't let her in because people can't be trusted and it's safer to accept certain solitude than to risk possible betrayal. I lock my door and sit on my bed and, as soon as I hear that the stairwell is silent, I take my helmet off and cry. The tears come like boulders, too big for my eyes. I am utterly overwhelmed by the loneliness of outer space, even though I have chosen to drift alone. My heart aches, longing to be held. I want to be seen, understood and known. I want help carrying my junk. And yet I want to keep people as far away from me as I can.

Aidan's dismissal at Christmas rings through my ears. *"It's always okay, isn't it? No point getting upset about it."*

I feel like a fool, caring so much over nothing.

My phone rings. I answer with a gulp. "Hello?"

"False alarm," my dad whispers. There's a slight lilt in his voice as though we are two adults confiding over a moody teenager. "She seems to have calmed down, thank goodness! She's ordering a takeaway."

Relief mingles with fury. "Okay."

"You doing anything fun tonight?"

"Just a party," I grunt.

"Oh right. Where's that, then?"

"Bar."

"Sorry?"

"The student bar." I don't feel like chatting right now. Angry Cat is close to flinging my phone across the room.

"Have a nice time! I'll call you as usual on Monday."

"Okay."

I curl up with Monkey Bear and cry and cry. It's as though there's a never ending abyss inside me. I'm scared I'll never climb out. Sorrow is drenched in shame. *What's wrong with me? Nothing even happened.*

My mother's voice sings in my ears as I trudge to the bar. *"You're too sensitive, Catrina. Don't make yourself cry. Smile. Don't slouch. Talk more. Be confident. Don't be silly."*

I pass some boys from Laurel. "Hey!" they shout. "Are you Catwoman or Supergirl?"

I attempt a smile. "I'm Super Cat."

They snigger. *I'm so stupid.*

Thunder Cat has lost her way and I arrive at the bar with Lost Cat and Squashed Cat far too close to the surface.

"Hey, Cat!" Annie waves as I head towards her. "I got you a blackcurrant soda."

"Thanks." I rummage around in my purse.

"Don't pay me!"

"Alright. Thanks."

I insert Play it Cool Cat into the driving seat before glancing around the room, taking in the array of wild and wonderful costumes. I pick out my housemates. Dotty Jay is shuffling around in a giant mermaid costume and Rory is accompanying her as an orange fish. Mad Jo has morphed into the freakiest clown I've ever seen and Wes has come as a toad. Elle has either forgotten to dress up or has come as a Barbie doll. Shay's costume is the most extravagant of all and every eye turns as she makes her entrance. She's come as a phoenix, her handmade costume ablaze with sequins and ribbons and dazzling frills. Wes the toad makes a beeline for her and, pretty soon, they're getting cosy on the dance floor.

Zachary is breakdancing in the middle of a circle, his cardboard angel wings bending as he spins across the floor. Ashley is dressed as a rag doll. She's watching Zachary intently, her blushes magnified by her painted red cheeks.

I wonder if my mother's takeaway has arrived. Wonder what she's having. Probably Captain Barry's boneless bucket. Her favourite. We had it for her birthday last year. She got angry about something and threw a plate. Aidan put his hands up to protect himself and she went hysterical because she thought he was about to hit her. She was gone for five days. She refused to return until Aidan said sorry. Aidan didn't think he had anything to be sorry for so I said it for him, over and over. *"I'm sorry, I'm sorry. Please forgive us. We love you. I'm sorry, I'm sorry."*

I quickly wipe my eyes.

Annie keeps staring at me. "Are you sure you're okay?"

"Of course. I'm fine." I take a large gulp of blackcurrant soda and wonder whether to go and dance.

She's summoning up the courage to say something. Finally, she asks, "Do you want me to pray for you?"

"Pray? What for?"

"I don't know. Anything. Zachary said—"

I turn so fast that I spill my drink. "Zachary said what?"

She blushes. "Just that we should pray for you."

"What for?" My mind is whirling. Blood fills my ears. Angry Cat loads her gun. My eyes dart to Zachary, showing off on the dance floor. *How dare he?*

The song comes to an end and Zachary leaps to his feet. He wipes the sweat from his forehead before stretching his legs and sauntering over. "Hi, Cat!"

I ignore him.

"Cat?"

I'm scared Angry Cat will explode in front of everybody. I storm out of the bar. Squashed Cat wants to be left alone but Thunder Cat is hoping he'll follow me, which he does.

"Cat? What's wrong? Hey, wait for me!"

Tears are burning my eyes but I force them away. This is not the time to be weak. I wait till we are halfway up the hill and out of earshot before turning to confront that backstabbing betrayer, Zachary Fenn. "I trusted you!"

He blinks at me, all angel eyes and innocent. "What?"

"The things I told you about my family... I thought I could trust you. How dare you tell Annie!"

"Woah, what are you talking about? I haven't told anybody anything, I promise!"

"Then why does Annie think she needs to pray for me?"

"We always pray for people. That's what Christians do." He gives a lopsided grin.

I feel an even fiercer surge of fury. "What for? Why do you have to interfere in people's lives?"

He adjusts his wings. I want to rip them off his back. Angry Cat couldn't care less who sees us. I call him all manner of names. I insult his clothes. His silly dancing. His trumpet playing. RoboCat is vaguely aware of how amusing we must look; an angel being challenged by a black cat.

"I'm sorry I've upset you, Cat. I didn't mean to—"

"You were talking about me!"

"Not in a bad way."

"What other way is there?"

"In nice ways! You're our friend. We were worried about you. It's clear you have a lot of issues going on."

"I don't have issues!" I scream.

Zachary puts his hands up. "Okay! You don't have issues. You're completely balanced..." I notice a smirk at the corner of his mouth.

"Are you laughing at me?"

"No!"

Silly Cat bursts into tears. "You are! You're being mean."

I turn to run away but Zachary grabs my arm. "I'm your friend, Cat. We were only talking about you because we care. You sometimes seem sad and we wish we could help."

I look at this boy, the only person in the world who knows my secrets. (Except for Leah and Jessa and Bex and Paige but they don't exist any more.) "I'm not sad! I'm fine."

"Let people in, Cat. Lots of people care about you. And lots more would want to, if you'd let them."

For one horrifying moment, Play it Cool Cat lifts up the visor and dares to look him in the eye. Bad choice. The boy has magic powers as powerful as mine. I crack and burst into tears all over again.

"Cat..." He holds his hand out.

I quickly adjust my cape. "I'm fine, Zachary. I'm sorry."

"It's alright. It's not your fault."

Oh but it is. It always is.

"I like your costume, by the way."

"I'm Super Cat," I say limply, feeling like the world's greatest idiot as I wait for him to make a joke.

But he just flaps his angel wings and says, "Amazing."

* 33 * Silly Cat is a bad loser

Zachary arrives at my door with a pile of board games.

I barely slept all night. I tossed and turned, unable to stop crying, feeling lonely and hopeless. And then I was bombarded by The Dream. It was more chaotic than ever, with a taunting voice asking on a loop, *"Where are your powers, Cat?"* I woke up ashamed and confused, as though there was something I ought to know. I can't decide whether I am pleased or peeved to find Zachary outside my door so early on a Saturday morning.

He rattles his boxes. "Want to play a game?"

Play it Cool Cat is about to fob him off. I'd planned to work on an essay, go over some lines for the Shakespeare Society, and finish reading a play. But, instead, Fun Cat stirs and says, "Alright! Hold on." I close the door and get dressed at lightning speed before reopening the door.

He trots into my room. "I've got a selection," he says, spreading his games out on the floor. "I wasn't sure what you'd prefer. There's chess if you fancy something brainy..."

I screw up my nose.

"...Some of the finest Eurogames if you're into strategy and player interaction... This one's fun."

I read the title on the box. *'Love Birds.'* "I don't believe in love," I remind him.

"You don't have to. It's nothing to do with love. It's a tile placement game with card drafting and resource gathering. On your turn you choose to sprinkle some seeds, play a bird, or approach a bush. Once you've played a matching pair of birds you can add a perch. And if you find the golden binoculars everything is doubled for that round but you can only use it once—"

I zone out. "Sounds confusing. And boring."

"It's not! It's really good once you understand it. It just takes some getting used to because there are so many cards. But it's one of my favourites and the artwork is amazing. Look..." He opens the box and thrusts a handful of cards at me.

I snort. "You're so weird, Zachary."

"I've also got some traditional dice games if you'd prefer to stick with luck."

Play it Cool Cat wants to snub his games but, before I can help it, Silly Cat arrives and pounces on an old favourite. "This one! Can I be the dog? I always wanted to be the dog but my brother never let me so I had to be the boot. Then the dog got lost and my parents thought I'd hidden it but I hadn't and Aidan refused to play, even though it turned out the dog was in his room all along. He'd hidden it and forgotten!"

Zachary looks bemused at my sudden outburst. "Of course you can be the dog," he says as he opens the tatty box of Monopoly. "I'm always the top hat!"

We set the board up and, as we roll the dice to see who should start, a sudden deluge of memories wash over me. I feel pangs of exhilaration, sorrow and nostalgia all at once. My own box of Monopoly has been gathering dust under my bed in Exeter for years. I can't remember when Aidan and I last played it. Actually, yes I can. The summer before Aidan started high school. Back when we were still friends. Aidan threw a fit because I wouldn't sell him Park Lane.

"I'm first!" I announce, signalling the dice. I gather them in my hands and give them a good shake. "Double sixes! Yes!"

We sprint round the board, picking up properties and playing community chest cards and spending our money. Silly Cat is joined by Thunder Cat and I have a whale of a time, building my empire and teasing Zachary for being so far behind. Then suddenly the dice turn on me and my luck runs out. I find myself in jail. I'm stuck for several rounds and Zachary races ahead.

"Aha!" He laughs as I jump out of jail and land straight onto one of his properties. "One hundred pounds, please!"

I frown and fling a handful of money at him.

A few rolls later, I'm back in jail. My excitement for the game has been replaced by a silent, brewing fury. Five minutes later, Silly Cat throws the board up.

"Cat!" Zachary gasps as I fling myself on my bed.

I don't mean to be a bad loser. I know it's only a game. But I'd landed on three of Zachary's properties in a row and was just about to do it again. Silly Cat exploded before I could stop her. "You stole all my money!" I wail. "It's not fair!" I am six years old and unable to contain myself.

"I didn't *steal*—" Zachary attempts.

"You did! And you took all the best properties. And you smiled when I missed out on Trafalgar Square."

He gives an incredulous laugh. "I'm sorry!"

Waves of shame crash over me. *Am I really crying over a game?* Silly Cat ebbs away and I sit up feeling stupid.

"Sorry," I mutter, hardly daring to look him in the eye.

He has a funny smile on his face. "Are you okay?"

"I just... don't like losing. Sorry." I slide off the bed and retrieve the board from the other side of the room. I gather up the houses that are scattered across the floor and hunt for Zachary's playing piece. I finally find it in a shoe.

"Do you want to play something else?" He indicates the weird-looking Eurogames.

"No, thanks." I try to be aloof but I don't think Play it Cool Cat will ever be able to show her face again. "I fancy a milkshake. Shall we go to the refectory?" I'm keen to leave this whole embarrassing episode behind.

"Sure. I'll just leave this here." He slides Monopoly under my bed with a grin. "We can play it again another day. I'll let you have Trafalgar Square next time."

As Fun Cat takes the reins and gives a casual laugh, I am aware of Silly Cat peering out behind my eyes. *He doesn't hate me for being weird. I had a tantrum over a game and he's not telling me off or running away. Does he like me?*

Angry Cat jumps in. *Don't be stupid. Nobody likes you. Not really. He just feels sorry for you.*

Play it Cool Cat pulls on her space helmet. "Come on."

Dotty Jay is in the hallway, cooking something in the microwave. She gives a goofy grin when she sees Zachary emerging from my room. "What are you two up to?"

"Playing games." I reply.

"Oh *really?*" She gives an irritating laugh.

"Board games." I usher Zachary out quickly. I don't want her catching sight of 'Love Birds' and making a joke.

After dumping the games in Zachary's room, we trot down the hill and into the refectory where I make a beeline for the fridge and my favourite banana milkshake. Zachary grabs two muffins, a yoghurt and a bottle of pop.

Windy Wendy greets us at the till with her usual grunt.

"I'll get that," Zachary says, taking my milkshake and adding it to his tray. He digs into his pocket for some money.

"It's fine." I wave my meal card. "I'll pay."

"Just for yours? Or for mine too?"

I laugh at his audacity. Obviously I meant for mine. "For all of it," I say instead, feeling like the most generous soul in the world. I mean, the food isn't exactly cheap and it's not my fault he's already spent his entire meal card. Plus, I already bought him a hot chocolate and a banana when it snowed.

"Treating you, is she?" Windy Wendy booms, raising an eyebrow at Zachary. "Isn't that lovely."

"She thinks we're together!" Zachary sniggers as we head to our usual table.

I roll my eyes. "Don't be stupid."

"Did you see Dotty Jay's face when I came out of your room? Her eyes nearly popped out of her head."

I frown and tuck my meal card away. Thunder Cat needs to make something clear. "You don't fancy me, do you?"

"No."

"Good. I would laugh in your face if you did."

"I'm sure you would."

"You'd tell me if you did, wouldn't you?"

"Of course." He reaches for the two muffins and hands one to me. "Don't worry. I know how you feel about relationships."

I nod. "You like Annie, don't you?"

"Annie?" He laughs. "Not like that. She's a good friend but not my type." He pauses before confessing, "I like Vanessa."

I am taken aback. "Who's Vanessa?"

"She's in the third year. She plays the clarinet. We were in a concert together last term."

"Oh. Well that's good then."

"Not really. She doesn't like me." He opens his bottle of pop and it explodes all over him.

I shove my chair sideways to avoid being hit, Thunder Cat roaring with laughter.

"Oh man!" Zachary shakes his hands and runs to the till.

Windy Wendy is waiting with a handful of napkins. "That's no way to impress the ladies," she sneers.

Zachary scuttles back to our table and I sip my milkshake, watching as he mops himself down. I wonder whether to comment on Vanessa, perhaps tease him for being so soft. But then I remember how gracious he was over Silly Cat's tantrum.

"So... Vanessa, hey?" I swallow the last bite of my muffin and lick my fingers. "How do you know she doesn't like you?"

Zachary blushes. "Because I wrote her a song and sang it at the Chamber Orchestra Christmas party."

"You wrote her a song?" I splutter.

"Yeah. I sang it in front of everyone." He grins and mimes playing the piano. "*Vanessa Vanessa, I long to impress her... Let me buy you a drink, it would be my pleasure...*"

As he sings the next few lines, Thunder Cat can't resist. "That's hilarious! I guess she wasn't impressed?"

"She was mortified. She hasn't spoken to me since."

"But you still like her?"

"Yeah. Silly, I know. I barely know her. I don't know whether to give up or try again. What do you think?"

"What do *I* think?" I scoff. "You know what I think! Love is a waste of time." I blow bubbles in the dregs of my milkshake. "But, if you do try again... Perhaps consider the lyrics, '*Vanessa Vanessa, I'm bound to depress her... If she buys me a drink I'll spill it all over myself!*'"

Zachary punches me on the arm. "Great. Thanks, Cat."

We laugh together.

Meanwhile, Play it Cool Cat slips off her space helmet and quietly fades away.

* 34 * Holy Cat saves the world

There's an awful commotion coming from Elle's room. I stand in the hallway, wincing at the sound of something smashing against a wall. Elle wasn't in class this morning. I didn't think anything of it. She's been known to skip classes after a night out. I edge down the corridor.

Crying. She's definitely crying.

"Elle?" I tap quietly on her door. "Elle? Are you in there?"

Stupid question.

Everything goes silent. She's going to pretend she's not there. I pause before knocking a little louder.

Nothing.

Just leave her to it, Angry Cat snaps. *She's a moody cow.*

Don't be so quick to judge, counsels Holy Cat. *You're just as bad at letting people in.*

I'm about to walk away when Elle's door opens the tiniest crack. She peers at me, her eyes all puffy.

I attempt a kind smile. "Are you okay?"

Another stupid question. I don't expect her to open up to me. I certainly wouldn't if things were the other way around.

"Reece broke up with me," she whispers.

So Dotty Jay's assessment was right. The two of them didn't make it to Easter. I have to admit, I thought it was something more serious than that. Fancy making all that noise over a boy. I thought her entire family had died or something. I intend to offer my condolences and make a swift exit but without meaning to I slip into Holy Cat and ask, "Do you want to talk about it?"

She looks at me like I'm the last person she wants to speak to. I almost apologise for offering. "Yeah, okay."

I swallow my surprise as she steps aside and invites me in. I've never been in Elle's room before. I expected it to be meticulous to match her uptight personality. But, even if it hadn't just suffered from a wild hullabaloo, I can tell Elle's room is anything but organised. Her bedding is mismatched, there are piles of unpaired shoes under the bed and none of her posters are straight. I expected it to be all prissy pink but it's mainly a dull shade of green. The bed is unmade so I perch on the edge of her chair, noting a smashed photo frame by the wardrobe. A shot of Elle and Reece snogging pokes through the glass. Elle plonks herself on her bed and stares at her hands.

Before I can figure out what to say, she blurts out, "He's the only guy I've ever slept with. He said he loved me otherwise I wouldn't of..."

I fix an attentive expression on my face as she divulges details of things that I, sheltered as I am, have no understanding of. Silly Cat is peeking, wide-eyed and embarrassed. I finger my phone through my pocket. I'm meant to be meeting Zachary for lunch but I can't text him to explain why I'm late. It would be incredibly rude to get out my phone while she's pouring her heart out.

She talks for ages. Angry Cat is peeved. *Typical Elle. Completely self-absorbed. She hasn't even checked if I've got things to do.* When she finishes, I respond with the only thing I can think of. "I'm sorry."

Sorry you were stupid enough to fall in love.

Sorry you've trashed your own room.

Sorry I zoned out while you were speaking.

She sighs. "How was class? Was Jodie cross I wasn't there?"

"Nobody noticed. I mean, we thought you were ill. We did some improvisation."

"I'm glad I missed that!"

"It was actually fun. Jodie gave us some great tips."

She sighs again. "I wish I was as confident as you, Cat."

I almost fall off the chair. "You're joking, right? I'm not... I'm... I mean, you were Little Betty!"

Elle scowls. "Ugh. I wish I'd never done that show."

I am incredulous. "Why would you say that? You were amazing! Everyone was so intimidated by you when we started the course. You're a real actor—"

"Everyone judges me! They think I'm a snob. I feel all this pressure, like people are hoping I'll slip up."

What am I meant to say to that? I mean, she *is* a snob, isn't she? Or was she just shy and insecure all this time?

"I'm sorry," I say again.

Sorry I judged you.
Sorry you're so sad.
Sorry I'm not better at knowing how to help.

My phone rings. "Just Zachary," I say nonchalantly. I press the answer button and tell him quickly, "Chatting with Elle. I'll call you in a bit." I hope he'll decipher the code. He knows Elle and I have never been friends. Hopefully he'll realise I'm in the middle of a good deed and haven't kept him waiting for nothing.

"Are you and Zachary an item?"

"No." I shove my phone away and wonder how to change the subject. Turns out I don't need to.

"My parents are getting divorced," Elle throws in suddenly.

I remember meeting her parents on our first day. Glamorous tall blonde lady and jolly pink-faced man. They'd seemed like such a happy family. I'd felt so jealous.

"I'm sorry," I mutter for the third time.

"It sucks. I'm seeing a counsellor. Jodie suggested it."

Sad Cat rears her head with a surge of envy mingled with self-pity. *Would Jodie help me, too, if I told her about my parents? Does Jodie like Elle more than me? Do they meet for dessert at the Grumpy Pig?*

Holy Cat shoves Sad Cat away. *This isn't about me.*

"Reece couldn't cope with me being sad," Elle continues. "He said I kept bringing the mood down."

The voices of Leah and Jessa and Bex and Paige echo inside.

"What's happened to the real Cat?"

"We can't carry all of this."

"We've got our exams to think about."

"My mum's evil," Elle continues.

I blink and say nothing.

"She said it's my own fault for getting with Reece because she warned me he was bad news. But that's because he was from Cliffside and didn't go to university. She never bothered to get to know him. I bet your mum is lovely. I bet she wouldn't brag to everybody about you being Little Betty and then wonder why you get so nervous about having to impress everyone."

I still say nothing. Somewhere deep inside, Sad Cat is making me feel all muddled. I force myself to pay attention, to nod and make appropriate noises. I follow Elle's gaze as she stares at the smashed photo frame.

"Want me to help you tidy up?" I offer.

"It's okay."

"At least let me help put your books back." I stoop to collect a clumsy pile by the desk.

"They were already like that! I'll sort it out later."

"Okay." I get to my feet, sensing that my work is done.

Elle follows me to her door and flings her arms around me. "Thank you, Cat. You've saved my life."

Holy Cat takes this literally. I feel a pang of horror at the thought that I almost killed her by walking off and ignoring her.

"No offence, but I thought you were a weirdo when we first met. Especially when you wore that random butterfly hoodie for the whole of Fresher's Week. But you listen so well and sometimes I just want someone to listen, you know what I mean?" Tears are rolling down her cheeks.

I wipe a stray bit of her spit out of my eye. I usually wait for permission to speak. Here she is verbally throwing up on me. Angry Cat is appalled. But Holy Cat is wide awake. *Elle needs a friend to listen? I can be a friend. I'll be the bestest friend ever.*

In that moment, Elle rockets up the ranks of my *Favourite People in Willow,* knocking Shay out of fifth position behind Zachary, Annie, Dotty Jay and Mad Jo. Call me shallow; perhaps I just feel sorry for her. Perhaps I feel guilty for my past ambivalence. Perhaps I still haven't forgiven Shay for her sly comments about me and Zachary. Or perhaps I just like being needed.

Definitely not. I hate being needed, Angry Cat muses. *Look at her. Going on and on as if she's the centre of the universe. As if nobody else has problems.*

Still, Holy Cat is clear on her mission. *Be friends with Elle. Check in on her. Keep her alive.*

Because it has always been my job to save the world.

* 35 * Scaredy Cat wrecks the scene

The days go merrily by and the gloom of winter is washed away by the first whispers of spring. Flowers have popped up round campus. I recognise tulips and daffodils but there are others whose names I don't know, vibrant pinks and lilacs and yellows bursting forth like tiny dancers celebrating everything that is wonderful in my life. Things like the view from my window of lambs skipping across the hills. The fact that the mornings are lighter when I make my pilgrimage to the library. And getting a good grade for the Theatre of Fact piece against all the odds.

Zachary and I spend most of our free time together and I learn there is far more to Zachary Conway Fenn than the brash breakdancing trumpeter he pretends to be. He cries at sad films. He grew up on a farm and has witnessed countless baby lambs being born. He can drive a tractor and milk a cow. When he was little, he fell on a basket of eggs, causing his sister Rachel to give him the bizarre nickname 'Eggnog.' To this day, he's known as 'Eggnog' or 'Eggy' amongst his extended family. He's visited eleven countries but Berney Arms in Norfolk is still his favourite place in the world. He has five cats. He used to sing in a choir. He's never broken a bone. His parents are happily married. His life is perfect. I'm not jealous at all. I have no desire to milk a cow. Even so, I can't help but wonder what it would be like to be called Eggnog by a big sister called Rachel.

I'm making slow progress on the trumpet but even Dotty Jay says I'm improving. I had a successful trip to Wakefield with Annie and found the perfect dress for Chantelle's wedding. And I've finally beaten Zachary at Monopoly. I am Fun Cat by day and Silly Cat by night, whiling away the hours talking to Jodie. This past week we've danced round Fairy Land, speculated over why my Uncle Richard moved to Canada and eaten cheesecake at the Grumpy Pig. In My Head, I mean. In Real Life, Jodie has only spoken to me three times. Twice to ask how I was (I said I was okay) and once to praise my efforts in an improv exercise.

I am idly checking FriendWeb when I learn my mother is in hospital. *'Not again!'* reads her status update from an hour ago. 'Another ambulance journey. Why me?' She has tagged her location as the Royal Devon and Exeter Hospital.

I feel a shot of panic as I scroll down the post. Messages of concern are pouring in but my mother hasn't replied to anybody. *She can't be seriously ill,* I reason. *There wouldn't be time to post on FriendWeb if she was.*

Angry Cat wrestles with Scaredy Cat. *Why is she making a drama of it by having me find out on FriendWeb instead of telling me?*

My thumb shakes as I send her a text. *'Just saw your FriendWeb update. Are you OK?'*

Holy Cat feels a surge of guilt. I've only rung my mum once all term. I've spoken to her more than that; she comes on the line most Mondays during my father's scheduled call. But that's not the same. That's not me being a good daughter and calling of my own accord. Did I even thank her for her latest parcel? She sent me a t-shirt from her and Keith's holiday to France. It says *'I rocked the Seine in Paris.'* It's neon orange.

Her reply comes through. *'Got rushed to hospital.'*

I breathe a sigh of relief that she's still alive and well enough to be checking her phone. *'What happened? Are you OK?'*

'Collapsed in Tesco. Just waiting for the doctor now.'

I keep texting as she drip-feeds me the information.

'How did you collapse? How are you feeling?'

'Just my heart. Don't worry!'

Of course I'm going to worry if she's collapsing without a known cause. Some Spanish words come to mind. It's my mother's prayer— the one she always mutters when she's stressed. *Or is it a spell?* I often say it for luck. I've tried over the years to heal my mum, clinging to the vain hope that Chantelle's theory about us having magic powers could have some truth to it. I recite the prayer now, willing her heart to be strong. Then my dad rings in a panic because he's worried about her and needs to make sure I am worrying too. Which I am, I assure him.

"She collapsed in the fruit aisle. Thank goodness she wasn't driving. Can you pray for her right away?"

"I am, I am..." I repeat the prayer silently, the burden to keep her alive as pressing as the burden to stop her running away.

"I don't know what I'm going to do, Cat! I can't think straight with all this stress..."

Once I've tended sufficiently to his needs, I hang up and pace my room, Scaredy Cat getting the better of me.

I don't want her to die. What if she dies?

I locate the Paris t-shirt which I'd shoved carelessly under my bed. I put it on. Anything to feel like I am connected to my mother in her hour of need. She tries so hard. Always gives me what she didn't have. Material stuff, I mean. Tears well up. I desperately want to talk to Zachary. He would understand my crazy mix of emotions but he's busy at a trumpet lesson.

I recite the Spanish words over and over before attempting a prayer in English. "Oh God, please look after my mum..." I look out of the window, searching for a sign, but the sky is empty.

Holy Cat is wracked with shame. *You behave like you don't believe in God. You can't crawl to him for help now.*

But Scaredy Cat is desperate so I go and knock on Annie's door. Play it Cool Cat forces a smile when she answers. "Sorry to bother you but I wondered if you could say a quick prayer for my mum? She's in hospital and I know you have more credit with God than I do so..." I stop before I choke up.

Annie looks at me with wide-eyed astonishment. "Oh, Cat! Of course I'll pray. I'll pray right now."

"Thanks, yeah, whenever."

I'm about to head back to my room when she says, "Hold my hand and I'll pray with you now."

"Oh I don't need to... Unless the prayer works better if..." I swallow the rock in my throat. "Sorry. I don't mean to get emotional. I'm just worried about her."

"Of course you are!" She gives me a big hug before grabbing my hands and praying. "Hey Jesus, please look after Cat's mum. Please send your healing power wherever she needs it..."

"Her heart," I mutter.

"Her heart," Annie echoes. "Please heal her heart and fix anything that's wrong. Thank you very much. I love you. Amen." Her tone is so casual, so expectant. Fancy telling God you love him. I can't contain myself. I burst into tears.

Annie gives me another hug before whispering, "Shall we go for a walk? Clear your head a bit?"

I wipe my face. "Alright."

We pass Elle on our way past the mansion and I force a smile and wave. I know she bore her soul to me recently but I have no intention of doing the same. I don't want to be needy and I look ugly when I cry. Plus her parents are getting divorced and her boyfriend slept with her and dumped her. She's got way too much going on.

We walk past Fairy Land without stopping to jump then head up through the woods and into the fields where the spring lambs are munching grass. Annie comments on the weather, the trees, the lambs. I can tell she's struggling to know how to help me. I feel embarrassed for causing her discomfort. I force Play it Cool Cat to the front, desperately stomping Scaredy Cat away. I soon feel guilty. My mother has collapsed many times before. I'm leading Annie on to think that it's going to be anything serious this time. She'll be home soon. She's probably home already.

I'm about to tell Annie that I'm sorry for overreacting when she says, "I like your t-shirt."

"Oh. I..." I shake my head. I'd forgotten I was wearing it.

"Have you been to Paris?"

"No... My mum sent it. She went last month." I don't add that she went with Keith because my dad won't travel. I don't add that I don't like the t-shirt. I don't add that I don't like any of my mother's gifts. Instead, I open FriendWeb and show her a selfie of my mother posing at the Eiffel tower.

Annie squints and cups a hand round my phone to shield it from the sun. "She looks happy. You must be very close."

My eyes fill with tears before I can put on my mask.

"Sorry. I don't mean to worry you."

"No, it's not... I'm not..." I gulp before blurting out, "We're not that close. I wish we were but we're not."

"Oh... I'm sorry, Cat."

I flap a hand. "No need to be sorry. Not your fault!"

She stops suddenly and sits on a fallen tree trunk, motioning for me to join her. "Do you want to talk about it?"

I should say no but instead I murmur, "It's complicated."

"How?"

I sit beside her and trace round a knobbly bit of bark. "Because I know my mum wants us to be close. And I do too. But there's just so much... So much that feels broken and we never talk about it..."

She keeps staring at me so, compelled to fill the silence, Scaredy Cat carries on speaking. I tell her about how my mother acts in unpredictable ways. I confess that she is both the person I love the most and the person I fear the most. I explain that I get confused because, although I love her, I feel all kinds of murky ugly stuff too. It's like a load is rolling off my shoulders. Like ice is melting in my chest and giving me space to breathe. Like I am not actually alone, after all, and I do have friends that care. But I'm a little afraid that I won't know when to shut up. I glance at Annie, trying to read any signs of disgust or boredom but she just stares at me, rapt and full of concern. So I carry on and Scaredy Cat feels lighter when I'm done. I look at my feet and wait awkwardly.

Shame starts to creep over me as Annie goes on staring. Eventually, she says quietly, "Can I tell you what you missed at *If God made a way?*"

It takes me a moment to figure out what she's talking about. Then I remember the Christian Union meetings from last term. "Okay," I say uneasily, trying not to show how hurt I am by the sudden change of subject. *I knew I shouldn't have spoken.*

She jiggles before turning to face me. "You remember the first session? *If God made the world?*"

I look into her beaming eyes and shrug.

"If God made the world then everything belongs to him and he's in control. Remember that? Remember what Nina said?"

I try not to cry.

"And then *If God made you...*" Annie grins before launching into a mini preach about God knowing all the hairs on our heads and having a reason for making us. "I've been praying for you loads, Cat," she says eagerly. "Praying that we'd get an opportunity to talk about this stuff."

I resist the urge to frown. This wasn't so much an 'opportunity' as her shoehorning it in.

"And that brings us to *If God made a way!*" She's practically spitting at me. "If God made a way then there's a meaning for everything and death is not the end and all your sins can be wiped out and you never have to be alone because Jesus has sorted everything out and he's always watching over you and he wants to be your best friend forever—" She finally comes up for air. "So... What do you think?"

"About...?"

"About God. The meaning of life. Jesus loving you."

I exhale through my nose. "I know all the stories. And I believe in God, sort of. I mean, there has to be something out there. But I don't... I don't know about specifics."

She peers at me. "If you wanted to go to Heaven, would you know how to get there?"

I should think so, Angry Cat whispers wryly. *I reckon the full bottle of Gelsemium would do it.*

I don't say this, of course. I just shrug again.

"Can I tell you more about Jesus? About the cross and what he did for you?"

I don't see the point in resisting. I shift on the log and try to look interested as she waffles on.

"You can pray to Jesus any time, Cat," she concludes. "He will hear you and come straight to you. God can do anything! He's so amazing and he'll never let you down."

I clench my fists, Angry Cat reeling. *She's so simple. A typical type five.*

God isn't like that. Sad Cat wails inside. *I prayed so many times for God to stop my mum leaving. I prayed for him to heal her, help her, mend my parents' marriage, help me be a better daughter. He did nothing. NOTHING. If God is out there, he's not so willing and lovely as Annie believes.*

Annie peers at me. "Have you got any questions?"

Questions! Angry Cat scoffs. *Oh, have I got any questions?*

I force a smile. "No. No questions. You explained it fine."

* 36 * Angry Cat doesn't want to see photos of poorly mothers

My discomfort is amplified on our way back through campus when we pass Charlotte and Ruth from the Christian Union. I often see them around campus and Fun Cat always waves or stops to exchange pleasantries. But it's hard to find Fun Cat when I'm stuck being Scaredy Cat. Play it Cool Cat will have to do.

"Oh hi!" I say as Ruth catches my eye.

"Hey, Cat! How are you?"

"I'm fine!" I sing back. "How are you?"

"Good, thanks. We're about to go to Wakefield."

"Great! Have a lovely time. Bye—"

Annie taps me on the arm. "Do you want to ask them to pray for your mum?"

Squashed Cat catapults into the passenger seat, petrified that Annie's about to repeat all the awful things I just told her. Play it Cool Cat keeps the wheel, just about, and my nonchalant expression gives nothing away. "It's alright," I insist. "They're off to Wakefield. The bus will be here soon."

"We're getting a lift with Nina," Ruth says. "So we've got plenty of time. We can pray!"

"Is everything okay?" asks Charlotte.

I'm furious at Annie but Play it Cool Cat goes on smiling. "Oh, my mum's a bit unwell. That's all."

"She's in hospital," Annie adds.

"It happens sometimes. Just her heart playing up."

"Oh no! Of course we'll pray," says Charlotte.

I try not to grimace as Ruth adds, "We'll pray right now."

The next thing I know, the four of us are holding hands and Ruth and Charlotte are spouting religious words in voices that are far too loud for the middle of campus. I say a prayer of my own. *Please God, don't let anybody walk past. Don't let Jodie see me and think I'm a freak.*

I employ RoboCat to tune the world out. They finally stop praying and Play it Cool Cat forces another indifferent smile. "Thanks."

I try to leave again but Ruth calls me back. "Oh, Cat. I saw a picture for you when we were praying."

"You saw a what?"

"A picture. God sometimes gives his children pictures when they pray and—"

I zone out again.

I don't hear anything Ruth says until she concludes with, "There's a door you need to go through. It will be scary but God will be with you."

I blink at her. I suppose that might have made sense if I'd been listening. But I don't dare ask her to repeat it.

Silly Cat feels a sudden pang of longing. *Can some people actually hear messages from God? Like some kind of superpower? I should ask them if they can pray for me to have a magic power too. The power to heal. Life would be so much easier if I could stop people from hurting.*

But if Ruth can hear from God, Charlotte definitely can't. She shoots me a look of pity before saying, "I bet your mum is lovely, Cat. You must be so worried. I don't know how I'd cope if anything happened to my mum. She was horribly sick with Covid last year and it completely ruined Christmas. I'll keep praying for your mum."

I swallow. "Thank you." I should feel grateful. But I don't. I feel irritated. She thinks we're speaking the same language when we talk about sick mothers and Christmas being ruined. She assumes I'm as close to my mother as she is to hers. Well, I wouldn't be middle class, well-spoken, high achieving or sheltered if I didn't have a happy home life, would I? Broken people look broken. Angry Cat is shrieking inside and it's like a room is being trashed inside my brain. I don't want them to assume I have nice parents. *So, what then? Do I want them to think my parents are awful?* Holy Cat feels ashamed. *Of course not. My parents do their best.*

I feel lonelier than ever as Ruth and Charlotte say goodbye.

"You alright?" Annie nudges me.

"Yes. Fine. You?"

At that moment, Zachary exits the mansion, fresh from his trumpet lesson, his instrument slung on his shoulder. He gallops towards us. "Hey! What are you up to?"

Play it Cool Cat feels oddly uncomfortable whenever Zachary's around. It's like I lose all ability to fake being fine. She steps aside and Sad Cat takes her place. "My mum's in hospital," I say quietly. "Her heart again."

"Oh." Zachary holds my gaze before taking my hand and giving me a little squeeze. That squeeze tells me that he understands perfectly. The anxiety. The confusion. The messiness of love and why I want nothing to do with it. "I'm sorry, Cat. I'll pray for her."

I am torn between wanting to scowl and wanting to sob. "Not now," I beg. "Pray on your own later."

I feel small and fragile as the three of us head to the refectory. Annie offers to grab some cookies while Zachary and I secure our usual table. I slide into a seat and check my phone. There are some messages from my parents which I missed while Annie and I were walking. My heart pounds as I open them.

'Blood clot! I could have died!' my mum announces proudly. She's sent a photo of herself in a hospital bed, canula in one hand, waving with the other.

In another message, my dad gives all the details. *'Utterly terrifying... Could've been fatal... emergency treatment... medication for the next few months... Chantelle's wedding coming up, bound to be stressful...'*

I skim it before turning back to the picture of my mother. The sight of all the hospital equipment makes me dizzy.

"Everything okay?" Zachary asks.

I hold my phone up and show him the photo before scrolling to my dad's message and holding that one up too.

He reads it slowly before asking, "How do you feel?"

Holy Cat wants to be a good daughter and say something kind. "I'm glad she's alright," I mutter.

I start to type a message to my mother. *'I'm so sorry to hear about the blood clot. How are you now?'*

But Angry Cat snarls in my head, *Doesn't she realise how it makes me feel seeing such a photo? Is she totally oblivious to my feelings? Or does she enjoy trying to scare me? What kind of mother—*

But I love her! Holy Cat insists. *I don't want her to die. I love her more than anyone in the world. I would use every wish and magic power to save her.*

I turn back to my father's message. I can hear his anguished voice. I can see him pacing, flapping about, consumed with his fears. Devoted. Endlessly devoted to my mother.

Angry Cat feels another surge of fury. *It's all about them. Always, always all about them.*

Then a shot of shame, so deep and so devastating. *I'm such an awful daughter. My mum nearly died and I'm about to eat a cookie. I should get a train and go and see her.*

"Are you okay?" Zachary interrupts the raging tug of war.

I'm not sure how to answer. Nobody ever asks me that. It's never about me. "I'm glad she's alright," I repeat.

Still, I cannot silence the fears. *What if they hadn't treated her in time? What if they missed something? What if she forgets to take the medicine? What if it happens again?*

"Has she had a clot before?"

I think before confessing, "I don't know." I feel awful. I should know. Why don't I know? I bite my lip as tears rush to my eyes. I can't remember all the details but I remember how I felt every time she was suddenly taken ill. The terror. The confusion. The guilt. Had I caused it? Should I have spotted something was wrong? Why couldn't I heal her?

"It's alright," he assures me. "You don't need to know."

"I love her," I insist. I don't know who I am trying to persuade more: him or me.

"I know you do."

"But it's..."

"Complicated, I know."

"And that's why I don't..." I almost choke on the lump that has appeared in my throat. "Why I don't..." I can't get the words out. "Why I don't believe..." I whisper.

"I know." He finishes the words for me. "In love."

* 37 * Sad Cat takes the biggest risk of her life

I have learnt never to relax because something bad always happens when I do. Like the frivolous fun I had at Exmoor Zoo, the first ever time my mum ran away. I was jumping too exuberantly with Aidan and he crashed into her. I have learnt that keeping the peace requires constant diligence and things go wrong if I take my eye off the ball. But, even so, even with all that I know, sometimes I forget to be good or to say my magic prayers. Sometimes I let my guard down and start having fun.

Today is one of those days.

I've had reckless fun all week. We're doing mask work in class and Fun Cat has had a riot. I've given *'Love Birds'* a go and it turns out I am a genius when it comes to abstract Eurogames. (Either that or Zachary let me win so that Silly Cat wouldn't throw the board up.) There are two days left until the Easter holidays and my suitcase is packed, ready for Chantelle's wedding at the weekend. Thunder Cat is in the middle of teasing Zachary as I wallop him at Monopoly. Then my phone rings.

"Cat, she's gone! I don't know what to do!"

The bottom falls out of my world. Again.

Again.

Again.

I want to scream at my dad, *"Leave me alone! Stop dragging me into this! Carry your own junk!"*

But I don't. I can't. I have to fix it.

"I don't know what to do," he repeats. "I'm on the edge!"

My throat tightens. I try to switch into RoboCat but I can't. Perhaps it's because Zachary is peering at me, raising an eyebrow and mouthing the words, *"Are you okay?"*

I swallow and turn the volume down on my phone.

"Cat? Are you there? Did you hear me? She's gone. Flew into a rage because I said a picture wasn't hung straight. Almost hit me with the hammer. This is it. This will finish me off."

I gulp again. I can't speak.

Zachary shoots me another quizzical glance and I shake my head, shoving my spare hand into my eyes to crush the tears that are forming. My head goes dizzy and I become Lost Cat, losing connection with the world.

My dad squawks on and I say, "Hmmm."

I feel a hand on mine. I open my eyes and stare into Zachary's sorry face. He gently takes my phone away.

I watch dumbly as he puts the phone to his ear and says, "Hello? Cat's dad? This is Cat's friend, Zachary." He sounds really grown up all of a sudden, nothing like the cheeky teenager who was just about to lose at Monopoly.

I hear my dad's frantic demands. "Who are you? I was talking to Cat. This is a family emergency!"

"I'm sorry," Zachary cuts him off. "I'm not going to let you talk to Cat like that. She's really upset—"

"Let me speak to my daughter!"

"I'm afraid she's busy right now."

I have gone numb. I hear my father making threats: he's on the verge of killing himself and if Zachary doesn't give me the phone back he'll be personally responsible.

"What you do is your own choice," Zachary informs him. "Goodbye." He hangs up the phone and lets out a long breath.

"What did you just do?" I whisper. I snatch my phone and prepare to call my father back, Lost Cat morphing into Squashed Cat, panic rising like vomit.

"Cat... Don't call him."

"You don't understand! He'll kill himself!"

"He won't."

"He will!"

"He hasn't yet."

"That's because I always talk him out of it. I sort things out. I help get my mum back. I can't just *ignore* him."

"Cat, wait one second!"

I pause, my thumb hovering over my phone. One second might be too late.

"You can call him if you really want to. But... Just think about it. He probably won't kill himself—"

"He might!"

"—but if he does, it's not your fault. It's completely his own choice and responsibility."

I blink at him. He may as well be speaking French.

"He'll kill himself," I repeat. "He's got close before. He's smashed his head on the wall and thrown himself down the stairs and if I hadn't—"

"It wasn't up to you to keep him alive. It wasn't then and it isn't now."

"But I don't want him to die. I don't want her to leave." I bury my head in my hands and sob.

Zachary shuffles up close to me and wraps me in a giant bear hug. I get snot all over his yellow hoodie but it's already stained from his beans at dinner so hopefully he won't mind. "It's not your fault, Cat," he murmurs. "It was never your fault. And you don't have to fix it now."

I look down at my phone. I'm surprised my father hasn't tried to call me back. Perhaps he's dead already. I struggle to catch my breath as I stare at the Monopoly board. Stupid frivolous fun. I glance back at my phone and then up into Zachary's kind face. Some nameless part of me believes he is talking sense but I cannot silence the cries from Squashed Cat and Scaredy Cat, not to mention the accusations from Holy Cat.

"I'll answer if he rings again," I say, my voice hoarse as though I have been screaming. "But I won't call him back."

Zachary pats me. "Well done, Cat. That's really brave."

Holy Cat yells at me that it isn't brave at all. It's selfish and irresponsible and the next call I receive will be from Aidan telling me that our father has hung himself.

"Do you want to finish our game? Take your mind off things?"

I'm about to say no. I can't play games at a time like this. But then I reconsider and say, "Okay."

So we play on. I win but the victory feels empty. Then we play a few rounds of 'Love Birds.' I forget all the rules but Zachary lets me win anyway. Then we play Snap. Then Battleships. Then Buckaroo. Then I ask Zachary to teach me how to play Chess because I don't want the evening to end yet. I don't want to go to sleep and face the darkness alone.

Zachary seems to understand without me saying a word. Usually, he'll yawn and stretch at some point around midnight and announce he's off to bed. But not tonight. He indulges my request for another game and another and another. We play into the dead of night, neither of us keeping track of who's winning. I check my phone at regular intervals just in case I've missed it ringing. But there are no messages, no emails. Nothing. At some point, we hear the campus clock dinging to announce that it's three in the morning. Still Zachary keeps vigil with me. Still my phone does not ring.

I picture my mother on the run. Where has she gone this time? To her friend, Angie's? Unlikely. She likes to pretend to Angie that everything is fine. To Keith's? He's seen her in a rage before. They joke about it sometimes. But she says his house is smelly because of his dog so I'm not sure she'd take all her belongings there. Perhaps she has friends I've never met. Or perhaps she's gone to a hotel. Or perhaps she's on a plane across the world. Perhaps she found a rocket and has vanished into the stars. Perhaps I'll never see her again.

I picture my father dead. Surrounded by his own blood. A tear-stained note announcing it was my fault for not caring.

And my brother? I feel a wave of guilt. Shouldn't I at least text to see whether he's okay? Surely he'd have rung if anything had happened? Unless our dad has killed him too. A fresh flood of tears explode out of my face and Zachary gives me another of his bear hugs.

At half five, my eyes are drooping. Zachary has fallen asleep in the middle of his turn and is snoring at the foot of my desk. I abandon our half-finished game of 'Love Birds' and curl up on my bed. My alarm wakes me two hours later. Zachary has gone. He must have crept out after I fell asleep. Our game is still spread out on the floor. I tread round it and reach for my phone. Nothing.

I stuff Squashed Cat away and slowly dress for class.

Zachary meets me on the front step and walks with me down the hill. "Did your dad call?"

"No. Do you think he's alright?"

"Probably."

Squashed Cat resurfaces. *Only probably? What have I done? Zachary reckoned it was for the best. But what does he know? Stupid Eggnog!*

I check my phone again. "Should I call him now?"

"I wouldn't. But it's up to you."

I chew my thumb. *What would a good daughter do?*

"What if he's dead? Maybe I shouldn't go to my lesson."

"Well..." Zachary replies matter-of-factly, "If he's already dead, then you may as well go to your lesson first and find out later." He gives a wry smile. "I mean, if he's already dead, nothing will change between now and lunchtime."

I am torn between laughing and crying at his logic. I can't silence the swirling panic that screams at me that I might have just killed my father. Yet, at the same time, Silly Cat is adamant that I don't want to miss any of Jodie's classes. I love my course. And I love Jodie. And it's not fair of my father to ruin my course by dying.

I toss my phone back into my bag. "See you later."

We part in the corridor and I force a steely expression onto my face, switching into RoboCat as I make my way to Primrose. The noise hits me as I enter the room. I am grateful we are doing mask work. As soon as Jodie lets us loose, I pick the mask with the longest nose. I figure the nose will give me some extra distance so nobody can get too close to me. My mask signifies that I am a type of character called Zanni. A typical Zanni is a servant, a clown and a buffoon. The longer the nose, the stupider the character. Fantastic.

I prance about, pretending to revel in the laughter of my classmates while tears trickle down my cheeks, hidden from sight by the grotesque mask.

"Brilliant, Cat!" Jodie shouts at one point.

I freeze, mid-roly-poly. Silly Cat has butterflies at the sound of Jodie's praise. Sad Cat wants to whip off my mask so that she can see I am only playing at being the fool. I'm not enjoying it really. I am not okay.

I am conflicted. Do I want Jodie to see me crying or not?

Course not, says Angry Cat. *Don't let anyone see you.*

Don't make a fuss, adds Holy Cat.

And yet the endless mask work is draining. I can't see properly and I'm about to trip over my nose.

The lesson comes to an end and I linger by the table at the front, running a hand over all the twisted shiny masks. Perhaps next time I'll try being Pierrot, the sad clown. Then I could cry to my heart's content and everyone would just applaud me for being a good actor.

I shoot a glance at Jodie, hoping to catch her eye. She looks busy and barely acknowledges me. Just a brief "Thanks," as I gather the masks into a pile and put them by her bag.

I slowly do up my shoes, thinking about how Elle said she spoke to Jodie about her parents' divorce. Spoke to her how? Like got her attention after class one day and stayed behind for a heart to heart? Like what? Like, *"Excuse me, Jodie. Have you got a moment?"*

But what if Jodie only has capacity for one needy student? I don't want her to think I'm an attention seeker.

Perhaps, if she asks specifically, like if she says, *"You seem a bit down, Cat,"* or, *"Is there anything on your mind?"*

That would be permission to be real, wouldn't it?

A regular *"How are you?"* is just politeness. Nobody expects to be told the truth.

I take my time getting to my feet.

"See you, Jodie!" Cooking Clemmie calls as she leaves.

"Coming for a cig?" asks Smoking Sienna, her arm linked in Dancing Donna's.

Jodie bats a hand. "Not today, thanks. I've got some stuff going on that I need to sort out." She pulls a face and carries on packing up her bag.

Well that settles it.

She's got stuff going on. I can't add my rubbish to her burdens. That would be selfish.

* 38 * Squashed Cat explodes

Zachary was right. My dad did not kill himself.

Somehow, he got himself through it. Somehow, my mother came home without my intervention. I don't even know what happened because my dad didn't bother to tell me. I only know it got resolved because I finally sent Aidan a text last night.

'Everything okay? Dad rang yesterday about something going on?'

"Yeah. No big deal. Mum was in a mood all day but she was back before EastEnders.'

The revelation that everything was wrapped up long before I went to bed— probably before me and Zachary even finished talking about it— causes a cascade of confusing emotions to smash through me. There's relief, of course, that my mum is home and nobody died. There's also astonishment because I am genuinely surprised that my abstaining from fixing things did not cause the entire universe to implode. And then there's anger. Like, if it was *that* easy to resolve without me, then what have I been doing all my life?

No, it's not anger. That's far too mild. It's more like Rage.

Rage at being taken for a ride all these years, believing that my father's suicide was inevitable if I didn't immediately jump to attention, laying my own needs aside to tend to his. As though my feelings do not matter. As though it is the role of a child to be the mother to her parents. As though I am an endless sponge, able to soak up everything that's thrown at me without drowning. Without complaining. Without breaking.

Rage. The kind of Rage that makes me want to smash things. But there's no time to think about it because they will be here to collect me in approximately fifteen minutes.

I'm sitting on Annie's picnic blanket on the patch of grass outside Willow, enjoying the weather which has suddenly brightened, playing cards with Zachary and Annie and wishing I didn't have to leave so early. Most of my housemates aren't leaving until Sunday and I'm gutted that

I'll miss out on the last two days together. I've been looking forward to Chantelle's wedding for weeks but, now that it's about to happen, all I feel is dread.

I pick at my newly painted turquoise nails. Shay completely forgot that she was meant to be doing them and said, "What's up, Cat?" when I turned up at her door this morning.

Copy Cat felt shy about reminding her, especially because I could see Wes reclining topless on her bed. So I muttered, "Just saying Happy Easter. I'm off today."

Then I ran back to my floor and asked Dotty Jay to do them instead. She wasn't very neat but she was full of enthusiasm. Apparently, I've got perfectly straight fingers and gorgeous cuticles.

"You could totally be a hand model, Cat!" Dotty Jay raved as she painted each nail.

I chuckled. As if Catrina Carla will need a back-up job. Still, I felt rather chuffed. Dotty Jay is an expert on most things. If she says my hands are special then they must be.

"Time for one more round?" Zachary asks, scooping up the deck of cards and shuffling them with one hand.

I watch him out of the corner of my eye as he deals the cards. He wasn't remotely surprised when I told him my father hadn't died. He just nodded as if to say, *"Told you there was nothing to worry about!"*

I wish I knew what it felt like not to be frightened. Aidan never seems to worry either. Why am I so stupid?

I pick up my cards and put them in order. Then my stomach lurches as my parents' car appears at the top of the hill. I put the cards down. "Oh. No time after all."

My mum is waving from the passenger window and my dad has his twitchy face on. I rise to greet them and the familiar prickles of anxiety awaken in my chest, amplified by the fact that Zachary and Annie are both beside me, knowing far, far too much. I feel like I am the worst traitor in the world as I wave to my family, playing the role of loving daughter. I shoot a glance at Zachary but he's his normal smiley self as my parents step out of the car.

"Hello, Baby!" my mother rushes towards me.

My heart flinches, as it always does when my mother hugs me. Then I spot that she's wearing the scarf I gave her for Christmas. The scarf she was so dismissive of because has 'lots of scarves already.'

"You're wearing the scarf from me!" I note, feeling pleased.

"Of course I am, silly! It's my favourite. I always wear it." She says this as though I am daft for being surprised. As though it ought to have been obvious that she loved it all along. She waves cheerily to Zachary and Annie.

Even though she met them at the end of last term, I know she won't have any memory of them so I tell her quickly, "These are my friends. Annie and Zachary."

My dad steps out of the car with a big sigh, as though he has just survived something colossal like an earthquake. Or a pandemic. Or a car journey with my mother. If he remembers Zachary's name from their little phone exchange, he doesn't let on.

"Hello Annie and Zachary!" My mother coos at them as though they are small children. "How are you both?" I've seen her do this with old people and foreigners. It's like she doesn't think they'll understand if she speaks in her normal voice.

"Fine, thanks! Good to see you!" they both chime politely.

My father ambles towards me with his usual greeting: "I must go to the toilet."

I nod and point to Willow's open doorway.

"Can you show me where it is?"

"You've been before. The little room at the end of my corridor."

"The little one..." He furrows his brow like it's a complicated maths puzzle. "You couldn't just show me, could you?"

I try not to grit my teeth. "Just go to the room with the toilet. The bedrooms have people's names on. It's pretty obvious."

"Or you can use the toilet on my floor," Zachary offers. "It's the same room, just on the ground floor."

My father looks like he's been told to get a tube across London.

"He won't be able to understand that!" my mother titters. "He's really stupid!"

I force a smile because that's what I'm meant to do. It's all Squashed Cat knows to do. Then I say, "Where's Aidan?" even though I can see him sitting in the car, eyes glued to his phone. I'm stupid like that. I say dumb things when Fun Cat disappears.

Zachary shows my father to the toilet on the ground floor while Annie helps me load my bags into the car. My new dress is on a hanger inside a see-through plastic bag. I lie it flat over my luggage so it won't crease. I sense my mother looking at it.

"What's that?"

I try to sound cheerful. "My dress for Chantelle's wedding."

She sniffs. "It's got funny sleeves."

"I like it," I insist, feeling ugly. I don't add that Annie helped me choose it. No need to drag poor Annie into my mother's disapproval.

"Well, it's you who's wearing it," my mother says carelessly. "If you're happy, that's the main thing."

"I am," I say, feeling the least happy I have felt all day.

"We'd better get going," my dad announces when he returns from the toilet. "Still got a long drive ahead of us."

I don't want to leave Zachary and Annie. But nor do I want them socialising with my parents for much longer. I hug them before sliding into the back of the car beside my brother.

Mad Jo skips past. "Have a good Easter, Cat!"

"Thanks. You too."

"Have a good Easter, Cat's friend!" my mother trills, giving Mad Jo a merry wave as she gets into the car.

Mad Jo grins at me and I know her grin says, *"Aww! Your mum is so sweet!"*

"Have a nice time!" yells Annie through my closed window.

"Hope the wedding goes okay," Zachary adds and I note that his smile isn't as cheery as Annie's.

Our car speeds up the hill, leaving them behind. I wave until they are out of sight before sighing and allowing Fun Cat to clock out for the next few weeks.

I've googled it. The journey from Forest Hall to Aunt Sonya's house in Glasgow is almost the exact same distance as the journey from Forest Hall to Exeter. I brace myself for the journey being a repeat of the one at Christmas, just with different scenery. But actually my mum falls asleep before we even reach Leeds. Perhaps she's exhausted from the journey up from Exeter. Or her health scare. Or her recent angry episode. Soon my brother dozes off too and the car is quiet apart from the sound of snoring and the roar of the road outside. My dad glances at them both before looking at me in the mirror. "I've felt really low this week," he confides in me.

I purse my lips and look away. "I'm sorry to hear that," I say, my cool exterior masking the fizzing in my head.

When I steal a glance, I see that he's still trying to catch my eye in the mirror. I'm supposed to ask what's wrong. Then I'm meant to try to fix it. That's the game we usually play. I look away again. Angry Cat is resolute. Not today. Not now that I know he can survive without my desperate efforts.

I pretend to be asleep. I talk to Jodie in My Head all the way to Carlisle. *I wish she was my cousin and that I could be a bridesmaid at her wedding. I wish. I wish.*

My mother stirs as we pull into a service station for dinner. There's considerable tension as we gobble down some greasy food and bundle back into the car for the final stretch.

We pull into Aunt Sonya's estate just after half ten.

"Number thirty eight. There! That one!"

"I can see it."

"Slow down, then. For goodness sake... Here. Stop!"

My father turns off the engine and gives a mighty sigh.

"Why couldn't we stay in a hotel?" Aidan pipes up.

I shoot him a glance, imploring him not to ask such sensible questions.

"I wanted to," says our mum. "Your father was too stingy."

Our father tuts. "We both agreed that we didn't want to waste money on a hotel when your sister has got plenty of space for us here!"

'Plenty of space' is quite an overstatement. It turns out Aunt Sonya has one spare room, a bumpy sofa in the living room and a utility room where the dog sleeps.

Aunt Tracey answers the door and gives us a clap. "You made it then! Mr Panic managed without having a nervous breakdown?" She looks older than when I last saw her. She's got a white streak in her hair and wrinkles by her eyes. "Alright, Cat?"

"Alright," Squashed Cat squeaks back.

"We're in the kitchen!" Aunt Sonya calls from the back of the house.

My dad turns on the spot, looking helpless, until Aunt Tracey points a finger. "Down there. Round the corner."

We traipse down the hallway and into the kitchen where Aunt Sonya and Chantelle are standing by a stack of buns at a table. Aunt Sonya has a tube of icing in her hand and is busy scrawling the initials 'C' and 'H' over a pile of pink cupcakes.

"You made it before midnight!" my aunt squawks.

"We were sure you wouldn't!" my cousin exclaims. She reminds us that this visit is long overdue by adding, "I can't believe I have to get married before you bother to visit us."

Chantelle is wearing a tight pink nightdress that shows off her blossoming baby bump. My mother makes a beeline for it.

"Look at you!" she screeches, cupping a hand over Chantelle's belly and pressing her mouth up close. "Hello little baby! Don't come out yet! Your mummy's getting married tomorrow." Then she lunges at her sister and they hug and scream as though they are the best of friends.

I trot over to hug Chantelle. Even though this is my family and I ought to feel confident around them, I can't shift gears out of Squashed Cat.

"Cat! It's so good to see you!"

"You too. And, er, congratulations and everything."

Aidan lingers in the doorway, looking sullen as usual.

He goes bright red as Chantelle grabs him and gives him a giant hug, her skimpy nightdress leaving very little to the imagination. "Gimme a hug, cousin!"

Aidan shimmies away, glancing around helplessly.

"Chris isn't here," Chantelle informs him, misreading his discomfort. "He's at a friend's tonight so Aunt Tracey could have his room. You've got the living room, Cat. And you're in with Ned, Aidan. Sorry."

My brother looks alarmed. "Who's Ned?"

Aunt Sonya roars with laughter. "Just the dog, Aidan! Bless him. Look at his face! You didn't think I had a new lover called Ned, did you?"

Aidan scowls, not bothering to hide his annoyance. Copy Cat grins, working extra hard for the both of us.

Chantelle announces that she's off to bed. "This is the last time I'll go to sleep before I become a married woman!" she squeals, grabbing me by the arm and jumping up and down. Copy Cat dances around with her until she lets go of me.

"I think I'll go to bed too," I say. Nobody pays attention so I slip away and start setting up camp in the living room.

My dad creeps in while I'm putting on my pyjamas.

"Dad! I'm changing!"

"As I was saying earlier, I've been feeling low recently..."

I pretend to be looking for something in my bag. "Oh dear. I hope you feel better soon."

He inhales. "I suppose you're tired now."

"Yup."

"Alright. Perhaps tomorrow we can find a bit of time to have a chat. I can tell you what's going on and you can do that thing where you psychoanalyse me."

I once attended a New Year's celebration in which, due to a mishap by Exeter City council, thirty minutes of fireworks got released all at once, resulting in a violent and terrifying frenzy of explosions which threatened to set the whole night sky on fire. That's what happens in my head as I whip round to face my father. "What? The thing where I *psychoanalyse* you? You mean you're doing it on purpose? All these years, I thought you were just stupid. But you're telling me you deliberately see me as your shrink?"

My dad's face contorts, like a child being beaten. "Don't shout," he pleads. "Keep your voice down—"

But I can't keep my voice down. Catherine wheels and rockets are whizzing through my brain, sparks are flying, firecrackers are banging in my ears.

The door swings open and my mum marches in, eyes blazing. "What's going on?" she demands. "Why are you shouting at your dad?"

My dad's frightened glance warns, *"Look what you've done! Don't upset her. You'll set her off."*

The blood fills my ears as Squashed Cat freezes. "Sorry," I mumble, swallowing the boulder in my throat. "I feel ill."

"Oh, you're ill?" My father jumps on this. It's a convenient excuse for my rudeness. "What's wrong?"

"That's why you should eat properly," my mum scolds me.

"I do eat properly," I mutter.

"You only had a burger at dinner."

No use telling her that she bought it for me.

"Have you been taking your vitamins?" My dad peers at me. "Perhaps you're not getting enough sleep. Have you had some late nights?"

I want to say, *"Yes, I've had a few late nights. One when I couldn't get that canula photo out of my head. Oh, and another when you threatened me with killing yourself."*

"You need to get good sleep, Cat," my mum says. "Otherwise you'll be ugly. See, look?" She almost jabs me in the eye. "You've got horrible shadows right there."

I pull away and murmur, "I was just about to go to sleep."

My mum turns to my dad. "Leave her now. Let her sleep."

The two of them leave and I hear my mum's careless laughter echoing down the hallway as they re-join my aunts in the kitchen. I crawl onto the sofa and pull an old grey blanket up to my chin. The blanket has silhouettes of dogs all over it and it smells of dog too. It probably belongs to the dog. Still, at least I'm not actually sleeping with it like Aidan.

Tears trickle down my cheeks as I stare at the shadows around the room. On the mantlepiece, there's a small silver frame with a photo of Chantelle, Chris, my brother and me standing on a giant mound of sand on Exmouth beach. We have the exact same photo in our kitchen. So familiar. Yet so unknown. Like strangers who share blood and a surname. Except Chantelle's surname is Cox, not Berger. And tomorrow it will be Hamza.

Why was I so excited about Chantelle's wedding? Now we're here, I just want it to be over. I squeeze my eyes shut and take a few deep breaths, remnants of fireworks still smouldering in my brain.

But it's not all bleak. In the darkness, Silly Cat is singing. Because there is one thing I am looking forward to more than anything. Tomorrow I will finally meet my cousin, Avery.

* 39 * Silly Cat gets her wish

When I was little, before I stopped believing in love, I sometimes put a white pillowcase over the back of my head and pretended to be a bride. Occasionally Aidan could be persuaded to play the role of my husband but, usually, my teddy had to do. I would prop up my mother's crucifix in the living room and pretend it was a church and I would walk slowly down the aisle singing, *'Lavender's blue, dilly dilly.'*

Chantelle's wedding is nothing like that.

For a start, she's not wearing white. She's in a tight pink dress much like the nightdress she was wearing last night. To start with, I actually thought it *was* her nightdress. Her husband-to-be, Haroon, is in a kilt. I noticed my mother smirking when he first walked in. Secondly, they make their vows in a registry office, not a church, and Uncle Martin spoils the mood by glaring at Aunt Sonya all the way down the aisle. Thirdly, their celebration anthem is not an old children's rhyme. It's *'Sex on Fire.'*

But none of that is important. The only important thing in Silly Cat's world right now is the fact that I am sitting next to my cousin, Avery. We are on Table 2 at the reception in a social club in what Aunt Tracey describes as the grottiest part of Glasgow. She and my mother keep making snide glances at the top table and whispering together.

My mother is looking very glamorous as usual. She's wearing a white dress which you're not supposed to do at weddings, but perhaps she doesn't know.

Uncle Richard is next to my father. I am pretty sure he is an uptight and practical type four. He's smiling but in a guarded sort of way, like he's not really here. When he arrived, my mother ran screeching to him and threw her arms around him, camera in hand ready for a selfie. He gave her a swift peck on the cheek and shook my father's hand. Now he's nodding along to whatever my dad is saying, a finger over his mouth as though he's determined to stay silent. Even though he is three years younger than my mum, he looks quite a bit older as his hair is completely grey.

My cousin Jackson sits on the other side of him. He is twelve and rather precocious. He keeps announcing weird facts to the table, oblivious to the sneers he's getting from Aidan and Chris. "Did you know a banana is actually a berry?" And, "Did you know honey is actually bee vomit?" And, "Did you know there can be meat from up to one hundred cows in just one fast food burger?"

"And did you know I prefer to eat my food without someone jabbering away in my ear?" Chris mutters.

It's the first time I've seen Aidan laugh in months.

I steal a glance at Avery. I hope she hasn't noticed Chris and Aidan mocking her brother. She's busy slicing her chicken kiev into tiny equal sized pieces. She takes so long that most people are on to dessert before she's done.

When she walked into the registry office this morning, Silly Cat wanted to run over screeching, like my mum had done with Uncle Richard. Play it Cool Cat was a lot more reserved and I hung back until she caught my eye. But then she'd given me such a wide and wonderful smile and whispered, "Hey!" as though she'd been longing to meet me as badly as I'd been longing to meet her.

So Silly Cat barged Play it Cool Cat out of the way and scampered over, squealing, "Oh my gosh! Avery! I'm so happy you're here!"

And she kept on grinning and said in the most beautiful accent, "Me too. I've always wanted to come to England."

It didn't seem the moment to tell her she was actually in Scotland. Our embrace wasn't quite how I imagined it. Mainly because she was kind of bony to hug. She's very fragile, almost waiflike. I was scared of crushing her.

There's a meticulous edge to her that reminds me of Elle, albeit a brunette and tanned version. I don't think she's exactly like Elle though. I reckon she's more of a whimsical type two. A little passive. A little melancholy. She doesn't engage with any of the chat around the table. I watch her and try to think of something to talk about. There should be so much to ask and so much to tell. But my mind is blank. I'm feeling insecure in my dress with the stupid sleeves and I've chewed my nails so much that they are already badly chipped.

My mum keeps taking photos and telling everyone to smile. She leans across the table, waving her camera. "Richard! Smile!"

Uncle Richard's eyes flicker slightly but he still doesn't say anything. Holy Cat feels a pang of pity for my mother. She's trying to connect but her brother won't let her in. And then I feel afraid. Am I looking at mine and Aidan's future? Have I been a good enough sister to him? Do I irritate him? Will he flee across the world one day?

"Cheer up, Cat!" Aunt Sonya says loudly, giving me a shake on her way to the buffet table. "You'll get your turn!"

I scowl as she waddles away. "I don't want to get married," I snap.

"You don't want to get married?" Avery finally looks up from her plate.

"Of course you want to get married!" my mum exclaims, taking another photo. Then she announces to the whole table, "Cat has a boyfriend."

"What? No, I don't!"

"That boy. What's his name? Zebedee?"

"It's Zachary and he's not my boyfriend!"

My mum roars with laughter.

Aunt Sonya passes us on her way back from the buffet table. "Oh, Cat, I didn't upset you, did I? You look even more miserable than ever."

"Leave her alone," says Aunt Tracey. "That's just how Cat looks." She reaches over and pats me on the arm. "I remember visiting when you were little. You never smiled! Always so serious."

I pull my arm away. I try to smile. To prove her wrong. But she's right. I never smiled. I was always so serious. Shame she never tried to understand why.

"So, Avery..." Aunt Tracey turns to my cousin. "What are you doing these days? Are you at college? Or do you work?"

Avery puts her cutlery down. "I'm working at the moment to save up for a training course."

"And what course is that?"

"It's a Masters in *Surviving in Hostile Climates*. I plan to live on Mars one day, you know, if we ever find a way to support life there."

"Mars?" I repeat. "Wow..." I give a Silly Cat smile and take a sip of lemonade.

When Avery's not looking, Aunt Tracey taps the side of her head and mouths *"Cuckoo!"*

Copy Cat returns her smile but I feel dreadful. My mum always said Avery went a little funny after her parents' break up. It's terribly disappointing to have her insanity confirmed.

At the top table, Uncle Martin is clanging two glasses together to get everybody's attention. We turn in our seats to listen to the speeches. Uncle Martin's is long and full of snide comments directed at my aunt. RoboCat zones out only to wake up in the middle of Haroon's speech at the words, "And for our next trick, my wife will soon be producing a mini human from inside her belly!"

As everybody cheers, Avery snorts and says in a loud whisper, "Maybe their baby will be the chosen one!"

Across the table, Uncle Richard shoots her a furious look. It's the most animated he's been all day.

I want to ask her what she's talking about. As Haroon concludes his speech with a toast, Silly Cat closes her eyes and makes a wish. *Please let me get some time alone with Avery.*

The best man takes the mic and kicks off his speech with a lewd joke. Silly Cat recoils. I want to put my fingers in my ears. Fortunately, God or the universe or my fairy godmother is listening and my wish is about to be granted.

Avery nudges me. "Do you know where the washroom is?"

I seize my chance. "I need to go too. I'll look with you."

So the two of us set off down a hallway and, even though I spot a sign telling us the toilets are left, I allow Avery to lead us the wrong way and out into the car park.

"This can't be right." Avery pouts and looks around. "Still, it's good to get some fresh air. It's hot in there, isn't it?"

I hadn't noticed but I fan myself and nod. "Hey, Avery..." I try to sound casual. "What did you mean just then? About Chantelle and Haroon's baby being the chosen one?"

"Oh you know..." She waves a bony hand. "You must know? You mean you *don't* know?"

"Don't know what?"

She perches on a nearby railing. "About our grandfather being a healer. And how his magic powers were meant to be handed down but skipped our parents' generation so is still waiting to be unlocked."

My heart stops beating. "It's true?" Silly Cat is wide-eyed. "They really had magic powers?"

"Course it wasn't true!" Avery roars with laughter and I spot two silver fillings at the back of her mouth. "They were just demented. And they did a whole load of crazy stuff to try to gain more powers."

I join her on the railing. "Like what?"

"You know... Rituals, mixing herbs, chants, sacrifices..."

"Sacrifices? You mean like pigeons?"

She snorts. "Sure. Why not?"

"Something bigger? Cows?"

"Think bigger."

"Bigger than a cow? An elephant?"

"Sorry, not bigger. Better. Purer. What has the most valuable blood?" She lowers her voice. "Or should I say *who?*"

A chill goes through me. "People?" I squeak.

Avery's grey eyes stare unblinking at mine.

"So... That's why they came to England? They were murderers?" This is even crazier than Chantelle's theory about a wizard chasing after our grandfather.

Avery jumps off the railing. "I've said too much. Promise you won't say a word to anybody?"

Great. Another family secret to lock away in the filing cabinet of my heart.

"Let's find the washroom." She waltzes back indoors.

I stumble back to the reception. The best man is still waffling on but I don't take anything in. All I can think about is the possibility that I have evil inside me.

It can't be true, Holy Cat insists. *Nobody is that bad.*

Oh it's true, says Angry Cat.

Baby Cat starts crying. But how would Angry Cat know?

Perhaps Avery is deranged, like Mum and Aunt Tracey believe. Maybe she's just telling stories to try to fill the gaps in her history. I mean, she's making preparations for living on Mars. You can't get more deluded than that.

Our family has a history of running away. Our grandparents fled Colombia. Her father fled England. And she wants to go to Mars. And yet... What were they all running away *from?* And why did Uncle Richard give her that warning glance? And why am I suddenly feeling panicky and remembering the taunts of the woman in The Dream hissing, *"Where are your powers, Cat?"*

I want to ask my dad what he knows. He'll keep my confidence. He has to because he'd never risk upsetting my mum. I sidle up to him later when he's on his own.

Everyone else has gathered to watch Chantelle and Haroon cut their cake. Haroon holds the knife in the air and pretends to slice Chantelle's head off. As everybody laughs, the sharp blade twinkles in the light. A memory stirs. My mum running towards our neighbour, Duncan Anderson, with a knife, screaming, *"I will kill you!"* I'm in my white nightie. Feeling sick.

I nudge my dad. I plan to ask what he knows about my mother's early childhood in Colombia but instead I blurt out, "Did we used to know someone called Duncan Anderson?"

My father thinks for a moment before laughing to himself. "Oh yes, he was a funny man. He lived down the road."

A funny man? Like a comedian?

Duncan Anderson is sitting beside me on the sofa. He's drawing pictures and promises I can have one. It's a lovely drawing. I really want it. "Did he babysit for me?"

I don't notice my mother appearing beside us. "What are you talking about?"

"Cat was just asking about Duncan Anderson," my dad says. "Remember him? He used to live down the road."

My heart is thumping. Some instinct warns me to shut the conversation down but my dad is totally useless at telepathy.

"Cat wants to know if he ever babysat."

My mother's eyes flash. "No, he didn't."

"Are you sure?" my dad ploughs on. "Because I remember we went to the cinema once—"

"No," she snaps. "We hardly knew him. He moved away when Aidan was a baby. He never came into our house."

Then why do I know his name? And why do I remember sitting next to him on our sofa? And why is my mother angry at me for asking?

* 40 * Holy Cat goes through a door

Good Friday. My mother has positioned her crucifix in the middle of the dining table so that we can remember Jesus dying while we eat.

We survived the wedding and the long journey back to Exeter. There are so many things I wish I'd asked Avery while I had the chance. But it's too late now. She's back in Canada and, statistically speaking, we're unlikely to meet again for another eighteen years.

My mum is in a good mood today. She's showing me the photobooks she's made commemorating Chantelle's wedding. She's going to send one to Chantelle, one to Aunt Sonya, one to Aunt Tracey and one to Uncle Richard. I wish I could be Fun Cat but only Copy Cat is available. I smile and nod and tell her it's a lovely idea. I don't dare mention she has spelt 'Haroon' wrong.

I can't stop thinking about Avery's disclosure and the random memories of Duncan Anderson and my mother's anger when I mentioned his name and the creepy voice asking where my powers are. While I'd like to dismiss Avery as a total loon, I can't shake off the niggling feeling that deep down I already *know* she is right. I have so many questions pounding round my brain. I'm scared that I'll explode like I did with my father.

Sad Cat is close to the surface. I want to cry. Because my mum is in a good mood and I'm sorry that I'm only faking it. Because the idea of her making a photobook for an event she was so offended at seems strange and sad. Because I know she's keeping secrets from me and I wish she trusted me. Because I wish there wasn't a wall between us. Because I don't know how to be myself around her. I want to crawl into her lap and ask for a hug. I want her to make it all okay, like I've just fallen over and need a plaster. But she can't make it okay because the wound is on the inside, deep inside my heart, and I don't have the words to explain why it hurts.

So I smile and nod and stare at the crucifix. Jesus looks weak and damaged, hanging half-naked on the cross. What kind of a God would humiliate himself like that? Still, Holy Cat recites a quick prayer because I don't want Jesus to be cross with me on his special death day.

My mum is busy writing an inscription in each of the photobooks. She spells *'Haroon'* wrong in a whole new way then looks up and grins. "What do you think?"

I keep smiling. "Great. It looks great."

"Did I spell his name right?"

I pause. If I say no, she might get upset. But if I say yes, she might realise she spelt it wrong on the cover.

Finally, I say, "I think it's spelt *'H.A.R.O.O.N.'*" I don't just *think* this. I know it for a fact. But it's always best to feign uncertainty around my mother.

"So I did it wrong..." She turns to the front. "And on the cover! I did it wrong there too?"

"Oh, did you? Oh yeah..."

You can never tell with my mum whether something like this might tip her over the edge. I am relieved beyond words when she throws her head back and laughs. One of her wild, carefree life-is-wonderful laughs. "I can't believe it! What was I thinking? I called him *'Harpoon!'* That's a gun isn't it?"

"Um... I think it's a spear."

She gives another enormous belly laugh.

And for a moment, Fun Cat laughs too.

I feel a surge of love. *I love my mum.*

I'm hit by a desperate pang of longing and, out of nowhere, I remember the cryptic message Ruth gave me when she prayed for my mother. *"There's a door you need to go through. It will be scary but God will be with you."*

I'd thought it was nonsense when she said it. But suddenly it feels like a clue to something important.

What door? It's a symbol, surely? But of what?

As I keep watching my mother, Holy Cat thinks, *Perhaps she longs for connection as much as I do. Perhaps she wishes we were closer too. And maybe we can be if we just talk about things. Maybe if I was able to share some of the things that have upset me over the years I wouldn't hold it all against her any more. Maybe she just needs the chance to say sorry and to hear me say that it's okay. That I forgive her. That I will always love her. Maybe I can heal her after all.*

Once I've had this idea, I can't think about anything else.

This is what Ruth meant, I'm sure of it. Go through a door: Be honest. Be brave. Be real. Take a risk at connection and God will make sure it turns out well. I feel a rush of excitement and, by the time my mother has packaged up her photobooks, I have made up my mind. I will talk to her. I will make everything okay. I will do it tonight.

I send Zachary a text. *'Remember I told you about that weird advice Ruth gave me? Well I've cracked the code! I just need to talk to my mum and be honest with her about how I'm feeling! I know she wants us to be close really.'*

He replies, *'Wow! That's great. I'll pray for you.'*

I take the plunge at seven twenty. My dad and Aidan are out at a football match so we have plenty of time for a heart to heart without anybody interrupting.

My mother is in her room, reading. I have high hopes as I knock on her door. "Can we talk about something?"

She pats her bed. "Of course, Baby! Come and sit down."

Holy Cat feels a strange giddiness as I plonk myself down beside her. I am about to mend our relationship. I am about to clear the slate so we can start again.

"Is it that boy?" she whispers. "Zebedee. Is he being nasty to you?" There's a flash of excitement in her eyes, as though the prospect of me being unhappy gives her a thrill.

"What? No, I... No. It's nothing to do with Zachary."

"Oh. What's wrong, then?"

I take a deep breath. I have temporary brain freeze and the script that Holy Cat and RoboCat spent the afternoon carefully crafting has disappeared from my mind.

"Is it your course? Have you failed a module? You're not pregnant, are you?"

"No! Nothing like that! It's just... I want to talk about us."

"Us?" A cloud drifts across her face as I prepare to break her heart. Her poorly heart. I feel confused and appalled, like I'm making something out of nothing. Like there's nothing wrong with our relationship after all. Like it's all in my head.

I try to smile. "There's so much on my mind, so many sad memories from the past, and I forgive you but I think we just need to talk..." This wasn't in my original script. I was meant to lay a stronger foundation of love and happy memories before I mentioned sadness or forgiveness.

"I'm listening." My mother folds her arms.

"Okay... Um... I get nervous around you sometimes... I find it hard when you're angry... And all the times you've left... I get sad thinking about it."

She sniffs and looks away. "Nobody's perfect, Cat. You can't expect people to be perfect. We all make mistakes. You're not so perfect yourself."

"I know. I don't expect—"

"I'd do anything for you. You know I'd do anything for you."

"I know! You do loads for me and I'm so grateful. I just thought if I could be real with you..." My voice squeaks and disappears. I stare at my model hands and chip off the remaining specks of turquoise nail polish.

What am I doing? Holy Cat screams. *Why am I hurting her?*

"I'm sorry," I mutter. "I haven't explained it right. I want to be myself with you and I don't know how. I love you very much. And I know you love me too. But I always feel like you're criticising me or that you might suddenly get angry—"

She swears. "Of course I'm going to get angry if you come in here accusing me of things. I thought you were coming to have a nice chat with me." Before I can find my tongue, she blows her lid. "You don't even care that I've been ill, do you? I could've died and you don't even care!"

No, no, no! I care! Of course I care.

"After everything I've done for you and this is what you have to say to me? That I'm a horrible mother. Is that it?" Angry tears pour down her cheeks.

"No! You're not horrible. I didn't mean... I'm sorry—"

"I hate your friends! They've poisoned you against me! I saw the way they were looking at me when we came to collect you. I bet Zebedee's the reason you're not eating properly. I told Angie you were starving yourself like Avery."

I can't keep up. She's not making any sense. "I'm not... I don't... My friends aren't... I'm sorry... I love you—"

"I don't want you to love me," she spits. "I want you to respect me."

My throat goes tight. I can't breathe. I'm trying. I'm really trying. I can love her. Unconditional love. I'll protect her. Keep her secrets safe. Welcome her back with open arms. Again and again and again. Swallow my pain and my need to be seen. Forgive and forgive and forgive. But respect her? Respect *this?* I don't know how.

"I do, I do," I whimper. "I do respect you." My heart is shattering into pieces. I've done it wrong. I was meant to fix everything but, somehow, I did it wrong.

"You're so ungrateful!" She carries on screaming at me. "What did I do to deserve a daughter like you? You treat me like a slave, expecting me to cook and clean and buy you things. I bought you four Easter eggs, you know..."

Tears sting my eyes. I've ruined it. Ruined everything.

"You have no idea what I've been through. No idea what my parents did to me..."

She starts to tell me.

Unspeakable things.

The kind of things that break a person.

She spits it out in a disjointed, incoherent babble. Incomplete fragments. Wisps of memories. Eyes accusing, as though I am to blame for the torment she carries. As though she expected me to save her, to heal her, and instead I am a disappointment. I have made her life worse by having my own needs. I am selfish. Hateful. Uncaring.

As she carries on screaming, RoboCat drowns the world out and my head goes light and dizzy as though I am floating out of my body. I can see my mother's enraged face but her words seem so far away. I feel like I'm about to pass out. I kind of want to, actually. Sad Cat feels this would be a very good moment to die.

A picture comes to my mind. It's of me as a little girl, standing at the front door with my arms spread wide. Tears stream down my cheeks with the desperate desire to stop my mother from leaving. *I love you. I love you. I love you. I love you. I'm sorry. I'm sorry. I'm sorry. I'm sorry. Please, please, please, please don't go.* Then, a question, *I love you? I love you? I love you? I love you?*

The tears keep flowing but my emotions drain away. I feel numb. Empty. Nothing.

The picture in my mind widens. I see that little girl who learnt how to save the world by the age of seven, who never rebelled or complained, who absorbed the shame of those who were meant to protect her, who believed the lie that it was all her fault. Standing in the doorway, begging, *"Please don't go!"* and promising to try harder.

A realisation strikes my heart like lightning and for one blazing moment I have clarity.

She does not love me.

My whole life, I have done all I could to never let her leave. Believing I could save her, if only I was good enough. Trusting she was sorry really but didn't know how to tell me. Daring to believe that she loved me deep down and that I was selfish for feeling sad.

But it turns out there is nothing deep down.

She does not love me.

THIS is my mother.

As she rages on, I make a choice.

In my mind's eye, I see myself stepping away from the door. *I let you go, Mum. I will not beg you to stay. For the first time in my life, I let you leave.*

Then I get up and walk out of her room.

****

ACT THREE

In which Cat creates a castle, writes a letter and puts the universe together.

****

* 41 * RoboCat gets a train

The thing about broken hearts is that you don't just die as soon as they shatter. You somehow have to go on existing, even as the pain is bleeding into every bit of you.

Exeter won the football match. Their first win in ages. My dad and brother arrive home just before eleven, happier than I've heard them in years. No idea that I've set off a bomb.

I lie in the dark, tears gushing like rivers and pooling on my pillow, as I cling to Monkey Bear.

My father trots up the stairs, shouting that they've won. It's hard not to feel guilty. I hear muffled voices in my parents' bedroom followed by the sound of my mother sobbing. My dad's voice rises and falls in baffled and desperate tones. "She wouldn't have meant..."

"She did! ...Horrible... Can't believe it..."

My door opens and I quickly turn to the side and breathe loudly, pretending to be asleep. My dad sniffs in the doorway before closing the door again.

The next morning, the broken pieces of my heart are so sharp and heavy in my chest that it hurts to sit up.

My mother spends the morning locked in her room. For once, I am not desperate for her to emerge. I intend to stay in bed all day but my dad walks in before lunchtime.

"What happened?" he whispers.

"I was trying to be honest. I thought it would help."

"Are you crazy?"

Evidently, I am.

Crazy for believing that she loved me.

Crazy for believing change was possible.

And crazy for believing that the problem was *me*.

She does not love me, I remind myself in case Holy Cat is tempted to go and beg my mother for forgiveness. *She does not love me. And I let her go.*

I stare at the wall, tightly gripping Monkey Bear.

When I was little, back when Monkey Bear had a teddy bear's head, my father used to hold him by the neck and pretend he could speak.

"I know it's you talking, Daddy!" I would squeal. "I can see your lips moving?"

"Are you completely sure?" my father would reply with a glint his eye.

"Not *completely* sure," I would say. Because secretly I wanted my teddy to be alive. I wanted to believe in magic. I wanted to believe lies.

"I can't cope." My dad starts to cry.

I dig into my thigh with my spare hand. Nipping and nipping until my leg stings and I start to feel numb.

"Maybe you could try talking to her? Explain that it was a misunderstanding. Please?" When I ignore him, he whimpers and shuts my door. As soon as he's gone, I let go of the tears I've been holding and weep into my pillow.

I remember something my mother once said.

I was standing at the door crying because I didn't want her to leave. "I need you," I had cried.

"Don't be stupid," she'd replied. "It's time to grow up."

Time to grow up.

I am too old for talking teddies.

Too old for magic.

Too old for lies.

I feel Sad Cat spiralling into despair. A huge shriek is threatening to come screaming out of me. I shut my eyes and squeeze her away. And then RoboCat arises and I pack my suitcase. I go through all my cupboards, rifling through every single possession and pulling out anything special. My first doll; the one with the lazy eye. My old diaries. My keepsake box with old photos and poems and the beetle from Aidan. A rock I painted in primary school. A troll necklace that I used to wear for luck. A set of Russian dolls decorated as princesses.

I fill an extra bag with clothes and old toys. Then I pause over my collection of shells from Exmouth beach. Too many. My moon lamp. Too big. My stripy rug. Replaceable. I can't take everything. I hoist my backpack onto my back and drag my bags out of my room, pausing at the door. I might never see this room again. I close the door, shutting in my childhood forever. Then I drag everything down the stairs and walk into the living room where my father is crying.

"I'm getting a train back to Forest Hall," I announce. "Are you going to drop me off at the station or should I get a bus?"

"What are you talking about? You're not going back today!"

"There's stuff going on at campus," I lie. "I need to get back for it." I know my dad will find it easier if he can convince himself I'm leaving for another reason.

"What stuff? What do you mean? Don't be silly—"

I put a hand up. "I'm going and that's final. Do you want to take me to the station or not? Oh, never mind. I'll get the bus." I start to drag my belongings back into the hallway. I have no idea which bus to get. But I'll do it if I have to. Or I'll walk. All the way back to Forest Hall. There's a courage that comes when you want to die. You don't care what happens so you're free to take risks.

Still, I am relieved when my father stops me at the door and says, "I'll take you. Please, just stop for a moment."

"The train is on the hour. If we go now, I can get the next one."

"Cat, please. I'll take you after lunch. Just stay for lunch. Don't go like this. I can't cope with it."

But I won't be moved with tears or bargaining. "I'm going now. Right now."

"Alright... Alright..." Huge tears roll down his nose. "Alright, I'll take you."

I drag my stuff to the car. "It's fine. I don't need help. I can carry everything myself." I heave it all into the boot.

I pretend not to notice my father sobbing and shaking as he gets into the driver's seat and starts the engine. I take one last glance at our house as we turn out of our street.

Goodbye Mother.

I turn ABBA on at full volume and close my eyes.

Aidan is out for the day. I feel a lump in my throat. How will I explain this to him? When will I see him again?

Don't think about it. RoboCat holds steady.

My dad cries all the way to the train station, begging me to change my mind. Warning me of what will happen. Blaming me if he dies or if she leaves. I block it all out. It's background noise. Not my life. We pull into the station and RoboCat says curtly, "Thank you for the lift. Goodbye."

He unbuckles his seatbelt.

"No need to get out. I can get my bags myself."

He gets out anyway. Trying one last time to deter me. Or, failing that, to smother me with a hug.

I prise his fingers off me. "Don't hug me, please."

His face contorts and he blubs, "You're horrible."

I pick up my bags. "Bye."

"Call when you get back. Okay? I love you? *I love you?*"

"Love you too." I don't mean it. I don't believe in love.

I don't look back. I march into the station and buy a ticket and locate the right platform and drag my bags to a carriage and find a seat on the train. And I don't let myself cry until the train is moving and it's too late to change my mind.

Zachary sent me a text last night to ask how things had gone. I didn't have the energy to reply so I do it now.

'Awfully. I'm getting a train back to Forest Hall.'

Seeing it in writing makes it suddenly real. RoboCat's tough wall cracks and I feel dizzy.

Zachary tries calling. Tears bubble out of my eyes. I want to die. *Stop it.*

I put my phone away without answering. Then I curl up and try to sleep. A picture pops into my head, like a movie in my mind. My mum is standing in a field and all the parts of me are around her, wearing red. One by one, we run away. RoboCat leads the charge, emotionless and sprinting. Angry Cat doesn't look back. Silly Cat and Scaredy Cat are holding hands. Sad Cat can't stop sobbing. Even Creative Cat is there. She puts her hands in red paint and makes handprints on my mother's dress before running to join the others. We run and run and run. And then the picture fades away.

I rub my eyes as the train stops at Taunton. A little girl bounds onto the carriage. "Mummy, let's sit here!" she squeals, bouncing into the seat across the aisle.

"Alright, Darling." A blonde mummy follows the girl into the seat, puts an arm around her, and offers her a snack.

Sad Cat wails in my head. *I want my mummy.*

Except not *my* mummy. A different one. One that would love me and see me and hold me. I want to feel special. I want to feel safe. The broken shards of my heart dig into my chest.

There is no love like a mother's love.

I choke back the tears and turn away from the lucky little girl and her mummy. Then I squeeze my eyes shut and try a prayer, the most honest prayer I have ever prayed. *God, if you are real, please help me. I don't want my life any more. You can have it. Please just help me.*

Nothing happens. Silence. Heaven is empty. Of course. It's Easter Saturday. The day that God is silent and everything good is dead in the ground.

I am taunted by the girl's shrieks of "Look, a horse, Mummy!" and, "Can I have a drink, Mummy?" all the way to Birmingham New Street. Sad Cat stares as they leave the train. The little girl skips carelessly down the platform as though she takes being loved for granted.

The train moves off again. Sad Cat goes to sleep and RoboCat resumes the journey, feeling and thinking very little as the train chugs on, pulling into Wakefield Westgate just before six o'clock. As I step out of the train station, I am relieved to discover that I recognise where I am. I'm able to find the bus stop with ease and, half an hour later, I step off the bus and onto the soft, steady soil of Forest Hall. The whole campus is empty. Everyone's at home with their families, enjoying the holidays and eating chocolate.

Inside my room, RoboCat crumples. I drop to the floor and weep. I have never cried so much. It's a loud, wailing, screeching kind of cry. The kind of crying you can only do when there's nobody around for miles and miles. The kind of crying that leaves you breathless and aching and squirming and pulling your hair out because you have no hope and nobody loves you in the entire world and you're all alone and you can't remember ever not being alone.

Time stands still. I cry forever.

Suddenly, there's a knock on my door.

I freeze, momentarily afraid.

"Hey, Cat. It's me."

I sprint to my door and throw it open. "Zachary!"

"I thought you might need this." He holds his arms out.

"Might need what?"

"This." He wraps his arms around me.

* 42 * Sad Cat is a freezer

"I'm sorry I didn't get you an Easter egg." I break the silence with this confession.

Zachary has been sitting quietly, a packet of crisps between us. "Don't worry. I didn't get you one either."

I still feel bad about it. That's the problem when you think it's your job to save the world. You feel responsible for things that don't even matter. "I would've done," I insist. "I usually remember that sort of thing." I think of the four giant eggs from my mother which I deliberately left behind.

"I'm really not bothered," he says carelessly. He goes on staring at me.

I force a shrug. "I'm fine, by the way." My voice cracks and shatters my mask.

"Do you want to talk about what happened?"

Do I want to talk about it? What's the right answer? Holy Cat feels like I should respectfully decline in order to spare him my emotions. But Sad Cat is desperate, utterly desperate to speak. So I recount it all to him. My futile attempt at connection. My mother's furious outburst. Her accusations. My inability to explain myself. My decision to leave. To be the one who finally walks away. I feel relief and embarrassment at the untameable tears that accompany my words.

"I'm so sorry, Cat," he says when I'm done.

I wipe my face and try to shrug it all away. "It's okay. It's just realising... She doesn't love me." I try to say this matter-of-factly, willing RoboCat back into the driving seat. "She never really loved me. That's all."

Zachary doesn't say anything and I avoid his gaze because the pity in his eyes makes me feel so small and ugly.

My phone rings. It's my father. I ignore it.

"I'm so stupid. I thought I was meant to go through a door. I thought God was going to do something nice."

Zachary inhales sharply, as though about to speak, then reconsiders. "You're not stupid," he says finally.

"I *am* stupid. I used to collect paperclips... Look..." I pull my collection out of one of my bags. "So stupid. Don't know why I brought them..." Sad Cat is unsteady. If I'm not careful, I will listen to the nagging voice that says I am selfish and have done a horrible thing. The voice that sounds an awful lot like my mother. I try to summon up Thunder Cat. *I don't care. I don't need anyone. I am Catrina Carla. Independent. Self-sufficient. Strong. An orphan.*

A tear slides down my nose. Feelings are horrible. It was much easier when I was RoboCat, calmly packing my suitcase. I wish I could cut my heart out and stamp away all emotion.

"I care too much," I mutter.

Zachary keeps staring at me. "The problem isn't that you care. What would you be if you didn't?"

I change the subject. "Shall we play a game?"

"If you want."

"I don't know. I don't know what I want."

My phone beeps with a text from my father.

'Are you back yet, Cat? Worried sick about you. Please let me know if you're alright.'

I grit my teeth and reply, *'I'm fine. Got back fine.'*

Then I switch my phone off.

"I managed to get a child's fare on the bus," I remark, smiling proudly. "The driver thought I was under sixteen, even though I was going to university. It's probably because I'm funny looking."

"You're not funny looking!"

"Course I am! Nobody ever knows where I'm from."

"That doesn't mean..." Zachary gives an incredulous laugh. "You see yourself in a distorted mirror, Cat. Like the ones you get in a funfair. You don't see yourself at all. You see a mess where other people see beauty."

"What people?" I scoff.

"Me. That's what I see. Somebody amazing... A warrior who never gives up..."

"Don't be so weird. You don't fancy me, do you?"

"You know I don't! You're my little sister."

"Little! Your birthday isn't till July, is it? Mine's in May. I'm older."

"You're still my little sister." He pats me on the head. "Maturity isn't measured by the number of times you've been round the sun. Anyway, I care about you. You're my best friend and I want to protect you. Like a big brother."

I frown. As flattered as I am at his offer of being my big brother, it's an older sister that I want.

"Alright, twins," he concedes. "Is that better?"

"We're not related at all, Zachary." My voice cracks. "We have different parents. Different backgrounds. Different everything. We share nothing at all."

"That's not true. We share this... Forest Hall. The memories we're making. This moment. This packet of crisps."

Tears are threatening to spill again. Damn emotion.

"We're a unit," Zachary continues, twisting his face to try to make me laugh. "We go together. Like a fridge-freezer."

"What?"

"I'm the fridge."

"Why?"

"It's bigger."

I blink at him. *What is he talking about? Best friend? Twins? A unit? A fridge-freezer?* I lose myself as a multitude of thoughts hurtle through my brain like trains on crooked tracks destined for a collision.

I really should have brought him an Easter egg.
He wears that yellow hoody all the time.
He came all the way here for me.
I don't believe in love.
I'm hungry.
I want my mummy.
I have no mummy.
Perhaps I'm not funny looking.
I should have brought my moon lamp.
Did I do the right thing?
Let's just play a game and pretend to be fine.
I'm all alone.
Except I'm not.
He's quite funny actually.
I want a hug.
I've never had a best friend before.

"Fine. You can be the fridge." I say. "The freezer's cooler."

* 43 * Fun Cat has gone away

The nights are horrible. Baby Cat wails and Sad Cat sobs and Angry Cat rages and there is no peaceful part of me at all. I toss and turn for hours on end, alternating between talking to Jodie in My Head and crying inconsolably. And, every night, after I have cried all the tears that I can, there is the stillness at the end of the world.

But the days are alright. I suppose. I'm not sure. I'm feeling pretty numb, actually. Even when I'm laughing. Or beating Zachary at a game. It's as though Thunder Cat has a bitter edge to her. Sometimes I feel invincible. Like I can run along the wall beside the lake without fear of falling off. Because, in the words of Peter Pan, dying would be a grand adventure.

Zachary and I go on many walks. We have a picnic under the weeping willow. We bounce in Fairy Land. We play a new board game called *'Flying Monkeys.'* We raid the vending machines. We watch a film or three. It's all alright.

I unpack my bags and place my treasures in a line along my shelf; my doll with the lazy eye, my keepsake box, my rock, my troll necklace, my Russian dolls, my paperclip collection. I keep my old diaries hidden at the back of the wardrobe where nobody will see them. I don't even want to see them.

I sent my brother a text: *'Sorry I left without saying goodbye.'* He responded with a thumbs up. Typical. He probably didn't even realise I had gone. He won't miss me.

Our housemates return. Nobody notices that I am not the same person that left at the end of last term. Dotty Jay and Annie rescue a hedgehog from a building site and keep it in the kitchen as a pet until Bob the housing officer finds out and goes berserk. Rory replaces the rope on his tree swing. Mad Jo makes some earrings out of her baby teeth. Shay and the dancers get completely wasted out on the pull in Wakefield. I think Shay and Wes have broken up. Or perhaps they never officially got together in the first place. I don't know. Who cares.

Fun Cat is definitely in hiding. And Sad Cat just won't shut up. Even when I'm pretending to be fine with Annie or Dotty Jay, she's jabbering away in my ears, threatening to betray me with a stray tear or choked-up voice. There's a crater of sadness lodged in my chest, making it hard to breathe. Perhaps I will die. I wonder what people will say about me after I'm gone.

"You'd never know she was feeling so sad."

"She was weird."

"She was ungrateful."

"It's always the quiet ones."

Elle needs someone to listen to her because her parents' divorce is final. She accosts me in the hallway one morning on my way to the toilet. "Divorce is done. Worst Easter ever."

I switch into Holy Cat. "How are you doing?"

She sniffs. "Feeling pretty rubbish."

I tilt my head to the side. "I'm so sorry."

"Dad's been sending me photos of his new flat. He said I can visit him any time. But I don't know if I want to, you know?"

I want to wee. Leave me alone. Stop dumping on me. I need to wee. Let me wee.

But Holy Cat just gives a sympathetic nod and asks more questions. When Elle's done and I'm spent, I creep back to my room and crawl under my covers and give a silent shriek.

I don't care about anyone or anything. No matter how much Holy Cat pretends. I am stuck on mute in black and white while everyone else lives in colour. And I am plagued by the accusation that this is all my fault for thinking I could make things okay by talking about my feelings.

I wish I had never gone through that door.

* 44 * Sad Cat needs some attention

I'm devastated. Jodie has had a haircut. She looks nothing like herself. It's way too short. Jodie in My Head would never opt for such a style. I feel completely disorientated when I see her at the refectory.

"Hey, Cat!"

I've been talking to Jodie in My Head non-stop. It makes seeing Jodie in Real Life far more painful and bewildering. Especially when she pops up looking like *that.*

I clutch my lemon mousse and force a smile, pretending I am pleased to see her but not obsessed. Not thinking about her day and night and trying to find her on FriendWeb.

"Oh, hey, Jodie." I take my place in the queue, my neck feeling hot as I turn my back on her. I immediately kick myself for scurrying away so quickly. I should've pretended to be browsing the salad bar. Or followed her to the hot food section.

As luck would have it, Jodie picks up a plate of lasagne from Windy Wendy before joining the queue behind me. "How's it going?" She nods towards my lemon mousse. "I hope you're eating well. I know what it's like to be a student!"

I'm thrilled that our interaction isn't over and angle myself slightly to face her. Her new haircut bobs about under her ears, screaming at me, *'You don't know me at all!'*

Of course I'm not eating well. But it feels attention seeking to admit to that.

A memory stirs. The time my mum was gone for a week and I staged a hunger strike until she returned. Sad Cat hoped my dad would pause his own grief and tend to mine. Just for a moment. One meal, maybe. But instead he wrung his hands and said, "Perhaps it's a good thing. Perhaps she'll come home if she finds out you're dying."

Before that day, I had considered becoming anorexic like Avery. My mum said she was doing it for attention. But when your world is falling apart you kind of need some attention, don't you? My parents never seemed to think so. With my dad's response came The Big Realisation: It will never be about me. I could cry. I could starve myself. I could probably even die. My mother would still take centre stage.

Jodie keeps smiling at me.

I wonder what it would be like to open up and tell her everything. But where would I even start? My throat tightens. Sad Cat is on the brink, ready to break down. I want to let go and have a good cry. But what if I can't turn the tap off? I don't want to ruin her boots with my mess. Maybe I could—

Shut up. Angry Cat wants to keep everyone out. It is incredibly vital that nobody is allowed anywhere near me.

Still, a part of me feels like this entire episode with my parents would be okay— worth it, even— if only I had Jodie. If only she would say, "Hey, Cat. Do you want to come and hang out with me?" Or, "Hey, Cat. I really want to be your big sister." Or, "Hey, Cat. Can I give you a hug?"

Don't be so stupid!

I know I'm needy with Jodie in My Head but I'm sure Jodie in Real Life wouldn't like it. I expect she would be repulsed if she knew how much I thought about her.

Don't cry! Don't cry! Pretend to be fine.

I try to think of something to say. I could ask what the next module is. But I know full well it's Theatre of the Absurd. I've already read all the books on the reading list and checked out several more from the library. I could ask where she got her boots from. But they're not really my style and she might think I'm mocking her. I could compliment her on her new haircut but I might burst into tears. I could offer to pay for her lasagne or make a joke about the lemon mousse. I could ask whether she wants to have lunch with me.

Loser!

I quickly wipe the corner of my eye. "I'm okay," I say.

I want her to ask. I want her to pry. I want her to read the signs, the clues in my eyes. But she doesn't. Nobody ever does. Perhaps I truly am a fantastic actress after all.

* 45 * Angry Cat writes a poem

The evening before the new term starts, I turn my phone back on and, within minutes, it starts to ring. The word *'Home'* dances across the screen and, for the briefest moment, Silly Cat feels a pang of hope. Perhaps it's my mum. Perhaps she's had time to calm down. Perhaps she's ready to reconnect. Perhaps some of what I said has slipped through the fortress of her heart and taken root.

But no. It's my father. His voice is terse, as though he's speaking to somebody unreasonable. "Ah, you're there now. I've been trying to ring all week... Are you feeling *alright?*" He speaks slowly and loudly.

"I'm okay."

He mistakes my coolness for carelessness. "Well I'm not okay at all. Your mum hasn't stopped crying. She says you don't love her. After everything she's done for you. She took you everywhere when you were little: to the library, swimming, to feed the ducks..." He repeats accusations that she's thrown at me a thousand times. *No idea how hard she tries. Never seem to appreciate anything. Always keeping them at a distance.*

I feel the physical sensation of my heart breaking. Agony. Like a knife twisting inside. I change the subject. There are things I've been desperate to ask. "Were my grandparents healers?"

"What? You know they were civil servants."

"Not your parents. *Hers.*" And because I'm too frustrated to censor myself, I add, "Did they do sacrifices and try to get magic powers."

He splutters down the line. "Don't ask such silly questions."

"Is that a yes or a no?"

"I don't know. Does it matter? It's nothing to do with you."

"It's everything to do with me," I snap. There are secrets that belong to me. Heirlooms with my name on. Inherited debt. Their blood running through me.

"I don't *know*," he says again. "You know how secretive your mother is. That's not why she's upset, is it? You didn't go asking about her past?"

"Course not." I clench my fists. "I didn't mean to upset her. I was trying to help us get closer." I feel a surge of courage as I add, "You *know* what she's like. You *know* it wasn't my fault. You do know that, don't you? Why don't you stand up for me?"

He sighs. "It was a daft misunderstanding. I wish you hadn't overreacted."

"Overreacted?" I spit the word out. "What should I have done? Say sorry even though I was the one being yelled at? Beg for forgiveness? Pretend to be fine?"

"*I don't know!* I don't understand it at all." He stops and sobs. "I'm sure I'll get cancer with all this stress."

"Can't you even *try* to see things from my perspective?" I plead. "Can't you think about me for one tiny moment?"

"Oh, of course! Nobody thinks about me! Nobody realises how suicidal this is all making me!"

"Shut up!" Angry Cat roars into action. "Stop playing the victim and blaming me for your own issues." My dad whimpers but I keep shouting. "I am not selfish! I am not ungrateful!" Tears scream down my face. "It's you. Both of you! Not me! I am not the problem!"

"Cat! Why are you being so nasty? Why are you shouting at me? None of this is my fault!"

I can't stop shaking. My head feels hot and heavy and I want to smash something. Suddenly, I hear the stairwell door open and Holy Cat jumps in alarm. *What if somebody hears me?*

I am RoboCat. Feelings melt away. Nothing can touch me.

"Cat? Are you still there."

"Mmm."

"You know we love you. Let's not be silly."

I sniff deeply to stop Angry Cat resurfacing. "I have never felt loved by you."

"What? Don't be ridiculous! You know we—"

"You *think* you love me. But I have never *felt* loved by you. That's how I feel. You can't tell me I'm wrong. I'm not lying."

"I didn't say you were lying... I just... Of course we..." He pauses to digest my words. Or perhaps to erase them. "I know you've got a lot on your mind at the moment," he says finally. "University and exams and things."

"We don't have any exams. It's practical work and essays."

"Right... You know we're always here for you if you need anything. And we *do* love you."

I gaze out of my window at the hills beyond the mansion.

"I'll put some money in your account as usual. I'll do it tomorrow on my way to the supermarket."

"You can stop sending money. I don't need it."

"Don't be silly! Of course you need it."

I press my head against the window.

"I'll let you go now. I love you... Cat? I love you? *I love you?*"

"Love you. Goodbye."

I hang up and change the caller ID from *'Home'* to *'Mr and Mrs Berger.'* They will never be my home again.

I stare out of the window, ignoring the streaming hot tears that tickle my cheeks.

Don't feel. Don't feel anything.

Suddenly Angry Cat takes hold and, without thinking, I slam my head against my wardrobe.

It's wrong to be angry
You're wrong to be angry
Don't be angry, they said
It's bad to be angry
You're bad to be angry
Hide it till you're dead.

* 46 * Squashed Cat is pushed to the limit

The first week of the Summer term has been all about endurance and pushing ourselves to the limit.

On Monday, Jodie made us run around the room all lesson, yelling at us to go faster whenever anybody stopped. Pranjal was heaving and I was afraid he might have an asthma attack. I'm not sure how I'd cope if my favourite person in the world got thrown into jail for manslaughter.

On Tuesday, we had to perform angry monologues. Jodie picked on Donna and made her do the same few lines over and over. She kept saying, "That's not angry, show me angry…" until Donna flipped and burst into tears and shrieked her lines.

I felt really sorry for her until Jodie gave her a huge hug and exclaimed, "Well done! You did it!" as though Donna was the world's best actress and then I felt all jealous and daydreamed for the rest of the day about Jodie shouting at me instead.

On Wednesday, Jodie put us into pairs and had us stand nose to nose staring into each other's eyes for a full fifteen minutes. I was paired with Viktor. I stared at his grey eyes and tried to zone out but then Jodie said something which hurt my brain: "You only ever get this close to someone when you're about to kill them or kiss them." I felt sick when it was over.

On Thursday, we did trust exercises which included walking around the village in blindfolds and trusting our partners not to let us fall into the lake or get hit by a bus.

Friday morning.

We've barely sat down when Jodie says, "Right then. Theatre that shocks. Theatre that pushes the boundaries… Think blood, sex, violence. I want to see you naked."

I am horrified. Jodie in My Head would never say such a thing. In a sudden blinding instant, I see perfectly clearly that all of my daydreams about her loving me or revealing herself as my long lost sister are an utter delusion.

"I'm speaking metaphorically, obviously," Jodie adds with a grin. "But this is the time to be brave."

I sit on my hands, feeling my body shrinking into myself as Jodie puts us into groups. My throat constricts. My heart screams. *Don't cry. Don't cry.*

Then Jodie leads us through campus, depositing each group at a different location. Our final performance of the year will be a site specific piece. In other words, performed at a location on campus rather than in any of the theatres. Everybody is giddy like we're on a school trip, even though we are literally just walking round campus.

As she dumps each group, Jodie announces, "This will be your home for the next four weeks."

Elle's group are left outside the library, Pranjal's group get the giant copper man, and another group has a wooden sculpture near the bat cave. I feel sorry for Heidi's group who will be spending the next month wading in the lake.

My group is dropped off last. Silly Cat imagines that Jodie orchestrated it so that I'd be with her the longest. But the rest of me is still reeling from the realisation that I am a deluded fool. I am not special to Jodie. We will never be related. We won't even be friends. There is no long lost big sister out there looking for me. I am alone. I will always be alone. RoboCat comes forward to blank this revelation out so that I can maintain the appearance of normal.

I had hoped for Fairy Land but we've been abandoned in an area known as the quarry. It's basically a patch of mud surrounded on three sides by a jagged cliff. I've walked here several times with Zachary and it's nothing special. What's Jodie thinking?

On autopilot, Silly Cat starts a conversation with Jodie in My Head.

"Oh it's the best place of all!" Jodie in My Head is grinning.

Don't! I dig my nails into my hands and shoo Silly Cat away.

I'm with Donna, Rose, Kimberley and Will. Another lapse of judgement on Jodie's part. Why has she put me with all the loudmouths?

Because she doesn't care about you, Angry Cat taunts.

My chest tightens as I battle to keep Squashed Cat at bay.

After the usual grumbling that greets each new module, we gather on some rocks to discuss ideas.

"We should get a bathtub," says Donna. "And fill it with red paint so it looks like blood. We could be sitting in it when the audience arrives."

"Where would we get a bathtub?" Rose asks. "Not being funny but I'm skint. I can't afford to buy anything for this piece."

"They might have one in props?" suggests Kimberley.

I stare at the ground. I have watched over ninety performances since arriving at Forest Hall, RoboCat making it my goal to attend every presentation put on by the first, second and third year Acting students, as well as every performance by visiting theatre companies. I know for a fact there are two bathtubs in the props department. What's more, bathtubs filled with fake blood have featured in no less than seven performances put on by the third years. It's a bit of a thing, apparently.

"Oh!" Will punches the air as though he's had a brainwave. "We could get some entrails from the butcher. You know, all the bits they don't sell. Like intestines and things."

There's a pause, then Donna says, "And rub it on our faces?"

Play it Cool Cat is about to attempt a laugh but is interrupted by Kimberley who says, "Would anybody have a problem with being naked, because I totally wouldn't mind."

Donna scans the landscape. "We could pop up from behind that rock."

"Holding intestines," adds Will.

I squirm. "I don't really want..."

"Oh, I've got it!" Kimberley leaps up. "We could be behind a screen and pass brains and intestines between us. The audience would only see our silhouettes so it would look like a real body being ripped apart!"

Jodie reappears during this conversation and watches as Kimberley and Donna discuss the possibility of erecting a giant screen between the cliffs. It takes all my energy not to cry as the person I long for most in the world sits beside me.

"We're thinking of starting off naked behind a screen," Kimberley tells Jodie eagerly. "And we might see if the butchers can give us some stuff for free. Brains and lungs and things."

"It would look like a human body being pulled apart," Rose chips in.

"We could be cannibals!" Kimberley squeals.

I shoot Jodie a quick glance. Her usually stern demeanour looks more open than usual. She actually seems impressed with Kimberley's idea.

"But what would..." I try to speak but nobody hears me.

They talk about screens and nudity and whether it would be okay to throw a bloody heart at the audience.

What would be the point? Angry Cat screams in my head. *What would be the point in naked silhouettes and blood and entrails? Where's the story? The purpose? The meaning?*

"It could be a sacrifice," Will says darkly. "We could have candles all over the cliffs and the audience could walk in to a ceremony."

I gulp and look again to Jodie, silently begging her to intervene.

"Keep going, you guys," she says as she stands up. "Some good starting points here. I want to see your first two minutes on Monday morning." And with a nod and a wave, she is gone.

I might be sick. *Some good starting points? Who IS she?*

Squashed Cat takes over as my group keep talking. At some point, Kimberley asks if I'm okay with getting naked and, when I shake my head, makes a joke about how sheltered I am.

I feel like I'm about to be eaten by the cliffs.

I want to run away before I am sacrificed.

Nowhere is safe.

Worst of all, the morning's realisation smashes through RoboCat's defences and hits me again and again like a meteorite crashing to earth: *Jodie is a total stranger. I don't know her at all. She will never be my sister. Never fix the wounds from my mother. Never love me the way I daydream about. I'm an idiot for talking to Jodie in My Head. She doesn't exist. She never did and never will.*

* 47 * Cat out of Hell

I look in the mirror and I don't know who I am.

How did I get so old?

I never wanted to grow up.

How do I keep myself safe?

Silly Cat still wants to play mermaids.

My world is topsy turvy. When I was a child, complete strangers would remark that I possessed a maturity beyond my years. Now that I am pretty much an adult, everybody says I am sheltered. Naïve. Immature.

But I am Catrina Carla, destined for fame and then oblivion. Perhaps I should just let everything go. Run out roaring, get naked, rub entrails on my face. Who cares anyway? What am I so afraid of? Why am I trying to be good?

My phone beeps. I turn away from my alien reflection.

'Cat, something's wrong with Dad.'

My brother. He never texts me.

I leap onto my bed, sitting cross-legged as I tap out a rapid reply. *'What's happened? Are you OK?'*

'He's losing it. He started crying because the printer wasn't working and now he says he wants to die. What do I do?'

My heart melts. That's not a metaphor. I think it really does. I feel it seeping into my chest.

Years ago, my brother jumped on me when I was in the deep end of a swimming pool. I floundered under the effort of keeping us both afloat and we splashed about in terror until a stranger came and lifted us out. Even though we might've drowned without the intervention of this good Samaritan, I beat my fists against him, yelling, "Leave my brother alone!"

I was my brother's keeper. I tried so hard to protect him. Be strong for him. Save him. And now I have left him.

I hold my breath before replying, *'He's always been like that. Just leave him to it.'* I hit 'send' before adding, *'I'm sorry.'*

I stare out of my window while I await Aidan's response. I can feel Sad Cat and Squashed Cat in the hole which was once my heart but I drag RoboCat to the surface and try to zone out.

My phone beeps.

'I hate you Cat. You've broken our family.'

Aidan never used to worry because it would always be okay. But now it isn't. I've stopped playing the game.

For one millisecond, RoboCat holds the fort and I feel nothing. Then everything breaks. Despair erupts and I jump up and start hurling things around my room. I toss my phone to the floor, slam my fists into my desk, kick my chair into the wall. Baby Cat starts screaming and I punch the sides of my head, trying to shut her up. I want her to die.

A counsel is taking place in my head.

Make her stop. Make her stop crying! I can't cope! I can't cope! I can't cope!

Then Angry Cat says loudly, *We need to get rid of her.*

A cool, calm voice agrees. *Yes. That's what we need to do.*

You can't! Scaredy Cat quivers. *You can't kill Baby Cat! You would die too.*

I've got my life planned out! Thunder Cat pleads. *I'm gonna be a famous actress. Let me be a famous actress. Then we can end it all!*

But the cool, calm voice inside tells me that death is unavoidable. That nobody loves me. That I'd better do it quickly. Baby Cat wails even louder.

I charge across my room and stumble into the empty corridor where I tear the butterfly poster off my door. What an idiot. I am not a butterfly. I will never be happy or beautiful. Nobody sees. Nobody cares.

I walk in a daze to the alcove and throw open Dotty Jay's cupboard. I know what I am looking for. She's offered them to me before. Paracetamol. They will take the pain away.

The whole lot, the voice whispers. *Take them all.*

I grab a glass from the counter. Bizarrely, I have the presence of mind to wash it first, as though it would be vulgar to take an overdose with water from a dirty glass.

Tears obscure my vision as I fumble to open the packet.

My chest is pounding and Scaredy Cat begs, *No!*

Holy Cat warns me that I'll go to Hell.

Silly Cat is weeping.

Pain is not forever, another voice whispers.

I ignore any hint of fear or reason as I pop the first pill out and put it to my lips.

Stop! Scaredy Cat cries. *Stop!*

But I can't stop. I've tried. I've tried everything. I even tried God but he ignored me.

I shove the pill into my mouth and take a large gulp of water. My head spins as I swallow it. I feel a momentary wave of celebration. I can swallow pills!

I take the next one. Then the next.

Stop! Stop!

I can't I can't.

Keep going. Keep going.

I slide to the floor, shaking and weeping. I want to stop. I want to carry on. I want to live. I want to die. I want to be rescued. I want to be left alone.

I hear my dad's voice in my head. *"Don't waste them."*

And my mother. *"It's time to grow up."*

Stop! Stop!

Suddenly the door to our floor swings open. I lay face-down on the lino and curl into a ball. I feel numb, dumb, stupid, as somebody's footsteps come towards me.

"Cat? Are you alright?" It's Elle.

Elle! I have been such a pillar of strength to troubled Elle. Now revealed as a fraud. I'm a mess. A dangerous mess.

"Cat? What's going on?"

Voices within me tell me to get up, stop faking it, do something! Baby Cat is still crying. Holy Cat is utterly appalled. RoboCat is calmly reciting Mama Octopus lyrics.

'Just one slash and I'll be gone, one slip to oblivion...'

But I can't do anything. The me on the floor has accepted defeat. I want to switch into Play it Cool Cat and ask Elle how she's coping with her parents' divorce but Cat out of Hell screams that it's over. The façade is over. *I can't. I can't. I can't. I can't do this any more.*

* 48 * RoboCat lets it go

Some people say that when you get to Heaven, everyone you loved and lost on earth comes running out to greet you. That is very little comfort for me because there wouldn't be anybody.

Still, maybe it's always sunny in Heaven. Maybe the skies are filled with rainbows. Maybe you can eat whatever you like and swim without tiring and fly through the stars and speak with the animals. Maybe Heaven is a thousand times better than earth and we are fools for clinging to this mortal life so tightly.

But before Heaven, there is death. What's that like? We are often shocked when somebody dies, as though a dead person is somebody to be pitied. But we all have to go through it. What if it feels nice, like stepping into a warm bath or floating out of your body and into eternal bliss? What if angels arrive to escort you to your heavenly home? Or does it depend on how you lived? On what you did and what you believed?

Maybe it hurts like crazy. Like a caterpillar turning to mush inside its cocoon, melting as though consumed by a mighty fire, eaten alive, drowning and gasping, with no idea of the beauty that may or may not come in the morning.

Or maybe there's nothing. No Heaven or Hell, no thinking or feeling, like the reverse of being born.

Either way, it's of no consequence right now. You can't die from three paracetamol. All that happens is you feel like an idiot as you scrape yourself off the floor and go to bed alone.

I hear muttering outside my door the next morning. I roll over and check the time before sitting bolt upright. I'm supposed to be meeting Donna, Rose, Kimberley and Will in Wakefield in less than half an hour. We're going to beg for entrails from the butchers and rifle through the skips at the back of the supermarkets before going back to Wintergates to devise the first two minutes of our Theatre of the Absurd piece.

RoboCat leaps out of bed and dashes to get ready. I can't be late. RoboCat is never late. Never misses a class or an appointment. I whip my curtains open in time to see the bus chugging up the hill. *No!*

"Cat?" There's a light knock on my door. "Are you awake?"

I run to let Zachary in. "I'm late! I've missed the bus! I need to see if someone can give me a lift to Wakefield."

Squashed Cat is about to hyperventilate as RoboCat scans the inventory in my mind. *Tanisha has a car but she works on Saturday mornings. Faye and Arthur from my class both have cars but would it be audacious to ask them for a ride when we're hardly best friends? There's Nina from the Christian Union but she might try to talk to me about church. Perhaps I should get a taxi. But I need a female taxi driver because I must never be alone with a strange man. Or I could just get the next bus and send my group a message to say I'm going to be late—*

"Woah, woah," Zachary grabs my arm. "Are you alright?"

"I'm late. I can't believe I slept through my alarm. I never do that." I burst into tears.

"It's alright. It doesn't matter." He leads me to my bed and I plop down and start to shake.

"What's going on? Your room's a mess." Zachary leans over and picks up my chair from where I tossed it yesterday.

I stare at the wall before noticing Annie in my doorway. "What happened last night, Cat? Elle said you seemed a bit strange..."

I know for a fact Elle used the word 'deranged.' I heard her wittering to Annie outside my room before I drifted off.

I pull my blanket over myself. "I'm fine," I whisper. I am demure, shy, soft. Nothing like the wild creature in a rage last night.

They keep staring, oozing pity and confusion. Zachary straightens the library books on my desk.

"I'm fine," I repeat.

My mind is whirling. I need to get to Wakefield otherwise... *Otherwise what? I'll let my group down? I'll break my perfect record? The stars will fall from the sky?*

The universe will implode? Suddenly the whirling slows down and my frantic thoughts grow dim.

Let it go, RoboCat. Let it go.

I close my eyes and picture RoboCat walking away. Squashed Cat vanishes and I feel very tired. I don't care if I miss today's rehearsal or if I miss the entire module. I don't even care if I get kicked off the course of if I am never an actress.

"I want more sleep," I tell Annie and Zachary. I pick up my phone and send my group a message telling them that I am ill and won't be coming. It is strangely liberating.

Zachary backs out of my room. "Let us know when you wake up and we'll hang out."

I nod and yawn. "Okay."

The two of them close my door.

I bury myself in my blanket and sleep for another two hours. When I awake, I stare at the ceiling, thinking about nothing at all, before grabbing one of the books on my desk. It's entitled *'The Heart Laid Bare'* and it's by Alvin Arnold, one of the leading voices in Postmodern theatre. As I flick through it, a diagram of a dissected heart catches my attention and I pause to read.

'Shock them. Scare them. Provoke them. Rip your heart open and leave it pulsating and weeping in the spotlight, screaming, 'This is you!' What's the point of theatre unless it hands the audience a giant mirror and confronts them with their own damned humanity?'

I wrinkle my nose and let the book slide out of my hands. I don't even care when the page crumples. Perhaps I will be reckless and refrain from reading any more books this term.

Right on cue, Rose sends me a photo of all the goodies she and the others have picked up in Wakefield. There's a bag of sheep intestines, several packets of out of date cheese, some dust sheets and a giant cardboard tube that Will plans to use as a penis. Damned humanity at its finest.

* 49 * Thunder Cat and Not-So-Mad Jo

There's some wild pounding on my door followed by Mad Jo yelling, "Open up, Caz! I've got you a hot chocolate!"

I rub my temples and wonder whether to pretend to be asleep. I've not seen Mad Jo or most of my housemates since my little episode on Friday night. I didn't leave my room all day yesterday except for strategic trips to the bathroom when it sounded like the hallway was empty.

"Come on, Caz! I know you're awake. I heard you in the toilet before I left for my run." Mad Jo rattles my door handle.

I am both affronted and gladdened by her upbeat manner. Zachary and Annie have been speaking to me in quiet voices for the last day, as though I am a fragile leaf that could crumble under the slightest noise. I've told them very little about what happened on Friday other than the fact that I'd had 'a bit of a moment' and felt overwhelmed. They're at church this morning. They invited me but obviously I declined.

I quickly brush my hair before plodding to my door.

"Oh good, you're awake. I wasn't completely sure." Mad Jo hands me a paper cup filled with steaming liquid before kicking off her trainers and plonking herself in my chair.

I carefully prise the lid off the hot chocolate. I've not eaten in a day. It smells like bliss.

"Thanks," I mutter. "Sorry about the mess." I bat a hand at the state of my room.

I'm trying to be Play it Cool Cat but Mad Jo doesn't mince her words as she leans back and asks, "So, what's going on? Lose the plot on Friday, did you? Elle said you were lying on the kitchen floor shaking and then you ran off when she went to get help."

I squirm. "I had a bit of a moment, I guess." I attempt a chuckle. It comes out more like a whimper.

"What kind of a moment? I feel like I'm gonna scream and I need to throw a few plates, kind of moment? Or I wanna slit my wrists and jump out of the window, kind of moment?"

She starts to laugh before immediately sitting up straight and swearing. "Seriously, Caz? That bad?"

I feel stupid as I shrug and mumble, "Kind of."

"You wouldn't actually do anything, would you?"

"I... I don't know..." Evidently not. I bite my thumb before blurting out, "I took some of Dotty Jay's paracetamol." It is a huge relief to confess to this because all weekend I've been wondering whether the pills are doing some hidden damage inside me. I had half expected not to wake up on Saturday morning.

Mad Jo stares at me with hawk-like eyes. "How many did you take?"

I look at the floor. "Three."

She seems relieved. "Only three? That's alright, then."

I'm torn between relief and shame. *Only three? Not a proper effort.* I take a large sip of my hot chocolate and burn the roof of my mouth.

"Is it your course? Are you under pressure? Because we've got this huge exhibition coming up and I'm proper stressed about it so I totally understand."

"No. It's not my course."

"Oh. Have you told your parents?"

"No."

"They'd want to know you're struggling. Your mum's so sweet. She'd probably want to come and see you."

"Probably."

Yeah. She probably would. She'd be up in a flash if she thought I'd had a breakdown. She'd sweep me into her arms like a doting mother and wouldn't mention anything that had happened between us. Silly Cat feels a pang of longing. My mum would come, if I needed her. She'd get my dad to drive her. Or, if he didn't want to, she'd make Keith do it. *If I just call her and say sorry, everything would be okay.*

It's Thunder Cat who pulls me back to reality. "My mum isn't always sweet."

Mad Jo peers at me. "What's she like, then?"

"She's not speaking to me at the moment because I tried to talk to her about some stuff over Easter and she took it all the wrong way. She always thinks people are against her and she explodes over the tiniest thing..." Tears spring to my eyes. I put my drink down and rub a hand across my face.

Mad Jo doesn't ask whether I want to talk about it. She just dives right in. Her bluntness is both terrifying and exactly what I need. "So she's a bit of a narcissist?"

"I don't know... Maybe... I just never feel like I can be myself around her. She'll get angry suddenly and do horrible things..."

"Like what?"

I go on speaking, even though I have been programmed not to. I tell Mad Jo all about my mother's outburst, my dad's hysteria and how Aidan is cross with me. I tell her tales from my childhood, each one slipping through my lips like birds escaping from a cage. Downstairs, Bertie is playing haunting piano melodies. They drift up through my floor, warning me to be quiet. I can sense my mother's rage from two hundred and sixty four miles away. I put a hand to my mouth.

"So what happened on Friday?" Mad Jo rocks backwards on my chair and I'm half afraid that she'll tumble off the back of it.

I consider her for a moment. We've hung out most mornings and talked about all manner of things. I know a lot about her family and her artistic endeavours and her thoughts on religion and politics and who's hot around campus. But I've largely avoided revealing anything deep about myself.

There's a tug of war inside me as Holy Cat chastises me for drawing so much attention to myself. But then Thunder Cat makes a defiant move towards being more open. It's lonely having to be so strong all the time. Plus, I figure I've screwed everything up already. Annie and Zachary know I'm broken and now Elle has seen me in pieces. What's one more person knowing what a mess I am?

"I had all this noise in my head," I confess. "Like my brain was being trashed or something. I couldn't think straight. I heard these instructions saying that I needed to... Like the only choice was..." I shrug and look down.

"Does that happen a lot? Hearing voices?"

I bristle. "Crazy people hear voices."

She gives a long hum before suggesting, "What if it's just disconnected parts of you?"

I feel my face reddening. "Disconnected parts of me?" I repeat, aghast. "Like a split personality?"

"Maybe." She sounds so matter of fact about it, like she's diagnosing a sprained ankle or something.

My heart is pounding. I mean, I know I have different parts inside me. But everyone does to some extent, don't they? I'm only slightly different. Not completely *crazy* different.

There was a man who lived down our street who wore shorts in the winter and sat outside the corner shop muttering to himself. Sometimes he called himself Peter. Sometimes he called himself Paul. You could tell when he was Paul because he wore an old fishing hat. My parents used to joke about him. Everyone used to joke about him. He was the man with two faces. I'm not like *him. Am I?*

I told you to be quiet, rebukes Holy Cat.

"People laugh about that sort of thing," I stutter.

"Well, maybe they shouldn't," says Not-So-Mad Jo. "We all need love, don't we? The voices in our head are hard enough without other people adding to them. Maybe we should accept each other a little more. We've all got our stories."

My brain hurts. I hear Baby Cat whimpering and quickly shake my head.

"You alright?"

Without thinking, I blurt out, "Baby Cat keeps crying. She's so annoying."

My head goes foggy and my train of thought crashes into a cloud as Lost Cat presses a button and ejects Thunder Cat out of her seat. I've never told a single soul about all the parts of me before. I shouldn't say their names. It sounded creepy and crazy when I said 'Baby Cat' out loud.

"What do you do when she cries?" Jo sounds so unfazed that the fog is broken.

"What do you mean? I ignore her or tell her to stop."

"But babies cry when they need something. My little sister had colic for three months. It was awful for us but she was just trying to tell us she was in pain. So what does Baby Cat need?"

I squirm at the sound of Baby Cat's name being spoken by another. "I don't know." My voice sounds tiny and far away. "If she wants something, why doesn't she use words?"

"Because she's a baby! Babies can't speak, can they?" She says this as though it's the most obvious thing in the world. "Perhaps she's in pain and trying to tell you about it but doesn't have the words."

I feel defensive. Before a tear can escape, I snap, "What makes you such an expert? You don't know how—"

"My dad had some issues before he died." She shrugs in a way that makes me shut up immediately. "I've lurked on thousands of online forums over the years. So, yeah, I am a bit of an expert, actually. It's alright," she adds before I can apologise. "You didn't know. We all have secrets, don't we?"

I nod awkwardly as RoboCat tracks back over everything Mad Jo has ever told me about her family. Her mum remarried when she was eleven. Her stepfather is called Colin but for the first few months she called him 'Creepin'. He eventually won her over with a purple mountain bike and the two of them are pretty close now although she still calls him 'Creepin' if she's mad at him. She loves her half siblings but sometimes feels jealous of them. She's never mentioned her father. I feel awful. There I was, thinking I knew everything there was to know about Mad Jo. But I had no idea. I try to apologise again but she cuts me off.

"Have you tried being nice?"

"Pardon?"

"When Baby Cat cries. Have you tried being nice?"

"Nice to Baby Cat?"

"Yeah. And to all the parts of you. Be kind. Listen to them. Ask them what they need."

Kind to Baby Cat? Kind to Angry Cat and Sad Cat? Kind to Cat out of Hell?

"But I don't... I don't like all of them," I say weakly.

"They exist for a reason. And they're all part of you. And life's hard enough without waging war on yourself. Can I?" Without waiting for a reply, she picks up my cup and downs the rest of my hot chocolate.

I pretend to look out of the window. I'm going to sound terribly needy but I ask it anyway. "Do you think I'm weird?"

She laughs. "I think everybody's weird."

I look at this girl with the three watches and the streaky purple hair and the earrings made of her own teeth. Perhaps we are all mad in our own way. Perhaps we all have a Play it Cool version of ourselves.

"Why do you call yourself Mad Jo?" I demand. "Jocelyn is such a lovely name."

"Ahh, I was named after my aunt. Now, she *was* crazy." She chuckles to herself but doesn't elaborate.

Neither of us speaks for a while.

"Thanks for listening," I say finally. "And for not judging me."

"Why would I judge you?" She joins me at the window and gives me a big squeeze. "I don't think you're crazy, Caz. I think you're just sad. You've held so much in for so long. No wonder there's so much screaming going on in your head."

A big fat tear rolls down my cheek.

"Plus, we all have voices in our heads. You just give names to yours."

I turn back to the window. The view of the rolling hills brings a strange stillness to my soul. For one peaceful moment, there is silence inside.

* 50 * Fun Cat makes careless plans

I feel strangely buoyant when I get up on Monday. I think Fun Cat might be back. Friday night feels like forever ago. I almost can't remember what all the fuss was about.

I meet my group at the quarry and hold my nerve as they show me their bag of junk from Wakefield.

"We've already buried the intestines," Will says, pointing to a mound in front of the cliff. "You'll see them in a bit."

"We were thinking of camping here tonight," adds Rose. "Thought we might get some inspiration if we spent a whole night here. You up for it?"

I grin, Fun Cat thrilled at the prospect of an adventure. "Totally!"

There isn't time for them to teach me the two minutes they devised on Saturday so I sit in the audience when Jodie and our classmates arrive. Silly Cat feels a shiver of excitement as Jodie sits beside me.

"Hi Cat. Feeling better now?"

"Yeah."

I am hyper aware of my breathing, my blinking and the feel of my lap under my hands as we watch the performance.

After an ominous scream from Donna, my group step out from behind the cliff dressed in silk pyjamas. They walk single file to the mound of mud centre stage and silently dig up the guts that they buried earlier.

Fun Cat falters. Silly Cat wishes she could snuggle into Jodie's shoulder for a hug. I am embarrassed, afraid, sickened and frustrated all at once. There is no point reminding Silly Cat that Jodie will never be my sister. Silly Cat has no grasp of reality whatsoever.

The two minutes end with Will rubbing blood on his face.

Jodie arises and says brightly, "Right then, we'll cut across to the waterfall and watch the next group."

I tag along with my classmates, Silly Cat longing to keep up front with Jodie and Scaredy Cat choosing to drift at the back. By mid-morning we've done a tour of campus and watched each group's offering. There's a lot of screaming. A lot of blood and violence. And far too much nudity.

Elle's group fill their two minutes with Elle and Arthur shrieking while Clemmie and Poppy pound them with rotten fruit. I think Elle is avoiding me. She hasn't spoken to me since Friday night. I said hello to her this morning and she just did her funny old fake smile as though she was scared of me.

Sky and Sienna's group have secured the two baths from the props department. I spot Donna looking peeved.

Viktor lies on a tree stump, naked and wrapped in cling film. Kimberley and Donna chat behind their hands as he groans and writhes about. Rose suggests something to Will. I pray they're not getting any ideas.

It seems this module is one big competition to be as shocking and sordid as possible. What a depressing climax to an otherwise wonderful start to my acting career.

Jodie in Real Life is still a complete disappointment. She actually laughs when Viktor falls out of the cling film. Sad Cat feels bereft and abandoned. Still, I can't stop talking to Jodie in My Head and imagining she's on my side.

"There's got to be more than this! The point of theatre can't just be to provoke and be disgusting!"

"Oh there is, there is. You can do it, Cat. You're a star!"

But I'm not sure that I am a star after all.

That night, I prepare to camp with my group mere yards away from where the pile of entrails sat this morning.

I hate this. Why am I doing this? Copy Cat is pretending to be excited, not letting on for one moment that Squashed Cat is so dangerously close. That's the problem with making decisions as Fun Cat. If she disappears by the time an event comes round then it's the less sociable parts of me who have to live with the consequences.

I had debated saying I felt unwell again. But I couldn't risk them coming up with more ideas without me. I needn't have worried. It doesn't look like they plan on rehearsing. All they've done so far is smoke and drink. The hours pass with me feeling like I don't belong and yet not particularly wanting to belong either. I've got my pyjamas on under my clothes but, now that I'm here, I no longer want to show off Thunder Cat's neon pink koala night shirt.

Finally, I am able to unroll Dotty Jay's sleeping bag and pretend to go to sleep. I don't sleep, obviously. I'm out in the wild, surrounded by drunks who I don't know very well. One is a boy who recently rubbed animal guts on his own face.

At some point in the dead of night, I find myself needing a wee. I toss and turn and cross my legs until I can't bear it any longer. Then I wiggle out of the sleeping bag and tiptoe past the sleeping bodies beside me. I plod into a nearby patch of trees where I do my business, careful not to pee on my wellies. Then, without thinking, I keep walking instead of turning back.

I walk towards a tree stump, one that Zachary and I have sat on many times, and I look up and stare at the stars. Out here in the middle of nowhere, they are so bright and plentiful. I understand why Zachary finds them so captivating. I locate The Plough and Betelgeuse and The Seven Sisters. I brush away a tear. *I wish I had seven sisters.*

I talk to Jodie in My Head.

I try counting the stars.

I twist my head and search for different patterns.

Some of those stars have hung there for thousands of years, twinkling through war and death and famine. Time passes but they still twinkle.

I exhale into the wind.

There's so much suffering in the world, all playing out under the same sun and moon and stars. It feels so self-indulgent to make a song and dance about my own private heartaches. *Who cares? Especially when so many others are hurting so much more?*

The silence of the sky is suffocating. The vast heavens seem full and yet so empty. *Is anybody out there? Does anything matter? Do I matter? Do my tears matter? I could ask for a sign but what if I miss it or deceive myself?*

I am mush.

My old life in Exeter feels very far away and I know I can never return. I am no longer a caterpillar but I'm certainly not a butterfly either.

I am mush.

Turns out change is not as easy as donning a butterfly hoodie and announcing I've arrived. Real change is painful and messy because if you want to be reborn, you first have to die. I feel tearful and yet oddly serene. I would never usually have the courage to sit alone in the dark for so long but there's no sign of Squashed Cat slipping into a panic. I'm okay. The stars are nice. Soothing. They whisper of an endless universe and lights that never end.

I am mush. And that doesn't have to be a bad thing. Mush means possibility.

I could literally become anything right now.

I shift position and lean back onto my elbows.

But who do I want to be?

I'm not sure how long I sit there, thinking about what a mess I am, how small and lonely I feel and how huge and crazy the universe is. But, at some point, two remarkable things happen. The first is that I have a sudden brilliant idea for our piece. It's so good that I want to sprint back to camp and wake everybody up. Before I can move, the second remarkable thing happens.

A voice speaks to me.

* 51 * Sad Cat meets The Star Maker

"Who does love say you are?"

When I say I heard a voice, I don't mean a big booming voice or a creepy command like what crazy people hear. But I do mean something louder than a thought. Something outside of me. Something out there in the dark night.

"Who does love say you are?"

I pause, my heart beating fast. Every bit of me looks up to see who has spoken. I wonder if this is some new part that I am yet to identify. Perhaps Cosmic Cat or Wise Cat?

"I don't believe in love," I say quietly.

"But I believe in you."

I look around, half expecting to see Will or Donna watching or laughing. But the woods around me are empty.

I want to ask, "Who are you?" but I haven't got the words.

The voice answers anyway. *"I am the Star Maker."*

God suddenly feels really close. Like close enough to punch. Angry Cat rears her head and snarls, *Leave me alone.*

But Sad Cat is curious enough to stay. And Silly Cat feels a longing so deep and so painful that I almost fall to my knees.

"I don't believe in love," I blurt out again.

"That doesn't stop love existing."

"I don't believe in love," I say for the third time.

"Love will never stop fighting for you."

I squeeze my fingers into my eyes as waves of sadness crash over me.

The voice speaks again. It is a gentle whisper in my mind, dancing between my ears. *"How are stars formed?"*

I think back to my astronomy lessons with Zachary. "Can't remember."

"Great pressure."

Pictures flash through my mind. My mother leaving. Face blazing. My father weeping. Banging his head against the wall. Saying sorry again and again and again. Standing by the front door with my arms outstretched. Aidan jumping on me in the swimming pool. A suitcase too heavy for me to hold.

The Star Maker continues, *"Nobody is born scared or ashamed. You were made for love. You weren't meant to break into pieces. But you did. Many times. And, each time you did, a new star was born. Every star has its story. Every star is there for a reason. And I love each one. I set them in space and I know them by name."*

I frown. Is he still talking about the big balls of rock up in space or is this some kind of metaphor?

"I see you, Cat. I see the parts that you want to hide. I see the great beauty that was birthed through pain. I see you and I love you. Every part of you." Then he adds, *"Pain is not forever."*

This is too much for Sad Cat. I bury my head in my hands and cry and cry. I'm crying because it feels like pain *is* forever, like loneliness and sorrow is all I've ever known. But I'm also crying because there is something so very comforting about the hope that one day the pain might end.

"Pain is finite but joy will never cease. One day you will understand."

Angry Cat recoils. *How is that meant to help me? How am I meant to be comforted by the idea that I was supposed to be something better but got split apart by great pressure? You see me? So what? Why didn't you stop me from breaking? You say you love me but where have you been my whole life?*

My attention is caught by a flash across the sky. A shooting star. I rub my head. I know, from what Zachary has told me, that some stars are bigger or brighter or older or younger. When they come together in groups, they create a constellation, a picture of who they are as one: The Saucepan, for example, or The Great Dog. So what is the picture of all my parts put together? Who is Cat, the real Cat? Am I a saucepan or a dog or a butterfly or a spoon?

Who would I be if I hadn't broken? wonders Sad Cat.

Creative Cat chips in, *Finding yourself is hard enough when you're stood in one place. When pieces of you are scattered across the universe it's impossible.*

The Star Maker whispers, *"Every star has its story. Every star is there for a reason. Communication brings connection."*

Baby Cat starts crying. Great. All I wanted to do was have a wee. Suddenly I'm sitting on the ground, talking to myself, comparing myself to lumps of rock up in space.

I'm such an idiot.

Baby Cat wails some more.

Shut up, Baby Cat! Use words!

But the counsel of Mad Jo— I mean my housemate, Sensible Jocelyn— springs to mind. *"She's a baby! Babies can't speak, can they? Perhaps she's in pain and trying to tell you about it but doesn't have the words."*

I look across the sky at a very bright star hanging over the fields. Sirius, I think. Unless I can pretend, just for a moment, that it's not.

I bite my lip before mumbling, "Baby Cat, you're a star... I see you. I'm listening. What do you need?"

* 52 * Scaredy Cat finds her voice

I wait until after lunch to tell my group about my brilliant idea. They were too hungover this morning. Now's my chance. Jodie's coming in half an hour, expecting to see progress, and everybody's sober and slightly afraid. We passed Elle's group earlier and saw them cowering as Jodie yelled at them for being lazy. The same miserable fate will be ours unless we have something to show her.

"We've got nothing. Literally nothing!" Donna moans as she picks up an empty vodka bottle and stashes it in her bag.

"I can't believe we spent a whole night here and didn't come up with any ideas," Rose adds.

I clear my throat.

"It's fine," says Will. "We can wing it. It's postmodern theatre. It doesn't have to make sense. Grab that cardboard tube... We can stuff it with cheese."

I clear my throat again. I'm stuck somewhere between Scaredy Cat and Copy Cat. I'm desperate for Fun Cat or Thunder Cat to take over but I can't find them.

I look up into the cloudless blue sky, searching for courage. Not a star in sight.

Baby Cat didn't reply last night and, in the cold light of day, I feel rather silly about it all. Clearly there was no divine voice giving me wisdom in the dark. My parts are not stars and nothing special happens if they all come together.

"Guys, we've got twenty minutes." Donna taps her watch. "We need to think of something or Jodie's gonna kill us."

"I've got an idea," I blurt out, shoving my hands in my pockets to stop them shaking. I try to organise my thoughts into the coherent brainwave that I had in the night. "I know everybody's trying to be as shocking as possible because Alvin Arnold was all about pushing boundaries and confronting the audience with their own damned humanity—"

Kimberley starts laughing. "Did you just say *damned,* Cat? I've never heard you swear before." She gives me a patronising smirk as though she's both shocked and impressed at sheltered little me.

"It's us! We're a bad influence," says Donna. "Poor Cat having to spend the night with us lot. I bet she was terrified!"

"Especially when you cracked out the weed," scoffs Kimberley.

Will guffaws. "I doubt she realised what it was."

I hadn't. Well, that explains the voice. I was high by osmosis.

"Aww leave her alone," says Rose. "She can't help being so innocent."

"Anyway!" I yell.

They look at me and Scaredy Cat almost shrinks back.

"Anyway..." I repeat a little quieter. "Blood and nakedness might've worked when Alvin Arnold did it, you know, a hundred years ago or whatever. Because it was a new idea back then. But now... I don't know... I think it's overdone. I've watched nearly a hundred performances since September—"

Will lets out a whistle.

"—and loads of them have had blood and screaming in them. There's nothing original or exciting about it. Why don't we do something different? Something really surprising. Something that immerses the audience in beauty instead of..." I think about the entrails and Viktor wrapped in clingfilm. "...something that makes them sick. Plus, once you've seen ten performances with blood and baths and nakedness, it stops being shocking. Don't you think?"

"What do you mean?" asks Rose.

"Well, I had this idea..." My heart thunders in my chest as I stand up to make my case. "Imagine a world without change. Without feelings or day or night or birth or death. Just existing in an endless void. The characters would have to create everything for themselves... Artificial weather, seasons, night, emotions. Even time wouldn't exist so they'd have to manufacture it for themselves. They'd have to imagine what it's like to get old or die."

I thought they'd be sold by this point but they're all just staring at me.

I think fast. "Imagine a big string running down here from up there..." I run to the side of the cliff. "We could start by unveiling the day by pulling up a giant yellow umbrella. Deliberately constructed by workers. A fake sun. An entire fake world. And then..." I dash over to a spot of mud. "They could plant fake flowers. All fake because nothing real or new would ever grow. And there wouldn't be any such thing as happiness or sadness or love so the characters would try to make themselves feel these things but really they would feel nothing. So maybe they would have a funeral for somebody with lots of dramatic weeping but then that person would just get up again and go on existing."

"What about the cardboard tube?" asks Will. "And the cheese and the dustsheets?"

"Throw them away. We wouldn't need them."

He looks affronted. "But I had big plans for that tube."

Kimberley snorts.

"We could create the weather," I continue. "Surround the audience with wind or rain or snow."

Will gives a hum. "How would that work?"

"I don't know yet but it would look really beautiful."

Donna taps her watch. "I hate to say it but we haven't got much time left."

Scaredy Cat swallows every ounce of fear to make one final plea. "It would be obvious that the characters were trying to feel alive in a world where nothing grows and nothing changes. We'd be presenting a world without all the things that makes us human... That would really confront the audience with their own humanity." I pause before adding, "Their own *damned* humanity."

Kimberley grins.

Rose nods. "I like it."

I feel a flutter of excitement.

Donna looks at Will and he shrugs. "Sounds a bit naff. Everyone else will be pushing boundaries and we'll be dancing around with fake snow."

I'm about to reply when Jodie arrives.

Will swears under his breath. "Just gotta wing it, guys. Pass me the tube."

"Good afternoon!" Jodie sings. "How are you getting on?"

There's a pause and then Donna says, "We've had a new idea. It's a bit of a change of direction."

Jodie raises an eyebrow.

Scaredy Cat goes utterly tongue-tied. I sit on a rock and say nothing as my group share my idea as if it was their own.

"A world where nothing changes and nobody experiences anything unless they create it," says Rose.

"So we would make everything, literally everything," Kimberley jumps in. "We'd maybe start with a big fake sun. Then go through a whole day trying to create all the experiences that makes someone feel human."

"Even giving birth and dying and falling in love," says Rose.

"And the weather," adds Donna. "Rain, wind, snow."

I sneak a peek at Jodie. She's beaming.

"Fantastic! I can't wait to see that." She laughs to herself. "How are you going to make snow?"

"We don't know yet," Donna says quickly. "But we'll think of something."

Jodie nods. "Always the best way. Start with what you'd like to do if anything was possible and work backwards from there." She gets up and pats her hips. "Well done. See you later. Now I need to go and check on those losers by the bat cave. Last time I saw them they were sitting around doing nothing." And with a curt nod, she's gone.

I feel like I might cry. I'm glad she liked my idea but I feel so stupid for staying silent. Now she'll think I'm just a loser who sits around doing nothing.

"Wow, she actually liked that idea," says Kimberley.

"Nice one, Cat!" says Rose.

I attempt a smile. "So you're up for it?"

"Yeah!" The girls nod.

"Will?" I look at him. "You okay with it? You don't mind throwing away the cheese and the dustsheets and the tube?"

Will scratches his chin. "Well, let's not be hasty... We might be able to make snow from the dust sheets."

I smile. A real smile that starts deep inside. "Cool."

That evening, I pass Jodie on my way out of the refectory.

"Alright, Cat?"

"I'm okay, thanks."

"How was the rest of the afternoon? Did you make much progress?"

"Yeah. We thought about how we'd get the sun to rise and we had a few ideas about the snow."

"Sounds great."

"Thanks." I turn to go.

"Oh, Cat?"

I turn back.

"I know that was you. The whole change of direction." She smiles. "I'm so proud. You're a star."

I give a sheepish smile, as though I am not remotely bothered by the praise. As though ecstasy isn't surging through me like a shot of morphine bringing life to my weary bones. As though there isn't a wild party erupting with Fun Cat and Thunder Cat and Silly Cat dancing the conga, Creative Cat wearing a crown at the head of the line.

Jodie's words echo as I gallop up the hill. *You're a star! You're a star! You're a star!"*

If only I could ditch all the rubbish and broken and needy parts of me and be a star all the time.

* 53 * Creative Cat makes a castle

It turns out I can talk to the Star Maker even when I'm not looking at the stars. I tried it last night when I was lying in bed. I asked, "Can you still see me?"

And he replied, *"I see you, Cat."*

I still don't know whether the Star Maker is a real somebody out there or just some sagacious part of me. There's some comfort in believing it's the former; like maybe God is actually out there and actually cares for me. But there's a chance it's just another split part of me and I'm only talking to myself. Then again, if that's the case, this new part of me must be very clever.

This afternoon, while I'm bouncing around Fairy Land, an image of Scaredy Cat comes to my mind. It's as though she has come to talk to me. I pause mid-bounce and close my eyes. I see myself watching as Scaredy Cat shows me something. Five plastic coins. Stolen from nursery.

I remember. I took them by mistake. I thought they were mine. My mother called me stupid when she found out. She said I should've known they weren't mine. She shut me in my room for being naughty. But I hadn't known. They looked the same as mine until I got them home. I didn't mean to be stupid. I didn't mean to be naughty. I hid them under my wardrobe and they're still there. From that day on, I hid my mistakes from my mother. And Scaredy Cat was born.

I feel Scaredy Cat's shame as I take the coins from her. And, just as I am wondering what I'm supposed to do with this memory, I hear the Star Maker say, *"Bring her here to the present. Let her bounce with you for a while."*

So I do. In my imagination, I imagine Scaredy Cat holding hands with me and bouncing with me on the dusty ground of Forest Hall. I see her grinning with amazement as the music rings out around us. Then she lets go of my hands and whirls around, as though encountering a world that is bigger than the moment when she got stuck.

The Star Maker says, *"Your mother's inability to love you properly was not because you weren't lovable."*

I stop and think about that. *Is it true? Am I loveable?*

Course not, Angry Cat snarls.

I broke my family, Sad Cat adds. *Aidan hates me. I always mess things up.*

Shame hangs in the breeze until the Star Maker whispers, *"You did not break your family. You broke your silence."*

Something flickers inside me. Before I can contemplate these words, Silly Cat appears and asks if she can bounce too. So I imagine the three of us jumping together— me, Silly Cat and Scaredy Cat— and afterwards I lie on the ground and imagine them both beside me. It feels strange, yet somehow thrilling, as though I am sort of making friends with myself.

I run back to Willow and grab a notebook and write it all down. Then I go to bed thinking about all my different parts and, when I'm unable to sleep at three in the morning, I kneel on my desk and open my curtains. I stare at the sky and imagine my parts as stars.

"Silly Cat, you're a star. Scaredy Cat, you're a star. And Fun Cat and Thunder Cat and Creative Cat, you're all stars..."

Baby Cat starts crying.

"Baby Cat, you're a star... A wonderful shining star."

And before Angry Cat howls, I add, "Angry Cat, you're a star... And Squashed Cat and Lost Cat and Copy Cat... You're all stars. Play it Cool Cat, you're a star. RoboCat, you're a star. Holy Cat, you're a star. Sad Cat, you're a star... Cat out of Hell... You're a star... Apparently." I feel both daft and peaceful, like many eyes are on me and many stories are about to be told.

Over the next few days, I have conversations with my parts and RoboCat compiles everything in my notebook.

Scaredy Cat was born on the day I took the coins. Silly Cat was created to provide a space for magic and fantasy so I could hold on to the hope that one day I would be rescued. Thunder Cat emerged during high school, when audacious ambition was paramount to my survival. Sad Cat's job is to hold all of my despair and Lost Cat ensures that the rest of me can function without continually breaking down. Fun Cat's world is all rosy which is why she can never be present in a crisis and barely remembers them afterwards.

By the weekend, I have filled the entire notebook.

I am confused over who is the real me. Suddenly Normal Cat seems like a blank canvas while all the other parts are vibrant and emotional. I thought I needed to make all the others disappear, but who would I be if they did? Who would I be without Silly Cat's daydreams or Thunder Cat's courage or RoboCat's amazing memory?

I'm not even sure which me is speaking right now. I think it's Creative Cat. I'm certainly feeling buzzed. Ideas keep pouring out of me in rehearsals and our piece is taking shape beautifully. The only trouble is, I'm very tired. My parts are noisy. They're constantly vying for attention, like a class of rowdy children, all eager to share their stories. I need a place to *contain* everyone so they're not all whirling around me.

Eventually, I have the good idea of creating a castle in my mind for everyone to live in. There are activities in the castle to keep everyone busy when they're not active in the *world outside*. Everybody has their own room, except for Silly Cat and Scaredy Cat who wanted to share. Baby Cat is too young to be left alone so Holy Cat is looking after her. And Lost Cat and Squashed Cat mainly stay in a special quiet room surrounded by white flowers where they can rest.

Everyone comes together for meals, although it's mainly Copy Cat who does the cooking because she was the only one paying attention to any of Dotty Jay's microwave recipes. Thunder Cat asked for a dance studio so I added one at the back of the castle. There are narwhals in the lake for Silly Cat. In the middle of the castle is a library where my different parts can share their stories. RoboCat ensures it's all kept in order. RoboCat also has her own noticeboard where everybody can leave notes. This morning, Fun Cat wrote, *'Hi RoboCat! Thanks for tidying everything!'* That was a lovely moment. At bedtime, Thunder Cat reads to the little ones and Fun Cat tucks them in.

Every morning, a tannoy system calls out messages for everyone to hear. They are things the Star Maker has told us: *'You are loved. You are seen. You're a star.'*

Sometimes I cause the tannoy system to ring out through the day, particularly if I am feeling unsettled. For example, in today's rehearsal, Will started making crude jokes when we were discussing how our characters might try to experience love. Play it Cool Cat took the little ones to play in the castle and Thunder Cat came to the front to tell Will to shut up.

I record everything in my notebook with notes and doodles from each part of me, although I still can't work out what picture my full constellation is supposed to form.

One afternoon, I feel a sudden urge to play piano. After a bit of probing, I think it's Holy Cat with something to say. So I trot along to the mansion and find an empty music room. I've always wanted to learn piano but my mum said it would be too hard. I glare at the keys before slamming a clumsy hand down. Pretty soon I'm pounding away, making a wild commotion, expressing all the wordless things my heart has never dared to confess. I realise how much Holy Cat has held in over the years. How painful it's been trying to be a good daughter. How much shame is involved when there's no grace to fail. Tears roll down my cheeks as I hammer away, making up melodies about trying to be perfect and the stars and the desperate longing I felt when I believed somebody bigger than me was watching.

And whether it's just my imagination or whether the Star Maker is truly speaking, a response comes to my messy music-making. *"You did the best you could with the resources you had. Anyone would have done the same. It wasn't your fault."* I add another message to the castle's daily tannoy system: *'It wasn't your fault.'* Then I lean back and give a happy sigh because Holy Cat feels heard and seen.

For the rest of the week, I barely speak to Jodie in My Head. I'm far too busy in the castle. There's a wonderful connection growing between my different parts— well, most of them. I don't dare seek out Cat out of Hell. And Angry Cat still gets cross whenever Baby Cat cries. I'm trying to be patient and I keep telling Baby Cat I'm listening but it's pretty hard, especially when Angry Cat claims she's just doing it for attention and that there isn't a story to tell.

Nevertheless, the storm inside me seems to have quietened down. I am curious where I was once full of angst. I am actually beginning to *like* parts of me. Everything is lovely until the night before my birthday when Angry Cat burns the castle down.

* 54 * Holy Cat still isn't sure

It's Zachary's fault.

He starts by asking, "Do you believe in God?"

"Huh?" I look up from my pasta bake.

It's the first hot day of the year and we're eating dinner on the grass outside the mansion.

"I know you don't want to go to church so I assume you don't... But what about deep down? If you had to make a decision?"

Holy Cat wants to say, *"Of course I do!"*

But the question infuriates Angry Cat. *What does it matter whether I believe or not? My parents believe in God. They go to church. My mum has a lucky crucifix. It's not like they're heathens like Uncle Martin who left Aunt Sonya for his dental hygienist. But believing in God isn't enough. Believing doesn't mean he'll help you. Believing doesn't mean that you're good people or that you'll raise happy children.*

I've thought about God quite a bit recently. Especially because the Star Maker— if he's real— seems very different to the God of my youth. *That* God was aloof and angry. *That* God demanded perfection. *That* God would've had strong opinions about Rory's new boyfriend and Mad Jo's experimental art.

So who is the Star Maker? Somebody more real than the God I grew up with? Or a heretical, distorted delusion? A fantasy like the castle in my mind? Holy Cat cannot be sure.

"Don't know," I say before changing the subject. "Did I do the right thing with my parents?"

I've been wondering about this all week. Ever since my mother posted a meme on FriendWeb with the words, *'You only get one mother. Be sure to tell her you love her.'* All my convictions evaporated the moment I saw it. And the next day, my mother unfriended me from FriendWeb.

Zachary looks at me, spaghetti sauce dripping down his chin. "What was the alternative?"

I jab my polystyrene box with my fork. "I could've stayed instead of getting the train back. I could've apologised to my mum and said it was a misunderstanding."

"What would have happened if you'd done that?"

"I suppose she'd have calmed down after a day or two and forgiven me."

"Then what?"

"Then we'd have carried on as if nothing had happened."

"It's not nothing though, is it? Your whole life you've had to pretend that everything is nothing."

"But I'm supposed to forgive, aren't I? I know bits of the Bible. *Turn the other cheek. Honour your parents.* Am I overreacting?"

"I don't think so. I think you're protecting yourself."

I stab the pasta, seeing how much I can fit on the fork. "Even now, I could phone her or send an email... Isn't that what a good daughter would do?"

Zachary wipes his chin. "Do you really want to know what I think?"

I brace and turn to face him. "Yeah."

"I think you're more broken than you realise. You make excuses for them. You've held in your pain in order to protect them. You've hidden the truth, even from yourself."

More broken than I realise. What does that mean? Mentally unstable? Weak? Crazy? "What should I do, then?"

"What do you want to do?"

I feel a surge of irritation. "I'm asking what the *right* thing is. I want to do the *right* thing."

Zachary guzzles the last of his spaghetti and crushes his takeaway box. "It's your choice, Cat. You get to choose."

"No, I don't!"

I don't have a choice. Not really. My mother has always been the loudest voice in all my decisions because the wrong choice is punished with rage or silence. My father needs me and gives me no choice about it. He demands I drop everything to carry him. Takes up every inch of space without checking it's alright. Drowns me in his tears and uses me as a towel. Walks in when I'm changing. I can't even have a shower without him banging on the door demanding to be let in to use the toilet.

The inappropriateness of this suddenly hits me and I'm furious. Furious at the lack of choice. Furious at the lack of space. Furious at being dismissed. Denied. Being told that I'm the selfish one. Being expected to show respect but never receive it. Furious that they do not, cannot, will not *see* me.

And yet, Holy Cat whispers. *They try their best. Forgive them. Forgive them.*

"They don't mean to hurt me," I say quietly.

"People rarely do."

"What would *you* do?" I demand. "If it was your mum. Would you call her?"

"I don't know. My mum would never behave like yours." A stab to my heart. "But, if she did, I don't think I'd call her right now." He sounds so relaxed, as though the solution is simple. As though I'm a fool for not seeing things clearly.

I feel a pounding anger in my chest. "So I should just do nothing? What if she dies?"

"She will at some point."

"I mean what if she dies while we're not talking. Won't I regret all this wasted time?"

Zachary gives a shrug and repeats, "I don't know."

I scowl and toss my food aside. "For the record, I prayed on the train when I came back after Easter. I told God he could have my life if he helped me. But it doesn't count for anything, does it?"

Zachary looks at me with wide-eyed surprise.

"In certain situations, God does nothing," I carry on. "He doesn't interfere with gravity or sports events or broken families. He just lets us play on." I sniff and look away, careful not to let Zachary see that I'm welling up.

He's silent for a while and then he says, "Perhaps God is closer than you realise. He led you to have that conversation with your mum. He told you to go through that door."

I snort. "Stupidest advice ever. It all went wrong."

"Did it? I think God knew that needed to happen."

I am enraged. "Why?"

"He wanted to help you... To show you the truth so you could start to be set free. He loves you—"

"It's easy for you. You had a nice upbringing. Of course you believe in a nice, happy God."

I spot Jodie in the distance, leaving the mansion. It takes everything in me not to let Silly Cat burst into tears. *If God loved me, he could've given me a big sister. Someone like Jodie to protect me and tell me every day that I'm a star.*

Zachary clears his throat. "The Bible says that God is close to the broken-hearted."

Yeah right. I remember Jodie's kiss or kill exercise. Close enough to watch us bleeding. Close enough to smell our tears. Close enough to intervene. But so silent.

"Maybe he's given me to you. To show you a little of his love." Zachary shoots me a hopeful smile.

I give a bitter laugh. "Yeah. Thanks."

"I heard a really good preach once..." I groan but Zachary waffles on. "This guy was talking about how we go through tough times and have no idea what God is doing through it all. But he always has a plan. And, the main thing was..." He stops and thinks. "The main message was... You cannot fulfil your destiny without your history."

I sniff. So is all this pain essential for the creation of Catrina Carla, famous actress? Perhaps. Famous people are often unhinged.

Thunder Cat takes charge and changes the subject again. "It's my birthday tomorrow!"

"Oh yeah. That reminds me..." He rummages around in his pocket before producing something about the size of a bar of soap wrapped in purple paper. "This is for tomorrow."

"Why are you giving it to me now? Give it to me tomorrow, you wally!"

"I have to give it to you now... It will become clear. Just don't open it until... Until the right time. You'll know..."

I give a bemused chuckle and toss it into my bag.

Then Zachary blurts out, "Vanessa asked me out."

"Who?" My mind is blank. "Oh! *Vanessa!* Clarinet girl. Good for you."

He looks shifty for a moment. "I said no."

"Why? I thought you were obsessed with her." I snigger. "Or have you finally realised that love is a waste of time?"

"No... I just... I realised that if I went out with her then I wouldn't be able to spend so much time with *you.*"

I mull this over. I'm rather flattered. And grateful. I'd hate to lose him to some mysterious third year. "Oh right. Thanks." I start to unwrap my cookie but he's staring intently. "What?"

"What's going on with us, Cat?"

"What do you mean?"

Something in his face makes my stomach lurch. "Oh Zachary," I force a laugh. "You don't fancy me, do you?"

"No," he says quickly. "It's just... Sometimes I wonder... I mean... I just think..."

I drop my half-opened cookie. "What?"

"I think maybe we love each other." He mumbles the words in one jumbled breath.

I zone out as one of the scripts from our first term floats through my mind.

"I'm not sure what you're saying, Mitch."

"I'm saying that I love you, Sarah..."

"Don't mess me about, Mitch. Please don't do this."

Then I tune in to the castle in my mind and imagine Silly Cat and Scaredy Cat playing chase in the garden. Climbing trees. Riding horses. Making candyfloss out of clouds.

"Cat?"

"I don't know what you're talking about, Zachary. You know I don't believe in love."

His face goes red. "Then what is this?" he demands, pointing a finger from himself to me. "What's going on between us if it's not love?"

"It's friendship. You're just a friend. No more special than anybody else. You're no closer to me than Rory or Bertie."

He frowns. "That's not true, Cat. I'm sure that whatever I feel, we both feel it."

I pack my things away. I've lost all appetite for the cookie. "I told you I didn't believe in love," I mutter. "So don't get offended now. If you think you fancy me then it's your own stupid fault. I've been perfectly clear with you."

"Cat!" He reaches for my shoulder but I shrug him off and get to my feet. He scrambles up and says more urgently, "Cat." His face is intense as he stands tall before me.

Close enough to kiss.

Close enough to kill.

"Cat," he whispers. "I love you."

Without a moment's pause, Angry Cat rises up and punches him in the face.

* 55 * Angry Cat on fire

What a complete idiot. He doesn't even know me. He has no clue about the castle in my head or the stupid thoughts that go through my mind. He wouldn't say he loved me if he really knew me. Why the heck does he want to ruin everything?

I thought we were friends.

Stupid fridge freezer.

I'm just crazy.

Crazy.

My head is hot and tight as I storm back to Willow.

I pass Ruth and Charlotte from the Christian Union. They wave from a bench but Angry Cat has no time for politeness and Play it Cool Cat winces inside as I scowl and stamp on.

When I reach my room, I slam my door loudly and fling my bag onto my bed, my mind filled with murderous thoughts. *I'm bad like my parents. There's no hope. I have murder in my blood. I cannot be anything but evil.*

I drop down and pound the floor over and over.

In my mind, I see myself wrecking the castle. Destroying everything Creative Cat worked so hard to create. Smashing mirrors, tearing up books, kicking toys, setting fire to the bedrooms. Fun Cat and Holy Cat sprint to save the little ones. Baby Cat cries. RoboCat tries in vain to salvage a few possessions before it all burns. And, after her longest stint on the outside, Creative Cat promptly disappears. The idea of a castle immediately seems completely stupid. A load of rubbish. Just my imagination.

Angry Cat rants on, consumed by fire.

It's a fantasy; all the different parts of you being friends and working together. You're making it up. Attention seeker. Nobody cares. There's no Star Maker. No hope. Give up.

Cat out of Hell waits in the wings. Watching the flames.

Give up. Give up.

I'm too weird. Too broken. My story makes no sense.

* 56 * Baby Cat speaks

My fitful sleep is invaded by The Dream.

I am sinking, spinning, squirming. Trying to get away. As always, the mysterious woman has her hold on me and I am stuck between dreaming and waking in a lucid but groggy state. If I could just give her what she wants then love would be available and love would be given. But I can't. So Baby Cat cries. When it ends, I am so angry at being disturbed by this dream *yet again* that I let out a shriek and exclaim, "Just tell me what's going on, Baby Cat! *Why* do you keep crying?"

And a voice says, *Do you want to remember?*

And I scream, *"Yes!"*

Instantly, it's as though I am being pulled backwards through a tunnel. Everything goes dark. I'm not sure if I'm dreaming or awake. I feel myself splitting into two. There is the me of the present day who is curious and alert and thrilled to finally be on the cusp of an answer. And there is a me that is very young, only a toddler, who is overwhelmed and terrified and tiny.

I hear words from my mother's special prayer. *Or was it a spell?* Then I see fleeting images that start to become solid.

My mother is there.

And Duncan Anderson from down the road.

I am watching and I am feeling. The older me and the younger me. Both co-existing in one place. The one who is observing and the one who is experiencing.

And then I remember.

Unspeakable things.

The kind of things that break a person.

For a moment, I see my mother clearly.

Trying so hard.

Determined to give her daughter the things she never had. Believing there was magic in her veins, if only the right ritual could be found.

But the spell didn't work.

And the neighbour couldn't be trusted.

And she was unable, after all, to give what she never had.

And how she hates me for it.

Because she's trapped in a prison and I was meant to set her free.

I feel the pain. The terror of the little me.

And when it is over, I run to her. I scoop Baby Cat into my arms and hold her tight. I want to hold her and keep her safe forever. And, as I hug her and comfort her and wipe away her tears, I sense her peace as she melts into me and she and I become one. How brave she has been all these years, holding on to that memory and keeping it from the rest of me.

How brave. How small. How scared. How sacred.

I sit up in bed and turn my lamp on, my whole body wet with sweat. I don't know how I feel about my mother right now. But I don't hate Baby Cat any more.

* 57 * Silly Cat on a treasure hunt

A few hours later, I am awoken by loud ringing. I sit up in a panicked daze. *What is that?* It's still very dark and my phone tells me that it's half past four. *Is it the fire alarm?*

I finally realise the ringing is coming from my bag and, upon further investigation, more precisely from the purple package Zachary gave me at dinner time. *What on earth?*

I carefully unwrap the parcel, afraid that it's about to explode, and out tumbles a phone. A super old one by the looks of it. I'm still fragile from my strange experience in the night and can't be sure this is not another dream. I hold the phone at arm's length, completely mystified. Then I notice the words *'Happy birthday Super Cat!'* dancing across the screen. It takes me a long time to register that since the phone is ringing it must mean there's somebody on the other end. I flip the lid and utter a cautious, "Hello?"

"Oh good! You're awake!" Dotty Jay's bright voice only adds to my confusion. "Your first clue is in the microwave. And hurry, sunrise is in twenty five minutes." Before I can say a word, she hangs up.

I blink at the phone. Then, as Dotty Jay's instructions solidify in my mind, I dash out of my room and lunge at the microwave. A piece of pink card, shaped like a jigsaw piece, sits on a plate. I pull it out and turn it over.

'Find me where leaves meet the floor,
Be my friend and cry no more.'

I read it twice before murmuring, "The weeping willow..."

I fetch my shoes before scampering down the stairs. Silly Cat feels a combination of awe and fear as I clutch my clue and head for the field. Birds are singing in the trees, cheering me on. I leap over the fence and spot Annie sitting under the weeping willow, a huge beam splattered across her face.

I gallop towards her. "This is crazy! What's going on?"

She just giggles, hands me another clue, and sprints away.

I wonder whether to chase after her. But then I look down at the second clue.

'You'd better not think of quitting yet,
Your Irish pal is getting wet!'

"The waterfall!" I squeal to nobody in particular.

I run across the field and through the gate where I find a bleary-eyed Shay waiting by the waterfall. She silently hands me her clue and then dashes off just like Annie did.

I read the clue as fast as I can before bolting down the track. I hurry as though I'm in a race, even though it's plain that this is all for me and nobody's going to be grabbing the clues before me. Silly Cat is beside herself. This is the most incredible thing that has ever happened to me!

Shay's clue leads me to Ashley at the bat cave. Next is Dotty Jay by one of the metal sculptures. Mad Jo is under the bridge. Then there's Tanisha inside the laundry room. Rory is outside the dance studio. Bertie is lurking in a porch at the back of the mansion. I clutch the jigsaw pieces tightly, determined not to lose a single one. I crack Bertie's clue and run eagerly to the music block where I find Zachary standing on a log. I momentarily forget that the last contact we had was me punching him in the face. Then I notice the bruise between his eyes and feel a flush of embarrassment. I avoid eye contact as he hands me his clue before running off.

'Nine clues you've found, this one's the last,
Put them together and catch us fast!'

I kneel down and spread my clues out, noticing for the first time that one letter of each clue is bolder than the rest.

I smile to myself. "Fairy Land." Then I sprint all the way down the hill to my favourite place on campus where my housemates are waiting in a giant huddle.

"Happy birthday, Cat!" they yell as I arrive.

"You made it!" Dotty Jay points at the dazzling sunrise that is breaking around us.

I wipe my eyes. I went to bed believing nobody liked me. That I was too messed up to ever belong. But here I am on my nineteenth birthday surrounded by nine friends who cared enough to organise a treasure hunt and wake up before the crack of dawn to put it into place. Shay is complaining about being up so early. But she's here and she's taking photos. Ashley is sitting on a bench in her oversized grey scarf. She's a nice girl. I should hang out with her more often. Everyone is jabbering at me. They want to tell me how long they've been planning it and all the little hiccups along the way. The old phone was Bertie's and everyone was worried the battery wouldn't last the night. Rory overslept and only just reached the dance studio before me. I wasn't answering my door last night so Annie was concerned I might be unwell. Mad Jo proudly informs me that she created all the clues.

"I helped!" Zachary chips in. "I said we should end it at Fairy Land."

I want to say thank you, but the words get stuck in my throat. I'm Play it Cool Cat instead, shooting him a mere nod.

Rory whips out his guitar and leads a rendition of the birthday song as Dotty Jay produces a cake, one of her microwave masterpieces.

Mad Jo lights the nineteen candles. "Make a wish, Caz!"

Silly Cat trembles. *What should I wish for?*

My birthday wish has always been *'I wish my mum wouldn't run away and I wish my dad wouldn't kill himself.'* That's really two wishes. Greedy.

Last night's dream-experience shudders through me and Sad Cat stirs. *Is my mum thinking about me? Elle's not here. Why doesn't she like me? Who am I?*

In the pause, the wind blows my candles out and leaves me wishless.

After the cake, there are presents. Zachary hands me something small and square and I unwrap it. It's a notebook. On the front is a picture of the night sky. On the inside, Zachary has filled most of the pages with hand drawn constellations. I feel a tightness in my chest as I stare at it.

Shay leans over and coos, "Ooh, what is it?"

"Just a notebook," I say.

I see the flicker of hurt across Zachary's face.

Just a notebook. Just a friend.

* 58 * Sad Cat receives a gift

After a pleasant day of rehearsing and the general fuzzy feeling that comes from having a birthday, I find Zachary waiting for me outside my room.

"Hey. I picked up your post."

"Oh. Thanks." I hadn't bothered to check whether anybody had sent me anything. I didn't want Bob to comment on my recent absence of parcels from home.

I look at the card and small packet in Zachary's outstretched hand. That's my dad's writing on the card. I don't recognise the scrawl on the packet. It's certainly not from my mother. I take them from Zachary and unlock my door. He follows me in and I'm not sure whether I am pleased or irritated by this.

"Are you having a nice birthday?"

"Yeah. Thanks for the treasure hunt and the notebook."

"You're welcome. Look... Yesterday... I'm sorry if I pushed you. I know how you feel about love..." He perches awkwardly on my desk.

"Okay. Thanks."

He frowns as though disappointed. "It didn't seem like you," he mutters, letting out a whistle. "You got into such a rage. Like that night when you thought I'd been talking about you. Sometimes you seem like a whole other person." Zachary studies me and every part of me wants to hide.

"I get cross sometimes," I stutter.

"You were a bit scary, Cat."

Silly Cat pouts and says petulantly, "I'm not scary." *Not nasty. Not real rage. Not making people frightened.*

Even so, I hear my dad's accusation. *"Sometimes you're just like your mum."*

Holy Cat is appalled. *Am I? Am I just like my mother?*

"I'm just saying it hurt. And not just my face." He rubs the top of his nose. "You haven't even said sorry."

I feel a surge of anger. "You don't have to be my friend! I don't make you hang out with me. If you're going to judge me, you can go away." Angry Cat is teetering on the edge, very close to affirming that I am indeed a scary monster.

Zachary's face drops and he looks out of my window.

I know I should say sorry but it's not fair. I always have to say sorry. Inside my head, there's a battle between parts of me who feel awful and parts of me who hate him. Sad Cat wants to tell him about last night's revelation from Baby Cat and melt into one of his giant bear hugs. Thunder Cat wants to poke him and sing, *"Let's play a game!"* Holy Cat wants to say, *"I love the notebook and I really don't deserve it."* But I am paralysed under Angry Cat's direction and feel there is nothing to do except freeze him out. Punish him for falling in love. For causing me to feel... I don't know. Confused and afraid and unsure of what we've begun. Push him far, far away. Be all alone and let nobody in. Trust nobody. Have a heart of stone so nothing can touch me.

I stare at the card and packet in my hand and do nothing.

Finally, Zachary says quietly, "I think what we have is more than friendship. And I think you feel it too. But I won't push you. We can just be friends and I'll wait for you."

"Don't be a hero, Zachary," I say, my voice flat. "You don't know me. I'm not a good person."

Inside, Angry Cat taunts, *I'm crazy. Just crazy.* It sounds like my mother's voice. *There's no hope. I should end things now before I make such an awful mess of so many people's lives.*

"You're a great person, Cat. You just don't realise it."

I scowl. I wish he would stop being nice to me. If he would yell at me I wouldn't have to feel so guilty about hurting him.

"Do you want to do anything special tonight—"

"I'm tired. I've got a performance on Thursday."

"The one at the quarry? Can I come watch?"

"I can't stop you. It's open to anyone."

"Would you like me to come?"

"I don't mind. Whatever." I step towards my door, hinting that he should leave. I am Lost Cat, driven by Angry Cat. I feel nothing, nothing, nothing.

"Cat... I think we need to talk. I didn't mean to—"

"No, I don't need to." I turn away. I won't cry on my birthday. Chantelle once told me that if you cry on your birthday you'll cry every day for the next year. I thought she was right. I thought that was why I was always so miserable.

"I need some space," I say. "I'll be fine in a few days."

"A few days?" He exhales. "Okay…" Even though I'm the one being rude, the way he sighs as he leaves offends me.

I close my door behind him and turn to the card and the parcel. Card first. Mystery parcel second. Delaying gratification is Holy Cat's speciality.

The card is mainly pink. It reads, *'To a special daughter.'* It has cartoony mice in flowerpots and a poem that I don't bother to read. My dad writes that he's put some money in my bank account. He's signed the card *'From Mum and Dad'* even though I'll bet she's not seen it. I drop it on the floor and rip open the parcel. A silver-plated necklace falls out and lands on my foot. I pick it up, my stomach turning at the sight of the shiny bird hanging from the chain. It's the necklace I gave to Aidan years ago. The one that was a reference to his favourite book, *'The Bravest.'* So he did keep it! Why is he giving it back to me? Is he clearing out all trace of me? Trying to make me feel guilty?

There's a card included. The picture is of a cat wearing sunglasses. My throat feels dry as I open it.

'Happy birthday, Cat. Have The Bravest day. From Aidan.'

A sob starts in my chest and brings me to my knees. My brother has never given me a card before. He usually just adds his name to the one from my parents. He sent this himself. He thought of me. I'm not forgotten. Perhaps forgiven.

Sad Cat stirs with a pang of longing.

A breath of life. A ray of hope. A tiny shard of ice melting. A way back home. Perhaps. Perhaps.

* 59 * Creative Cat rises from the ashes

'Oh to be alive! To be human!'
These words greet our audience, chalked along the cliff, as they assemble at the quarry on Thursday evening. Our group is the last to perform and some of our classmates arrive in rags or covered in fake blood.

Will and Donna are perched on a rock. Kimberley and Rose are on the ground. And I'm curled up in a nook in the cliff. We are wearing white hooded overalls as we toss and turn, as though trying to sleep. I sneak a peek into the crowd and spot Zachary and Annie at the side by Jodie. I squeeze my eyes shut and get myself into the zone. *Our final performance of the year. Let's do this.*

Once everyone has gathered and the murmuring has died down, Will jumps down from the rock and makes a loud crowing sound like a rooster announcing the morning. Halfway through, he chokes and squawks before trying again.

The audience laughs. They sound both bemused and a little wary. This is understandable considering that so far this evening they have been pelted with rotten fruit by Elle's group, shouted at by Otis, spat on by Pranjal, witnessed a number of violent acts, ordered to lay face down on the mud and exposed to several naked bodies.

As Will continues to crow, the rest of us arise and give loud fake yawns before opening the big yellow umbrella that signifies the sun. We hook it up to our rudimentary pulley system (a rope strung over a branch) and shield our eyes as Rose pulls it up the cliff and secures the rope in place. Our 'day', and our performance, has begun.

The whole thing, all twenty four minutes of it, flies by and any trace of uncertainty melts away as it becomes clear that the audience are enthralled. There is gasping and cooing in all the right places and even moments of light applause, like when we dig up a pile of bibs and bottles and booties and construct a giant 'baby' in the scene depicting the longing for new life. Creative Cat is aglow, enjoying the thrill of knowing we're shocking the audience with an experience of something beautiful. We float from scene to scene portraying life events through a variety of creative means. As the space is so vast, we use limited dialogue. The whole piece is one big visual spectacle.

We reach the scene where we explore love and I feel myself faltering slightly as I am positioned very close to Zachary. I force myself to look beyond his head as I join my group in reciting the same Shakespeare quote over and over.

"Love sought is good but given unsought is better."

We recite it until the words grow empty and lifeless. Then we turn and recite it to each other, offering forced hugs as we do so.

Next, I join Kimberley in running through the audience and thrusting bundles of white balloons into the hands of the nearest spectators. "Blow your balloon up. Pass it on," I say, indicating that they need to share the balloons with those around them.

Amidst curious whispers, the balloons are blown up.

I pull a bobble hat out of my pocket and put it on. Then the rest of our group come and join us, wearing gloves and scarves and we all yell, "Snowball fight!"

I grab a balloon from Elle and throw it into the air. Within seconds, white balloons are bopping and bobbing like snow falling in slow motion. Everyone is whooping and giggling as they toss balloons to and fro. Zachary catches my eye and lobs a balloon towards me. As I bat it back to him, I can't help but remember our careless wrestle in the snow. I turn away and pick up a stray balloon by Jodie's feet. I throw it shyly to her and she grins as she catches it.

Then Donna appears carrying a giant blue umbrella. I stop in my tracks, along with the rest of my group, and stare at her. The audience soon follow suit and every white balloon falls to the ground. By now, the light is starting to fade. Donna has a torch hidden inside the umbrella which she turns on as she holds the open brolly high.

Kimberley, Rose, Will and I line up and follow Donna as she leads a solemn procession to the cliff. Once there, Rose steps forward and unties the rope holding the yellow umbrella, sending it tumbling to the floor. She replaces it with the blue umbrella before pulling the rope to raise the new moon. The rest of us have positioned ourselves under the hidden multitude of fairy lights that we meticulously hung up earlier. The props department may have been all out of baths and red paint but they had twenty packets of battery operated fairy lights just begging to be borrowed. We flick them on in unison and a thousand tiny bulbs erupt like flickering stars in a perfect circle all around the audience.

There's an audible gasp followed by the sound of Heidi crying. Then Will hoots like an owl as the five of us slowly bow our heads and resume the positions that we had at the start of our piece; tossing and turning and longing for a sleep that never comes.

After a weighty pause, the audience burst into wild cheers. It's by far the noisiest cheer of the night and Terry Marvel loudly proclaims that it's the best Theatre of the Absurd piece in the entire history of Forest Hall.

I spot Jodie beaming and I hear someone say, "That was extraordinary."

I close my eyes and breathe in the ecstasy of the applause. For once in my life, I am grateful for all the rubbish going on inside me. I'm sure I couldn't create anything extraordinary if I was only ordinary.

Finally, I climb down from my nook and look out for Zachary and Annie. I spot them a little way away, admiring the fairy lights.

I slip away before they see me.

* 60 * Play it Cool Cat chooses a different path

I intend to run straight home but I am intercepted on my way past the mansion by Ruth from the Christian Union who is coming out of the laundry room.

"Oh wow! Cat! I was literally just thinking about you." She says this as though our meeting is divinely inspired.

I force a smile and go to rush on. It's starting to rain.

"I was praying for you—" My insides squirm as Ruth continues uninvited. "And I got a picture for you from God."

I bristle. Her last message from God didn't exactly help me. Play it Cool Cat smiles politely. "Oh?"

"Basically there was this huge trophy room that was totally abandoned. It was full of silver trophies that needed shining but they had been forgotten about."

I force another smile as I say curtly, "I get it. I'm like forgotten silver that has value but looks grubby." *Lovely*.

"No, I wasn't going to say that." Ruth shakes her head. "These are the trophies you've won from the battles you've endured. You have no idea. You earned them for your courage. You survived, Cat." She shrugs. "I mean... I have no idea if that means anything to you or not. But it's what I felt God saying. That he knows what you've battled and he sees you."

Play it Cool Cat nods. "Thanks. I'll ponder that."

Tears spill out of my eyes the moment I've turned.

God knows what I've battled and he sees me. Really?

I run all the way to my room.

God sees me.

I curl up behind my door and weep, a great dam breaking in my chest. Boulders and rocks and shards of glass are being swept away as Ruth's words light a candle inside me.

I close my eyes and rebuild my castle. I make it bigger and better than before and I watch as the different parts of me arrive and make themselves at home. Thunder Cat announces her arrival loudly and races to the new dance studio. Silly Cat and Scaredy Cat skip in holding hands. RoboCat gets busy arranging the books in the new library.

Then I create a secret passage behind the library and add a trophy room. I imagine everyone stepping inside the trophy room and admiring the shiny silverware. There are cups and medals and rosettes and crowns and a huge giant trophy with Baby Cat's name on. A tear rolls down my cheek as I watch her hugging it and smiling.

I get up off the floor and plod towards my shelf. I pick up my Russian dolls and open them one by one, breathing in the familiar woody smell. I assemble each doll in a line until I get to the tiniest princess, a funny-shaped bean in a painted white dress. I sit for ages on my bed, holding her with my eyes shut and tears flowing, soaking up the sensation of feeling safe and contained. Nobody will ever hurt Baby Cat again.

When I open my eyes, my gaze lands on the notebook that Zachary gave me for my birthday. It's been sitting on my desk all week. I pick it up and casually flick through it. Star systems and constellations dance before my eyes. The Saucepan, The Hunter, The Northern Cross, Betelgeuse, The Seven Sisters. All the ones he's taught me and many more. He's used silver pens and special glitter to make it all stand out. I tilt each page from side to side and watch it sparkle. The boy sure is talented.

Right on cue, he texts.

'Hey Cat, where did you go? Great job on your show. The stars at the end were incredible!'

I feel a pang of something painful. Irritation? Longing? Guilt? I'm not sure. I raise my thumb, ready to reply. But Play it Cool Cat halts. I want to be aloof. *I'll reply later.*

I turn back to the notebook. At the end, there are a handful of blank pages. I grab a pencil and start to doodle.

Baby Cat as a teeny tiny princess.

Thunder Cat with my special autograph.

Fun Cat singing.

Silly Cat with wings.

Holy Cat with a halo.

Sad Cat as one single solitary tear.

All stars in space. Drifting. Or maybe dancing. I wish I had some glitter. I draw a faint line between each one, like some kind of cosmic dot to dot. I still don't know what my constellation is. Who am I when all my parts join together?

Who do you want to be?

The question comes from some place deeper than I can reach and causes me to shiver. Do I really get a choice? I'm bound by my genetics, aren't I? Tied to a legacy. Set on a path. Chained to my family. Destined to fail. What will be, will be. No hope.

I stare blankly at the back of my door. It's plastered with quotes which Thunder Cat eagerly transcribed during my first term. My eyes land on one by Krispin Staniscofskin in *'The Truthful Actor'*:

'There are no prisons greater than the ones of our own making. The voices that tell us we are stuck when we are not. The chains of doubt and fear and unbelief. The refusal to look beyond one's feet and step into the light. For truly we are all powerful enough to create an entire universe. You are only limited by what you believe.'

I have highlighted *'create an entire universe'* and underlined it several times. I felt pretty mighty at the time. But now...? Can I believe that change is possible? That something so ugly as a caterpillar could truly grow wings and fly? Do I dare to be different even if it feels strange? Go against the voices that tell me I am broken? Run a new race. Change paths. Be reborn. Break the cycle of trauma. Re-write my story. Create a new legacy. Pass a different baton on. To dream. To hope.

To say sorry. Something my mother never does.

Before I can lose my nerve, I pick up my phone and reply to Zachary.

'I'm sorry I punched you. You're so nice to me and I'm often mean to you. I tease you or make silly jokes or pretend I don't care. The truth is you're the kindest friend I've ever had and you're really special to me. I just don't say it. Sometimes I feel like a different person. It's like there are lots of voices in my head and some of them aren't nice. There's an angry part of me that I should never let out. She's horrible. I'm horrible. I want to be nice but sometimes I can't help it.

Parts of me are bad. I'm no good for you. I really appreciate everything you've done for me but I don't want to hurt you so it's probably best if we don't spend so much time together. I hope you understand.'

Tears obscure my vision and I can't see to write anything else so I send it without even checking it over.

A few minutes later, there's a knock on my door.

I freeze, a tug of war erupting within me. Do I let him in? Into my room? My mind? My heart?

Yes, yes, yes! Fun Cat cries. And Thunder Cat. And Silly Cat.

No, no, no. I can't. I won't. Angry Cat is furious and frightened.

I sit frozen, doing nothing, waiting for him to go away. Then I feel devastated when he does. I curl into a ball and cover my head, willing myself to disappear. I break into choking sobs because what if I have succeeded in pushing him away? I want him and yet I don't. I am desperate and terrified. I'm too much and not enough and I cannot be trusted.

Suddenly I hear a rustling noise and a piece of paper slides under my door.

I quietly slip off my bed and go to retrieve it, my heart thumping as I read Zachary's tidy writing.

'I love you. Every part of you.'

* 61 * Angry Cat's true name

I am writhing on the floor, hating Angry Cat.

Love isn't real. Love isn't real.

Go away.

Don't leave me.

I grip onto Zachary's note, fighting Angry Cat's command to tear it into shreds.

I don't believe in love. Push him away.

I roll onto my back and let the tears dribble down the sides of my cheeks as I stare at another Krispin Staniscofskin quote on the back of my door.

'There is nothing superfluous in a good story. No word is careless. Every character, whether big or small, has its distinct and irreplaceable role in holding the piece together.'

I read it several times because, at first, the words have no meaning. What role could Angry Cat possibly have in my life besides to fill me with rage and distress? She doesn't hold me together. She tears me apart from the inside. She consumes me with fury. Lashes out without thinking. Assembles walls and turrets and chains.

But then I am reminded of something the Star Maker said: *"Every star has its story. Every star is there for a reason. Communication brings connection."*

I don't like every part of me. Far from it. And there are parts of me I have no desire to speak to at all. But maybe I should try a little harder. Maybe Angry Cat is there for a reason. A reason beyond the torment.

I close my eyes and face the rabid dog inside me. "Angry Cat. Your feelings are important. Thank you for the role you play..."

I don't mean it and have to resist the urge to smash my face into the floor. But, as I force myself to go on, I notice a slight shift inside me. It's like she's listening. Softening somehow. And my heart sort of softens too.

"I want to be your friend," I tell her slowly and deliberately. "I want to know your story."

She's transformed from the posture of a snarling dog to one of a whimpering puppy. No longer scary. Just scared.

"I love you, Angry Cat," I whisper. "We're on the same team. Please be my friend."

The blood rushes to my brain and Angry Cat comes to the surface.

And suddenly I am breaking down and it's like being thrown from a plane. I am free falling, tossed by the wind and plummeting down. I am totally unravelling and it's both terrifying and so healing because finally I can speak clearly. Finally somebody wants to listen. Finally you can see me.

It was the year I turned fourteen.

My mother had a hysterectomy after years of unresolved pain. While she was in theatre, my father told me her health issues had been the cause of her unpredictable behaviour. He promised, PROMISED, things would get better.

But she got into blazing rage a mere week later.

Screaming that she hated us.

Screaming that she would leave and never come back.

And he just snivelled and blubbered and blamed me and Aidan for setting her off.

Nothing had changed. It was all a lie.

False promises. False hope.

I hated them. And I locked myself in the bathroom and cried and cried and I told myself, 'Remember this moment. If you ever find yourself falling in love, walk away. Because this is love. This horrible, twisted loneliness. This is love.'

So I don't let people in. I can't. It's not safe. I'm not safe. I need to keep myself safe.

And I'm angry.

But I'm never allowed to be angry.

It's never about me.

Let it be about me.

Let me be angry.

Let me cry.

I see myself in front of the castle, feeling like an outcast. I don't belong in this family.

Holy Cat comes to me. For once, her eyes are not full of judgement. For once she really sees me and she kneels beside me and puts her hand in mine. *I keep trying to forgive them,* she says quietly. *I keep trying but I can't do it. You get angry whenever I try.*

Because pain has to be felt before it can be released, I tell her desperately. *You keep stuffing it away. Let me feel it, Holy Cat. Don't just tell me to forgive. Let my feelings be acknowledged. Even God gets angry sometimes. Even God flooded the world with his tears.*

Her eyes meet mine and she nods and starts to weep. *I'm sorry, Angry Cat. I'm sorry for not letting you cry.*

Then other parts gather round. Fun Cat and Play it Cool Cat. Thunder Cat and Creative Cat. All the ones who hated me most. And they say, *We're sorry, Angry Cat. You're allowed to be angry. We're sorry.*

Tears of relief almost drown me as I beg them, *Don't call me Angry Cat. Call me by my real name. Call me Grief.*

Of course I believe in love. That's why it hurts so much.

We're all born believing in love.

Created to receive it.

Ready to soak up all the love we are given.

Broken without it.

I hoped and hoped and hoped.

I waited and waited and tried so hard.

Call me Grief.

Grief is all the tears I never got to cry.

Grief is all the words unspoken.

Grief is all the love we never got to share.

Grief is all the promises that were broken.

Grief is all the time that will never be replaced and all the impossible tomorrows.

Grief is everything that should have been but wasn't.

And why not?

Did God not want it for me?

Did I not deserve it?

Did I do something wrong?

Fun Cat reaches for my hand and helps me to my feet. She leads me into the castle and into the trophy room.

Look, she whispers. *These are all for you.*

There's a whole cabinet filled to the brim with gold medals.

For courage and loyalty towards your comrades, Creative Cat whispers. *You were only trying to protect us.*

"Because every part has a story," whispers the Star Maker. *"Every part has good intentions. Every part is essential."*

At last— feeling what I feel and knowing what I know and being allowed to exist— I can put my sword down.

"But I don't know what to do now," I sob into the filthy carpet. "I can't let Zachary in. I can't. It's too scary. I will hurt him. He will hurt me."

I scream a tangled, suffocated scream.

Remember this moment. If you ever find yourself falling in love, walk away. Because this is love. This horrible, twisted loneliness. This is love.

"I have to let him go. Push him away until he loves somebody else. But then I'll lose him forever. And I want him to stay. Oh!" I cry and cry and cry, a ball of snot and choking tears. "Oh, Star Maker, if you're real... Help me..."

I beg him. Perfect, wise, all-knowing Star Maker.

Help me. Help me.

Nothing happens.

I sob into the deep, silent abyss.

And then everything happens.

A wave of divine peace rolls over me. Peace like nothing I have ever known. Peace that I could not possibly create. A shooting star right into my soul.

And with it, piercing clarity.

Zachary loves me.

I love Zachary.

And finally I see what my constellation should be. It's a heart, whole and undivided. Full and free. A heart created for love. Ready for love. Love that is available and waiting to be given. Love that has been pursuing me even though I sought it not.

I sprint out of my room, down the stairwell and into the boys' corridor where I pound on Zachary's door.

No reply.

"He just left," Mike says as he opens the fridge.

"Left?" I pant. "Where's he gone?"

He gives me a funny look. "Calm down. Just the Merry Bar. Someone's birthday from his course."

I nod and race back down the hall, my socks clinging to something sticky. I leave Willow and lunge into the dark night, running desperately down the hill. The rain is falling fast and I'm not wearing a coat or shoes but I don't care. I run through puddles and over slippery grass, eyes darting back and forth because this is the most crucial moment of my life.

And there he is.

Head down, hood up, passing Ash and Cedar as he marches into the rain alone.

"Zachary!" He doesn't hear me so I shout louder. *"Zachary!"*

He turns and cups a hand to his brow, squinting as I pelt towards him.

"Woah, Cat! Are you alright? What's going on?"

I hold him tight. Up close.

Close enough to kill.

Close enough to kiss.

Love could kill me. Love could heal me.

Love could break me. Love could make me.

Oh to be alive! To be human!

"I'm alright, Zachary Fenn," I murmur as I wrap my arms around him. "I just need to give you this."

* 62 * Silly Cat says goodbye to Jodie

Everybody's still talking about our Theatre of the Absurd piece.

Jodie greets me at the door of Primrose the next morning. "Hey Super Star Cat! How's it going?"

"Good."

She raises an eyebrow. "That's the first time you've not just said *'Okay'!*"

I give a coy smile. "Yeah I'm... I'm good." I want to linger and say something else but I don't know what. Several of my classmates are coming in behind me so I just scuttle to my usual place on the floor.

On my way, Clemmie says, "I loved your piece, Cat."

Heidi says, "It was enchanting."

And Otis offers me a high five.

Jodie gets our attention. "Good morning everyone! Let me start by saying a huge well done for your performances yesterday. There were some incredible moments of genius and I couldn't be more proud."

Play it Cool Cat wears a humble smile.

"You've worked so hard this year. I can't believe how fast the time has flown." Jodie clears her throat. She looks rather choked up and I'm thrilled that she's been so impacted by me. I mean us.

"Next year it gets serious as your grades will count towards your final degree but, if this year is anything to go by, I know there's a bright future ahead for all of you— both here at Forest Hall and beyond." She waves a hand to signify the many wild and wonderful paths we might choose.

I feel like I'm levitating slightly. I drift into a daydream in which Catrina Carla thanks Jodie for her years of support when picking up the Best Actress award at the Oscars.

"So you have two weeks left of term..." I pull myself back to the present as Jodie picks up some flyers. "Your first year is officially over so none of this is compulsory. You can stay in bed until the holidays if you want to. However I think you could have a whole heap of fun if you take advantage of what's being offered to you..." She waves the flyers. "There will be two workshops a day for the next fortnight covering a shedload of skills... Sword fighting, accents, a visiting physical theatre company, juggling, choral work..."

Thunder Cat is ecstatic. I've mentally signed up for the lot.

But then Jodie drops the bombshell. "So I hope you'll enjoy that. Unfortunately I won't get to see any of it as I'm leaving Forest Hall at the end of today. I have a new job at a college in London and I have a few things to organise before the summer."

I think the world stops turning.

There are cries of surprise around the room.

"You're leaving?" says Donna.

"But you're the best!" says Otis.

Jodie gives one of her strained smiles, just like she did at the start of our first term when she was a scary ice queen. "Trust me, I'd loved to have stayed if there was a job here for me." She sounds slightly bitter but doesn't elaborate. "Anyway, I don't have anything planned for this morning. I just wanted to make sure I'd had a chance to say goodbye. So, unless you want a lesson, you're free to go and enjoy the sunshine. Just remember to pick up your final grades from that chair on the way out."

To my dismay, most people take her up on this. They get up, chattering eagerly, grab their things and go, some with yells of thanks towards Jodie and others barely blinking as they leave her presence for the very last time. I feel like I have lost sensation in my legs. If I move, the tears that are precariously balanced in the corners of my eyes will come crashing out of me. I sit and wait, wondering if Jodie will do a lesson just for me. But it soon becomes evident that the offer was rhetorical.

The class is over.

Our last ever lesson with Jodie.

Our last precious hour over without warning.

I get slowly to my feet, trying not to wobble. Trying not to give myself away. Waiting till I am the last student in the room before edging towards the door.

Jodie catches my eye and smiles.

I want to tell her how much she has meant to me. How her encouragement has been a lifeline. How I wish she was my big sister. How I've been carrying so much in my head. How I wish she could stay. *Stay forever. Please don't leave me.* But it's too much. I'm too much.

All I can manage is a pitiful, "I'll miss you."

She keeps smiling. "Drop me an email sometime and let me know how you're doing. I know you'll be great."

The tears dribble out of my eyes. She won't be here for my second year? How will I survive without her?

As if reading my mind, she says, "You can do it, Cat. Everything you need is inside you." She sighs as she looks around. "I'll miss this place. It's so special."

I nod and wipe my eyes with the back of my hand. I know she said she would've stayed if she could. But that can't be true. Why wouldn't there be a job here for her? She's amazing. She must have found something better in London.

"Will your Forest Hall email address still work after you've left?" I ask hoarsely. Course it won't. I just feel like a stalker asking for her private one.

"No. I'll give you my personal one..." She scribbles on the back of one of the workshop flyers.

I pick up my grades from the chair. I've ended the year with a first. Not that it counts for anything. This year was just preparation. Next year we start from scratch. Without Jodie.

She opens the door for me and I say, "Thanks," as we step into the corridor.

"Bye Cat."

"Bye."

Then she turns to go up the mansion staircase, towards the offices, not even looking back.

I stumble out of the building in a daze, clinging to the flyer as though it's gold even though RoboCat has already committed her email address to memory. My grades feel like nothing compared to this scrap of paper with Jodie's hasty scrawl on. I will keep it forever.

I run all the way up the hill and straight to my room to have a big cry. Jodie in Real Life is leaving me. But I can't help it. Jodie in My Head will stick around for a while longer. I daydream about her returning next year and saying it was all a mistake. That she was offered a job here after all. That she's going to be our tutor for the whole year again. That she chose my class specially. Because she simply couldn't bear to miss what I might get up to. Tears roll down my cheeks and soak Monkey Bear as I wish and wish and wish that things could be different.

And yes, Silly Cat is deluded. I keep telling myself that our real life interactions have been fleeting and limited. Jodie may have been kind and witty and wise but she has also worn a mask. A tutor's mask. An actor's mask. A professional mask. And I have not seen the Jodie beyond that mask. Her faults or failures. Her fears or insecurities. Her regrets or secret heartaches. Everything that makes her truly human. Everything that makes her Real.

So I *know* that most of what I will miss is what I have imagined. The idea of being known. Being seen. Being mothered. I *know* Jodie can never be my sister or my mother or my saviour. I also know, deep down, that one day she will be replaced, just as Monica and Evelyn and Sadie and Sandra and Davina were once replaced before her. One day Jodie from Forest Hall will be a fond memory. Somebody that I used to know.

But still, she will always have a place in my heart and maybe, Silly Cat hopes, maybe I will always have a place in hers. Maybe, when she turned to go up the stairs, maybe she shed a little tear too.

Maybe.

* 63 * Sad Cat writes a letter

My cousin Chantelle has given birth to a little girl called Asterix. There are photos all over FriendWeb. Chantelle looks as though she has aged about ten years. Like she has suddenly become a mother. I mean on some deep heart level, not just biologically. She's not even wearing any make-up. She's just staring with doting affection at the squashy-faced tiny human in her arms as though her life has found its meaning.

I look up the name. It means *'Little Star.'* Sweet.

My phone beeps and a text flashes up on the screen.

'Hi Baby. How are you? Just letting you know Chantelle had her baby. A girl called Astrid.'

I feel a stabbing pain inside. I put my phone down and close my eyes and check in with all my parts. How do I feel? *Hopeful. Scared. Angry. Relieved. Distraught. Conflicted.*

I take out my Russian dolls and line them up one by one. *Every part of me is valid. Every feeling is allowed.*

I uncover the last doll and hold her tenderly. Even now, I don't know what to make of what Baby Cat showed me on my birthday. Pieces of the jigsaw are missing. It's so frustrating not having all the answers. I keep trying to push it away but shadows follow me wherever I go. And the trouble with shadows is that they stretch and distort and, without a true source of light, it's not clear what they're even a shadow of.

I pick up my phone and re-read my mother's text.

She loves me. She loves me not. Does she love me?

I am frozen, unsure how to respond. Unsure of what I want. I tear some paper out of a notebook and start to doodle. I draw stars and hearts and crying children. I draw caterpillars and butterflies and angry eyes and ugly scars and Monkey Bear with his head torn off. I draw a bird flying through a storm and a boy playing a trumpet and a secret castle on a cloud. Then I write.

'Dear Mum
I am sad about how things are between us. I tried to talk to you at Easter and you got angry. Now you're texting me

as though everything is okay and I know I'm supposed to stuff away what I feel and embrace you like nothing has happened. I have never been allowed to be angry with you. I have never been able to be honest. We never talk about feelings. Not my feelings anyway. It's always about you. You always have to be right, respected, the centre of attention. When does it get to be about me?

I try so hard to please you but it's never enough. You get cross when I'm sad. You dismiss me when I'm happy. I don't feel safe with you. I don't know who I am when you're around. I have feared losing you my entire life. And that fear has caused me to put up with anything you throw at me. You don't realise how much you have hurt me. You don't know how much it cost me to stay silent. And how much courage it took to speak up.

I wasn't trying to hurt you. I was trying to make things better between us because things have never been okay even though we pretend. I was giving you an opportunity to get closer to me and I'm sad you didn't take it. I'm even sadder that you believed I had wronged you. I've tried to be the perfect daughter all my life but you don't see it. You talk about all the sacrifices you've made for me but you don't see what I have sacrificed to try to earn your love. All the times I've swallowed my feelings, opinions and pain.

I know there are secrets. I know things happened that you don't want to talk about— in your life and in mine. I wish we could have a loving heart to heart and be REAL, but you've never been that kind of mother. I've spent my life feeling ashamed of myself but I'm finally realising I was not the problem after all. You didn't deserve the awful things you went through and I'm sorry that life broke you. But because of your pain you've only ever seen me through a broken lens. And because of your pain, you broke me too.

You were my first love and I'll always love you. But you taught me not to love myself.

Your daughter.'

I don't know if I'll send it. My mother isn't capable of changing. Not right now, anyway. If I want things to be different, I'll have to change myself. I fold the letter into a tiny square. I could burn it. Like how my mother burns stuff when she's fallen out with someone. But Bob the housing officer would never forgive me if I set fire to Willow. Especially following his most recent fire safety lecture after Wes put a packet of crisps in the microwave. And anyway, I want to be different. I want to change my story. I won't become my mother. I won't burn the things that hurt me.

I weep as I hide the letter in one of my old diaries at the back of my wardrobe. While I'm there, I pull out the nearest diary and skim through it. It's from sixth form. My wild handwriting jumps out at me, screaming for attention: Thunder Cat's reckless ambitions interspersed with Sad Cat's wails of sorrow. An old photo falls out. It's of me and my mum in the hospital when I was born. It's almost identical to the ones of Chantelle and Asterix. Same hospital set up. Same breathless wonder. Same doting gaze. Same potential.

The photo is slightly crumpled. That's because I once kept it in my pocket for several days when my mother vanished during the Dark Days. I run a finger across the old photo. My mother was so young when she had me. Barely even twenty. A mere child herself, like Chantelle. She looks so besotted with me. So pleased to see me. In love. How did it all go wrong? Mothers don't really want to hurt their children, do they? I'm sure she had good intentions. Tried her best. Couldn't help it. Still can't help it. Just can't see.

She loves me. She loves me not.

Is it me or is it her? Am I owed an apology or should I somehow try harder still? Things would be a whole lot easier if she was *unwilling* to love me instead of being unable.

My thumb shakes as I text my reply. *'I know. I saw the photos on FriendWeb. I'm doing fine thanks. Hope you are too.'* I don't correct her on the baby's name. Nor do I ask if she plans to add me as a FriendWeb friend again.

She loves me. She loves me not.

But perhaps that's not the point. She has never loved me the way I needed to be loved. Because true love shouldn't break you.

I take one last peek at the old photo and suddenly I feel sorry for her. Sorry that she couldn't overcome her past. Sorry that she has missed out. Missed out on knowing me.

And my father. Absent from this baby photo. Absent in so many ways. Too consumed with appeasing my mother to be present for me. I know so little about him. He had a whole life before I was born. Perhaps something happened to break him. Perhaps he just isn't very resilient. Perhaps the fact of the matter is that he *does* love me; he just loves my mother more. I can't fix them or ever be enough. I was never meant to. It doesn't depend on me. Her anger was never about me. Her eyes filled with rage whoever she was looking at. His depression was never mine to carry. They would've been this way with or without me. I am not responsible. It's not my fault. And I'm not going to play their game any more.

I send a message into my castle, loud and clear, on the tannoy system: *'You are worthy of love. You have rights. A right to speak. A right to feel whatever you feel. A right to be safe. A right to say no. A right to choose.'*

And yes, it would be so much easier if they were unwilling to love me rather than unable. But true villains are rare. Nobody is black and white. There is good in everyone. There is evil in everyone. I am Sad Cat and I am Fun Cat. I am Creative Cat and I am Lost Cat. I am Holy Cat and I am Angry Cat. And sometimes I am Cat out of Hell.

No relationship is black and white either. We had some good times. It just wasn't enough. Perhaps one day I'll be able to see all the colours dancing amongst the shades of grey. Perhaps I'll smile when I remember my father talking through my teddy or my mother's laugh as she sings karaoke. The cakes she made. The clothes she mended. Special times at the library or feeding the ducks. Layers of pass the parcel painstakingly wrapped. Cheese toasties. Rhubarb fool. Jumping with glee through the wave machine. A magician for my birthday. A gentle embrace on the day I was born. Eyes that promised love. Hands that never meant to harm. A heart that aches for connection.

There is more than one way to tell a story. Perhaps my mother's tale would show her in a different light. In another story she would be a hero or a victim or a saint. But this is my story. And I'm telling it in the only way I am able.

* 64 * Fun Cat will survive

Within minutes of me replying to my mother, my dad phones. We've not spoken all term but here he is, triumphantly acknowledging that contact between myself and my mother has been made.

I puff out my cheeks before answering. "Hello."

"Oh, hello! You're there!" His voice is bright and cheerful, as though hoping everything has been swept far enough under the carpet to never trouble him again. "Just checking when you want me to collect you for the summer?"

"I don't need you to, thanks."

"Sorry?"

"I haven't decided what I'm doing yet. But I won't be going to Exeter at the end of term."

"What are you talking about?"

"I might stay with some friends for a bit. I don't know yet."

As a matter of fact, I have many options for the summer. Annie's parents are going on a cruise so she's invited me to stay at hers. Mad Jo and Tanisha are moving to a house in Wakefield. A real house with an oven and a living room. They've said I can stay on their sofa anytime. Or I could go to Norfolk and see the farm Zachary grew up on. Meet his sheep and have a ride on his tractor.

"Don't be daft!" my dad makes a noise that's a cross between a splutter and a guffaw. "You've got to come home. We all want to see you."

I falter for a moment. He makes it sound as though I'd be heartless not to. *What should I do? Should I go home? For how long? What would a good daughter do?*

I know what Zachary would say: *What do you* want *to do?*

I interrupt my father's pleas.

"I might come down at some point." *Might.*

"I need to know *when* so I can make plans."

"I won't need you to collect me. If I come, I'll get the train."

"Train!"

"And I'll bring Zachary."

"Who?"

"My friend."

Bertie is playing piano downstairs. I tune out my dad and focus on the music. It sounds beautiful. Perhaps I'll learn how to play.

"Mum's bought you a dress, by the way. And apparently Tracey is planning to visit in a few weeks, so you'll want to be back for that. And don't forget the football season starts on the second weekend of August so I won't be able to come and get you then..."

I listen to the tannoy in my head.

'You are loved.

You are seen.

You're a star.

It wasn't your fault.

You are worthy of love.

You have rights.

A right to speak.

A right to feel whatever you feel.

A right to be safe.

A right to say no.

A right to choose.'

And I decide that any voice that doesn't sound like these must be rejected.

There's a knock at my door.

"I've got to go," I tell my dad.

"Let me know, won't you?"

"Yup."

Zachary pokes his head round my unlocked door. "Ready for dinner?"

"I love you," my dad warbles down the line. *"I love you?"*

I catch eyes with Zachary as I end the call and toss my phone onto the bed.

You did not break your family. You broke your silence.

"Love you."

Zachary holds out his hand and I take it.

$$*******************************$$

Curtain Call

In which Cat finds her wings and takes her final bow.

$$*******************************$$

* 65 *

"So, what have you got for me?" Dotty Jay stands in my doorway with an outstretched hand.

It's the last day before the holidays and she's organising a time capsule. I grin and give her the pile of artefacts I've gathered: My plastic lemon from Fresher's Week. A photo of me, Zachary, Mad Jo and Dotty Jay singing *'I will survive'* at the Merry Bar open mic. The *'Reserved'* sign from our Christmas meal at the Grumpy Pig. The filming schedule for the Mama Octopus music video. A receipt from the refectory. A list of all the library books I've read this year. The first puzzle piece from my birthday treasure hunt. A shrivelled up white balloon from my Theatre of the Absurd piece. And a letter to myself which I have sealed with lots of tape because I don't want Dotty Jay to get nosy and read it before me.

"Ooh a letter to your future self. Good idea." Dotty Jay stuffs my offerings into her duffel bag before exclaiming, "We'll have a big reunion in seven years when I turn thirty!"

I do the maths. I'll be twenty six. Feels like forever away. I've only planned up to twenty five.

Dotty Jay peers into my room and lets out a whistle. My belongings are in a heap by the radiator. Everything else is as bare as the day I arrived. Bed stripped. Shelves empty. Naked desk. Patchy green carpet. The echoey walls are stained with grey marks from my blue tack and the whole room feels lifeless, as though nothing has happened here at all. Or perhaps it's a broken cocoon, in which everything has happened. An old shell no longer needed by the new creation that has taken flight.

Dotty Jay peers into my empty wardrobe to see what I've written. My cheeks burn as she reads my inscription. *"Last day of an amazing year. Here's to every star in the sky."* She traces my curly autograph with a finger and says, "Cryptic."

I shrug and close the wardrobe door.

I'll be back in Willow in September but I'm moving to Dotty Jay's room, number 8. I don't like the ghosts in the pipes in mine. Zachary and Annie are returning to campus too but most of our housemates are moving to Wakefield to live like proper grown-ups. I'm not ready for that yet. There's something safe and comforting about living on campus, with Bob to sort out any housing issues and Windy Wendy and her crew providing hot meals at the refectory. Plus, the stars are brighter in the countryside.

"I'll miss this place," Dotty Jay says wistfully as she peers out of my window. "I wonder what your new housemates will be like."

I stand beside her.

I wonder. What lies ahead?

I've made a decision about the summer. I'm going to start at Annie's house in Leeds. I've promised I'll go to church with her on Sunday and I'm actually looking forward to it in a weird sort of way. Then, next week, I'm going to get a train to Norfolk all by myself. I'll get the 11.11 from Leeds train station. Then I'll change at Peterborough and again at Norwich and arrive in Berney Arms by the early evening. Zachary's going to meet me on the platform. We'll play games and climb trees and spend a day watching seals on Horsey beach.

"This is for you, by the way." Dotty Jay whips out a rolled up piece of paper.

I unfold it and smile. It's a butterfly painted in what smells like nail polish. "It's beautiful. Thank you." I place it by my bags. I'll put it on my door next year to replace the one I destroyed.

Then Dotty Jay's on and off boyfriend, Daryl, appears on the landing and says, "Ready, Dot?"

She pats me on the arm. "Right. I'm off. Nice knowing you."

My legs are wobbly as I follow the two of them down the stairs. It feels like only yesterday that Dotty Jay sprang into my life, the first to greet me at Forest Hall, squashing my pillows with her exuberance and declaring that I was a type three. She seemed like such a weirdo on that first day. But now I'd count her as one of the most precious people I've ever met. Strange, beautiful, kind, fantastic.

I feel full of regret. Where did the year go? I wish I could start over and spend more time with Dotty Jay. Now she's moving back to Birmingham, never to return. Hoping to find work in a bar, wiping tables by day and singing jazz by night, while continuing her studies in Music Therapy. I wonder how she'll get on. I wonder where she'll live and who her friends will be and how long she and Daryl will stay together this time. Most of all, I wonder whether she'll ever find her type seven. Ever find the one who is perfect, humble, divine. Totally good and totally pure. Full of love, no darkness at all. The one I'm learning to call the Star Maker.

I watch as Dotty Jay and Daryl load her belongings into Daryl's beaten up car. The back seat is crammed to bursting and several tins of beans fall out as Daryl opens the boot. Dotty Jay winces as he attaches her guitar haphazardly to a makeshift roof rack and secures it with bungee ropes.

"Sheesh, Daz! That's my most prized possession."

He grunts and asks if she'd rather walk.

There's a shout behind us and Zachary comes running out of Willow carrying a rock and a melted spatula. "Am I too late?" he asks before thrusting his strange treasures at Dotty Jay.

She raises an eyebrow. "What's this?"

"It's a rock from the waterfall and a spatula that I accidentally cooked on my camping stove. For the time capsule."

"Ahh! Nice." She plonks them on the parcel shelf, much to Daryl's annoyance. Then she turns to me and I see that her eyes are wet. "I'm gonna miss you, Cat!" She throws her arms around me.

"I'm gonna miss you too," I blub. "Keep in touch."

"Try and stop me! I'll come visit in the Autumn. Remember to take the first years on a late night walk to Fairy Land and show them Rory's swing."

"I will! I will!"

She gives me one last hug before squeezing into the passenger seat. Smoke chugs out of the exhaust as Daryl starts the engine and accelerates up the hill. I wave until the car turns the corner and then I sigh and let my hand drop. Zachary puts his arm around me.

Elle walks past carrying her duvet. "Aww, look at you two. I knew you'd get together. It's not fair. You didn't even want to fall in love."

I try to smile at her. My mother always warned me that life isn't fair. And maybe it isn't. But sometimes it is. Sometimes there's hope in unexpected places. Shooting stars on a dark night. Friends when you least deserve them.

"Have a nice summer, Elle," I say.

She sniffs, as hostile as on our first day.

I feel a pang of offence. But then I spot Elle's mother waiting impatiently beside a pink sports car. Hands on hips. Urging Elle to hurry up. A tall, bearded redhead by her side.

I cannot judge anybody. I don't know what's in their suitcase. I don't know what battles they have fought. I don't know what it has cost them. Just existing.

The trophies with their names on.

The castles in their minds.

The stars that make up their story.

We all bear scars. Some are visible, shameful, grotesque. Some are hidden and nobody sees. Some may fade but never completely go away. Whether we wear them with pride or horror or disgrace or denial, they are all evidence of pain. We all bleed. We are all more broken than we realise. Nobody has it all together. Nobody has all the answers. We all need love.

Zachary squeezes my hand. "What did you give Dotty Jay for her time capsule?"

"Loads of things..." I count them off on my fingers. "My lemon.... A balloon... A letter to my future self."

"Nice. What did you write? You know Dotty Jay will probably forget and leave our stuff rotting somewhere!"

I laugh. "Probably." It doesn't matter. I'm keeping everything that counts.

We turn down the hill and head to the refectory. I still have three pounds and sixteen pence on my meal card. I'll treat Zachary to some chips.

We pass Ruth and Charlotte from the Christian Union and exchange pleasantries. I consider telling Ruth that her trophy room picture has had a huge impact on me. But, in the end, I don't say anything. I'm not sure why. Perhaps it's because I still have so many questions. Sometimes things feel clear and sometimes they don't. Sometimes I believe and sometimes I doubt. I still don't fully understand what happened to Baby Cat— I mean to *me*. I have a feeling that there's more to discover. Squashed Cat keeps tugging on me like she's got a story to tell. And I have no idea what to do about Cat out of Hell. Suddenly the future is a blank and scary canvas and there's no map to lead me. A wave of worry crashes over me as Ruth and Charlotte wish me a good summer and walk on.

But then I sense the Star Maker whispering, *"There is more for you to discover, little one. And when you are ready we will face it together."*

We reach the refectory and Zachary gives me a playful nudge as we squeeze through the door at the same time.

So perhaps this is not a story about how I broke. Perhaps this is a story about how I started to heal.

Maybe I am not a type or a number.

Maybe I cannot be defined.

Maybe I am all the stars in the sky.

All the colours of the rainbow.

Every snowflake on a winter's morning.

A thousand sunrises waiting to shine.

A love song waiting to be sung.

Maybe I am one of a kind.

And maybe I am just like everybody else.

I hope. I fear. I fly. I fall. I am lost. I am found. I am and I am not. I am braver than I thought but more fragile too. I am worthy of love. I am loved. And I love.

Maybe one day I'll be a famous actress and orchestrate Thunder Cat's grand plan.

Or maybe I'll learn how to drive and travel the world and Zachary will help carry my laundry.

Maybe I'll get a proper job and move into a house with an oven. And learn how to cook. And take up running. And make friends with the neighbours. And get a piano and play music with Zachary. And beat him at Monopoly. And watch the sunrise in the snow.

Then one day I'll get an email out of the blue from somebody called Dorothy Jayne. It will say *'It is time.'*

And then I'll remember.

And we'll get together.
And I'll look through my old treasures.
And I'll read my letter.
And maybe— maybe— I'll realise I have found my way.

'Hey Cat,

It's me. I mean you. By the time you read this, I will be gone. You'll have grown up into somebody new. A butterfly, perhaps.

What are you up to? Are you famous yet? Did you do something crazy like marry Zachary? If you did, I bet he's reading this over your shoulder. Have you got children? Note to self: I really like the name Jocelyn.

I can't give you much advice because you're older and hopefully wiser than me but here's what I learnt this year:

1.   *You're more brilliant than you realise.*
2.   *It's possible to cook almost anything in a microwave.*
3.   *The stars are really beautiful if you take time to pay them attention.*

Anyway, I hope you're happy. And I hope you didn't quit. And I hope that I am not completely gone. That maybe you've kept me in your heart or something. If you did, I want to say thank you. Thank you for seeing me. For listening to my story. For letting me shine for a moment.

Love from Cat

of Willow, Forest Hall, and all the stars in the universe and beyond.'